Praise for *The English Monster*:

'Subtle, clever and satisfying, *The English Monster* is historical detective fiction with an X-Files twist. Shepherd's extraordinary imagination offers us slavers, pirates, murderers – and the birth of modern Britain. Wonderful' Shelley Harris, author of R&J pick *Jubilee*

'Vividly realised . . . show[s] a flair for enlivening historical events with vivid characters . . . An original, imaginative investigation into some of the most disturbing episodes of the nation's history' *Times Literary Supplement*

'A brilliantly imagined historical crime novel that evokes such creations as Shardlake and *Jonathan Strange & Mr Norrell*' *Sun*

'Atmospheric, gruesome and compelling. With Shepherd as their quartermaster, readers who enjoyed *Perfume* by Patrick Süskind will find plenty on this voyage to appal and intrigue them' Katie Ward, author of *Girl Reading*

'*The English Monster* is a refreshing example of intelligent and cleverly constructed historical fiction which also has a tantalising plot' Essie Fox, author of *The Somnambulist*

'There is a dark twist – a spot of black-magical realism, if you like – about half way through Lloyd Shepherd's first novel that this reviewer has no desire to ruin for readers. In fact, so delicious and unexpected is this turn of events that it moves a book that is already part detective fiction, part historical novel and part pirate adventure into entirely new territory, adding themes of national philosophy and moral turpitude to a story as rich in ideas as it is in intrigue . . . If all this sounds ambitious to the point of audacious for a debut novel, then suffice to say that Shepherd pulls it off . . . *The English Monster* becomes as vivid an education as it is an entertainment. None of which is to mention that devilish twist in this tale' *Independent on Sunday*

'*The English Monster* has a terrific idea at its core . . . The book becomes a joyously, flamboyantly melodramatic scamper' *Guardian*

'*The English Monster* is a riveting police procedural, a thrilling tale of life at sea, and an evocative piece of historical re-creation – all with an intriguing element of the fantastic that makes it irresistible. This is a novel that surprised and astounded me time and again' Felix Palma, *New York Times* bestselling author of *The Map of Time*

'Lloyd Shepherd's novel, *The English Monster*, dramatizes one of the most shocking of all real life crimes, the Ratcliffe Highway Murders of 1811, in which two families were brutally slaughtered . . . Shepherd really gets under the skin of Regency London . . . An ambitious novel' *Daily Telegraph*

'Marvellous; what a concept and what a feel he has for both eras – I can smell old Wapping when I read it. First-class stuff' Robert Low, author of *The Oathsworn* series and *The Kingdom* series

'This gripping novel puts a fantastical spin on the old tale of terror . . . his yarn is rich in atmosphere, taking us into smoky riverside inns, candle-lit panelled parlours and out into the rough streets around London's docks . . . the power of the novel lies in its symbolism' *Financial Times*

'As much as it is detective novel, historical tract, and magical tale, *The English Monster* is also a polemic . . . A truly superb book, succeeding on every level. As a crime novel, it is unorthodox but rewarding. As a work of historical fiction, it serves up an evocative dose of swashbuckling, crime fighting and social commentary. As polemic, it mercilessly slices open the British soul, and deserves to provoke not just thought but debate. This is a five-star triumph from a writer with skills that belie his debutant status; buy it, and buy it now' *bookgeeks.co.uk*

'You can practically lick the sea salt off these pages. What an exuberant, daring, swashbuckling, deftly written, savagely delivered story. Love the gothic, Frankensteinesque twist but I'm saying no more. Reminded me a bit of David Mitchell in parts. Patrick O'Brian, too . . . Lots of thematic ideas here, bursting at the seams to get your historical teeth into'
D. E. Meredith, author of *The Devil's Ribbon*

THE ENGLISH MONSTER

or

The Melancholy Transactions of William Ablass

LLOYD SHEPHERD

SIMON & SCHUSTER

London · New York · Sydney · Toronto · New Delhi

A CBS COMPANY

First published in Great Britain by Simon & Schuster UK Ltd, 2012
Paperback edition published by Simon & Schuster UK Ltd, 2012
A CBS COMPANY

1 3 5 7 9 10 8 6 4 2

Simon & Schuster UK Ltd
1st Floor
222 Gray's Inn Road
London
WC1X 8HB

www.simonandschuster.co.uk

Simon & Schuster Australia, Sydney
Simon & Schuster India, New Delhi

A CIP catalogue record for this book
is available from the British Library

ISBN 978-0-85720-537-7

Typeset by M Rules
Printed and bound by CPI Group (UK) Ltd, Croydon, CR0 4YY

For Louise

They have good ships and are greedy folk with more freedom than is good for them.

Guzmán de Silva,
Spanish ambassador to England, 1566

21 JUNE 1585

The ancient road began at the Tower and ran east to west along a terrace of gravel. To the east it disappeared into the flat treeless horizon of the estuary, merging into the earth just as the earth merged into the sea at the muddy edge of England.

As it left London, this road, which in only a few years would become a highway, formed the northern boundary of a dreary region of swampy land. The great river, as it bent south then north again, formed the southern edge of this semicircle of marshland. It had been drained and flooded, drained and flooded half-a-dozen times in the previous fifty years, while England burned Protestants then Catholics and then Protestants again. This place could not seem to decide if it was of the river or of the earth. The ancient name for the misbegotten half-land was Wapping. No one could remember where the name came from.

In recent years small wharves and little clusters of houses had appeared along the riverbank at Wapping. The rich men who funded the buildings decided that houses and wharves would do a better job of keeping out the river than the sea walls they'd been building for decades in their vain attempts to reclaim the land from the waters. And, more to the point, a wharf generated more profit than a wall.

During the days men made themselves busy around the dozens of boats that moored up along the wharves, the vessels settling down into the riverbed when the tide went out and rising again as it flooded back in, washing up against the wood-and-brick pilings. The pickings were not rich. London's most lucrative trade still headed further upstream towards the wharves that operated within the city walls, but a new grey economy was emerging here downstream at Wapping.

Beyond this sliver of moneymaking and building, back behind the wharves, between the river and the road, were the marshes. The occasional flood still occurred, sweeping away families and livelihoods as well as the property of the men of business. This dank, oozing landscape, unpromising and undeveloped, was the result of the river's inundations. The ground was low, lower than sea level in some places, rising up to the bluff along which the road ran to the north. A man could stand there in the marshes, his feet sinking into the mud, and look to the backs of the wharves and warehouses along the river and imagine that they were floating on water.

There was a gap in the riverside development, and in this gap stood a group of gallows. The gallows lived on borrowed time – already there were complaints that this place of execution was dragging down the land value of investments. Could it not be moved downstream a bit, perhaps to Ratcliffe, somewhere benighted and undeveloped where men of business were not trying to attract custom? But for now the gallows still stood. On this midsummer's eve there were six river pirates hanging there.

The gallows were right at the water's edge, set in amongst the wharves. The six unfortunates hanging from the ropes had been caught after leaping aboard a barge in the river. It had been their sixth attack in four weeks and it was to be their last. The local lightermen and watermen had banded together to bait a trap for them, putting out stories that a barge with wool intended for France and Spain would be travelling downstream that day. When the pirates had clambered onboard, a group of twenty river men hidden beneath sails had emerged and captured them, but sadly not before the pirates, or at least, reported most of the ambushers, the apparent captain of the pirates, whose knife had flashed more quickly and more viciously than those of his crew, had sent three of the Wapping lightermen into the embrace of the old river, their throats slashed and their eyes empty. Eventually the men overcame the pirates and after some cursory discussions with what passed for the authorities in this new outpost they decided upon a customary punishment. The pirates were hanged at Execution Dock, where they would be left for three tides as a signal to others (and perhaps an offering to the river) before being cut down and disposed of.

The river was already rising for the first of these three tides when the leader of the pirates heard a clatter of hoofs on the mixture of mud and stones that constituted the main street here in Wapping, running along the curve of the river behind the wharves. A mighty carriage, it sounded like. The clatter stopped, and he heard the sound of a carriage door slamming. A few minutes later, some squelching footsteps as a man approached. The pirate kept his eyes prudently closed as the footsteps stopped, perhaps directly in front of him. Within two hours, the river would be up to the chins of the men on the gallows, before falling back again.

Carefully, the pirate opened one eye halfway. He saw the swaying feet of his dead shipmates on either side of him, and opened the eye a little further. His visitor was standing on the foreshore, dressed in the Dutch style, all sombre black and white, the clothes effortlessly wealthier than the new gay and gaudy fashions that were rippling out from the English Queen's court.

The visitor cleared his throat and spat. The pirate heard a small splash in the water, and his careful eyes caught the sun as it glittered on a thick lump of green phlegm which appeared and spun around in the water as it commenced its journey down to Tilbury. The visitor glanced up and behind at the gallows, and the pirate closed his eyes quickly. He resolved to keep his eyes that way as the visitor started to speak, in rich aristocratic tones with just the hint of a clammy Dutch accent.

'Quite a view they've given you. Desirable waterfront property, I'd say.'

The pirate said nothing, obviously. The creaking of the gallows was the only sound as he and his men swung gently in the soft summer breeze. Miles and miles upstream, it was a beautiful evening among the willow trees and reeds at Runnymede and Richmond, where the aristocrats played at court and love and wrote poetry to each other. The sun was setting in the opulent west. But here, to the east of the metropolis, the dominant colours were greys and browns. Mud and water, not trees and flowers.

The thought seemed to make the visitor positively cheerful. He put his hands behind his back and actually rose up on his toes at the vista before him. 'Someday all this will be very desirable property, captain. When my father built his wall here, he had a vision of a new suburb, with the river kept out and the land turned into meadows and orchards. He wanted this to be the prettiest part of London. And all within sight of that dreadful Tower.'

It occurred to the pirate to wonder why the Dutchman was speaking when, as far as the man knew, there was no one there alive to listen to him.

The visitor spoke again, and even with his eyes closed the pirate captain had the impression that the Dutchman had turned his back on the river and was facing him. Almost as if he were speaking to him. Perhaps he was practising an address.

'You'll be the last, captain. The last crew to be hanged on this so-called Execution Dock. It's keeping the developers away, this grisly habit, and this land is valuable. A hundred years, maybe two hundred, this'll be the busiest port in the world. Trade is coming, captain. Trade. Not petty thievery or the ridiculous swapping of bits of unmade cloth for bits of food 'n' drink. The world's wealth is out there waiting to be bought and sold, and unlike most of my countrymen I predict that the buying and selling will happen here, in London, not in Antwerp or Rotterdam. Wapping's going to flourish. It's going to become the hub on which the world turns. You'll go down in history, captain. The last pirate to be hanged at Wapping. My congratulations.'

Another movement, and then the sound of the visitor walking back to his carriage. The slamming door, the 'hai!' of the coachman, and the snap of hoofs and wheels on the road back into London. And then only the sound of the creaking gallows again.

The tide rose, and later it fell. It rose and it fell three times. When the locals came to cut them down, they were disconcerted to find only five pirates hanging from the gallows. The sixth – the *captain* – had gone.

[illegible] and [illegible]
[illegible] impression that the Dutch had
[illegible]
[illegible]
[illegible] before [illegible]
[illegible]
[illegible]
[illegible]
[illegible] Joint Trade [illegible]
[illegible]
[illegible]
[illegible]
[illegible]
[illegible]
[illegible]

[illegible]

[illegible]

BOOK 1

Drake

As I was a-walking down Ratcliffe Highway
A flash looking packet I chanced for to see
I hailed her in English, she answered me clear
I'm from the Blue Anchor bound for the Black Bear
Sing too relye addie, sing too relye ay.

She had up her colours, her masthead was low
She was round in the counter and bluff in the bow
She was blowing along with the wind blowing free
She clewed up her courses and waited for me

I tipped up my flipper, I took her in tow
And yardarm to yardarm away we did go
She lowered her topsail, t'gansail and all
Her lily-white hand on my reef-tackle fall

I said, 'My fair maiden, it's time to give o'er
For twixt wind and water you've run me ashore
My shot locker's empty, my powder's all spent
I can't fire a shot for it's choked round the vent'

Here's luck to the girl with the black curly locks
Here's luck to the girl who run Jack on the rocks
Here's luck to the doctor who eased all his pain
He's squared his mainyards, he's a-cruising again.

(traditional, nineteenth century)

7 DECEMBER 1811

On a dark cloudy Saturday night in December, a young woman slams a freshly painted door on the front of number 29, a smart little house which faces north onto the old road from London, the Ratcliffe Highway. As the door crashes shut she can be heard to mutter a sharp, salty obscenity to herself, before looking around quickly to see if anyone is listening. Nobody is.

The young woman, barely more than a girl, is called Margaret Jewell, and the house belongs to her employer Timothy Marr, a former sailor who has been busy making the beginnings of a name for himself as a linen draper and supplier to the great ships which pour in and out of the new dock, back down the hill behind the house below the high ground which supports the Highway.

Margaret is a plain-looking sensible girl of seventeen years who is now blushing to herself, enlivened by the shocking language she has just used and savouring the privacy of the moment. She has been learning more and more of these choice words in the weeks since she joined the Marr household, just by listening to the men who roll around on the streets around the dock (and they do, she quickly realised, actually *roll*, their gait rocking from side to side even when they are sober). She has taken to mouthing these words silently, rolling the forbidden syllables around her teenage tongue to savour the taste. They are windswept and thrilling, as are many of the dirty, dishevelled, rolling men she carefully avoids while out walking on the pavements of Shadwell and Wapping.

There is nothing windswept or thrilling about her employer, alas, despite his maritime history. Most of the time Timothy Marr simply exasperates Margaret. She finds his priggish fussiness annoying beyond words, and tonight is not the first time she has slammed his front door. Margaret has no father. The position with the Marrs was her escape route from her mother, whom she has left behind in a deserted little Essex cottage out towards the estuary, weeping into her washing. But now Margaret feels stifled again, and the truth is that she finds Timothy Marr ridiculous, a self-consciously upright paragon of virtue plying his trade among men who look like they would cut your throat as soon as speak to you. She cannot understand why Marr has not opened a little grocer's shop somewhere genteel like St Albans or Richmond. He seems to spend a large part of his time bemoaning the lack of quality among the denizens of the Highway, displaying a strange kind of snobbishness which even Margaret's young ears find discordant and vaguely comical.

It has been a painfully long and hard Saturday. It is always the hardest day of the week, but something about today has been especially vicious. Marr started the day in a foul temper, shouting at his wife as Margaret emerged from her bed and then shouting at Margaret about some inconsequential nothing which she has already forgotten. He only got worse as the day wore on, despite the steady stream of customers into his shop.

Normally, Marr's moods rise and fall with the traffic through his shop's door. A busy day will typically see him cheerful and raucous, trying (and failing) to make jokes with Margaret and the shop boy James Gowen. A quiet day will find him sullen, anxious and short-tempered. Margaret does not yet understand the pressures on a self-made man to make something more of himself, particularly a man like Marr, who is the first of his family to have anything resembling a social position.

None of this matters to Margaret, who already considers herself as someone rather separate from the common herd. She is a girl capable of rich fantasies. Her mother gave her the gift of reading in the years after her father's death, patiently taking her through the pages of the handful of books that were in their cottage, ignoring Margaret's tantrums, wanting to give her daughter something unique and still rare. This gift has given Margaret access to the dreams of others, and like many secret female readers she has for some time been leading a double-life imagined from within the pages of a novel, in her case Ann Radcliffe's *The Mysteries of Udolpho* (her copy, dog-eared and fretted over, lies beneath her bed where Mrs Marr discovered it once, picking it up with a curious frown before smiling to herself and placing it back where she found it). Walking the streets during the day Margaret sometimes looks at a tall, disreputable man and imagines he is Valancourt, come to London to whisk Emily St Aubert (Margaret Jewell, as is) away to Toulouse. If the man looks back the vision creeps away in a cloud of excited shame, and she looks down at her feet and hurries on.

Of course, these are childish visions, and there is an emerging part of Margaret that finds these visions ridiculous. It is this part of her which will carry out this infuriating midnight errand despite everything, which will not allow her to just walk back to the house after half an hour and pretend the oyster shop and the bakers are closed. But she is also still a girl, and it is this girl that swears elaborately as she turns away from the door and then blushes, the words hot on the tongue.

Margaret heads westwards along the Ratcliffe Highway. At this end of the Highway, nearest to the city, the houses are tidy and newly built, and within them reside many respectable people who are already in bed, Saturday or no. Much of this housing sprang up after the fire of 1794, which swept through Wapping and Shadwell and was a national emergency, the government forced to provide temporary shelter in military tents even while they were needed for the Revolutionary Wars sweeping across Europe.

London's fires are like those in a forest, destroying the old and clearing the ground for the new. The property developers followed the fire and low, smart houses began to appear like new growth within a burned wood. This little wave of new housing reaches another few hundred yards further east down the Highway, away from the city, before crashing on the rocks of the old depravities at Wapping and St Paul's, where the new grid-like streets give way to clusters of sinewy lanes crammed together between empty land owned by the London Dock Company. Guarding the boundary line between the new and the ancient is the stern white mountain of St George in the East. The church exerts a brooding presence on the local people, as if it had been dropped down into this place by angels with gigantic schemes.

Walking along the straight pavement towards the city, Margaret sees the bird-like Olney, the parish watchman, come out of his ramshackle hutch on the pavement and begin walking towards her. His steps are uncertain, and as he gets closer her sensitive nose picks up his smell even over the odours of salt and tar and fish and rigging which blow over the wall from the dock.

The man is drunk again. No surprise there. Almost all the watchmen she's ever come across in her young life have been drunk from the moment the sun went down to the moment it came up again. After which time they were generally asleep.

Olney raises his cap to her as he passes, and seems about to say something, but thankfully her momentum takes her past the confused old fool. She continues down the road.

She has two errands – to buy some oysters from Taylor's, and to settle the baker's bill. The oysters were Celia Marr's idea, something to please her husband and maybe coax him out of his foul mood. Celia tacked on the oysters as Margaret left the house, despatched by Mr Marr to pay the baker, which is a fool's errand. Margaret knows the baker will be closed at this time of the evening. It is just an excuse to get her out of the house. Marr has made no secret about how very irritating he has found her all day. She'd overheard a conversation between Marr and his wife, some days before, in which Marr complained about there being 'too many bloody children in this house'. She supposes she is one of the 'children'. She is a year older than James, the shop boy, who is now helping the Marrs to close up. The new baby, a few months old, has seemingly been crying without stop since he emerged from his mother's womb. Margaret is sick of the noise from the cellar, where the baby sleeps. The child is the most miserable excuse for an infant she's ever come across.

The creaking masts of the ships in the dock are quieter than normal tonight – there is no breeze to buffet them – and the moisture in the air dampens the occasional cry from behind the wall that divides the dock from Pennington Street, just behind the row of houses to her left. But the absence of other common noises only makes the sound of her footsteps ring out even more, and Margaret feels a familiar little stab of anxiety, so familiar that it passes almost without notice. Any young woman walking along the fringes of the dark heart of the Ratcliffe Highway would recognise it.

She comes to Taylor's, the oyster shop, and is surprised, despite herself, to find it closed. The shop would normally be open even at this late hour, selling Whitstable oysters to the shopkeepers and merchants of the surrounding streets, who typically don't end their day until midnight on a Saturday. But now the shop is closed up and apparently empty, and looks like it has been so for some time. Muttering another little furtive obscenity to herself, Margaret turns around and walks back towards Timothy Marr's shop. The baker's is on the other side of number 29, eastwards along the Highway and then down John Hill towards the dock.

She overtakes Olney the watchman as she approaches Marr's shop again, but he doesn't notice her. He is gazing, apparently awestruck but probably just confused, at the pale-white steeple of St George in the East which rises up ahead of him. Margaret slips by the watchman as quietly as possible, silently praying to whatever God is in residence in the church tonight to stop the drunk old watchman from conversing with her.

She gets past him safely, and peers quickly into Marr's shop as she walks past it in the other direction. Marr is still busy setting things straight, and she hears him bark an instruction at young James, whose shape hurries past the inside of the window carrying an enormous box. She smiles to herself. Maybe she won't hurry back this evening. Without breaking step, she carries on down the Highway, and turns right into John Hill, which runs down the hill from the ridge of the Highway and ends against the wall of the dock.

And, of course, the baker's is closed. Like Taylor's the oyster shop, it has an air of finality about it, as if it had never opened. Its shutters are closed and tight, like every shutter in the neighbourhood will be in an hour or so's time. This area might be moderately respectable, but people aren't stupid; this is the Ratcliffe Highway, after all, and the residents round here are only too aware of the unending disorder a few hundred yards further east, where the lunatics, the thieves, the drunks and the prostitutes congregate down towards Wapping and Old Gravel Lane, and are more than likely to chance their arm with a quick smash-and-grab on respectable households.

But what to do? She feels a strong reluctance to return to number 29 with neither errand completed. She can imagine what the reaction will be to that. Suddenly, she remembers another oyster shop, around the corner on Pennington Street. She might even be able to gain some credit by finding oysters on her own initiative, at least with Mrs Marr. She walks down the remainder of John Hill.

In front of her, running from left to right along the far side of Pennington Street, she can see the dark, hulking presence of the dock wall, a prison-like expanse protecting the wealth within the new London Dock on the other side. The dock is as full as ever, and the tops of the tallest masts are visible over the top of the wall and the warehouses within.

It is not her night. The second oyster shop is as closed as the first. Feeling brave, she crosses the road to stand next to the wall of the dock. Underneath it the darkness is even deeper, and she places her hand on the new brickwork as she has done many times before, as if she could absorb some narrative from inside. She closes her eyes and imagines herself on the shore of a tropical country, sand beneath her naked feet and the sound of gulls screeching above.

If you put your ear to the dock wall, you can hear the river. It is the bassnote to all the other noises of the dock – the shouting men, the creaking timber, the splashes and the crashes and the thunder of barrels rolling down planks and into cellars.

This is the counterpoint to the bass of the river: the music of trade.

Because here, in this dock, is where the chattels of a ravished, crushed world are poured out. Wine and brandy (even now it pours in, even while Boney bestrides Europe). Tobacco from the New World. Rice and tea from the Far East. All of it tumbles down into the vast vaults that encircle the dock, the most expansive man-made underground areas in the world. The Pyramids contain only a fraction of the volume of these massive capacities. Trade built them, trade fills them, and trade empties them.

It is six years since the dock opened, nine years since men started digging out the damp marshy soil. Eleven acres of scrubby dwellings were cleared to make way for the clean lines of the new dock. The vaults take up another eighteen acres, creeping underneath the homes of Wapping and Shadwell and St Paul's, where people go about their days only feet above casks, pipes, barrels, hogsheads and butts, containing tobacco, tea and enough wine to float a navy.

Above the ground, the dock is a gleaming display of the finest English brickwork, and follows the brutal aesthetic of its architect, Daniel Alexander, who has also just given the country Dartmoor Gaol. Within its walls a mighty machine has been built, well run and ruthlessly protected. Every day lumpers and porters and sailors pour out of the dock to meet the grocers and innkeepers and boarding-house women and prostitutes who sate their thirsts, fill their stomachs and attend to their immortal souls and animal desires, while victuallers and chandlers and coopers and drapers sell the goods which will equip their ships for new voyages.

For six years this economic organism has been spreading itself, pushing itself out northwards and eastwards. Its intensities have deepened and its sensibilities have coarsened. Only one language is understood, the language of trade, and even religion has had to give way against the tide. God has left Wapping, say many of the locals, and the Devil himself fancies his chances down here on the dock.

Saturday night will be the Devil's night, when idle minds and hands turn their thoughts to sin. Even innocents can feel this, and Margaret opens her eyes suddenly from her dreamy revelry of sun and sand, thinking she hears something new and discordant in the night air, above and beyond the mutterings of the dock.

The quality of the night has changed. It has closed in, and her mind replays the sound she thought she'd heard, but she is unable to process it. A hum? The buzzing of bees? She takes her hand away from the wall, turns around, and begins to walk back to Marr's shop, defeated in her errands but somehow anxious to be home.

The watchman, Olney, is nowhere to be seen when she gets back to the door. The shop is in darkness, the shutters up. She pulls the bell, and hears it ring inside the shop, and waits. She pulls the bell again. And waits. She places her ear to the wood and can hear nothing, but it is a pregnant nothing, as if the house were waiting for something to happen. She bangs on the door and, despite herself, calls out.

'Mr Marr! Mr Marr! It is Margaret!'

She places her ear against the door once more, and from inside she hears a faint noise, the creak of a footstep on the stair. She pulls away, relieved that someone is coming. The strange fears that had momentarily surfaced in her mind start to ebb away. She waits for the sound of the bolt being pulled on the inside of the door. It doesn't come. She leans towards the door again, and hears the faint, sharp cry of a baby. Something about the noise recalls the strange sound she'd thought she'd heard by the dock, and the wave of fear in her head (an authentic fear, not one learned from the gothic extremities of a novel) crashes in again, and she begins to strike the door.

'Mr Marr! Mr Marr! Let me in please, Mr Marr! It is Margaret.'

A hand falls on her shoulder, and she whirls around, the shout frozen in her throat. Behind her stands a short, stinking stranger who puts his toothless face into hers and yells at her:

'Hear the noise, filly! Hear it in your head! It'll wake us all!'

He steps back, and Margaret leans away as well, her head brushing against Timothy Marr's door. The drunk man falls backwards into the street, sprawled headlong, and apparently falls asleep. Margaret feels a rigid stiffness in her stomach and a growing softness in her knees. She puts her hand against the door and forces herself to stay upright. She takes several deep, slow breaths. She regains herself, and turns back to the door.

Its solid, freshly painted surface intimidates her, and suddenly she feels hopeless and abandoned and exposed. She looks up and down the street, and sees, maybe a hundred yards away, old Olney emerging from a side street and beginning his slow, stumbling progress towards her. Then the panic breaks through and now she is striking the door with both hands, furiously and unthinkingly.

'Mr Marr! Mr Marr! Mr Marr!'

OCTOBER 1564

Out on the edge of the dark moor, with winter coming on, a young man lay stretched out beneath an ancient leather coat, composing a letter in his mind.

My sweet Kate

Tomorrow, I will reach Plymouth. My travelling partner, the old Tin-Man, tells me we are only three miles away now, and I fancy I can already smell a change in the air. Perhaps it is the sea? It is certainly exciting. It smells of Opportunity.

God willing, I will find a Room for the night and a Table on which I can write down these words to you. It still feels wonderfully strange to write. I have a good supply of quills to sharpen, and the jar of ink is nearly full. Can it really be less than a fortnight since I left you in Stanton St John? Even my daily Letter to you is not enough to make much difference to the supplies your Father gave me.

Writing was a skill hard-earned, even with the help of you and your Father. But it is why I am here tonight, shivering by the side of this old Road with an ancient Tin-Man for company. He saw me writing, in an alehouse in Tavistock. He looked at me like I was some kind of Faery when he first saw me pull out the implements. I told him I was writing to my Wife and Beloved, but it did not take away the Wonder from his eyes. I believe he has never once seen another Person write something down for any other purpose than that of Commerce. I seem to him to have magical Powers.

So, we fell to talking, and I told him of my destination and he offered to guide me, saying he knew the quickest way to Plymouth and would help me enter the town. And as I was so concerned with missing the Ship, I readily accepted. And now, tomorrow, I arrive in Plymouth, and the next part of my Journey begins.

I believe I may not be able to write to you again for many weeks. Or perhaps I will write again tomorrow. Who knows? Who knows when the Ship leaves, or even if it has already left? Who knows if this is a Fool's errand or the beginning of our lives together? I may come back with Money. I may come back with Nothing. But I am determined that I must at least try to provide the means for us to create our Future. Your Father is a generous, large-hearted man, and I think of him, indeed, as being the equal of the Father I lost. My Mother's gratitude to him was a warmth which eased her passing. But Sons must grow beyond their Fathers, even when those Fathers are substitutes.

Money, or Nothing. These are the two Destinations I head towards. I come back with one of these, or I do not come back at all.

I know you are frightened by this Journey, my sweet. I am frightened too. But if all goes well, I will come back a Man, having left a Boy. A Man with Prospects and with the Resources to meet them. A Man, in short, with Money. Tomorrow, Plymouth welcomes me, and I welcome all that Plymouth may bring.

I love you. Wherever in the wide World my Journey takes me, that love will be with me.
Billy

The next day was market day in Plymouth, and the gulls knew it. There were clouds of them hanging over the town ahead of him, and he had never seen such screeching raucous creatures in the sky before. The silent clouds of starlings over the woods of Stanton St John would soar away from such a racket. It was only the first of that day's marvels.

The old tin-man's packhorse raised its sad eyes up to the gulls, but seemed incapable of surprise after so many years of trudging the ancient ridge road from Tavistock that fell down from the treeless edges of the moor into the punchy self-confident little town below. Half-a-dozen half-empty sacks of tin weighed down the spine of the old horse. The old man himself didn't look up from the cold, damp dirt below him. He had kept his eyes on the road for much of the journey, unsteady on his ancient feet as he was, but he still fell down three or four times a day, in a flurry of pagan curses and foul-smelling clothes. He was too old to be doing this journey, it occurred to Billy. He was the oldest human Billy had ever seen. He was perhaps fifty, almost two decades older than Kate's father.

The road had been descending for some time, and below the gulls Billy could see the compact walled town, a church spire climbing up almost to touch the bellies of the birds which squawked their welcome. Although the ground remembered it was October, maintaining autumn's damp, it was a dry day for so late in the year, essentially clear, and down the hill and over the roofs of the houses Billy could see the unfamiliar vertical sight of masts. The wind brought a new smell into his nostrils, a cold, fresh, salty smell. There had been a forewarning of that sharp tang the previous day, but now it came on hard and strong. Plymouth sat at the edge of the whole world, and the scent of it brought the world sharply into focus.

He felt profoundly excited. He felt like crying. He felt sick.

He touched the side of his face, again, the place where Kate had kissed him, two weeks before. 'For luck,' she'd said, and now he said it again as he walked past the first houses, on the edge of the town. 'For luck.'

Luck had been a constant companion these past few weeks. He'd travelled more than a hundred and fifty miles from Oxfordshire, sleeping in fields most evenings, occasionally taken in by a well-meaning farmer's wife with perhaps the trace of an old sparkle in her eyes. Finally, he'd skirted the north side of the moor and had reached Tavistock, where he'd met the decrepit tin-man.

Kate's father had been adamant – stay away from the towns, and don't go near Dartmoor on your own. If you do, you'll die. And yet the only way into Plymouth from the north was along the edge of Dartmoor and through Tavistock, breaking both of Kate's father's admonitions. So Billy had been relieved when the tin-man had approached him in the inn and told him about ancient paths known only to farmers and tin-men. He spoke like that, too: 'ancient paths known only to farmers, young 'un', as if his every utterance was to be written down within a Celtic myth. Billy had grasped the chance, even though these 'ancient ways' turned out to be no more than the main north–south road into Plymouth which had been tramped up and down for centuries past.

In any case, Plymouth hadn't been designed for those arriving on foot. Plymouth sat on the water, and was only notionally attached to the rest of the country behind it. If you didn't have a way of getting there by boat, well then Plymouth had little time for you. If you weren't travelling by water, really, what sort of a person could you be? In recent decades,

Plymouth had been the stage for dozens of epic encounters, between England and France, England and Spain, England and the Hanseatic League, England and anyone with a ship full of treasure who thought they could slip by the hungry chancers of Devon and Cornwall without at least a nibble of piracy. Fowey, westwards down the coast, was the home of a more vicious collection of thieves and smugglers. In Plymouth the chancers dressed well and cloaked themselves in mercantile respectability. Like London, the town was run by and for its merchants. Its aldermen were cut from a particular swashbuckling cloth, and looked longingly (and greedily) out across the ocean, out to where the Spaniards and Portuguese were busy carving out empires and hollowing out mountains of gold and silver. It was from Plymouth that the English followed them, and it was back to Plymouth that the plunder of countless acts of derring-do had begun to return.

Billy and the tin-man (no boat, but a trusty packhorse) entered the town through Old North Gate. There were men at this gate writing down the names of those who entered and left, and he felt a momentary tug of fear (*avoid the towns*, said Kate's father again urgently), but the old tin-man grunted at the men and Billy was waved through, apparently as someone the old man would vouch for.

Once inside the walls of the town, everything changed. Rows of houses started to bunch up like young men in an alehouse, and the spaces between these rows of houses started to organise themselves into something like paved pathways. These are streets, Billy realised. Streets like they have in Oxford itself.

And as these streets and rows of houses began to crowd in, Plymouth rose up to meet Billy's eyes and ears and nose. It was a whirl of shouting voices, human and animal smells and blurry-bright magnificent colours. Having spent the last few days with only the sounds of the moor to keep him company, and the swaying rattling of the packhorse and the tin-man, the torrent of sensation was overwhelming. Now there were people everywhere, a river of humans scurrying down to the Market Cross to indulge in the passion of all Englishmen and Englishwomen: the buying and selling of *stuff*.

Everywhere he looked, money was changing hands, and if not money some other item of exchange. People swirled around the street. If you sniffed the air, it smelled of deals.

Billy turned towards the tin-man to ask directions, but the man was gone, along with his packhorse, and Billy whispered a farewell under his breath, along with a quiet Polish *Ave Maria*, like his mother had described his father doing.

A woman heard him whisper the little prayer and glanced at him curiously. Plymouth-dwellers were notoriously alert to the presence of spies in their town, and with a fresh Protestant queen on the throne Roman Catholic homilies rather stood out. But he smiled his charming smile and her face melted, as faces (particularly female faces) generally did around young Billy Ablass. He was a fine-looking young man, tall with dark hair and pale, smooth skin. His teeth were whiter and straighter than they had any business being, and his blue eyes (inherited from his Slavic father) were crystal-clear.

He'd now reached the Market Cross itself, and he stopped for a moment. His heart was still racing with the richness of the experience, but the *Ave Maria* and the woman's smile had quietened his mind somewhat. He needed to get to the Mitre – that was the alehouse Kate's father had told him about, the place where he'd find the captain. Normally, Billy would not have been remotely concerned about asking for directions, but the paradox of these crowds had already hit him: he felt alone and very obviously out of place, and for a moment imagined all the faces of the crowd turned to him, the stranger from far away.

And there she was again, the woman he'd smiled at, coming back into view behind a horse, so he smiled again and approached her.

'Excuse me, ma'am. I'm searching for the Mitre, if you would know where that would be.'

Her smile remained, but it was puzzled – his accent was unplaceable. Not Devon, certainly. Somerset, perhaps? Dorchester? Surely not as far as Oxford!

'And why would a handsome young thing like you be looking for the Mitre?' she said, determined to keep him in conversation for a while. Her rich Devon vowels made her seem impossibly exotic to Billy, her accent even stronger than that of the farmer. Her seductive tone might have given him pause, but Billy didn't hesitate to roll out his learned-by-heart story.

'My uncle Jack is a brewer, from Abingdon. He wants to sell his beer in Plymouth, and has asked me to visit the local alehouses to see if they might be prepared to sell his fine ale. I'm to talk to them all. Starting with the Mitre,' he added hurriedly, afraid she might direct him to another tavern.

He'd remembered the fictional details, and felt a small lift of pride. The woman was smiling even more broadly now, as if he'd just told her the finest joke this side of the Tamar.

'Well, quite the man of business, aren't we?' she said. 'And all the way from Abingdon? Why, you must have been travelling for weeks, young fellow. The Mitre's in the street down there, towards the harbour.' She pointed to a gap in the buildings that surrounded the Market Cross. 'But you'll have no joy with your uncle's fine ales, which I'm sure are the nectar of the gods themselves, judging by his fine nephew. The Mitre's run by old Coakley, and that nasty old bugger will only sell ale from Devon. He makes a point of it.'

He thanked the woman, who laughed again at his formality before continuing on her way.

He looked at the houses she'd pointed at, and they were (again!) the most opulent things he'd ever seen, their leaded windows glittering in the unseasonal sun. In one of the open windows, a gorgeous young creature sat watching the crowds below and combing her long red hair. He took no joy in her appearance, because she reminded him of Kate, and of how long it would be before he saw her again. She noticed him, though, and for a moment she imagined eloping to Exeter and heading for the golden pavements of London with the gorgeous, serious-faced stranger.

He struggled across the stream of market traders and visitors, and walked down the street the woman had indicated. It was a small, crooked place, smelling of shit and cows and, within and above the other smells, the mysterious scent of some foreign spice that lent all the other odours an impossible glamour. There were still people here, so many people, but in the shadows they stopped being faces and voices and turned into presences. Up ahead, a gaggle of shadowy men stood outside one of the buildings, and above them swung a childishly simple picture of a bishop's mitre.

The men outside the inn ignored him as he pushed through them, and Billy thought in passing that this was the first time he'd deliberately touched a stranger and been ignored by him in return. Half-a-dozen strangers, at that. Another new sliver of experience. Perhaps he was already a changed man, even after so little time.

He passed through a low-arched doorway and, to his surprise, emerged into a small open courtyard with a cloister down one side and a staircase at the end, beneath which was a door. It didn't look like any inn he had ever seen before, but he headed for the door and went inside.

Within there was a genuine gloom, one that reminded him of the local alehouse back at home on a winter's night when the fire was on and a few candles served to light the room. But this gloom was not particularly cosy; indeed, there was something church-like about it. In one corner a man sat on his own with a few candles and a massive pewter beer-jug, an open ledger in front of him. The man seemed to give off his own light, or rather to be reflecting and amplifying the light from the sturdy candles in front of him. He wore an amazingly impressive ruff on top of something possibly more alien than anything Billy had seen thus far – a purple doublet with gold stitching and brass studs, each the size of a sheep's eye and each polished, so that the man looked like a map of the stars. He was the most impossibly exotic human Billy had ever seen.

Billy approached what seemed in the gloom to be a bear cleaning a huge earthenware jug in front of a new-looking hatch in the wall. A man, of course, but a man so huge and so hairy that Billy could not get his first impression out of his mind, that the landlord of this place was a huge Russian bear with a thick mane on its head and a beard hanging down from its impressive jaw. The man's massive fat hairy fingers moving surprisingly delicately over the jug. He didn't look up at Billy.

Billy found it took some courage to speak to him.

'Excuse me, sir. I'm looking for someone, and was told I might find him here.'

The hairy man said nothing, but something about the way he moved his head indicated that Billy could at least carry on speaking.

'I'm looking for John Hawkyns.'

At that, the hairy man looked directly at Billy. He was interested now, although Billy sensed this might not be for reasons entirely beneficial to him.

'Yer lookin' for John 'Awkyns, are ye?' said the man. His

accent grated on Billy's ears. It was harder and harsher than the sandpapered-down warmth of Oxford. He'd not heard anything quite like it before. Even the old farmer hadn't sounded like this. Letters were dropped from the beginnings and ends of words, and the whole thing sounded chopped and mangled and turned in on itself. Aggression seemed to be the cable that strung the words together.

'Yes, sir.'

'And why would ye think Mr 'Awkyns would want ye to find 'im, eh?'

Billy wondered if he would get anywhere with this beast of a man, but then another voice cut in.

'Now, now, Coakley. Mr Hawkyns can decide such things for himself.'

After the harsh rasping of Coakley, as Billy now guessed the hairy giant to be, this new voice was rich, elegantly polished and sardonic, and even without turning Billy knew it must come from the glamorous man with the candles and the ledger. Billy turned to look in that direction, and saw the stranger was smiling, almost rapturously, at him. He preceded his next utterance with a theatrical wink towards Billy.

'Really, Coakley, I don't know how they are wont to do things in London, but here in the Queen's Harbour of Plymouth we like to make young strangers feel welcome. Particularly such well put-together young strangers. Pour the boy a drink and get him to come over here.'

Coakley smirked as he poured beer into a pewter jug, and handed it to Billy with a leer. 'Sip i' slowly, stranger,' he muttered as he handed it over. 'Few too many of these and ye'll find yourself tied to a mainmast. And no' in' the regular way, if you ge' my meanin'.'

Billy did not get his meaning, but didn't say so, preferring instead to adopt his newly learned attitude of polite caution in the face of strangers saying inexplicable things. He took the ale and walked over to the man with the ledger and the splendid clothes, who was still smiling at him with an expansive, welcoming ease. Everything about the man oozed splendour and munificence, and something about him made Billy think of the young girl brushing her hair in the window of the expensive house.

'Sit down, young fellow, sit down,' said the rich man. 'Now. I do know this John Hawkyns whom you are seeking. What would you have him speak to you about?'

That smile remained in place, and the hands were folded on top of the thick, heavy leather ledger. The studs in the man's doublet flickered like beacon fires on the hills above Plymouth, warning of encroaching danger.

'I've a letter for him, sir.'

'Really? How tremendously exciting. So let's see this letter, my lad.'

Billy reached inside his jerkin. For half a second he could not feel the letter and an impossible world of failure opened up, a world in which he returned to Stanton St John with nothing, with no money at all, and Kate's father lost the tenancy of the manor farm and left the village, taking Kate with him, and Billy roamed the country, a worthless serf, away from Kate and away from his dreams of money and all that came with it. But then he felt the corner of the thick parchment, pulled out the letter, and stopped.

The stranger was staring at Billy, his smile now smaller but still there, his head tipped back slightly and his eyes almost closed, like a cat waiting for a mouse to jump.

'Can you smile, sir?' the rich man asked, suddenly, before Billy had a chance to show him the letter.

'Smile?'

'Yes, dammit, smile. I'd like to see you smile. If I were to say that Coakley here was a London man and came here to avoid three different women who mystifyingly wanted to spend their lives with him, would that make you smile?'

Despite himself, Billy did smile. The man's easy, arrogant charm was so beautiful to observe, while being so patently lethal.

'My God, you do smile, sir. Exceptionally so.' But Billy stopped smiling immediately. He felt something cold in his gut, and found that he had some steel inside him when it came to matters of negotiation. He kept a hold on the letter.

'If you please sir, I'd rather give the letter to Mr Hawkyns directly, sir. The man who gave it to me said specifically that I should give it to Mr Hawkyns and only Mr Hawkyns.'

The man's smile was still in place, but its personality had changed. The nose had pinched, the eyes compressed. He now looked like he might bite Billy's head off and spit it into his beer.

'You have a bloody nerve, boy. I say give me the letter and I'll give it to Hawkyns.'

'And if you please, sir, I say that in all conscience I cannot, having been instructed to give it to Mr Hawkyns directly.'

The rich man leaned forward, the hands rising together and the index fingers pointing directly between Billy's eyes. His eyes were flat and dangerous.

'Young men from the country arrive in Plymouth all the time. And young men disappear as well . . .'

'Now, now, enough, Tregarthen. Leave the lad alone.'

Another man had emerged from the gloom of the inn and had placed his hand on the shoulder of the first. Although he spoke quietly, and had emerged as if from smoke, his presence changed the room. The atmosphere of threatening bonhomie disappeared. Undercurrents vanished. Billy relaxed, despite himself.

'Get me a beer, Coakley. And another for this pillar of the community Tregarthen. Now, this letter, lad.'

'Mr Hawkyns?'

The man nodded as he sat down, and his natural authority was such that without a qualm Billy handed him the heavy precious letter which he'd husbanded so carefully on the journey from Oxfordshire. Billy watched Hawkyns as he read the letter. The man wore a doublet and a ruff like the man he'd called Tregarthen, but where the other's clothes were all ostentation and show, Hawkyns's outfit was relatively subdued but still, deliberately, very expensive. Even to Billy's untrained bucolic eyes, his clothes were obviously much more costly than those worn by his comrade. This was a man who dressed not to influence or to impress, but to dominate and to control. His hair was dark and cut short, his dark beard pointed in the Spanish manner, his nose long and straight. Hawkyns's eyes were almost black, as far as Billy could detect here in the gloom of the Mitre. The candle glittered in them as he read the letter.

He finished reading.

'The hand is barbaric, but I'd expect that from a man like White. You are his son-in-law, yes?'

'Yes, sir.'

'Well, lad, your father-in-law is a presumptuous rogue to have written a letter like this to one such as I. I've just returned from a private audience with Elizabeth herself. I'd like to know why I should grant the request of a bloody Oxfordshire farmer who seems to be under the impertinent impression that I owe him a favour.'

'Yes, sir. He helped you with a horse, sir.'

'Yes, he did. As he should have done for a superior.'

'He said you'd say something like that, Mr Hawkyns.'

'Did he now?'

'Yes, sir. And he said to tell you that the horse he lent you came back lame, and is now good for nothing more than a Frenchman's supper.'

There was silence at that. Hawkyns did not laugh, smile or rage. He kept his eyes steadily on Billy's, and Billy did not look away, and perhaps that more than anything meant he did not have to turn around and travel home with nothing. They glared at each other for five seconds, ten, fifteen, but Billy held on, grimly, until Hawkyns's expression finally softened and he raised one well-groomed eyebrow.

'Extraordinary. Well, one must admire the man's backbone. Does it run in the family?'

'Sir?'

'You're married to John White's daughter?'

'Yes, sir.'

'And who is your father?'

'Now deceased, sir, as is my mother. My father I never knew. He was a Polish sailor.'

'Polish? How does a Polish sailor end up siring a son in Oxfordshire? As far away from the sea as a man can get, I would imagine.'

'He ... Well, he performed some services for a powerful man in old King Henry's court, sir. His reward was a small property in Stanton St John.'

Billy stopped, unsure of how much more he should say on the subject of services and powerful men. Hawkyns caught his hesitation and weighed it up for a second, possibly intrigued.

'No doubt, but a detail I didn't request,' he said, eventually. 'You'll learn to only respond to direct questions when speaking to a commander, lad.'

'Yes, sir.'

'Have you sailed before?'

'No, sir.'

'No, sir. Then what bloody use are you to me?'

Billy said nothing. After not flinching from Hawkyns's gaze earlier, it was the second good decision he'd made that day. Hawkyns sipped his beer, considered something, and then looked at Billy again as if he'd just arrived. The hard face now appeared almost friendly, and Billy once again realised that this man had a certain power to make people do what he wanted just by looking at them the right way.

'You've come a long way, lad. And that on itself says something about you. You can join my crew as a seaman. We sail in three days. The *Jesus of Lübeck*. You can't miss it.'

Billy worried about this. He was pretty sure he could, actually, miss it.

'If you please, sir, how might I be sure it's the right ship?'

Hawkyns laughed.

'You'll be sure because it'll be the biggest fucking thing you've ever seen.'

8 DECEMBER 1811: 2 A.M.

Charles Horton, waterman-constable of the River Thames Police Office, takes almost a half-hour to walk from the Police Office building at Wapping Stairs to the Ratcliffe Highway. His errand is urgent, but there is nevertheless the not insignificant fact of the new dock lying between him and the most direct route to his destination.

The shortest way now available thus takes him around the southeastern corner of the dock, through the heart of Wapping itself – along Old Gravel Lane, with its alehouses both respectable and dissolute. Despite the late hour there are still people mulling around on the street. Sunday may have begun, but most of those out are no respecters of religious tradition. Drunken sailors collide into equally drunken lumpers and watermen before collapsing into a thumping heap; prostitutes keep an eye on the alehouse exits in the hope of picking up a lone, lonely seaman who has still kept hold of some of his money; the occasional gentleman picks his way gingerly through the sodden lower orders on his way back from an evening roughing it on the waterfront. It is in most senses a normal Saturday night in Dockland.

But there is something else too, and Horton, a Wapping man (but a Margate boy), can smell the difference as soon as he walks out into the street. He has been working a night shift at the Police Office, something he does rarely unless traffic is particularly heavy out on the river, so it was fortunate that he was there to receive the excitable boy who'd arrived with news from the Ratcliffe Highway. Horton, who has an easy way with children, employs a small network of excitable boys with open ears and watchful eyes throughout Wapping and Shadwell, and has lost count of the times a juicy nugget of intelligence has worked its way down to the riverside office from a backstreet to the north or east.

Now, out in the street, it's clear to Horton's finely tuned senses that the same news carried to him by his boy has already begun to work its way into the shared consciousness of Wapping, and soon some of these people (the ones who can still walk, at least) will be making their way in the same direction for a look-see. Only alcohol and the late hour are slowing them down, but before long raw human curiosity will overcome those obstacles. He walks fast to beat them to it.

Horton is a tall man in his forties, dressed tonight for work on the river in a dark pea coat and even darker trousers, a dark shirt and woollen jumper beneath the coat, and a dark hat on his head. His eyes are dark, his skin pale, his hair as dark as his clothes. Despite his size, he has a near-invisible quality about him, the same near-invisible quality as a watchful excitable boy who wishes to make himself useful. He bumps into no one's shoulders, trips over no one's feet, and no one notices him as he flits through the common herd. He walks, and he listens, and he hears the sound of Wapping growling in its cups.

At the end of Old Gravel Lane he turns left onto the Highway, and even from here he can see the beginnings of a small crowd mulling around the house at number 29. As he approaches, he sees that perhaps fifty people have already gathered outside. He starts to push his way through, shouting out who he is as the crowd gets thicker. The smell of gin and ale and unwashed clothes is heavy in the air. Even shouting he struggles to be heard, but still eases his way through.

Finally he breaks through to a clearer space around the front door of the neat little house. The space is a respectful one, left intact by the growing crowd despite their excitement and their intoxication. A young girl is sitting on the pavement weeping in the almost silent, exhausted way of a woman who has been crying for some time and is almost worn out. A group of men is standing around her but somewhat away from her, as if embarrassed by her display. Horton recognises one of them: Olney, one of the local parish watchmen. He pulls the old man aside.

Olney is drunk, as is to be expected of a watchman at this time of night, but seems to be relatively alert. Horton grabs his upper arm and speaks directly into his ear. The crowd becomes quieter, recognising the appearance of authority even when it dresses in a pea coat, trying to hear what he is saying.

'Olney – what has happened here?'

'Murder, Officer Horton. Foul, foul murder.'

The watchman begins to weep, and not for the first time this evening, reckons Horton. He has seen the old man cry before. He becomes sentimental and maudlin when he has been drinking, and he drinks most of the time. It is the normal way for a Shadwell watchman to behave, and Horton does not judge him for it.

'In the house?' asks Horton, still gripping the old man's arm, still whispering urgently.

'Yes. Yes, sir.'

'Witnesses?'

'The girl. And him. Murray.'

Olney, still weeping, points a shaky finger towards one of the men standing around the sobbing girl. The man is looking back over Horton's shoulder, away from the girl, gazing at something. His lips are moving and Horton thinks he hears a fragment of prayer. Horton glances back behind himself, in the same direction as the man is looking, and sees the white tower of St George in the East. He had walked right by it on the way here and had not even glanced up at it, scurrying along underneath its pale gaze.

He turns back to Olney. He is still gripping the old watchman's arm.

'Anyone inside?'

'No.'

'No constables or magistrates from Shadwell?'

'No.'

'Have you been in?'

The old man looks at him.

'Not for all the world.'

At that, Horton lets go of Olney's arm, and walks up to the man the watchman has identified. The man's lips stop moving as Horton steps towards him, but while they are speaking the man keeps his back turned to the house and his eyes keep flicking over Horton's shoulders towards the unavoidable bulk of the church.

'Murray?'

'Yes. John Murray. I live nex' door.'

'You've seen what has happened?'

'I've been . . . inside, is all.'

'How did you get in?'

'Back of the 'ouse. Through the back.'

'Show me.'

Murray's eyes flicker and focus on Horton.

'I'll show ye. But I'm not goin' in again.'

He leads Horton away. As they pass the sobbing girl on the street, Horton sees her glance up at him. A young girl, maybe sixteen or seventeen. Long red curly hair. Her eyes almost as red as her hair with the crying, but at the same time full of a knowledge newly acquired. Her mouth opens in a small 'o' as if she is going to say something, ask for his help or his guidance perhaps, but she says nothing, and then the crowd closes around her, eager for a glimpse and perhaps a touch of the eyewitness.

Some of the crowd break off and follow Murray and Horton down the street. A man shouts 'Oi, you!' but Horton ignores that. There will be more and more of it before long.

The two men and their small accompanying flock come to a gate between two blocks of houses, which Murray opens and goes through. Horton turns to the small crowd as he passes through the gate and shuts it behind him.

'No one is to follow me, on the authority of John Harriott, magistrate of the Thames River Police Office. Stay here.'

The flock grumbles, with one male voice particularly vocal, the same one as before. But Horton shuts the gate behind him and no one attempts to follow. He and Murray are in the passageway between the two blocks. Murray is waiting for him, silhouetted by moonlight.

'You're with the River Office?' Murray asks. 'Not Shadwell?'

'Shadwell will be here, I'm sure,' Horton says. 'Now show me where you got in.'

The end of the passage opens into a semi-private, rather bleak little square, more of a yard really, onto which face the backs of perhaps twenty houses. Murray turns left and walks back past two or three of these trim little houses. He stops at one of them.

'This is it. Timothy Marr's 'ouse.' He pronounces the name *timoffee*.

A chest-high fence runs along the back of the Marrs' yard, broken by a gate, which is open. Horton steps through it, and then pauses. He turns back to Murray.

'Tell me what happened, as quickly as you can.'

The man's face is white but his voice is steady. A good witness, it occurs to Horton. Should one be needed.

'I live coupla doors away. I 'eard noises from the 'ouse, some shoutin' and furniture crashin'. It's no' uncommon, though. But then I 'eard the girl shoutin' at the front door. She couldn't ge' in, no one was answ'rin' 'er. The watchman, Olney, 'e came and started ringin' at the door too. I come round the back 'ere, saw a light on. I shouted back roun' to Olney an' the girl that the light was on, an' she screamed at me to get in 'n' check they was all right. So I go' in the 'ouse. And I saw 'em.'

'What did you see?'

'They're all dead.'

Murray's voice cracks slightly now, and he looks at the ground. Horton turns away from him and walks through the gate towards the house. A single light is shining from a back room. It seems to be waiting for him.

The back door to 29 Ratcliffe Highway is open, and he steps into the downstairs hallway, out of the cold December air. On his left is the kitchen, then there is an open door with steps leading down to the cellar. Ahead of him, down the hallway, a half-open door beyond which, he supposes, is Timothy Marr's shop. To his right is a steep flight of stairs, and there he sees the source of the light he could see from the street: a candle has been left alight, at the top of the stairs. He climbs the stairs and picks it up. It is nearly burnt out. He wonders if Murray left it there, so deliberately at the top of the stair, and if not Murray, then who? Considering this, he carries the candle into one of the bedrooms. Anyone standing at the bottom of the stairs would have believed they were seeing a miracle, a candle floating by itself down the upper landing, as Horton's dark clothes make him almost invisible in the gloom.

In the bedroom, the flickering light picks out a heavy implement leaning against the wall, but there is no one in there. Horton tells himself to come back and check on the room when he has examined the rest of the house. He turns, checks the other bedrooms (they are empty) and heads back down the stairs.

A quality of watchfulness has come over him, a close attentiveness to the details of everything he sees and touches. He is not aware of this. He is not aware of anything at all beyond the shapes and textures and patterns of the dark little house. He approaches the half-open door which leads into the shop. It is propped open by a body. Horton passes his candle over the body's face. It is a young man, maybe even a boy. The eyes are open. The head has been smashed in, and as Horton's candle moves across the body and towards the shop beyond he catches a glimpse of bloodstains and thick, stodgy matter splattered up the wall behind. It is thick enough to cast its own lumpy shadows in the candle flicker.

Horton steps over the body and into the shop beyond. He can see the shapes of people moving outside on the Highway in the glass above the front door and through the blinds in the window. He discovers a woman dead on the floor between the counter and the door, and a man behind the counter. The woman's head has also been smashed in, but in the gloom Horton cannot see immediately where the wounds on the man are. He looks around the shop. It is clean and tidy, as if the victims had just completed closing up when they were attacked. The only thing on the counter is a ripping chisel, which

Horton picks up. It looks clean and well-cared-for, even in the gloom. Unused. For anything.

He continues to search. Back in the hallway he opens the cellar door and walks down the steps. He sees a cot in a corner and passes his candle over the top of it. He has to stop himself involuntarily dropping the candle into the wrecked, dead face of the baby within.

8 DECEMBER 1811: 7 A.M.

John Harriott is watching the river as it rolls by his office window. The office of the magistrate of the Thames River Police. *His* office. It is early morning on a rising tide, the busiest time of day for the river, with new ships pouring into the Pool in front of him and into the dock behind where Harriott stands. Even on a Sunday they continue to appear from downstream, one after another, an endless succession of vessels of different shapes and sizes, squeezed together like horses after a race.

Harriott is a short, stout man approaching seventy. He is dressed in white breeches which ride high up on his solid globe of a belly. The breeches and his white wig are in stark contrast to the redness of his face and the maritime blue of his tailcoat. His jaw juts out of his well-fed face towards the window as he watches the river. He has slept for barely three hours, and looks like what he is: a throwback to a time before Napoleon, to the era of Washington and Jefferson and the elder Pitt, when England meandered magnificently towards an empire.

His eyes may be on the river, but John Harriott's well-stocked mind has travelled somewhere else. He is remembering his second trip to pre-Revolution America, between his stints as a midshipman in the navy and an officer in the East India Company militia. He is remembering a particular squaw of the Oneida tribe, who had saved him from some jealous braves. He is remembering her tantalising brown skin and fierce white teeth and the way she leaned into him when they talked, and the places this led to, and the well-founded reasons for the jealousy of the braves. He is remembering the sun through the trees and the sound of happy women chattering in the shadows. He is remembering how much he missed England back then, and is wondering at how much he misses America now. He feels a newly familiar sense of torpor creeping over him, like the Asian illness which nearly took his life forty years ago. His half-dead left leg itches. His mind has temporarily wandered away from the subject at hand, as it does with a frequency he no longer notices.

Behind him, his waterman-constable, Charles Horton, is leaning over a table on which lies a fearsome heavy instrument, which Horton is examining, end to end. It is a maul, a common tool of the waterfront, the same size as an axe, at the end of which is a heavy iron mallet on one side, and a long iron spike on the other. The instrument can be used as both a hammer and a pickaxe, although on this particular maul the tip of the spike has been snapped off.

It is the object Horton saw leaning against the wall in the bedroom at 29 Ratcliffe Highway. He has carried it back from the house wrapped in a sheet taken from one of the bedrooms, and has presented it quietly but deliberately to Harriott, while describing the scene at Timothy Marr's house with precise urgency. He has just finished talking.

Harriott had listened closely for a while to Constable

Horton's narrative, but soon had to turn away to face the window. The maul was exerting an awful compulsion on him. The shape of the murderous instrument sits on his eye like the imprint of a midday Indian sun. Horton's calm description of the maul's barbaric usage has turned this particular tool into something Viking and appalling. Through the window Harriott watches a group of lumpers dragging bags of coal along a wharf, and suddenly envies them their work. He remembers sailing, remembers the activity of the hands and the brain, and the inability to think of anything else, the needlessness of anxiety when all your brain wanted to do was to pass your hands over and over each other in an endless whirr of doing.

He turns back to the room. Horton is still looking at the maul, but he does not touch it. He is concerned with not disturbing the – *oh dear God* – the evidence which still clings to the flat surface of the mallet-shaped side of the maul, a nightmare of blood and hair and other matter.

Constable Horton is, to Harriott's eyes at least, an exceptional man but an occasionally rather odd one, and he is displaying his capacity for oddness right at this moment, pondering the maul, eating it with his eyes, searching for some kind of message on its hard iron extremities. Horton is *inspecting* the maul, as if a close examination could render up information contained within it. As usual, Harriott finds himself to be vaguely uncomfortable with this. It seems somehow wrong to pour such intense attention into such a terrible instrument, as if by doing so the inspector could somehow be infected with the evil that wielded the thing in the first place. But Harriott has also come to realise that Constable Horton's attentiveness yields results. The man can discover answers to unfathomable questions which no other man in the River Thames Police Office can. Harriott only recently came up with a word to describe what it is Horton does. It is *detection*.

Of course the questions for which Harriott and Horton have been seeking answers have normally been of a mercantile nature. A cargo gone missing. A ship sabotaged. A barge raided. Needless to say there have been murders over the thirteen years since Harriott first formed the River Police Office. When sitting down to dinner at Whitehall and Westminster, Harriott has heard Wapping described as the worst place in the world. Powerful and wealthy men have questioned him remorselessly, eager for every nugget of awfulness he can provide on the subject of the human monsters over whom he watches. Harriott always obliges, a natural showman – as a younger man he had once promenaded a herd of Russian sheep through Lord Holland's dining room just to raise a chuckle from the assembled ladies. That memory now pops into his head, another pleasant sliver of reminiscence from a more gilded time, and he turns again to see Horton inspecting the accursed instrument, and considers that this crime is not of a mercantile nature at all. It has a flavour of something else entirely.

'How much sleep have you had, Horton?' Harriott's voice is port-and-cigars gruff, but he finds himself speaking almost for the sake of saying something. Why in heaven should he worry about how much sleep the man has had? There have been savage murders. Something must be done. Sleep should be the last thing on his mind.

But I am an old man . . .

Constable Horton glances up at him, and Harriott sees that the man has barely registered the question. There is an absent look in his mind; the brain is whirring behind the forehead. Horton is busy – now, how had the man described it to Harriott once? Oh, yes. He is busy *making connections*.

'I haven't slept, sir,' Horton replies. 'I wanted to get the details down on paper for you by first thing this morning. I can sleep later.'

Ah yes. The young man of action. I remember him.

'But your wife. Abigail, isn't it? She will be concerned about you.'

Horton does not reply.

'And no one from Shadwell was at the scene of these murders?'

'Not that I saw, sir, no.'

'But it's their area, not ours.'

'Indeed, sir. Odd.'

'Not really. They don't have the same calibre of men up there as we do, Horton.'

Harriott puffs out his chest at this in a military manner, but his officer says nothing to the compliment. He continues to gaze at the hellish maul. Harriott grows exasperated with himself and with the unheeding intensity of his officer. He slaps the table with his knuckle, and Constable Horton perceptibly starts. The old man places his fingers in the pockets of his waistcoat and turns back to the window, forcing himself to be businesslike. *No more daydreaming, Harriott. Get on with it, whoever's jurisdiction it is.*

'So, we have four murders,' he says. 'Two adults, a shop boy, and a baby.'

'Yes, sir.'

'Notable elements of the murders: their savagery, the small window of time the murderers had in which to undertake them, and the fact that nothing is apparently missing from the premises.'

'Nothing that we've been able to ascertain, sir, no.'

'Witnesses: the shop girl, who had been out of the house; the old watchman who sounds about as reliable as any old watchman of the area can be expected to be; the neighbour Murray who discovered the bodies.'

'Yes, sir. Murray seems the surest of them. The girl was still hysterical when I left her, and the watchman had clearly been drunk.'

'Yes. As I say, as one would expect from a watchman.'

'And then there's this story from Pennington Street.'

'Yes. Reports of a *gang* of men running out of an empty house.'

'Yes, sir. The witness concerned states that he heard men running out of the house. If they were the perpetrators, they could have left the house via the back, run through the square and come back through the empty house.'

'And the clues within the house itself are simply this … instrument here. And a ripping chisel.'

'Yes, sir. But the chisel is clean. I don't see how it could have been used in the murders, although its very presence is rather perplexing. The babe's throat was clearly cut with a knife, and we found no knife. The maul was in an upstairs room, away from the bodies. It had been left leaning against the wall. As if someone had put it down while doing something else, and then forgot about it in the rush to escape.'

Not for the first time, Harriott feels uneasy at the process of Constable Horton's deductive reasoning. The man's imagining of the scene is something he will never get used to. Harriott is a man who needs action and interrogation and movement. This fantasising of the event makes him profoundly uncomfortable.

This decides him.

'I'm going to visit the house.'

'As you wish, sir.'

'Make sure the maul is guarded, Horton. We will in all probability have to deliver it up to those fools at Shadwell before the end of the day. But let's see if we can't make some progress on this before they get their fingers on it.'

Harriott leaves Constable Horton inspecting the maul. He grabs his hat and greatcoat and walks out of the River Police Office onto Wapping Street. Warehouses tower on either side of him as he walks east. The streets have changed character since Horton walked them a few hours previously. There is still detritus from the night-folk, but these desperate individuals have mainly given way to working people, scurrying to the dock, to the river, to the shops and boarding houses and workshops and warehouses in Wapping and beyond, even on the Lord's day. Some of them look like they are heading for church, most likely the recently built St John's which nestles up against the south side of the dock. There is a pervading stench from an open sewage ditch which empties into the Thames; its odour settles onto everything. Nonetheless, in the years since the River Police Office opened, Harriott has become comfortable with the air here. It has something of the feel of his drowned island farm in Essex, the one that nearly bankrupted him when it gave way to the sea. Wapping itself had been saved from the sea during Elizabeth's reign by a clever Dutchman, Cornelius Vanderdelf, who'd built a mile-long wall around the riverbank and had, eventually, turned the old marsh into rich meadowland. Harriott had enjoyed the historical circularity of that when he discovered it. He seems to be attracted to reclaimed land.

He passes shops and boarding houses, brass instruments glinting in windows next to elaborate foodstuffs and alien oilskin clothing. And alehouses. Alehouses everywhere. Behind him is the Town of Ramsgate, where the old hanging judge Jeffreys popped in for a drink in 1688 on his way out of the country. The mob surrounded him, and got him back to the Tower to die. Death and beer always hang heavy in the air in Wapping.

Then there is the inn that had been called the Devil's Tavern, now called the Prospect of Whitby after the ship permanently moored outside. Harriott himself has supped in there with his Freemasonry friends, who'd told him of their introduction of Samuel Johnson to Freemasonry in that very spot, where he'd joined the Dundee Lodge.

And hulking over the whole area, visible through gaps in the buildings like a canvas on which Wapping has been painted, the walls of the new dock and its surrounding warehouses. As an Englishman and a professional, Harriott had greatly approved of the general project for improvement which the dock represents. He had defended it to all, even to his wife Elizabeth, who had been concerned about the poor people who had been forced from the area to make way for the construction. 'Nonsense my dear,' Harriott had said, at dinner more than a decade ago, a glass of port in his hand and a table of guests hanging on his words. 'The dock represents the triumph of trade and commerce, and as a failed farmer, soldier and sailor, I warmly welcome the opportunity it brings to fail at something else!' At which there had been general chuckling, approbation and applause.

But even Harriott must admit that there is something massively dark about the dock, something of the gaol about its walls and the warehouses between it and the river, buildings which now glower over the High Street, each of them a good storey or more higher than the older buildings which cluster around the walls like supplicants at a cathedral. The dock is so enormous that it has effectively squeezed Wapping in against the river, with only a few streets now connecting the residents left behind with the rest of London. Wapping has itself been imprisoned by the same trade which gives it succour.

There is a little cluster of freshly minted housing, much of it still under construction, around the Pier Head entrance to the dock, genteel but in keeping with the new brick splendour of the development, and this is where Harriott has made his new home, within a polite little community of wealthy merchants and pillars of the community perched between river, dock and the ratholes of Wapping proper.

He turns back to look towards this new development, to where even now Elizabeth will be stirring for a new day, and sees the sight which never fails to catch his breath. A ship is entering the dock, and from here it looks like it is being wheeled through the streets, its masts sailing over the heads of the buildings, a ghostly mass creeping, apparently silently, through the noxious streets. He turns around again and continues his walk.

Following the same route as Horton before him, from Wapping Street he turns left up into Old Gravel Lane, a twisting, crowded tunnel of a place, made even more crowded by the clearing of buildings on either side of it to make space for the dock. At the end of the lane, running east to west, is the Highway.

The Ratcliffe Highway is a chattering river of people, even this early on a Sunday morning. The new lick of paint on many of the houses built after the fire can't hide the dirty underbelly of the place. For every respectable-looking shop window there are three or four bitter-looking women with painted faces and suggestive clothes standing around. For every one of these molls, there are three or four dark, dirty-looking men standing in the shadows of the buildings, eyeing the staggering sailors and dockers who, even in the early morning, are raging with gin and porter, their pockets jingling with change just waiting to be transferred to new ownership.

Harriott has not walked down this part of the Highway in some time. When he walks anywhere, it's normally along the

Wapping curve of the river, which has the Tower at one end and Limehouse at the other. The Highway, which joins those two points in a straight line to the north and thus defines the bow of Wapping, is not his domain. It is the responsibility of the three Shadwell magistrates, gentlemen who have done little to earn Harriott's good opinion or to demonstrate that they can effectively police this thumping, multifarious ribbon of commerce and human vice.

As Resident Magistrate of the River Police Office at Wapping, Harriott's attention is directed out towards the river rather than inland. The River Police Office is his creation; he founded it in 1798 as an independent public service, and as a means of convincing the government of the need for such a thing. Pilfering and worse was damaging the river trade, but Harriott's new independent creation was such a success in securing trade on the river that it only took a few months before the bewigged gentlemen of Whitehall were finally persuaded that the river trade needed official supervision, and the office became fully integrated as one of the new magistrate's offices.

There remains an intense squeamishness among Their Honourables that Trade, not Land, is making Britain Great, but even among the landed gentry a large number with plenty of zeroes gets attention. Harriott's office is now responsible for ensuring that the hundreds of thousands of pounds sterling which is traded between ship and shore on the river has some measure of protection. The government wrings its hands over the more general policing of London, lest it be accused of aping Bonaparte with a centralised force to keep the general peace. But the good old British love of individual liberty, even in the face of criminal anarchy, ceases to apply on the river. The river is money and it is trade, and if there is one thing London has learned in the centuries since the Romans decided to build a fort on a small hill surrounded by a muddy, meandering river, it is that money and trade will triumph over liberty any day of the week. Even Sunday.

So now Harriott looks upon the Highway with the eyes of someone who has brought a semblance of order to his own patch of authority, on the other side of the dock. The morning air has revived him, and out here among the crowds the memory of the frightful instrument of death can be pushed away. Here, all around, are the kind of villains Harriott is familiar with. He sees, as he always does when out walking, a population of criminals and ne'er-do-wells, all with an eye on the main chance and a hand in someone else's pocket. He sees trade, no doubt, but it is a species of trade which a man like Harriott – navy midshipman, East India Company lieutenant, farmer, inventor, magistrate – can only hold in contempt.

The crowd thickens as he approaches the draper's shop at number 29. He elbows his way through to the front almost nonchalantly, happy with the throng of bodies, passing through with a sailor's steadiness of feet and singleness of purpose, even with a virtually lame leg. The shop he can see as he gets closer to it is one of the new breed of Highway properties: clean, respectable, the ambition and diligence of its owner clear in the new wood around the window and the freshly painted door. On normal days, when there were not horrors concealed inside, he imagines the place would be cheerful and businesslike. Not today.

He barks at a pair of officers who are attending the door, who do not recognise his face but jump to attention when they hear him bellow his name. 'Magistrate John Harriott' are still words that thunder with some authority among the new lawkeepers of east London. They open the door for him, and he goes in.

There is a sepulchral air inside. The shutters have remained up, to keep out the prying eyes of the mob, so inside it is dark. A tall, heron-like figure is standing with a candle in the main area of the shop, just in front of the counter. The figure turns its face to him, and the candle lights up its cold features. A face like a rat sucking on a piece of lemon, Harriott has often thought, belonging to George Story, the senior magistrate at the Shadwell office. So they are finally here. The old man visibly winces when he sees Harriott.

'Ah,' he says. 'You.' His voice sounds like a man breathing down a pipe.

Harriott stays at the door. He feels he should be invited in, now that Story is here, but neither man speaks for a moment. Eventually, that breathing sound again, and with a sigh Story beckons him in.

'You should see the bodies,' says Story. 'Look.'

He moves his candle and there, on the shop floor, lies the body of a man.

'Marr,' says Story. 'The head of this doomed household.'

The flickering candle casts dancing shadows over Marr's ruined face, before Story brings the candle back up towards himself and Marr is cast back into darkness.

'I think it would be superfluous to say I have never seen anything like this, Harriott. But I will say it nevertheless. The Highway is a lawless place, an awful place. It has killed this respectable man. It has taken his entire family.'

Harriott still holds his own counsel, resisting the urge to point out who is responsible for constraining the 'lawlessness' of the Highway. He tries to look around, the image of Marr's face like a fresh wound in his mind. How can he get hold of a damned candle?

Story, meanwhile, is embarking on a soliloquy. The candle hops up and down in the gloom as he emphasises his words, as if standing at a lectern.

'I have been a Shadwell magistrate since 1792, Harriott.' The breathiness has left his voice as he picks up momentum. Old Story is fond of a monologue. 'In 1792, none of us had even heard of Napoleon Bonaparte. The French king was still alive. Our king had not yet been overtaken by his terrible illness of the mind and Mr Pitt was in the business of bringing order to this great nation. But since then we have slid back, Harriott. Slid back to barbarism. The war has turned us into a nation of savages, sick with bloodlust and greed. The king is mad again. It is the end of days, Harriott, the end of days. These murders are only a sign.'

Harriott ignores the older magistrate, as most men are wont to do when he is like this, and is hunting for a candle. He finds one on the counter and takes the candle from the other man's hand in order to light his own. Story barely seems to notice.

'These people weren't killed by men, Harriott. They were killed by monsters, by representatives of the age we find ourselves living in. Our only consolation is God and the grave. We shan't hunt these killers down.'

In the gloom, Harriott rolls his eyes. He bends down to Marr, and looks calmly at his injuries. He works his way to the back of the shop and finds Mrs Marr, and then James Gowen, and here he stops, because the flavour of the injuries is such that stopping is the only appropriate thing to do. The boy's head has been savaged. Harriott looks back at Story before heading downstairs. His hand shakes slightly with the thought of what he will find down there. Story stands at the top of the stairs and continues to hold forth, as if he were preaching from the mainmast of a ship.

'A baby, Harriott. What species of creature murders a baby? And why?'

OCTOBER 1564

Dear Kate

It is near midnight, and outside the window of my little room is Plymouth. A mad, Godless place enclosed by a wall and the sea. Imagine the Stanton St John alehouse, late on a Saturday night, and then make the alehouse a mile around, and fill it with salty creatures of every stripe, with appetites of every hue, all fixed on spending every coin they have on drink and on women.

Everything is for sale here. Even the women offer themselves for money. I had heard of such things, Kate, but the wonder of it still enthrals me. There is nothing, it seems, that cannot be turned into Money given the necessary circumstances to Trade.

I am hypnotised by the place. There is Opportunity on every single corner, Kate. It would make your head spin. Everywhere you look there is somebody going about the making of a fortune, and still more and more people pour into the place each day, all of them with an eye to Money and Destiny. In this, it is the place I thought it would be. The right place to start an adventure such as the one we have talked so long about.

We have travelled to Oxford together, you and I. We have been intoxicated by it. It made our head spin, the size of it, the clothes on the townspeople, the goods in the market. I remember you laughing and shouting with the extraordinary wonder of it. But Plymouth is something else. A kind of fairyland imagined by a drunken sailor.

The men here are a warning to me. They have no control of themselves. They appear on shore after months and even years at sea, often but not always with money in their pockets. And they seem hell-bent on destroying themselves once they come ashore, or at least on destroying their small piece of fortune. They show no husbandry whatsoever. The Money is there. Then the Money is gone. Why can they not see that the Money is a vessel? That it is the material of Life itself?

I do believe these men want nothing more than to end themselves. Their lives are, to be sure, miserable and careworn. But these miseries seem to me to be self-inflicted, to be nothing more than a lack of imagination and application. I shall not end up like them, Kate. I shall return with Money in my purse, enough money to buy a dozen pigs and to set us up on a small parcel of land of our own, close to your father's farm but far enough away for us to make our own lives together. I find myself dreaming of Woodperry and Peartree Lane Ground, up on the edge of the wood. We will be happy, and our fortunes will grow. Our children will be born and will add to our estate. And we will live long, happy lives, growing old together in the sure knowledge that we have been good and productive people. And at the end of our lives we shall bequeath an Estate upon our children, and our name shall be made in Perpetuity.

I sail tomorrow, my darling. This will be my last night in England for God knows how long. I will arrange for these letters to find their way to you, and, God willing, I will try and find ways to write to you from wherever God may carry me. I will carry your voice in my heart, your counsel in my head, and your face in all my dreams.

Billy

He had found the ship without any trouble at all, as Hawkyns had predicted, and it was indeed the biggest thing he'd ever seen. Its size dwarfed anything else in the harbour at Plymouth, and its reputation was just as large. Everyone knew, and Hawkyns made no attempt to hide, that the *Jesus of Lübeck* belonged to the Queen herself. Hawkyns had let it be widely known that he'd come to Plymouth directly, only a day or two before, from a private audience with Elizabeth at Enfield Palace.

Elizabeth's father Henry had bought the giant vessel off the Hanseatic League more than twenty years before, all 700 tons of her, and she was now an old, creaking Leviathan of a thing, patched up and repainted magnificently and ready to go on whatever mission Hawkyns had in mind. Her age, her almost comical size, her history, all seemed to contribute to the courtly message the young Queen was sending about this voyage. *Go with God's grace and my blessing*, it said. *But I'm taking a chance on you, Mr Hawkyns, and this ship's all you're getting, however ridiculous and ancient she seems to be.*

She'd been converted from a trading vessel to a fighting ship by the old king, and was formidable, with 26 guns and 4 masts. She was fat and squat, as fat and squat as old Bloody Mary, only two and a half times long as she was wide. At either end of the ship towered wooden castles, slapped onto the old merchant vessel to make the *Jesus* a more threatening fighting prospect. Even to Billy's uneducated eyes, the *Jesus* looked like a marine chimera: a stubby thing which also contrived to appear uncomfortably tall, as if she might fall over in a strong wind or if she turned too sharply.

The *Jesus* sat out there in the Pool with the three other ships in the Hawkyns fleet: the *Solomon*, a reasonable-sized 120-ton merchant ship, and two smaller vessels, the *Tiger* and the *Swallow*. Billy watched the ships for a while. To his untrained eyes they were a chaos of wood and rope and cloth, brightly coloured and somehow impossible. He tried to get a plan of the *Jesus* into his head, he tried to imagine what its cargo might be, and he tried to work out how he was supposed to get on board. Boats were making their way out to the fleet, and he saw a group of well-dressed gentlemen clambering up onto the *Jesus* from a pinnace, perhaps twenty of them.

He waited for the boat to empty and then make its way back to the quayside, where there were several small groups of rough-looking men standing around. With a final glance at the huge shape of the *Jesus*, Billy made his way over to one of these groups, towards which the pinnace from the *Jesus* was now returning. He did so with little enthusiasm. They looked as vicious a bunch of miscreants as it would be possible to imagine.

The men were gathered around a familiar-looking figure: Tregarthen, the glittering, venomous gentleman he'd encountered in the Mitre. He was yelling at the shabby men as they climbed down into the now-returned pinnace. A great many more of them were being squeezed in than the previous cargo of well-dressed gentlemen. Billy joined the huddle and soon discovered that this was no orderly queue. He was shoved aside half-a-dozen times before he realised that there was a hint of desperation about these men, an urgency to get onto the ship that pushed them on even as the memory of last night's liquor thumped in their skulls.

It's every man for himself, he thought. *None of these men are guaranteed a berth on this ship.*

Some of the men gazed hungrily out at the fleet and not one of them looked back towards the land. There were no loved ones there to wave them off. They could not wait to get off the land, and virtually leapt down into the pinnace as if the ground beneath their feet was red-hot.

With that thought, Billy screwed up his courage and began to barge and jostle with the rest of them. His desperation to get on board the great ship had its own incentives, and with the image of Kate clear in his mind, not to mention the thought of pig farms and Peartree Lane Ground, he shoved his way to the front in relatively short order, and suddenly he was face to face once more with Tregarthen.

Tregarthen chose to ignore Billy at first, making him wait while he barked at the men around Billy and, in some cases, behind him. Billy waited. He felt relaxed and, if possible under the weight of terror which had come over him when he first saw those gigantic wooden impossibilities sitting on the water, amused. His destiny was aboard the *Jesus*, it had already occurred to him. It seemed a nonsense even to consider that he might be placed on one of the other three ships. Nothing Tregarthen could do would change that.

Eventually, Tregarthen's eyes moved to his. They glittered with malignant mischief.

'Ah, our young friend from the Mitre,' he said, smiling that lupine smile. 'You found us then.'

'Yes, sir. I wish to present myself to the admiral, John Hawkyns, sir.' Words he'd been given by his father-in-law, but pompous, pious words which sparked hilarity among the men around him. A couple of them shoved him in the back, while he caught a whispered *pretty words, pretty boy* from his left. Tregarthen's grin grew wider.

'I'm sure *Admiral* John Hawkyns is excited by the prospect, young sir. But he is rather busy to be receiving guests, be they ever so grand. Step down into the boat, and I'll make it certain that you're taken care of.'

Billy made to step past him, but pulled up short at the feel of something hard and sharp in his side. He looked down to see Tregarthen's stiletto pressed to the side of his father's old Polish greatcoat. Tregarthen leaned in to whisper in his ear.

''Tis a shame I'm not to be travelling with you, boy.' His breath was warm and carried a disgusting whiff of ale and garlic. 'Me and my friend here, we'd have enjoyed your company.'

The sense of pressure in his side disappeared, the stiletto likewise, and then Billy half-clambered, half-tumbled down into the pinnace which, despite its size and the number of heavy men within it, yawned impossibly when Billy put a foot in, and he was convinced that he and all the other new sailors would be tipped into the Pool, and he remembered that he had never even considered the fact that he could not swim.

My first time on the water.

He tried to find a point of balance, his stomach flipping and his heart pounding. He sat down eventually, drawing scowls and muttering from the experienced sailors in the boat, and waited for the last few men to make their way down. Then they began to make their way out to the fleet.

The *Jesus* only grew bigger, and yet bigger, as they approached. If she had seemed massive from the shore, from the water she took on the appearance of a maritime cathedral. With every tug on the oars, the sides of the ship grew taller, and then they were touching the hull of the gigantic vessel, with rope ladders hanging down to meet them and carry them up a steep wall of wood and nails, against which Billy's feet slipped and scrabbled, the ladder swinging wildly as he made his way upwards, his tall frame swinging from side to side, laughter from the boat below and laughter from above. And then he was on the deck, and everywhere was a mess of movement and activity, the men from the shore seemingly springing into life the minute they stepped on deck and transforming themselves into disciplined seamen. He was grabbed by the collar, shoved towards some incomprehensible activity, and Billy became a sailor.

After several hours the *Jesus* and the other ships began to creep out of the harbour. Billy was bounced around from job to job, fetching, carrying, sweeping, stowing, the language of the ship already beginning to reverberate around his overflowing head – Hawkyns standing in full finery on the *quarterdeck*, in front of the rearmost *sterncastle*, while one of the men gathered before him (the *first mate*) called for the *foresail* to be *cut*. The wind caught the sail and one of the ropes (which were mystifyingly called *sheets*) whipped a pulley round, directly into the face of a young deckhand. The man's head was smashed to pieces instantly, and Billy and another deckhand were commanded to clear the blood and the brains off the deck and the rails.

At the end of that first day of wonders, which passed in a blur of alien-sounding words, slaps to the back of the head and occasional grudging acceptance of satisfaction, Billy was shown where to take some sleep. Most of the men slept on the floor, lying in apparent disarray on one of the two decks within the ship. Billy learned immediately that this seemingly random display of bodies was an illusion: every man had his spot, and even when sleeping he had a job allocated to him. Billy was shown a spot on the upper of the two decks, where he was introduced for the first time to his very own Bloody Mary, a falcon cannon which he was to sleep next to for the duration of the voyage, his head tapping against the cannon's wheel while he slept, the smell of the old Hanseatic wood full in his head. He was shown how to maintain the cannon, and dark imprecations were muttered at him about the consequences of the weapon malfunctioning if it were needed.

In the first hours and days of the voyage, rumours swirled around the ship as to their destination. The officers (a class of men who looked much the same as all the other men, Billy thought, the grandly dressed Hawkyns apart) kept their counsel, but down in the bowels of the ship, where a few hammocks swung in the corners and you could occasionally hear the quiet whimpering of terrified young boys on their first voyage, Billy listened in silently as the experienced sailors discussed the trip.

'It's New Spain,' said John Gilbert, a one-eyed seaman from Gloucester who had sailed across the Atlantic half-a-dozen times, and who had recently escaped from a French prison. 'Old 'Awkyns is off to singe some Spanish beards, and to grab some treasure.'

'In a ship the size of a bloody island?' scoffed Morgan Tillert, a Welshman with gambling debts who cheerfully admitted to being on the voyage only as long as was needed to earn enough to get free and clear so he could start gambling again, and who planned to jump ship as soon as he could afford to. 'Why does he need this monster to carry gold? And it'll be as much use as a fart in a hurricane if we get caught in a fight with Spaniards.'

'Hides,' said William Cornelius, who had spent the last eight years sailing sardine ships to and from Portugal. 'I hear hides can be bought on Hispaniola for pennies. He's going to get hides.'

'And pay for them with what?' asked Gilbert. 'He might be bringing something back to England, right enough, he might be. But he'll need to pay for it with something. Aztec gold, mates, Aztec gold. We're off to take some off those Spanish whoremongers, and steal the treasure from the mouth of the Roman Satan himself.'

Billy heard someone chuckling nearby. They were knowing and rather sophisticated chuckles, and they came from a young man of Billy's age, who followed the chuckles by whispering something under his breath. Billy caught the words 'African treasure' before the young man realised he was being watched and looked sharply at him. The man's eyes inspected him for a few seconds, and then the face softened and he smirked at Billy, nodding towards the older men in the shared contempt of the young for the old.

He wore a young man's wispy red beard, but it was well tended. He was dressed plainly but something about the smoothness of his skin and the whiteness of his teeth gave the impression that he was perhaps used to rather more opulent surroundings. William Cornelius noticed the smirk and was about to say something, before another man gave him a warning slap on the shoulder. The young man saw this and smiled insolently. He seemed impervious to the fear that Billy still felt – the fear of these strange, salty men talking a strange, salty language of rigs and yards and sheets which meant nothing to him at all.

Two days out from Plymouth, Billy and the insolent young man were told to take an inventory of the supplies down in the hold. Billy found this a surprising task for two such young crewmen. Surely it was vital that the information was correct and perhaps even confidential? He pointed this out to his new acquaintance, who smirked that smirk again. 'We can both read and we can both write,' he said (Billy had been spotted writing a letter to his Kate the night before, and word had got around already that there was another scholar below decks). 'Qualities much needed in those taking inventories.

Besides, Hawkyns doesn't want old hands ferreting about in here.'

The man's easy air and familiar way with the admiral's name struck Billy. All the crew were rude about the captain and his officers in their below-decks mutterings, but even they invested the word 'Hawkyns' with some kind of weight, as if speaking it in the wrong way might jinx their fortune. This young man had no such anxiety.

'He wants to keep things tight and keep things mysterious. Those fools up on deck have barely been down here. And look! Enough food to feed an army. Too much food for us. Why all the food?' And he tapped his nose, and then offered a hand. 'Francis Drake,' he said. 'Cousin of the commander, Mr Hawkyns.' And seeing the look in Billy's eyes, he nods: 'And thusly impervious to injury from those muttering idiots.'

Billy introduced himself. And made the immediate decision to stay within Drake's orbit. It seemed a safe place to be.

They got started with accounting the items down in the hold. There seemed to be three main groups of cargo. In one were the victuals for the crew: biscuits, dried beef and bacon, beer, peas, cider (no fruit, noticed Billy, whose diet in Stanton St John had been full of the stuff). Then were great piles of random but seemingly valuable materials: cloth, iron, wood and jewellery. This was obviously intended to be traded.

And then, a third category of cargo. Piles of dried beans and peas, set apart from the victuals for the crew. Neat bundles of plain, austere clothing – cotton shirts and simple shoes of varying sizes. An odd collection of wood of various lengths and thicknesses and thick, sailcloth-like material in bright colours which Billy could see no use for at all. All this was part hidden behind a set of bulwarks in the hold of the *Jesus*. Drake watched Billy assessing the nature of the cargo, and once again that knowing smirk appeared.

'Finding the cargo a bit *unusual*, are you?' he asked Billy.

Billy considered the question. He looked around. There was something odd, now he had come to look closely. He considered things further. Drake was asking the question with a certain air of bonhomie. Billy wondered if he was being tested.

'I do wonder,' said Billy, 'what those clothes and sacks of food might be for.'

'Do you, indeed?' asked Drake. 'And well might you. Well might you indeed.'

Drake grinned, mockingly applauding Billy, and said nothing else. Then he winked, and Billy carefully framed a half-smile back. Clearly, he was supposed to know what Drake was talking about. Equally clearly, he did not.

Billy learned quickly, about sails, trims and a clean deck, and about the loading and unloading of cannon, which they practised incessantly until Hawkyns was satisfied they could launch a broadside in short order. Many of the sailors muttered at this. 'We're here to trade, not to fight,' grumbled William Cornelius. 'What the bloody hell are we training like soldiers for?'

'There's Spaniards everywhere,' pointed out Morgan Tillert. 'We'll need to act like soldiers if one of those Papist bastards sets his ship on us.'

While they grumbled, Billy learned every line and curve on his own Bloody Mary, and she took it upon herself to burn his fingers in three places and his arm in two before they eventually reached a common understanding.

Hellfire and damnation were much in mind on board the *Jesus*. Every morning, the men would gather on the deck for a service of half an hour, and Hawkyns or the ship's master, Robert Barrett, would read from the prayer book. Every evening the crew would gather again to kneel around the mainmast while psalms and prayers were read out, normally by the quartermaster, William Sanders, a vicious Lutheran who would whip those not kneeling in good time with a thick rope. The master, Barrett, was almost as full of religion as Sanders, carrying his prayer book with him everywhere he went. Billy, who took religious instruction from his wife and father-in-law and whose learned Protestantism was mixed with a good deal of remembered Catholic instinct, remained practical – he followed the accepted rituals, and kept to himself whatever Roman impulses might remain within him. There were Catholics onboard, including among the gentlemen accompanying Hawkyns, but they kept quiet about their religion, and the old Hanseatic ship burned with Protestant fervour as it cut its way through the waves.

Three days out from Plymouth, Billy learned a great deal more about life at sea, and quickly too, when a huge storm came out of the north-east and battered the *Jesus* for an entire night, the waves higher than the castles fore and aft. Many of the men were convinced that the top-heavy vessel would tip over just as the old *Mary Rose* had done and send them tumbling into the wild Atlantic off Finisterre. The night passed in a freezing, sodden blur of activity, fear and exhaustion. The following morning, the *Swallow* had disappeared from the fleet. The inexperienced sailors kept an informal watch over the sea to try to find them, while the more experienced turned back into the ship and kept busy, muttering to themselves. A loss so early. Dark theories were voiced about Hawkyns's apparent lack of luck, a commodity which admirals were commonly held to need in abundance.

What remained of the fleet drew itself together and continued, out into the Bay of Biscay and down the coast of France. The following night the mood lifted again when the *Swallow* was rediscovered, thirty miles off Finisterre, and the mutterings about Hawkyns's luck ended. To find the *Swallow* again so soon after losing her felt like a divine benediction, as Mr Barrett made clear in his peroration from the mainmast the following morning. Days later, the fleet stopped for supplies and post-storm maintenance in Ferrol, in Galicia. Billy stepped ashore with Drake after two days of scrubbing and more counting of supplies on the *Jesus*. When Billy's tired feet did make it onto the Ferrol quayside his dull, lifeless head took a few moments to recognise two salient facts: that the land now felt more wobbly than the sea; and that this land was Spanish – was foreign, was not England.

A momentary panic set in, as he looked around the little harbour (little by Plymouth standards, in any case), expecting conquistadores in dagger-like helmets to emerge from the surrounding stores and bars and boarding houses. Wasn't Spain the enemy? Wasn't the King the former husband of Bloody Mary, killer of Protestants and hounder of, among others, his father? Shouldn't he be killing Spaniards?

Drake, smiling at the world as ever and smiling particularly cruelly at the obviously perplexed Billy, found them a bar and sat them down. He sipped from a jug of local wine, squeezed the buttock of the young girl serving them, and settled down for a history lesson.

'We hate Spaniards,' he explained. 'The Spaniard is a cruel, low-to-the-earth creature of base appetites and gargantuan ambition. We will singe their beards and steal their gold, we will make merry with their riches and lay their beautiful olive-skinned lasses over our legs. But while we make merry in this way, our Queen must play her own, very different part. She must dine and drink and flirt with the Spanish ambassador in England. She must at all times give the impression that England wants nothing more than to be stroked by her Spanish masters.

'While the Spaniard thinks that, we are safe. But if the Spaniard is roused, if he once organises himself into a fighting force, it will be a fearsome thing. But it will also be idiotic. The Spanish control everything from Madrid. They run the place on fear and on a rigid rulebook. No Spanish commander can so much as sneeze without having orders in triplicate from his King in Madrid. As if a king could know how to stop a ship from going down, or a company of soldiers from running away! We English are allowed a sight more leeway, thank the Lord. Our Queen does not wish to be a naval captain. She has men like Hawkyns to do that for her. Men with initiative, with brains and with ambition. Men who will slice you up without hesitation, but only if slicing you up is more rewarding than keeping you in one piece.

'So for now we lead the Spaniard a merry dance. Some of us hound their ships, but never officially, always in such a way that Elizabeth can flutter her glorious eyelids at the Spanish hound who attends her court, and can simper her innocence into his stinking unclean ears. While Spain believes England is fuckable, they will forgo fucking her. If you get my meaning.'

Initiative, brains, ambition.

Billy felt a sense of excitement, even entitlement. Didn't he have all those qualities, and in abundance? Didn't he thus deserve everything that was coming to an adventuring Englishman with his eye on the horizon and on the main chance?

Drake enjoyed his days in Ferrol, and Billy enjoyed being his companion. Drake had an inexhaustible capacity to charm barmaids and find small change to pay for drinks. Once, Billy caught Drake smirking to himself and tossing a small handful of coins in his hand, just after they had passed through a crowd of well-to-do Spanish traders. A man of high skill and flexible morality, was Francis Drake.

'Hawkyns is a master of action and exploit,' Drake said one day, while the two shared yet another bottle of Galician wine (Billy had developed a taste for wine in only a few days of trying – the tankards of cider and ale seemed a long way behind him). 'But his genius for adventure is exceeded only by his self-regard. He is motivated solely by greed and the desire for self-aggrandisement. He will come to a sticky end, mark my words, young William.'

Drake had taken to calling Billy 'young William', even though they were the same age, but Billy accepted it, in recognition of Drake's higher social standing and his obvious experience as a seaman. In any case, Drake's elaborate, dramatic language, which made everything he said sound like it was being readied for immortality within the form of a sonnet or perhaps one of the new dramas, demanded he adopt such arch conventions of speech.

Drake took little interest in Billy's reasons for being on the trip, other than recognising that Billy seemed solely motivated by money. Billy's questions always returned to this subject: what were they to trade? How much return could be expected? Drake just smiled when this question was asked, and gently mocked Billy for his stupidity and lack of imagination. Wasn't it obvious what they were going to trade? And as for the return, who could possibly tell, given that they were the first Englishmen to try it?

The ships left Ferrol and sailed out into the Atlantic, leaving Portugal on their larboard. They sailed south-south-west almost a thousand miles, and Billy began to find both his sea legs and his sense of distance. They passed Madeira off to starboard, and almost two weeks after leaving Ferrol, at the end of the first week in November, they were off Tenerife.

The little fleet anchored off the harbour of Adeje, and Hawkyns was lowered in a boat from the *Jesus* and rowed to the shore. A group of men could be seen waiting for him there, and after some shouting between the boat and the men on the shore the admiral was rowed up onto the beach. Drake and Billy watched them, and Drake pointed towards the eastern horizon. 'Africa,' he said. There was nothing visible, but just the sound of the word caused an immensity to shimmer just over the brim of the world, as if Drake had conjured the continent into reality just by saying its name.

There followed another hiatus, seven days of fixing and repairing but also of exploration. Billy and Drake continued their drinking sessions, discovering the local wine was even more palatable and sun-drenched than that of Galicia. They also discovered the girls of Tenerife, who seemed at once terrified and fascinated by the English interlopers. Drake fucked his way around three different girls in a week, but Billy was happy to just sit with them up on the hillside and listen to them giggle as he told them about Kate and Stanton St John using words they didn't understand, his face lit by the fires in the harbour below and by the Atlantic starlight.

During the stay, one man from the island was a frequent visitor to the *Jesus*, a wealthy individual who came on board when they'd first arrived in Adeje and whose welcome from Hawkyns was warm and familiar. 'Pedro de Ponte,' said Drake when Billy asked while they rested on the hillside. 'He's Hawkyns's agent on the island. They go back years. De Ponte's got his fingers all over this island: sugar plantation, fort, position on the council. His position here's much like the one the admiral holds back in Plymouth.'

'But why does Hawkyns need an agent in Tenerife?'

'Well, perhaps *agent* isn't quite the way to describe him. He's a contact, a friend. Maybe even a little bit of a spy. There's talk that Hawkyns has been schooling de Ponte in the new religion. And de Ponte's the one who put the idea of going to Africa into Hawkyns's head in the first place. He's got some experience of finding and harvesting African treasure.'

'Treasure?'

'Really, young William. You are quite the biggest idiot I have ever encountered. Now, pass that wine, and let's go and find some girls.'

After a week, the fleet sailed to Santa Cruz, and de Ponte sailed with them as a guest in the admiral's cabin. No explanation of his presence on the *Jesus* was given, nor was there any apparent reason for sailing sixty miles north from Adeje, where all the supplies needed for the trip were readily available. On the first night in Santa Cruz, Hawkyns and de Ponte and several other gentlemen from the ship were rowed ashore with half-a-dozen mysterious boxes which Billy hadn't seen before, and which did not come back with them when they returned to the ship. Even Drake didn't pretend to know what might be in those crates.

The next day, a shout went up from the watch, and Hawkyns came out on deck, with de Ponte, to see what had raised the alert. A pinnace was approaching the *Jesus*, and in it were a group of dark-robed figures which glided straight out of the Protestant tales English mothers told their misbehaving children. The Inquisition had arrived.

There were six of them (*one for each of those mysterious crates*, Billy thought to himself), and they climbed up onto the deck with some difficulty, their heavy robes an impediment to movement on the ship. Hawkyns came forward to greet them, and the crew watched sullenly as this unwelcome intrusion played out, their bones tingling with a fierce but anxious Protestant energy. The dark-robed figures were introduced and spoke to Hawkyns, with de Ponte acting as interpreter. The crew could hear very little of what was said. For Billy the worst part of the whole episode was the tense expression in Drake's face. Billy had never seen him look so worried.

A document was left with Hawkyns, served upon him by one of the black-robed figures with a good deal of threatening ceremony. Then the black-robed figures spread out and began to search the vessel. Hawkyns stepped up to the quarterdeck and spoke to the crew.

'Leave these creatures to do their work,' he said, and his voice, like Drake's face, was tight. 'We are accused of smuggling religious materials from England onto the island. There are no such materials on this ship, and thus none will be found. Let these *inquisitors* do their searching, and then they will be gone. I wish to have no fight with the officials on this island. Our mission is too important to allow us to be distracted by the interruptions of such as these.'

Beside him, de Ponte followed the black-robed figures with his eyes. Billy thought again of the crates on the boat the night before. The inquisitors passed through the ship, and in most cases the crewmen gave them plenty of room, as if they were leprous and infectious. Morgan Tillert, though, stood his ground against one, forcing the inquisitor to go around him. Tillert's fierce wide Welsh face paled as the inquisitor whispered some Latin mysteries into his ear as he passed.

After a half-hour the inquisitors regrouped on the deck and waved de Ponte to come to them. The supposedly all-powerful merchant and politician scurried towards them like a small boy caught stealing apples. One of the inquisitors spoke to him in the local language, and de Ponte looked even more worried, if such a thing were possible. Then the inquisitors turned and climbed down to their pinnace, which was soon heading back to land, the black robes within like a pool of oil crossing the surface of the waters. Within minutes, de Ponte had climbed down into his own boat, and the order to weigh anchor was given. The Hawkyns fleet sailed away from Santa Cruz, like a dog which had been slapped by its angry owner. The incident was never spoken of again.

10 DECEMBER 1811

Charles Horton chooses a seat at the back for the coroner's inquest, within the dark wood shadows of the Jolly Sailor. The upstairs room of the alehouse is appropriately gloomy for the purpose to which it is now being put, and its unlit edges mean it is a simple matter for Horton to slip in unnoticed by the people already there – the Shadwell magistrates, along with a few other officials and the witnesses. There are already a number of local people, some of whom Horton recognises, though he does not approach them.

He is here to watch proceedings rather than to participate in them. He has a great capacity for watching, does Waterman-Constable Charles Horton. It can drive his wife Abigail to distraction, those times when they are out walking and she catches his eye straying across the faces of those around them, taking them in, filing them away, apparently not listening to her but nonetheless still attentive. She can never catch him out. *What was I saying?* she will demand with mock asperity, and he will turn his eyes back on her and tell her just *precisely* what she was saying, a smile at the edges of his mouth.

There is a low but excited chatter inside the room. A man in old-fashioned breeches and tailcoat wearing an ancient powdered wig which makes him look like Dr Johnson (he could be, thinks Horton, an impoverished relation of Magistrate John Harriott) is preparing the table for the coroner, and he glances nervously at the growing number of local people filing in. His bovine, jowly face makes it clear what he is thinking: *Don't let any more of those people out there in here. Those people are not like us. They do not recognise the sanctity of officialdom.*

This much is true – the people of Wapping are certainly not behaving as if a great evil has been perpetrated in their midst. Or rather, their reaction is not that which is approved of or desired by the official agencies, which have only the shakiest of grips on the teeming little streets around both the Gravel Lanes and the Highway. Outside the Jolly Sailor the atmosphere is wild and excitable, and Constable Horton understands that the murders have, for these people, offered a break from the mundane. There is something of a party spirit in the air, the vast crowds chattering and laughing even while women turn pale and cry on each other's shoulders.

Horton has seen something much like this before. Not here in Wapping, but out on the Nore, the ancient estuary mustering point for the navy. 1797, and the crowds were gathering then, too, this time to watch the establishment take its just and timely revenge on the mutineer Richard Parker, leader of a small fleet of navy vessels which, for a few weeks, had appeared to have their calloused hands around Great Britain's windpipe. The Wapping crowd milling outside looks much like that crowd had looked to Horton when, as second lieutenant on the *Sandwich*, he had stood standing on deck, his gut filled with guilt and fear and remorse, as they hanged Parker from the yardarm on a specially built platform protruding out from the cathead. The ship's crew – or rather, what was left of it once the mutiny's ringleaders had been identified and taken away based on information from their shipmates (thus, the remorse in the young Charles Horton) – had come out on deck into the June sunshine, and Horton had looked towards the Sheerness shore to see the ramshackle scaffolds that had been put up to allow people to sit and watch the execution. They were heaving with humanity, those scaffolds, gentlemen and ladies jostling with watermen and dockers and sailors and farmers' wives, all craning their necks to get a glimpse of the monstrous Parker, who must have been little more than a stick figure to them, such was the distance. But, Horton now knows, people need to feel a part of something, of some common undertaking, and the execution of a miscreant feels like an act of social commonwealth. *Look at him, and look at us*, the crowds seemed to say then. *He is not like us. He is not one of us.*

Parker hadn't disappointed them. His wife, delayed by the tide, had pulled alongside the *Sandwich* in a rowing boat just as the moment of execution arrived, and she had called out to him. Somehow her clear voice had carried across the water, perhaps thanks to a romantically inclined God who had changed the direction of the wind. The hanging hood had not yet been pulled over Parker's eyes, and at the sound of her voice he had shouted something guttural and imprecise and had sprung forward and out from the cathead, before the final signal for his hanging had been given, before the crowd on the shore was ready. It was a final act of defiance which made the seamen on the mutinous ships look down at their respective decks and silently, sullenly applaud this final act of pointless yet somehow marvellous rebellion.

Leaning against the wooden panels of the Jolly Sailor, somehow so reminiscent of a grand navy ship, Horton can feel the dull itch in his back, his skin's memory of the fifty lashes he'd received as a member of that mutinous crew, a not-so-jolly sailor at all, and that other itch of guilt that rises from the knowledge of why there were only fifty lashes, of what he'd done to secure a second chance. That guilt is under the skin, and that itch is sharper.

The newspapers had stirred the pot of outrage at the mutiny in 1797, and they were assiduously doing the same now. The ghoulish crowds had been rolling down the Ratcliffe Highway since yesterday, when news of the Marr murders had hit the London papers. *The Times* and the *Chronicle*, in particular, have hooked attention (and sold a fair few extra copies, Horton wagers) with their painting of these murders as the worst, most depraved atrocity ever to unfold within the benighted confines of the sprawling city of London, the biggest city the world has ever seen and without any doubt the wickedest. Horton had only to walk a few hundred yards along Old Gravel Lane to the inquest, from the lodgings he shared with Abigail in Lower Gun Alley, but that was enough to show him that the Great Public Leviathan was up and out of its chair and scooping down the atmosphere with a gigantic spoon. He saw gentlemen buying drinks for watermen in the hope of gaining some precious nugget of colourful local insight (the watermen very happy to oblige, concocting elaborately invented tales of local evils), while the refined ladies who'd come along with them gazed with fierce fascination at the Wapping whores. Murder and horror, it appeared, were greater social levellers than anything Messrs Danton and Robespierre had managed in France.

The locus of this great chattering crowd is not this inquest. There is something far more visceral and appealing available further down the Highway, where the bodies of the Marrs have been laid out in their house. Anyone can get in to see them. Horton passed the house this morning, and going in found the landing chock-a-block with gawping ladies and wailing boarding-house keepers. The house stank of the mob and, increasingly, of the days-old bodies of the Marrs. Timothy Marr, whose freshly painted wooden shopfront was now notched and battered, would have been beside himself.

And while the crowds have gawped and the newspapers have thundered, the patchy apparatus of policing has been busy squabbling with itself. In the last twenty-four hours an especially technical word has been passed around between the panicked officials of Shadwell and the Home Office: *jurisdiction.* The murders happened in the parish of St George in the East, which is in the district covered by the Shadwell magistrates. Yet the river magistrate, John Harriott, in a flurry of his old energy, has seized the moment and the initiative, even though he is only technically responsible for crime on the river. Never one for pettifogging, Harriott has decided that the murders are so serious that all London's magistrates need to involve themselves. Neither the Home Office nor Shadwell quite agree.

Thus the evening after the murders Harriott had arranged for a handbill to be printed and distributed, offering a £20 reward for information about the perpetrators of the Marr murders (this, Horton would say, in the absence of anything resembling an investigation of the murders). The handbill has enraged the Shadwell magistrates, who have done nothing so deliberate themselves, what with old Story still reeling around talking about the end of days. His two fellow magistrates, Mr Markland and Mr Capper, complained bitterly and directly to Ryder, the Home Secretary himself. Harriott has long been the grit in the eye of the Home Office, the lunatic gentleman-farmer-sailor-soldier who follows no man's rules, who makes it up as he goes along, the very definition of a maverick. Harriott is detested in the corridors of Whitehall power, and Ryder, who inherited Harriott along with all the other little annoyances of his post, shares that detestation. So, while the bodies of Timothy Marr and his family lie on their beds in the tidy little house on the Highway, the servants of the public who are supposed to be investigating their deaths are quite busy enough, thank you, arguing about who does what.

This jurisdictional jousting is one reason for Constable Horton to make his way into the inquest – Shadwell's inquest – with care, seeking the shadows and avoiding the glances of the Shadwell magistrates who are already here. But now John Harriott arrives, and he makes no such acknowledgement. He thunders into the Jolly Sailor in much the same way as he had thundered into Moghul fortresses in India. The faces of the attending Shadwell magistrates see him and show their annoyance, but Harriott ignores them and takes up a seat in the front row of chairs. Horton, in his shadows, smiles to himself. *Good man.*

Harriott's defiance today is well earned, for despite the squealing of Shadwell and the Home Office it is becoming clear that all London's magistrates are indeed going to be involved in the Marrs' murders, whether or not they care to be. Suspects are pouring in to all seven magistrates' offices in the city, and the Home Secretary has been heard to mutter that if there are so many murderers in London's streets, why is there anyone still living? Throughout the metropolis, handbills are going up, descriptions of potential murderers are being circulated, the usual suspects (normally Irish, Jewish or Portuguese, or some exotic mixture of the three) are being rounded up by constables and police officers and magistrates who prefer to trawl for criminals rather than discover them.

While all these suspects clog up the arteries of London's stuttering policing systems, the Shadwell magistrates have been forced to write to tell Ryder that, in effect, the Shadwell office has paradoxically *nothing* to go on. Despite this, the Home Secretary, steadfast in his determination that the proper forms will be observed, has formally chastised Harriott and ordered the old man to assist Shadwell at their own instruction and to stop, at all costs, issuing handbills which are only likely to cause more fool's errands. Harriott has written a suitably grovelling response this morning – 'vexed with myself . . . run me into an error . . . discretionary powers were limited . . . I will take special care to keep my zeal within proper bounds.'

The lack of evidence, the debates between the offices, the rogue handbill: all of these have made the issue of the maul, the only apparent piece of concrete evidence in the case, all the more vexed for Harriott and Horton. Gently, ever so gently, Harriott has introduced the idea that his officer had removed a key piece of evidence from the Marr household immediately following the murder, well before any Shadwell officers arrived. With his relationship with the Home Secretary somewhat on edge, Harriott has been forced to play a little politics himself, speaking informally to the Shadwell magistrate Charles Markland and offering to make it clear that Shadwell, not the River Office, made the great breakthrough in the case and would claim the credit for it with the Home Office.

The nature of the breakthrough is pleasingly dramatic, more than enough to keep the Home Office satisfied for a few days. Before handing the maul over, Constable Horton made careful sketches of the maul, a thankless task given the devilish material on its face, but one which Horton accepted gladly, as it gave a chance for closer inspection. Wiping away some of the blood and the matter on the flat, mallet end of the tool, he had felt a warm surge of excitement as two letters were revealed in the face of the maul: 'JP', the shapes crudely hammered out in dots into the metal.

This is the information which Shadwell has been allowed to claim as its own (although, as Harriott said, it would probably lead to the arrest of everyone within a mile of the river with those initials). But it is also information which Horton has been allowed to chew on; a nugget to be shared down on the streets.

While Harriott has busied himself with fending off the politicians and consuming inordinate quantities of humble pie, his Constable Horton has been plunging into the twilight world of ramshackle boarding houses which cluster in and between the bottom ends of Old and New Gravel Lanes, in search of 'JP'.

These ramshackle houses are where the sailors dwell, in the gaps between voyages, sequestered in tiny rooms, their entire worldly possessions stuffed into heavy old sea-chests which they place at their feet while sleeping. Men of every nationality are squeezed into an endless succession of uneven rooms, stinking of gin and sometimes wrapped around a female, either a professional woman or a lovelorn sweetheart who has been pulled into the boarding house upon the sailor's return before being thrown back out into the world again when the sailor runs out of money and flees back to the forgiving, anonymous ocean.

Constable Horton's twilit activities do not constitute what John Harriott would have understood by 'looking into it', because this is not how policing is done. For Harriott, a police force is about protection, not detection. His original plans for the Thames River Police were predicated on a police force observing the river, and making arrests when said observations led to information about individuals or, more often than not, when a police officer witnessed a crime directly (at the time of the formation of his Police Office, Harriott reckoned there were 11,000 people involved in pilfering on the river, so witnessing a crime directly was not uncommon). The idea of going out and *discovering* criminals, of foraging around within the chaotic connections of the dock and the river, is as alien to

John Harriott (and, indeed, to almost all the other London magistrates) as a Napoleonic code of rights and wrongs.

In the day and a night since he started his investigations, Constable Horton has so far failed to discover who 'JP' might be, but he has discovered something else. Several sailors in Wapping knew of Timothy Marr by reputation. He had served on the East Indiaman the *Dover Castle*. One sailor (an ancient one-eyed man from Norfolk, with a single tooth and, of all things, a small, blond-haired daughter, with no sign of a mother or anyone to care for her when the old man went back to sea, as he surely would) claimed that Marr had made enemies, and had developed a reputation as a below-decks stool pigeon. When Horton pushed him, the sailor had little to add, and Horton saw that this was something the sailor felt rather than understood. Somewhere, a story had taken root that Marr was on the side of the officers and not of the crew, and such a reputation was hard to shift. Horton understands that only too well – the itch beneath his skin again.

From the back of the room Horton can see that Story, still the senior Shadwell magistrate, is working himself up to confront old Harriott, but then there is a flurry at the entrance to the room, and the coroner, John Unwin, appears, followed by the inquest jury. All are men, and all are pale and grim-faced. Most look at the ground, avoiding anyone's eye. They have come back from visiting the Marr household.

The jury take their seats, and Unwin commences proceedings. Horton knows the man well – he is solid and steady, a stickler for process, like all good coroners.

First the surgeon, a Mr Salter, lays out the medical facts, in neutral tones taken from anatomy textbooks and read out from a thick leather-bound ledger, within which, Horton wonders, must lie the terrible details of many more deaths. Mrs Marr: left side of the cranium shattered, temple-bone destroyed, wound from jaw to ear, wound at the back of the ear. Mr Marr: nose broken, bone at the base of his skull fractured, wound over left eye. James Gowen: skull smashed open and the brains spread down his neck and the adjacent wall. The baby, Timothy Marr the younger: the artery in his neck slashed from the mouth downwards and other marks of violence on the face. Across the room, John Harriott, who has seen ships wrecked on English rocks and women carried away by tigers, feels his eyes moisten and the old wound in his lame leg tighten as the descriptions are read out. Constable Horton has no such reaction. The facts are the facts. They help to bring the picture into focus, that is all. The itch has gone.

The only other witnesses are those that Harriott himself helped to interview at Shadwell, on the day after the murders: Margaret Jewell, the neighbour John Murray and the old watchman, Olney. The girl speaks calmly but almost inaudibly, and Horton is impressed by her self-possession, in such stark contrast to the raw-eyed young teenager on the pavement outside that benighted house. And Murray adds a new element to his story: that he heard a raised voice from the Marrs' home around midnight which sounded either afraid or angry, and could have been either a woman's voice or that of a boy. Olney, who seems to have been replenished by the jugs in the alehouse downstairs, embellishes his tale with his own detail: that the maul, which Horton had brought out of the house, was 'running with blood'. Story looks across at John Harriott at the mention of this evidence, but the old man takes no notice.

The coroner asks for the jury's verdict, and it is given: wilful murder, by person or persons unknown. The jury and the clerks make their way back downstairs, the clerks in particular looking terrified about what awaits them in the street. Constable Horton stays put for the moment, waiting for the

Shadwell magistrates to head back to their own offices, wishing to avoid any kind of confrontation, and notices Harriott doing the same. Story looks like he might be about to say something, but the descriptions of the bodies have had a chastening effect on the man. A horrified look is frozen in his face, and in the end he gives John Harriott a wide berth. The landlord of the Jolly Sailor, all the jollity blown out of his sails, begins to sort out the chairs and the tables, and Horton walks over and sits beside the old magistrate. He says nothing, waiting for Harriott to speak.

Some colour is coming back into the old man's cheeks, which had gone white with the evidence from the surgeon. He has placed his chin on top of his hands, which are folded on top of his walking stick. He stares into a middle distance, only glancing up to acknowledge Horton as the officer sits down. Eventually he speaks, his chin remaining on his hands.

'Monstrous descriptions, Horton. Monstrous. I barely know of anything the like of them.'

'Indeed, sir. The attack on the babe seems particularly inexplicable.'

'Unless they killed it to silence it.'

'Possibly. But something strikes me, sir.'

'What would that be?'

'No shouts, sir. Two adults and a boy killed, but not one of them raised a shout, apart from the one Murray thinks he may have heard. How was it done so quickly?'

The question would seem blasphemous and shocking to a Shadwell magistrate, but Harriott is sturdier than that.

'You have a theory?'

'Not in the least, sir. But it is odd.'

'Hmm. What next?'

'Well, sir, the Shadwell magistrates have apprehended someone I would like to know more about. Mr Pugh, a carpenter who was working on the shopfront and interior. They think he may be the owner of the chisel found in the store. I thought I might go along and listen in. I have had no luck in tracking down the owner of the maul.'

'Hmm. We should perhaps avoid attending any further interviews at the Shadwell office. Is there not someone who can give you information about the interview with Pugh?'

'I can find someone, sir.'

'I'm sure you can. That is likely to be better, I feel.'

'Yes, sir.'

Constable Horton stands, nods at the magistrate, and leaves. Harriott waits a little longer as the last few stragglers depart. Among the last to leave is Unwin the coroner, who raises his eyebrow when he catches a glance of Harriott before nodding grimly at him and leaving. Like all nods between Englishmen, this one carries an enormity of meaning. *We are sailing in uncharted waters*, it says.

DECEMBER 1564

'There's some of the bastards there!'

The blue-green waters of the great African estuary had almost certainly never heard a Welsh accent before that fine morning. Morgan Tillert yelled the words with all the excitement of a poor starving serf discovering a nugget of gold in a mountain stream. Men rushed to the rails of the *Tiger* to see what he had seen, and Hawkyns himself appeared immediately on the aft deck, immaculate and calm despite the heat.

There, on a spit of land in the great estuary, a crowd of black figures were looking back at the ship. They had been fishing in the river, several dozen of them, but now they gawped at the *Tiger* and the *Swallow*, the two smallest vessels in the Hawkyns fleet, which had made their careful way into the river estuary the day before.

For a moment, the two groups stared at one another. On board the *Tiger* there were several seconds of tense silence. But then Hawkyns barked an instruction, his officers began ordering their men into the boats, and the deck was awash with activity, as if an enemy vessel bent on war had come alongside.

Billy joined dozens of shipmates as they clambered into the various forms of armour which had been left in piles on deck since the previous day, ready for just this discovery.

None of the men, Billy included, had any doubt as to what Tillert had meant when he'd first shouted his alert. They knew what they were there to do, even if it had never been declared by Hawkyns or by any of his officers. Nods and winks and knowing guffaws were all Billy had seen and heard, but as the voyage had continued it had become more and more obvious what their target was. The chatter below decks had been excited: *black gold* was what they were after. The kind of gold that walked itself onto a ship, and off it again. And now here it was, staring back at them, apparently struck dumb and just waiting to be herded away.

Within minutes five boats were making their way across the immense blue-green estuary towards the spit of land which, as they approached, resolved itself into an island separated from the main riverbank by a narrow stretch of water. Billy's boat was the first to feel the sandy riverbed as the island rose up to meet it. The sailors clambered out, clumsy and stupid in their great metal costumes. There was a simple instruction from the second mate, a vicious bastard from Birmingham named Watson: 'Catch as many of them as you can, lads. If you have to kill a few to get at the rest, well, are we Englishmen, or are we not?'

'No, we're bloody not,' said Morgan Tillert, but he was grinning. They were all grinning. It felt like they were doing what they'd set out to do. Destiny was standing there on the shore, ready to be roped into a line and dragged onto the ships.

The armour they were wearing was a precaution, but it was a precaution hatched in the cool air of Northern Europe, and the men were quickly drenched in sweat. The armour presented another bigger and more pressing problem. The clanking and splashing of the metal-clad tin sailors terrified the Africans. They had been transfixed by the arrival of the ships and then by the little boats which separated themselves from the larger vessels, but now when the tin men began to crash out of the boats and into the surf, their metal shapes creaking and screaming under the strain, the Africans turned and fled, running and half-swimming back across the river waters, their shiny, strange faces and huge white eyes looking back over their shoulders as they disappeared into the scrubby jungle of the interior beyond the river.

The tin men could not follow. The metal suits were too heavy and ungainly to allow for crossing the river safely, and there was no time to get back into the boats and give chase. Billy and his shipmates hauled themselves up onto the island only to see the last of the Africans disappear into the undergrowth. The treasure was gone.

Watson screamed an oath towards the far riverbank, and several of the sailors could be heard muttering dark near-mutinous curses while others tore at their armour in frustration. But then Watson shouted again, as two black men reappeared from the undergrowth on the far shore and made their way gingerly towards the water.

Both groups watched each other for a moment – the tin men of Europe, the near-naked black men of Africa. And then the two black men, to the astonishment of the sailors, began to laugh and whoop and dance, waving what looked like longbows around their heads. Jet-black and near naked they were, and they were leaping around like merry demons.

The Europeans were being mocked. The two Africans had realised that the visitors could never reach them, and had returned to make fun of the ridiculous would-be kidnappers. Watson let rip an elaborate stream of Midlands obscenities, and ordered the men to line up and take aim.

The sailors were carrying harquebuses, long ungainly things which got water in them but which could still rip through flesh willingly enough on the one-in-three occasions they actually fired. On Watson's command, the tin men fired the guns at the capering Africans, and even with the inevitable misfires the sound of the successful shots was sudden and enormous. For a moment the great estuary was silent, as if the waves themselves had hushed to hear what this alien sound could be.

The blacks had been scared by the explosions from the guns and had stopped jumping about when they'd first heard the sound. But as far as they could see the mountainous noise of gunfire had only led to puffs of smoke unfolding around the guns of the sailors – the Africans hadn't noticed the sand jumping at their feet as the balls of lead buried themselves within it, or the leaves crackling behind them, or the little splashes of water in the river in front of them. These strange sticks made a vast echoing noise, but apparently did little else.

Watson lined the sailors up again, and ordered them to prepare to shoot a second time. As the tin men fiddled with the infernal unreliable guns, the Africans continued their enjoyment at the expense of the slow, plodding, metal strangers who'd come up onto their shore, apparently threatening but really about as scary as a pride of old, fat, toothless lions. As the guns were raised again, Billy heard someone say something.

'Run, you silly bastards. *Run.* Get *away* from here.'

Billy couldn't see who was speaking. The helmet he was wearing had a smaller angle of vision than the crack in the barn door through which he'd once watched a farmhand and a girl. It was hot inside the armour, hot enough to turn his skin into something wet and flowing. There was sweat dripping down every bend in his body. His excitement had given way to an intense irritation – with the armour, with Watson, with his harquebus, with the Africans, and with the stranger who now seemed to be urging their quarry into flight. Weren't they here to seize the Africans they could, and shoot the ones they couldn't? Wasn't this his destiny?

Watson barked at them in his miserable Midlands drone to fire at will, and again that cracking sound, bigger this time as, miracle of miracles, more than half of the guns actually fired. There was another one of those silences, and both of the Africans looked down as puffs of sand and explosions of water sprouted around them. A fraction of a second later, Billy heard a man's scream as one of the black men felt the effect of harquebus shot piercing his skin and bone. First he'd been dancing, and now a wound had exploded in him and pain had ripped through his leg. Billy had never seen a gun before this trip, either. But even so he'd known what guns could do, known it as he'd known that the water in the Cherwell was cold in winter. Just the shape of them was all he'd needed to understand what their purpose was. These two fools had no idea what they were up against. Or at least, they hadn't until now. The lesson was hard and sudden and excruciating.

The wounded man carried on screaming as his companion dragged him into the trees in the same direction as the others had fled. The tin men did not bother following them. The cries of the man they'd shot could be heard for several minutes before the two men were swallowed by the forest, and then the noise of the estuary reasserted itself, cleansed of the shrieks of gunshot and agony. Watson ordered the sailors to drop their weapons and return to the ships. Not a single African had been captured.

Half a day later the two ships that had sailed into the estuary – the *Tiger* and the *Swallow* – met up with the *Jesus* and the *Solomon*, both of which had stayed out on the ocean (as indeed had Francis Drake, who had winked at Billy and given the strong impression that he was in some way being left *in charge*), and Hawkyns issued the next order: sail south. And off they went, frustrated but also excited by the prospect that had opened up for them that day: a continent which teemed with African life, all of it capable of transmutation into gold and silver. If only they could catch it.

Billy watched the beautiful blue-green estuary fall away behind them, and felt something very like joy. Since the voyage began, he'd been troubled by the nagging doubt that perhaps this John Hawkyns was just a particularly well-funded chancer, without a plan or a clue, hoping for something to show up somewhere which would justify his voyage and the patronage of his Queen. That feeling had only grown as calamity had followed calamity, like the strange visit of the inquisitors and the scramble away from Tenerife.

A few days after that ignominious getaway, Billy had seen Africa for the first time. It had been the Barbary Coast, and it had looked dustily exotic and alien, but at the same time drained of any colour, shimmering in oranges and browns like a line of sand spread across the horizon. For five days they sailed south along that coast, looking for Portuguese to 'trade with', a euphemism that Billy only fully comprehended when Hawkyns sent his crew down to hide below decks on the *Jesus* as he prepared to enter the new, hastily built and ill-constructed harbour of Angla de Santa Ana. The smaller ships in the fleet waited outside on the open sea while the colossal *Jesus* burst into the harbour and opened fire on the cluster of Castilian and Portuguese boats, the crew's training in broadsides now explained, and Billy riding his own Bloody Mary into battle with a thrill and only one or two new burns.

Some Portuguese ships were sunk, most of the shot went into the water, but when the smoke cleared there was silence, allowing Hawkyns to shout from the forecastle: 'Halloo! The *English* are here! Do you dogs want to make some money, or do you want to be blown up?'

Such was the John Hawkyns method of negotiating trade. While Billy could admire the directness of the approach, he failed to comprehend how it would lead to riches for him or his shipmates. Very little real trading was done in Angla de Santa Ana – a few yards of cloth exchanged for some precious stones, little else – but the men seemed happy enough with the measure of humiliation they were able to deal out, particularly to the Portuguese, whom they viewed as short-arsed buffoons not fit to run an empire awarded to them by a rancid Catholic pontiff (or so said the master, Barrett, that evening at prayer, his Lutheranism now an engine of war).

The night after the one-sided gun battle with the two Africans, Hawkyns himself took evening prayer, and delivered a comely sermon on the need to bring Christianity, Luther's Christianity, to these benighted pagans, racked by disease and starvation, limited in understanding and capacity, needing only to be transported to the bosom of a good Christian home to be rewarded with at least a measure of eternal salvation (for how could savages, really, be headed for the very same celestial palaces as were good Englishmen?).

Two days after this, with Hawkyns's pretty justifications still being shared below decks with admiration and agreement, they anchored off an island which Hawkyns said was called Sambula, though it wasn't clear if this was a name he'd discovered or one he'd simply made up. The island was situated at the edge of another massive estuary, this time a huge expanse of water into which several gigantic rivers emptied. The island was fifteen miles long and five miles deep, and was a scrubby, rocky place on the seaward side. However, the landward side was green and fertile, with freshwater and a network of small rivers. And, as the ships' crews soon discovered, it was teeming with human life.

Half-a-dozen boats set off from the fleet, each carrying twenty men this time, without armour to weigh them down. Billy found himself in one of these, though again not with Drake, who once more seemed to have found something pressing with which to make himself busy on board ship. There seemed to have been other changes in strategy, too. Now only the more experienced men carried harquebuses; the younger, greener crew members, like Billy, were there to carry supplies and ropes.

As they rowed towards the shore, Billy saw a small gathering of black humans on the beach ahead, the rocky outcrop of the island looming behind them. The group was still, and every minute or so a new figure walked casually into it, swelling its numbers. By the time the three boats from the *Jesus* reached the shore, there were perhaps twenty people in the group, all of them standing still while they watched the sailors come ashore.

The lead officer in Billy's boat this time was Clinker Jerome, so named because his skin had been resewn so many times it looked like the hull of an old clinker-built boat. He had one eye and most of his nose was gone, as were most of his teeth. He was perhaps thirty-five, looked twice that age, and he had the most terrifying voice of any man Billy had ever heard, more terrifying than the master, the first mate or Hawkyns himself.

Clinker was the first to jump into the shallow water as Billy's boat beached, and was followed by the other sailors as he approached the group of black men, women and children standing on the shore. Two of the black men grinned, a man and a woman, and Billy noticed that their teeth were filed into points and that their skin, like Clinker's, was sewn together in some places like an old leather jerkin, but in their case this looked deliberate and decorative and almost beautiful. They were tall and muscular, their loins covered in simple cloth, the woman's breasts exposed, their dark skin shining like the surface of a still, deep pond. They chattered something at the approaching Englishmen, and the sound of the chatter was joyous and musical and profoundly welcoming.

Something hung heavy in the air as Clinker approached the group, something old and timeless, and Billy felt a roaring in his ears as of wind rushing down a tunnel, somewhere dark and close into which he'd crawled.

Here it comes. Here comes the thing we've been searching for.

Clinker reached the first African, the woman, and with one smooth movement which belied his creaking body he pulled back her head and cut through her throat, and then Billy heard something else – an inhuman roar, as if from a gigantic beast, and it was coming from Clinker, and then the other men from the ship were roaring too, and deep within the roar Billy heard his own voice, deep and screaming and tremendous. The black humans were falling away, jabbering and aghast, and Billy reached out and grabbed the arm of one of the men, his fingers closing around the Negro's thick upper arm, squeezing the bone and muscle within as something crackled between them, noticing the sharpened teeth which were bared partly in welcome and partly in the sudden onrush of terror . . .

. . . and Billy pulled the shrieking African down into the boat.

Later that day, as evening fell and the ships lay at anchor just off the island, it became time to take the inventory, so Billy went down to the hold and there found Drake, already counting and listing, walking between the dozens of black figures which lay chained together, naked (the simple cotton clothes and leather shoes which had been brought from England had not been needed, Hawkyns had decided – they could sell it on, these savages did not dress themselves, so why should Hawkyns pay to do so?). There had been children on the beach too, Billy remembered, but there were no children down in the hold, and very few females – only the youngest and strongest-looking of them had made it this far. Billy considered asking Drake where the other captured Africans might be – on another ship, perhaps? But then he realised that he knew, in effect, what had happened to the children and older women. Just mouths to feed on a long voyage.

Drake was standing, or rather crouching beneath the low ceiling, simply staring at the Negroes, watching them as they tried to move around and whispered quietly to each other. They did not cry or moan any longer (many had been screaming as they'd been shoved down into the hold).

'I have them where I want them,' said Drake, noticing Billy's arrival. 'They were a-wailing and a-moaning when they came down here, but I asked them forthrightly: wherefore do you moan? We have come to rescue you: to feed you and to take you to the bosom of a Christian family, to save your immortal soul in return for the labour of your body and the loyalty of your spirit. They jabbered away for a while. Not a single one of them can communicate with me. But I made my point, sometimes with the help of an open hand. They are quiet now. Look. Dozens of them, cleaned and made ready for our voyage across the Atlantic. We will feed them beans and peas and keep an eye on them. But look at this.'

Drake leaned down to one of the men, whose sharpened teeth flashed brightly in the gloom of the boat and who let forth a stream of African language which sounded, to Billy's ears, like the screeching of a monkey, all clicks and whoops and shrieks. The man's face was familiar – the Negro he'd grabbed first out on the island beach.

'Look at this, young William,' said Drake, grasping the man's foot. 'Look at what we're saving these savages from.' In the gloom, Billy could see an open sore at the man's ankle, and emerging from the wound, perhaps half an inch out of the skin, the white, eyeless head of a thin worm, squirming horribly as it pulled itself into the light. 'The worms of Guinea are passing strange, young William. These blacks should be grateful.'

They stared a little longer at the ugly thing, while the man moaned with something like pain.

'What do you think he's worth with that inside him?' asked Billy.

Drake grinned.

14 DECEMBER 1811

Four days after the inquest in the Jolly Sailor, John Harriott leaves his pristine and still somewhat-unfinished home at Wapping's Pier Head to head across town for dinner with his old friend and fellow-magistrate Aaron Graham. Harriott's wife is still accustoming herself to their soon-to-be excellent accommodation in the new building, which looks over the entrance to the dock from the river and houses many of the administrators and officers of the London Dock Company but which is still very much a work in progress. Elizabeth is Harriott's third wife, and unlike the two poor women who preceded her and who are now dead in the Essex earth, destroyed by the horrors of childbirth, she is a survivor, tolerant of the schemes which have seen her husband overcome by Essex rivers, London creditors and American farmhands only to bounce back again and again. The third Mrs Harriott has persevered this long by virtue of bottomless (if by now a little dry) wells of perseverance and patience, both with her husband and with fortune.

In truth the small apartments are the most luxurious

surroundings they have ever found themselves in; they feel like home, perhaps the final home for Elizabeth and her husband after their incessant journeying. She is looking forward to a quiet evening of reading, embroidery and correspondence, without the hectoring bluster of her husband and the recent 'insidious events' (as she insists upon calling them) to disturb her.

Aaron Graham is the magistrate of Bow Street in the fashionable West End of town, and as such has some right to consider himself the lead magistrate in London and Westminster, though no such seniority exists in official point of fact and in any case Graham would never be graceless enough to dwell upon it. But Bow Street still has a special status within the magistracy, thanks to the fifty-year-old tradition of Henry Fielding and his Runners.

Graham's lodgings are near his office, so Harriott must travel from the eastern edge of the metropolis to the western. He escapes Wapping via Old Gravel Lane, climbing up onto the old gravel bluff along which the Ratcliffe Highway makes its way into the city. Inevitably, he must pass Timothy Marr's shop, which is shut up and dark on this cold night. Harriott watches the little shop pass to his left, and then sinks back into his seat as the carriage heads west.

It is a cold night but there are crowds on the streets in the West End, better dressed and more purposeful than the oblivion-seekers of Wapping and Shadwell. Harriott always feels restless and vaguely disgusted in this part of town, this close to the politicians and the dukes and the influencers. Somewhere in these streets is Ryder, the Home Secretary, for whom Harriott's distaste has grown beyond all reckoning in the past week. And Ryder is just the latest in a long line of smooth intelligent men upon whom Harriott has run aground.

Nonetheless this is Aaron Graham's milieu, and Graham is a

good friend and an excellent companion, honest and diligent but otherwise totally unlike John Harriott. Indeed, rather more like Ryder than Harriott cares to admit. Graham dresses carefully in the latest fashions, affects a stylish air of insouciance and has a lightness of touch when it comes to conversation that makes him a favourite among the dining societies and parlours of the West End. His political nous may not be to Harriott's tastes, but it is always framed with such charm that the older man's hackles are rarely raised for long. Graham, for himself, admires Harriott more than any man he has ever met, and fervently wishes his old friend were more discreet and measured in his undertakings – he had raised a despairing eyebrow when he first heard of Harriott's handbill. The two of them dine regularly, and Graham's hand has been responsible for guiding the old farmer-sailor-soldier to a more effective sense of purpose and, did Harriott but know it, for shielding him from several attempts to unseat the River Thames magistrate and replace him with someone cut from a more amenable cloth.

Graham's lodgings on Great Queen Street throw light and heat out into the dark street as Harriott arrives, and the welcome inside is just as warm and bright. Harriott and Graham share an excellent meal that evening, discussing random administrative and political matters (when the name of Ryder is mentioned Harriott embarks on a screed of such maritime saltiness that Graham is forced to ask his servants to retire until it blows itself out). And, eventually, as the port reaches the table, the cigars are rolled out, and the servants clear away the dinner things, the conversation turns to the Ratcliffe Highway murders. Harriott wastes little time in bemoaning the lack of action at the Home Office and in Shadwell.

'And yet the reward, Harriott. It is unprecedented,' says Graham. The Home Office has just raised its price for information about the murders from £100 to £500. 'Ryder has made a bold move, particularly for one such as him. You surely cannot complain about his effort.'

Harriott grunts.

'It's ironic, is it not, Graham?' he says. 'Barely a week after I was forced to apologise for offering an amount which was a fraction of that sum. Had it come earlier, perhaps the reward would have been effective. As it is, there has been more than a week since the murders. Whatever information may be unearthed by this new sum is likely to be worse than useless.'

'Worse than useless, Harriott? How so?'

'The unprecedented amount serves no purpose other than to make it even more worthwhile for miscreants to invent information. It will create noise and bluster. We have more than enough of that. Have you not noted how many suspects the various offices have taken into custody? Not one of them has led to a firm avenue of inquiry. This setting of eye-catching rewards is no substitute for good police work.'

'Police work? What an extraordinary phrase. I take it that you mean the business of discovering who committed these atrocious crimes.'

'I mean that exactly, Graham. We are only beginning to scratch the surface of the methodologies of detection and evidence. There is much to be discovered in this area. The men at Shadwell have little idea of it. They expect the murderer will walk in with his hands in the air and an apology on his lips. Or, alternatively, they imagine that by arresting all and sundry they will somehow scoop up the killer, as a fisherman scoops up his catch in a net. Multiply that by seven other offices, all of whom are scooping up in the same fashion, and you have a very large catch indeed. 'Tis a shame there aren't any decent fish to eat in it.'

'So, you include my office in that, Harriott?'

'I do, sir. I do not include you in it, however. Despite your ironic grin and mischievous countenance, I know full well you understand what I am talking about.'

'What makes you so sure?'

'Your investigation of Mr Patch, and your discovery of him as the murderer of Mr Blight.'

'Ah, once again your attention to the niceties of my career flatters me, Harriott.'

'Not at all. It is my Waterman-Constable Horton who told me of the case. He is very much a student of your work.'

'Really? How very odd he must be.'

'He is exceptionally committed to the cause of reducing the miseries which plague honest men and women.'

'I am sure he is, although you make him sound like a politician. And I do know him rather well, as it happens. I have observed his work on several occasions. And I rather think he, like us, is genuinely motivated by other things than the simple doing of good.'

'I do not understand your meaning, sir.'

'Let me explain. You are first and foremost a seagoing man, Harriott. You started your career at sea. You are a man of action. Wherever you spy inaction, such as your perception of the inactivity at the Home Office in recent days, you become irritated and frustrated. You clench your fists and you slam them down on tables. I can see your fists now, and they look as tight and as white as a pair of fresh cauliflowers. You resent the inactivity of the Police Offices. The Shadwell magistrates enrage you because they are, essentially, passive men, Harriott, and you are the most active man I know. I believe if you go to bed not having completed a dozen tasks in any day you go to bed a deeply unhappy man. You stamp your mark on the world in a frenzy of doing.'

'I will accept your description even while I ignore your mocking tone, Graham.'

'My respectful thanks, old friend, and I meant no mocking by it. It is an extraordinary quality. I only raise the point to make another point. Constable Horton is not like you, Harriott. Horton sees the world as an intellectual puzzle. It is something to be worked out, like an interesting watch mechanism. Horton looks at the facts surrounding these murders rather as Plato looked at the shadows flickering on the walls of his cave – as indications of a reality which cannot be directly seen. Horton is not motivated by the wish to do good, he is motivated by the wish to receive gratification for working things out. Like all of us, including you, Harriott, he wishes to find ways of gratifying himself.'

'I rather suspect that you just described yourself, rather than my policeman.'

'That is perhaps the case. You are more deductive than I gave you credit for, my dear Harriott.'

'Your point is well taken, Graham. Horton and I are indeed trying to force the issue on this case, in our different ways. Horton spent yesterday at Shadwell observing their efforts to make something stick with this Pugh character.'

'Pugh?'

'He is a contractor, responsible for the cosmetic work on the Marr shop. The ripping chisel found on the shop counter was his. Pugh claims he hired a man named Cornelius Hart to work on the shop three weeks ago, and this man requested a chisel of the type found in the shop. Hart was also brought in to Shadwell, but was identified by a bricklayer who worked in the shop, and by the girl servant Margaret Jewell.'

'Why was the chisel on the counter?'

'Why? I suppose it was left there.'

'Left there? By whom?'

'By the carpenter, Hart.'

'But you said he did the work three weeks ago. Are we to

believe that the fastidious Mr Marr would have left a tool on his shop counter for three weeks? Surely it would have been put away. And why was it not missed?'

'You sound like Horton.'

'I shall take that as the greatest compliment, given what you have told me this evening.'

'Perhaps Marr took the chisel out to return it?'

'At midnight? Surely he wasn't planning to take it to Hart at that time of night?'

'Well, perhaps using your powers of deduction you might give me an idea of what did actually happen.'

'Well, I think it most likely that either the killer, or killers, brought it into the house as a tool for their crime, or Marr got it out for some other reason, perhaps to defend himself.'

'But no one heard any voices, raised or otherwise. And unlike the maul the chisel had no blood on it, so was not used in the crime.'

'Indeed. But it is there. That is the one single fact we're sure of – the chisel was on the counter.'

'Yes.'

'Then I do think it rather important, Harriott, that we find out what it was doing there.'

'We?'

'We, indeed. Since neither of us is *formally* permitted to work on this case, I think we may both be said to have an equal share in its investigation, if I may use such a word. Now, some port?'

'If you insist, my friend. Though I wouldn't want your crystal clear investigating faculties clouded by the rancid effects of alcohol.'

'Yes. Like all seamen, you are of course a model of temperance.'

APRIL 1565

Billy and Drake were looking for pearls.

The place in which they were looking, Rio de la Hacha, was a scrappy colonial town on the coast of Venezuela where the pearls grew to the size of hazelnuts, or so Drake had heard, and he'd found a local man who owned a boat and a team of slaves who dived for them. This wiry middle-aged Spaniard had just added to his little team by buying some more slaves from the Hawkyns fleet, squeezing their thighs to test for muscle and holding his hand over their mouths and noses to see which of them had the biggest lungs.

Billy had never seen a pearl, but even the sound of the word was thrilling and opulent. Drake was just excited by the prospect of more surreptitious wealth, although it had seemed clear to Billy for quite some time that Hawkyns's second cousin Francis Drake was set fair to make more money from this voyage than Billy could dream of making in an entire lifetime. Drake had the knack of being in the right place at the right time, and of being as far away from the wrong place when he needed to be. It had struck Billy that Drake's position on the voyage was rather more influential than the one he affected, that of the sophisticated but callow young distant cousin learning his trade. Billy was beginning to think Drake was there to keep an eye on the crew, an eye on the cargo, and both eyes on the interactions between the two. Hence their careful stocktaking, and Drake's long evenings spent watching the Negroes in their cots. He had even been learning their language.

They had met with the bad-tempered little pearl fisherman early that morning. Eight slaves were already sitting in the boat. One of them looked at Billy and pointed, opening his mouth to shout something, and Billy saw sharpened teeth and thought perhaps that he recognised the man. A slave from the *Jesus*, obviously, one of the two hundred or so they'd been selling in Rio de la Hacha since their arrival. The boat-owner smacked the African round the back of the head when he heard him speak, and the Negro's head fell forward. He made no further sound. Billy looked down to the man's feet and there, sure enough, was the questing head of the worm, now four or five inches longer and beginning to work its way down the African's foot. It made him feel sick, and he looked away.

Throughout their negotiations the boat-owner was surly and unhelpful, and Drake smirked at him. 'This Spanish coward is worried we're going to kill his family,' he told Billy, not bothering to lower his voice in front of the Spaniard. 'Isn't it marvellous how afraid they are of us?'

The boat-owner, and his fellow townsfolk, had learned pretty well to be afraid of English sailors. The John Hawkyns style of mercantile negotiation brooked little debate and was conducted under the shadow of cannon. Since arriving from Africa weeks before, Hawkyns and his fleet had bullied their way around much of the Caribbean and the coast of the

Spanish Main in an attempt to sell their slaves. They had taken on as many riches from the locals as they could get away with.

In the third week of March the fleet had arrived in the Caribbean. Before leaving Africa, thanks to the capture of several Portuguese caravels sixty miles up the Callowsa river, the number of ships had swollen to seven. The holds of these caravels had been filled with Africans and their crews had been tortured for information by Hawkyns and the gentlemen officers who sailed with him. Billy had heard the screams of the Portuguese from the caravels, and each scream had been accompanied by a cheer from the crew of the *Jesus*. When Hawkyns had finished with them, the Portuguese were thrown into the river waters.

They had spent many days raiding the island of Sambula for slaves after the initial successful attack. Every day for two weeks they went ashore, and perhaps two hundred Africans had been seized. But Hawkyns had been determined to seize more Africans with less effort, and the caravels provided both information and, crucially, more cargo space. The holds of the *Jesus* and the *Minion* were almost full, indeed were becoming dangerously overcrowded.

The Portuguese information led to an attack on a town further upriver, in which more Africans were seized. Before long the caravels were also filled up, and Hawkyns came down to view the cargo in the hold of the *Jesus*, ignoring Drake and Billy as he counted heads and muttered to himself. Billy thought he understood the equation Hawkyns was trying to calculate. He and Drake had already done it themselves. Pack the Africans in too tightly, and the contagions which were already leaping from slave to slave would jump ever more quickly. Pack them in too loosely, and there wouldn't be enough Negroes left to draw a profit (or at least as heavy a profit as they all would like) on the other side of the ocean. What was the optimum ratio of Africans to cargo space?

Billy did not know how many slaves were in the holds of the other ships, but he reckoned on more than a hundred down in the hold of the *Jesus*. Whatever the calculation was, Hawkyns decided this was the ideal amount, and they immediately set sail for the Spanish colonies of South America and the Caribbean.

Crossing the Atlantic took several weeks, and many Africans died during the voyage. Billy and Drake carefully totted up the totals each morning, removing the Africans who had died during the night or looked close to death and having them thrown overboard. But the losses seemed to be acceptable, and Hawkyns's equation had held – the number of surviving Africans was still thought to be high enough to bring healthy profits when they reached the Spanish colonies.

No one had been able to answer Billy's oft-repeated question, though: what were these slaves actually *worth*?

Their first stop was Dominica, where they took on fresh water, mainly for the Africans in the holds. At their next stop, the island of Margarita, the townspeople vanished when the Hawkyns fleet arrived, fearful of what he might do. They remembered previous English voyages to the region, and had been told stories of guns trained on towns, and secretaries and treasurers and governors run through for refusing to cooperate with those wanting to trade.

The fleet kept moving, hitting the Venezuelan coast at Cumaná, but finding the settlement there almost deserted they moved on to Santa Fe, where they took on supplies for the crew and for the slaves, although prospects for trade were still not promising enough for Hawkyns to set out his stall (quite literally, as Billy would discover). At Santa Fe they were approached by Arawak Indians, with whom the English traded trinkets such as beads and pewter for food – bread and corn and chickens and, most exotically of all, pineapples. Only a few crewmen went ashore for the transactions, and from the ship Billy watched the Indians emerge from the forest behind the shore, their dark hair gleaming in the sun and the light flashing on their painted skin. Some of the crew came back with stories of the Arawaks' poisoned arrows, which the Indians had been happy to show off and which were tipped with the venom of the local serpents.

Finally, at the significant colony of Burburata on the mainland coast, Hawkyns decided to set up shop, finding a settlement big enough to need slaves and rich enough to promise profit. Soon after the fleet anchored, he was rowed ashore to meet with the town officials. Drake went with him, and returned with details of the formal negotiations. The admiral had claimed to have been blown off course by storms, and had asked to be allowed to trade with the locals in order to replenish his much-needed supplies. His tale was delivered with part desperation, part charm and part threat – as he spoke to the local dignitaries, Hawkyns made sure his ships' guns were visible from the quay-side, ordering them made ready and polished up so the Caribbean sun flamed along their sides. It was a combination well tailored to unlock the incipient greed and fear of the locals.

Like all Spanish subjects on the Main the Burburata officials had been told many, many times by representatives of the crown that they were not to trade with Englishmen, and in particular this Englishman. Hawkyns was already well known among the bureaucrats and counsellors of Madrid, and Spain's ambassador to England had long ago sent word that a visit from this Plymouth adventurer should be expected. Madrid was clear: local trading monopolies were to be preserved. The economic wall which the Spanish court had erected around its empire would not be breached.

But then, Madrid was a very long way from Burburata.

Hawkyns persisted in his cajoling. He promised bribes for the governor of Venezuela (who just so happened to be the nephew of another official with whom Hawkyns had traded on a previous voyage, which was the kind of relationship which drove those same Madrid bureaucrats into elegant tantrums), but he also hinted that a ship the size of the *Jesus* with a big crew of lusty determined Englishmen was likely to turn nasty if his wishes weren't met. The threat became more defined, the charm sharper at the edges.

And while all this was happening, Africans were dying in the ship's hold. Sickness leapt from slave to slave, and the English sailors muttered angrily that if the Spaniards didn't give them a licence to trade soon, the merchandise would all be dead. Billy worried as much as anyone. If Hawkyns didn't get a move on, and get the slaves sold, he'd be returning to Kate with nothing.

Eventually, with one eye on Madrid but with a more immediate, and significantly greedier, eye on the treasure in the hold of the *Jesus*, the Burburata authorities agreed to issue a trading licence, with the authority of the governor of Venezuela. But in their determination to drive a bargain, they went too far, demanding that Hawkyns pay customs duty in advance and a sales tax on every African the English sold in the town.

At the mention of a tax, Hawkyns did what any self-respecting English merchant would do – he went to war. Dozens of crewmen were ordered into their armour, including Billy. Hawkyns carried on negotiating even as his men loaded their weapons, graciously saying he'd pay the sales tax but the customs duty was a Papist restraint on the God-given right of Englishmen to trade their goods. Gone was the easy charm. Now all was bulldog and belligerence.

As Drake passed this information out among the crew, the

sailors muttered about 'greedy fucking Spaniards' and complained that landlocked bureaucrats were going to take bread from their mouths, what with their disgusting haggling and procrastinating. When news of the demand for a sales tax and customs duty hit the lower decks of the *Jesus*, there was an explosion of outrage which caused the slaves in the hold to moan and scream in terror as the English stamped and hollered in frustration. Tax! Did those bastards on shore not know how hard they'd all *worked* for this?

Hawkyns knew how his men felt, and delivered a rousing speech to manipulate this anger and anxiety. Standing in his finest courtier's clothes (Hawkyns had remained smartly attired for the entire voyage – Drake told Billy that he'd brought fifty changes of clothes with him) the admiral gazed on the men ranged before him and, in the fine baritone Billy had first heard in a Plymouth tavern, reminded them of what was what.

'Men! My fine men! The finest men on the sea! We're off to yonder town to put on a little show for the King of Spain. Those whores in civic clothes are wetting themselves to make some money out of us. They know the treasure we carry and they know they need what we bring. But they're scared fellows. They're terrified. They think that the old woman Philip will cut off their heads and the Papist Inquisition will cut off their balls for trading with fine English Protestant seadogs such as us!'

The men on the deck roared. Billy roared along with them. Drake smirked, watching everything with that careful attention which marked all his observations of Hawkyns, as if he were witnessing a masterclass.

Hawkyns was warming to his task, and spread his arms out wide with blessed good fellowship, his fine white teeth flashing like the barrels of the guns below decks.

'So listen, my lads! The cowards and thieves have already

tried to fool us with their godless sales tax and their Papist custom duties, but no Englishman in the world is going to be stopped from his holy right to trade and commerce by a bunch of spineless Spanish women dressed as men. Now, here's the thing, lads. They want to trade. They surely do. But they want to make it look like we *made* them trade with us, so when their king's sodding bureaucrats crawl over here from Madrid or out of whichever sinkhole they breed in, and when those bureaucrats look at the town's accounts and say' – and with this Hawkyns adopted a comical, sneering approximation of a Spanish accent – '"What is *this*? You traded with Hawkyns?", the cowards who run this place will be able to squeal: "They made us do it! They made us trade! We did not want to, but what could we *do*?"'

The men laughed and cheered, stamping on the deck and waving daggers and swords. Hawkyns had stirred up a vicious potion of fury and comradeship. Billy would have cheerfully shot his weapon into the face of a Spaniard – be it man, woman or child – if there had been one to hand. And he was more than ready to do anything else the admiral might require of him.

With his men straining to be set loose on the town, Hawkyns wrapped up his performance.

'Now, this ship we stand on, you know who it belongs to. You know who owns the sails and the shrouds and the yards. *Elizabeth*, boys. And while we all wondered what kind of queen she would be, I'm here to tell you, lads, that she's made of the same vicious and unyielding stuff as her father was. And she can feel every stamp, every shot and every scream from the boards of this ship. Back in London, even now, she knows. She *knows*. And she has *expectations*. So armour on and guns up, and if we have to kill a few of the bastards to make it look more real, so be it! For God, for England, for Elizabeth, and for trade!'

Another roar from the deck, and then they were climbing into the boats and making their way into Burburata. Billy lost sight of Drake, but it didn't matter. The bloodlust was on him, if only for a while, and he crashed unhesitatingly into the town with his shipmates. A few skirmishes and the odd Spanish death later, and the authorities caved in (with some relief) to this show of Anglo-Saxon mercantile force. The fighting died down almost immediately, and the trading began, with a sense of relief and excitement.

From somewhere within the innards of the apparently endlessly bulwarked hold of the *Jesus* a strange contraption made an appearance. The strange lengths of wood and coloured sailcloth Billy had first seen with Drake just after they'd left Plymouth were explained. Canvas and struts were unfolded on the quayside and made up into a glaring and extraordinary anachronism: a merrily striped tent with a detachable awning, as might be seen in an English country fair. Within barely two hours of the supposed invasion of the town, Hawkyns could be heard gleefully laughing from the *Jesus* at the sight of an English summer market springing up on the dusty quayside of a New Spanish colony. Dejected and chained groups of slaves were lined up outside the tent and made to stand, one by one, on a small dais within as locals assessed them, grabbing their legs to feel the muscle and pulling back the lips from their teeth. The very few Negro families still together after the raids and the disease and the drownings were soon separated. Those older children who'd been brought with the men and the few women were acquired as individuals, and as good investments.

Over the next few days a great deal of trading was done. Locals from Burburata wandered up and down, the women in what served as finery in this Spanish outpost, the men complaining of the poor condition of the slaves but buying them anyway.

But trade was still not as good as it should have been. Billy's oft-repeated question – *what are they worth?* – had been answered, and the answer was: *not enough*. Most of the slaves were being sold for 90 pesos of gold. For perhaps the first time in the voyage, Drake looked tense. Hawkyns had reckoned on making 125 pesos or more per slave. The knowledge that he could be making a third more on each sale ate away at him like one of the Guinea worms that accompanied the slaves on board the ships.

Hawkyns decided to play another game. He ordered that the gaily coloured tent be packed up, raised the anchors and took the fleet out of the harbour of Burburata. The canny traders of the town were left bemoaning their cleverness. They'd been deliberately keeping the prices low because they suspected Hawkyns of selling his sickest, weakest slaves first – which indeed he had been. They wailed with anguish as the fleet made to leave. They still needed more slaves.

But the fleet's departure was the naval equivalent of a knowing wink during a market-stall haggle. After a few days, Hawkyns brought the fleet back and set up the stall again, and now slaves flew out of the hold and onto the plantations and into the mines of the Spanish locals. The prices were higher, and as demand began to ebb and prices began to fall again, Hawkyns packed up, for good this time, and headed for Rio de la Hacha. There were still many living Negroes in the holds of his fleet and he needed the best price for them.

Rio de la Hacha was not a wealthy place; it was certainly less promising than Burburata. The land was hard to cultivate, and only the pearl fishing brought in a regular income. But even this was enough to make it worth trading with, although the locals went through similar charades as their fellows in Burburata had: abandoning the town on his approach; sending officials to negotiate, said officials being easily persuaded to participate in another charade; Hawkyns claiming to have been blown off course and needing to trade to get supplies to get home; the locals replying that they would love to trade, really, but the King wouldn't let them.

If anything, the pretence in Rio de la Hacha was even more theatrical than in Burburata. The town authorities penned pretend letters of protest and Hawkyns pretended to be annoyed with them. He sent a pretend force to attack the town, and the townspeople pretended to surrender. Billy found the whole thing perplexing and frustrating, and the crew watched as Hawkyns's contempt for the Spanish grew and grew with every new play-act they put on. Drake found the whole thing delightfully amusing. But then Drake found a great many things delightfully amusing.

Finally, another all-clear was given, and the bucolic English stall was reconstructed in this new location. The whole town came out to the shop, in a pent-up frenzy of spending. For three days and three nights, the Hawkyns collapsible boutique was the fashionable place to be seen for the inhabitants of Rio de la Hacha. The final two hundred slaves were all sold, along with French wine and English flour, cakes, cloth and clothing and even lingerie. The town's royal treasurer, the mayor, the tax collector – all of them made it to the shop. Drake and Billy watched them from the deck of the *Jesus*, and Drake spat sardonically into the sea before declaiming: 'So much for the Inquisition – these sorry Papists are more concerned about missing out on a quick profit than sending their souls to damnation for all eternity.'

It was on the third day of this trading extravaganza that Billy and Drake had decided on their little pearl-diving expedition. Now their commandeered boat was ready, and they pulled out of the small harbour and into the wide mouth of the river. The boat-owner threw out a rudimentary anchor, and then started shoving the slaves out of the boat, each of them with a net tied to their waist and a couple of rocks tied to their legs to weigh them down. Drake and Billy helped him, grabbing the arms of the more reluctant ones and pulling them over the side and into the sea. The one with the sharpened teeth and the worm was particularly reluctant, gibbering something in his own language as Billy grabbed his arm before they threw him in, and waited for him to return.

After a minute or two, all the more experienced divers popped back onto the surface, spluttering and spitting but carrying sacks of oysters which their owner heaved into the boat. Some time later the newer slaves made it to the surface, with far fewer oysters and with their eyes rolling with fear. The owner heaved them into the boat, slapping their heads in irritation at the small catch they brought with them. The last slave, the one with the worm, was nowhere to be seen, and they watched as three or four shark fins began to circle.

This troubled Billy, but it troubled the boat-owner more. He shouted angrily at the other divers, slapping them around the head again and muttering angrily at Drake, who simply smirked.

'He's saying he wants his money back. He's saying we sold him a slave who doesn't swim. What an idiot.'

14 DECEMBER 1811

While John Harriott is dining with Aaron Graham, Waterman-Constable Charles Horton is indulging in a spot of what Graham would call, with smooth asperity, *police work*.

He is standing in the scrappy patch of land behind Timothy Marr's house. The backs of the tidy little houses look out onto this nondescript little space. If the square were in one of the new fashionable districts around Chelsea or Belgravia there would no doubt be some nicely planned planting, with a small wrought-iron fence to emphasise exclusivity. Here in the East End, it's just a patch of land, an accident of design, a scandalously under-used piece of scrub which will inevitably be built on in years, if not months, from now.

Horton has just come out of the rear of number 29, carrying some pages torn from Marr's order book which he is now folding and placing in a pocket of his pea coat as he ponders the scene. He found the order book in a metal box in the main bedroom of the house, shoved into a cupboard. It is a small miracle it was still there, so many people having traipsed through the house since the day of the murders. Horton supposes the Shadwell officers who'd been keeping an eye on the place had done a rather better job than he would have ever imagined.

Immediately after the murders, a local resident claimed to have found tracks across this little parcel of land, as if several men had run across the enclosed square to one of the houses opposite. John Murray, the first witness Horton had encountered, reported hearing the sound of men crashing through a house near his and Marr's property. Horton has today found himself wondering if there is evidence for any of this.

The houses are arranged in a rectangle, their fronts facing north onto the Ratcliffe Highway, south onto Pennington Street and the wall of the dock, and east and west onto the smaller connecting roads between Pennington Street and the Highway. There is no chance of finding any of the footprints again, if indeed they had ever been there. The ground has been churned up by an army of amateur investigators. In fact, there is one obvious route which tracks the muddiest parts of the soil, a proxy for the dozens of feet which have rehearsed the probable escape route of the murderers (perhaps they followed the original claimed footprints, perhaps they didn't). This muddy track heads southwards down the hill, directly towards the dock. But Horton is, for the moment, ignoring this muddy track. He is more interested in a house which faces out on Artichoke Hill, one of the roads running down from the Ratcliffe Highway to the wall of the dock. There is a house here that is close enough to John Murray's to have caused him to notice noises from it. Murray's house is on the corner of the square, and he would have been able to clearly hear men running through one of the Artichoke Hill properties. Also, this particular house is dark and unoccupied, and would be an obvious option for desperate men seeking a rapid exit from the square.

He walks to the back of the dark house. The back door is hanging open, and has clearly been forced more than once. It is a sad, ill-used thing, this door. Horton goes into the dark house, looks around him, and comes out again.

He walks through this little re-enactment five times, trying to use the mechanisms of walking to activate some connection in his mind. He loses all track of time in the process (his wife Abigail is at the little apartment in Lower Gun Alley even now, fretting over his ruined evening meal, angry at his absent-mindedness, resigned to his coming in at any hour with his eyes closed to anything but the melancholy considerations running through his head). He peers into every corner of the dark little house. He runs his fingers along shelves, between banisters, even underneath loose floorboards. There is not even any evidence of a previous tenant, let alone anything indicating a gaggle of men escaping the scene of a slaughter.

He comes out, he goes in again. This time he does not kneel or feel. He walks into the hall of the little house, which is in complete darkness. Through the wall he hears the sounds of a man and woman talking in the neighbouring house. Is that Murray's house? He thinks so, but can't remember for certain. He leans back on the banisters and feels them give slightly, with a creak. He looks back behind him up the hall, to the rear of the house, then brings his head round towards the front, and as he does so something catches the light from the moon which is shining through the large front window.

There is something on the dusty staircase, a couple of inches back from the edge and almost at his eye level. He stands up on tiptoe and gazes at it. It seems to be the edge of a thick silver coin. He ponders for a moment, then walks around to the foot of the stairs. He tests how safe the bottom step is but the house, whatever its state of cleanliness, is relatively new and fairly well built, and the staircase is firm. He walks up half-a-dozen steps, but cannot see the coin and for a moment considers whether or not he might have imagined it. But then he remembers the light from the moon, the light which he is now standing in, and steps to the side and the coin reveals itself again.

He stoops to pick it up. It is thick and heavy, but it is too dark to see it clearly. Horton walks back down the stairs and out of the front door, and stands where the moonlight allows him to take a closer look.

On one side of the coin is a picture of two pillars topped by crowns. Between the pillars the words PLU-SUL-TRA, and a number, 79. Around its edge the words POTOSI and CAROLUS II. On the other side is a cross quartered by dragons and lions.

It is a piece of eight, from Peru. Horton recognises the currency immediately, from his days as a sailor, and is perfectly capable of decoding the writing on it. Spanish colonial currency is still widely accepted in the far-flung corners of Spain's empire, even in the pockets of English power which have inserted themselves inside that ancient, creaking imperium. He has himself received Spanish doubloons and pieces of eight while travelling, even in places where Spanish power never reached. The coin is surprising, not least for its age (Horton guesses its date at 1679, given the number and the name of the King, Charles II), but not unprecedented.

Horton ponders the metal disc. What is it worth? A not inconsiderable amount, he thinks, even though the degraded Spanish currency has been very much frowned upon these last two or three decades. The purity of the silver guarantees a certain amount of value. How much, exactly? Perhaps enough for a new set of clothes for an ordinary lady, not so distinguished that she demands the finest things, but certainly aware of quality. A woman much like his wife, he thinks to himself, running his thumb around the uneven edge before placing the old coin in his pocket, and the thought of his wife makes him impatient to be home again. He taps the coin through the material of his trousers a couple of times with his fingers as he closes the front door of the house, looking up Artichoke Hill towards the Highway. The tower of St George in the East rises above the houses behind him, a very similar rectangle of houses to the one he has just been inside.

He has had his fill of the Highway for a day. He turns down the hill, towards the wall of the dock, and then stops again. He looks to his right and sees the wall meandering westwards, parallel to the Highway, towards the old city a mile or so beyond.

He turns away from the city and to his left and walks down towards Wapping, that great dock wall now on his right, and as he walks he runs his hand along its massive extent (his fingers passing the spot where Margaret Jewell pressed her own face to the wall several nights before). He wonders if he should put his head into some of the alehouses and make enquiries about who has been paying for their liquor with Spanish colonial coins.

But then he yawns. It is almost midnight, and it has been a long day. He turns right at the end of the wall, and trudges down Old Gravel Lane, towards Lower Gun Alley and Abigail. Nodding at a tall young man who is limping away from Wapping as their coats brush against each other, Waterman-Constable Charles Horton ends his investigation for this evening, and heads home.

MAY 1565

After several days, the Hawkyns fleet left Rio de la Hacha in some triumph, and on friendly terms with the locals. Hawkyns even had a testimonial from the town's treasurer inside his pocket. The mood on the ships was high. Trading had been a success, and now the crew looked forward to heading home and enjoying the fruits of their labours.

But in this they were disappointed. What followed instead were dozens of fruitless and frustrating days sailing around the islands of the Caribbean. Hawkyns spent much of this time standing on the aft castle, looking vaguely into the distance and drumming his fingers on the rail, as if pondering the meaning of existence, or at least the meaning of money. He seemed uncertain of what to do next. Were there still opportunities for money to be made, or should they now head home with what they had?

The crew continued to work the ship, with growing surliness, glancing at Hawkyns and his retinue of gentlemen and waiting for some signal as to what the admiral was up to. Over the course of a fortnight the little fleet pulled in to several different places – Margarita, Cartagena, Cabo de la Vela – but they had nothing significant left to trade. The Africans had almost all been sold; a disconsolate few remained to be taken back to England as gifts. The hold brimmed with the bounty they'd received in return: Indian gold and silver, pearls (Billy and Drake had pocketed six from their little expedition, and the value of one of these was worth more money than anything Billy had ever had his hands on), jewels and mountains of hides, taken from the island of Curaçao, where tens of thousands of cattle carcasses rotted in the sun and the Spaniards sold hides at ridiculously low prices.

This apparently aimless wandering became the soil for all sorts of below-decks rumours. Hawkyns was pondering another prize, said some, a different type of transaction, a more larcenous one even than those perpetrated on Burburata and Rio de la Hacha. The rumourmongers leant in, touched their noses and with immensely secretive authority swore blind that the admiral had his eye on the biggest prize of all: the Spanish treasure fleet, which sailed twice a year from Portobelo and Cartagena back to Spain, transporting the wealth of the Americas from the New World to the Old. It was due any moment. They weren't hanging about to trade; it was good old Plymouth piracy that Hawkyns had his eyes on.

Others nodded sagely, smirked to themselves at the idiocy of their shipmates, and whispered of Hawkyns's *real* aim, as they saw it, an even more exotic target: the fountain of youth of Ponce de León, believed to be a river within the Spanish territory of Florida. The ageing conquistador, it was said, had spent months trying to find the restorative waters told of by the local Indians, to cure his impotence. The combination of Indian mysticism and Spanish sexual dysfunction was too sweet not to interest a bored and sated crew of English sailors, and for a while the two rumours – treasure fleet versus fountain of youth –

rebounded off each other as the men muttered and groaned and itched with impatience.

Drake found the rumours ridiculous. 'Why would we have gone through those elaborate charades to avoid annoying the King of Spain? Why would we do that and then attempt to sink his treasure fleet? Hawkyns is not a stupid man. And as for a fountain of youth? Ponce de León was looking for gold, that is all. And he died of a wound in Havana.'

Billy, whose diplomatic sophistication was growing with every minute he spent with Drake, did not point out that Hawkyns had probably already succeeded in annoying the King of Spain greatly, and that the trading had gone on under the threat of cannon and sword.

But it soon appeared that Drake was right. Hawkyns seemed to have his eyes on a rather more prosaic prize – hides, the price of which had astonished the English and which would represent easy money to be made back home. They were heading for Hispaniola, where Hawkyns had acquired hides on his first trip to the region. But the currents were against them, the cloud came down, and for days they wandered aimlessly, the strong underlying current shoving the fleet along as if by some unseen giant hand, confounding the navigators and taking them up the side of Hispaniola and towards the channel between the giant island and the dangling peninsula of Florida. Below decks the excited chatter about a fountain of youth reached fever pitch, even while the officers struggled to find a way through the strange warm winds and rapid currents of the Caribbean.

One particularly aimless evening in the midst of this wandering, Drake and Billy were standing at the rail watching the stars, which had only reappeared from the clouds a few hours before. Billy touched the pearl in his pocket, which stayed there and never shifted, and imagined handing it to Kate on his return to Stanton St John. He thought of her fine blonde hair and high cheekbones. So strangely Slavic for such an English rose.

'I think I know where we're heading,' said Drake, with the customary smirk-and-wink.

'Hispaniola?' said Billy, disturbed from a reverie of Oxfordshire pig-farming.

'Possibly, for a bit. But I think we're actually in the business of finding a particular gift for the Queen.'

'A gift?'

'Yes. I think Hawkyns wants to give her the keys to Florida.'

'Florida? You mean the fountain of youth?'

Drake chuckled, but looked angry at the same time, and Billy saw (not for the first time) that there was steel inside this charming, immoral man, the steel of a future captain.

'No, young William, I do not mean the fountain of bloody youth. I mean the big chunk of land, across the water from here, which stretches out towards Hispaniola and Cuba, right out into the ocean. Like a sort of gate.'

'A gate?'

'That's right. A big bloody gate across the Caribbean, just waiting for a new gatekeeper.'

'And he wants to give it to Elizabeth?'

'Well, in a metaphysical sense. He wants to give her the keys. He wants to present maps and reports and information, everything she needs to send a fleet down here and take it.'

'Take it?'

'Yes, young William, take it. It's all very well, this exploring and trading, but England wants what Spain and Portugal have got. We want dominions and chattels and land. We can't let this ridiculous accident of history stand.'

Drake's hair was blown back slightly by the wind, and something about the set of his jaw and the sparkle in his eyes made Billy pay more particular attention. His friend suddenly seemed rather older than his years would suggest. Drake put his arm around Billy's shoulders, and with his other hand swept the horizon, a Devil offering empires to Billy's Christ, before his hand dropped back to the ship's rail.

'New times are coming, mark my words,' Drake continued. 'We've already broken with the Papists and with Rome. We've set our own course. Elizabeth might not say it – she might not even *think* it yet – but England's got the wind in its sails. France, too. You only need to look at how those pathetic Spanish colonists behaved to understand that they won't keep a grip on all this for much longer. They got lucky. They funded a Genoese chancer when no one else would, and the gamble paid off. It paid off *magnificently*. The Pope backed them and the Portuguese and between them those two carved up the world. We were too busy massacring each other in England and France over matters of doctrine to pay all this much attention.

'Out here, we're at the edge of something *enormous*, Billy. Ships like the *Jesus* will be legends to those who come after us. We're opening up the world, and mark my words, before much longer all these islands will be English or, just maybe, French. And Florida, over there, is the key. If we can grab it for ourselves, before the French do, the world's our oyster.' Drake removed his arm from Billy's shoulder, and with a practised wink opened his other hand to hand back the pearl he'd whisked out of Billy's pocket while they'd been talking. 'We're going to be rich.'

Eventually, as June reached its end, the little fleet found the right current and a helpful breeze and struggled towards Florida. For a few days, Hawkyns sailed them up and down the coast of the region, as seemingly aimless as before, but the commander spent endless days in his cabin and Billy began to see the truth of what Drake had said. Plans were being hatched. Charts were being scratched on parchment. Soundings were being taken, lists of water supplies recorded, and the crew made use of the time by taking boats out and capturing hundreds of birds and turtles from the Tortuga islands while they hunted for freshwater.

After three weeks, they finished exploring and turned south-east, intending to head for the harbour in Havana, but the weather had become treacherous in the meantime. The currents now made navigation impossible. Freshwater supplies began to run dangerously low, and below decks the talk was no longer of fountains of youth; it was of the recklessness of Hawkyns and the gentlemen who surrounded him. Sanders the quartermaster had been particularly busy with his rope, as some of the men began to drag their heels when it came time to pray. The admiral ordered a rush to be made for the string of islands that garlanded the tip of the Florida peninsula. Billy considered what Drake had said about Hawkyns offering Elizabeth the Keys to the Caribbean; it didn't feel like such a grand prize now. Panic was boiling through the crew.

Reefs prevented all but the smallest ship in the fleet getting too close to any of the islands, so twenty men or so were rowed out to the *Swallow*, the 30-ton pinnace, to act as exploratory parties to find freshwater. The group included Billy, though Drake had done a vanishing trick, as was his custom when there was dull exploration to be undertaken. The wind was vicious, and as the small pinnace worked its way into the islands the *Jesus* was forced to bear away from the reefs around the islands and almost instantly she seemed to disappear over the horizon under the influence of the vicious underlying current. The pinnace dropped off pairs of sailors at different islands, promising to return to pick them up on the trip back. Billy and a young man named Reynolds were dropped off at one unpromising-looking place, with a sandy beach backed by dense tropical bush. They were rowed in from the pinnace, walking up the beach when the water was shallow enough, and headed towards the undergrowth.

It was there they discovered the Spaniard's body.

15 DECEMBER 1811

John Harriott occupies an unyielding volume of cold, damp London air. He does not wear either of his dress uniforms – from the navy, or from the East India Company – for the simple reason that neither of them fit him any more. He stands at the edge of the Ratcliffe Highway, near St George in the East, and despite the crowds he is given respectful room. Many of the ordinary people know him by sight – the man who faced down the Irish watermen in the River Police riots of 1798 – and even those who don't know him can smell the authority on him the way they can smell gin on the breath of a man falling out of a tavern. He is sixty-six years old, fat and tired. And not for the first time in his flamboyant, buccaneering life, he is feeling not entirely in control of his destiny.

The Highway is lined, three or four deep, along both sides, all the way down from Timothy Marr's shop to the entrance of the St George in the East churchyard. Many of those in the crowd have been there since the early morning, despite the cold.

Harriott listens to them talking to each other, an energised whisper running through the gaps between people, smelling of fear, excitement and anticipation. He thinks there are significantly more women here than there are men, and many of them look like they are on a bit of an outing. Their clothes are a bit more spruce than normal, almost Sunday best, faces are scrubbed, hair is hidden under bonnets. Dotted amongst the locals is the occasional group of wealthier types, with their new hats and smoother coats, down from London for a little crime tourism amongst the lower orders. These groups lean in among themselves and occasionally belt out a laugh, unaware of and frankly unconcerned with the looks of scandalous disapproval this provokes among the ordinary people of Wapping and Shadwell.

Clouds of breath hang in the air over people's heads. Vaguely, Harriott can hear the creaking of masts and rigging over in the dock, its ships shifting gently in the misty breeze. Up here on the Highway they are almost level with the top of the dock wall, but within this wall sit warehouses which hide the ships even from the raised point of the Highway. Only their intricate masts are visible. The sounds of their movements bounce off the walls of the great white church behind him, and Harriott thinks of an old warship making its way through the fog off Newfoundland, alone and lost.

The bells of St George's ring one o'clock. Half an hour to go. He looks around for Constable Horton and soon spots him, standing within the crowd in his best clothes (the ones Constable Horton had stolen, unbeknownst to Harriott, in the desperate months after his departure from the navy. The jacket is pretty threadbare but still expensive-looking. Its legitimate owner was a city merchant with a big villa in Upper Norwood who had carelessly left a box of belongings on the steps leading to his front door when a starving, half-dressed and freezing

Horton had happened to be walking by). Within the crowd Harriott also sees some of the respectable gentility of Highway society, the shopkeepers and landlords and parish councillors without whom the organism would not function. There are even respectable brothel owners, their means of gathering wealth far less important to their neighbours than the simple fact that they own a business. For these people, ownership of a moneymaking instrument is itself a badge of respectability. The Highway is not so different from the great city.

The minutes pass. Harriott's mind wanders, back to America and a certain squaw, then to Indonesia via a frigate in the West Indies and a plague shipwreck on Mewstone Rock, followed by the capture of a xebeque off the coast of Barbary. The old magistrate's memory is not fading, but the boundaries between the events in his life are bleeding into one another. His capacity for clear thought is in a race to the death with his old, lame body. One of them must give out before too much longer.

Then there is a disturbance in the crowd down the Highway, around the Marr shop. The coffins are coming out of the house, all bar that of James Gowen who has been buried separately. The crowd gasps, and a few women begin weeping quietly to themselves. A group of them near the entrance to the church let up a particularly loud wail. Harriott, initially sceptical of this feminine lack of rectitude, softens when he hears someone say this group includes the mother and sisters of Timothy Marr.

It is only a few hundred yards from the house to the church. The coffins seem to bob around on the heads of the crowd as they make their way along. For a while, there is something approaching silence. Even the creaks from the dock seem to restrain themselves. And then a woman – perhaps Marr's mother – wails 'God, oh God', and that sparks off a new, bigger wave of muttering and weeping and shouting, and by the time the coffins have arrived at the church gates the mood of the crowd has changed into something louder and angrier. Vengeance is in the air as the mourning party enters the church: Marr's coffin first, then his wife and infant, then his father and mother, then his four sisters, then his brother, then a group of friends and mourners, including Margaret Jewell. She is not crying. But she is as pale as a ghost. Harriott would have put her age now at nearly thirty. It has been a long week for the young girl with rebellious thoughts.

Harriott follows some other luminaries and close friends into the church, where the Reverend Dr Farrington administers the funeral rites with, Harriott feels, a somewhat warmer sense of fellowship than is quite appropriate for either the occasion or for a distinguished man of the cloth. The service lasts more than an hour. Harriott has been to more than his share of funerals, and knows this is rather over-egging things. He suspects Farrington of enjoying his time in the limelight of public regard. At the end, Harriott shuffles out behind a tall young man with a pronounced limp, almost as pronounced as his own.

Outside, the coffins are lowered into an empty grave, and there is a final vengeful shout, male this time, before soil starts to be emptied down onto the hard wooden coffins. Above, the hard white edifice of Hawksmoor's church glowers at them all, and even the West End dandies in the crowd are shamed into a silence which is at least partly respectful.

MAY 1565

They'd clapped eyes on the Spaniard's body as soon as they'd walked up the beach. Reynolds had started muttering in that strange north country way of his as soon as they'd seen it, something about 'cannibals', a word Billy had never heard before, although it didn't seem to be the time to be requesting definitions. The body was laid out on the sand, apparently ceremonially, and around its neck was the dark brown necklace of a slit throat. In the centre of its chest was a cavity, from which the heart had been scooped out. Billy examined the thing from a few yards away, and came to the conclusion that the body had been placed there as a sign. It didn't look like a particularly welcoming sign. Even in its eviscerated state it was obvious that this was a Spanish body; the little beard was a giveaway, and up beyond the tree line they also discovered the Spaniard's helmet and breastplate and the remains of his leather tunic. There was even a little Bible.

He and Reynolds had considered, without discussion, a quick sprint back to the water to wave the pinnace back, but the wind had already blown the small ship away, and neither of them wanted to look like a coward in front of the other one by yelling across the water for assistance. They were young men, still, even after all the things they'd seen. And the motivation for their volunteering for this jaunt remained; if they were the ones who got back with news of a freshwater source, they'd receive warm praise from Hawkyns and, who knew? Perhaps a slightly larger share of whatever was in the hold. Taken together that was payment enough for putting up with mysterious bodies on tropical beaches.

So they sucked in their bellies, stuck out their chests and pretended a bravery they did not feel. They inspected the ominous ravaged body and the remains of its belongings, and then they spent a fruitless couple of hours cutting through the low-level undergrowth of the island's interior, trying to make their way through and find freshwater and, hopefully, a source of food. The foliage wasn't thick, but it had an annoying green persistence which at first enraged them before eventually exhausting them. They slashed at it with their ineffective swords, and occasionally they forced a way through, but the green stalks still scraped their legs with enough force to draw blood.

It was after three hours of exhausting and painful hacking and ripping that they spotted the bloodstained tree. It was in the middle of a clearing that looked ominously man-made within the recalcitrant green. The tree was on its own in the centre of the clearing, its pale bark stained deep brown from head-height down, and grooves ringing the tree at waist-level and inches above the ground. *In the right place to tie up a man*, Billy thought to himself, and something in Reynolds's slow face said that he too had reached something like the same kind of conclusion. And there was something about the way the vegetation lay that indicated a body had been dragged from the tree out towards the beach where they'd landed. The dead Spaniard, presumably.

They walked around the tree several times, inspecting it and becoming aware that men had indeed made this clearing, men had killed the Spaniard and that it was quite possible that these men were still around somewhere. There had been no time to share this thought with each other when the Indians appeared.

Billy wasn't sure exactly how he knew they were Indians, because they looked very different from the native savages he'd seen in Venezuela and at Rio de la Hacha. But their skin colour was the same, their eyes were similarly pinched and Asiatic, and their black hair shone, though less healthily than the Arawak he'd watched from the ship in Santa Fe.

There were four of them: three young men, and one very, very old woman, whose ancient face and stooped shoulders couldn't mask the fact that she was, apparently, far more hale and hearty than the three men who accompanied her. They were thin and shivering, and their eyes had a yellow sourness. Even from the edge of the clearing, Billy could smell death on them.

'God's teeth!' said Reynolds, instinctively moving behind the bloody tree. He held out his sword towards the three men. Billy didn't bother. He couldn't see any trouble coming from these sad, emaciated men. The old woman, though, was perhaps another matter.

She stepped confidently, if a little shakily on her ancient limbs, into the clearing. She was holding a staff that looked like a stiffened snake, thick and colourful with a snarling serpent's head, which she raised above her head, and began to speak in a strange, rasping tongue that meant nothing to Billy. A little after she started, one of the men started speaking as well, in something more recognisable to English ears.

'He's speaking Spanish,' said Reynolds, sounding miserable and scared, still holding out his sword.

'You speak Spanish,' said Billy. 'What's he saying?'

Reynolds lowered his sword and squinted at the male Indian, as if trying to read his lips. The renewed purpose seemed to have weakened his fear.

'Wait!' This to the old woman and the Indian man, who stopped talking for a moment and allowed Reynolds to catch up. Something about their calm patience, their wish to make themselves well understood, was professional and crisp. They looked like diligent (if near-dead) factors on an errand onshore to conduct a dockside transaction.

'He was speaking too fast, but I think he said something like "our people are dead". Over and over.' Reynolds indicated with his hand that the old woman should continue, and she did, the voice of the young man sounding the Spanish words behind her, slightly out of time. Reynolds tried to keep up.

'Yes, our people are dead, that's what they're saying, over and over, like a song. Oh, wait, now it's changed – something about boats carrying things that kill, no, carrying *death*, I think she means, or killers, or people who bring death, something like that. He says, I mean *she* says, their time has reached a finish or an end, and now they are leaving, but it's a strange word, more like that story from Egypt. *Exodus*, that's it. But the boats brought a great evil, a great wrong, and now they will place a curse on the ones who came here, they will allow one to escape, while one must stay and carry their curse back over the sea, to the place where the boats came from and to which they must one day return.'

Reynolds blinks, as if only just realising what he is saying.

'This sounds bad, mate, doesn't it? What do they mean?'

The old woman held up her arms, and the young man who was translating looked down at the ground, as if to shield his eyes. She raised her eyes to the sky, and Billy thought he could hear something, something like the hum of a congregation inside a chapel. He looked around him. Were there more people in the trees? The woman started to speak again.

'I can't hear him very well, what's that noise? Jesus, are there more of them? He's saying something about a power, a great power, she's calling to the great power to come down. She's talking about – what? – she's talking about a "half-lit place", about living in a half-lit place where nobody enters and nobody leaves, and she's asking the power, she's asking it to choose, to choose between ... Oh Christ, she's asking it to choose between us, to take one of us and to leave one of us in that place, to send the cursed one back with the evil that came with the ships ...'

Reynolds's voice changed then. It stopped stuttering and stammering and for a moment the embittered, self-pitying David Reynolds, man of Lancashire and son of a farmer, stood up straight and spoke with the authority of a Lutheran priest.

'Our people are dead.'

'Our people are dead.'

'Your ships have brought death to us.'

'Death is the ending we have all been taken to.'

'Our people are coming together again in the houses of the gods.'

'For the death you have brought us you must stay in this half-lit place.'

'Our people are dead.'

'Our people are dead.'

Reynolds's head whipped back at that last repeated dirge, a gurgle came from his throat and he fell to the ground. The humming from the trees stopped, like a blown-out candle. The three young Indians moved back into the trees, leaving the old woman staring at Billy. She said something in her local tongue, and her cold professional eyes softened momentarily with something like sympathy. And then Billy ran.

The trees were humming again and within them Billy could

see brown bodies running alongside him, running and humming. It was all around him, above, below, even within him, ringing off the bones in his chest. He ran with his hands over his ears, the vicious green growth slapping him in the face and eyes, but he didn't care and barely noticed. The humming turned into a whoosh, and it sounded like water sluicing into the air. Like water from a great fountain.

Within the humming, he could hear the chattering and screeching of those who were running alongside him, seemingly accompanying him rather than chasing. His own breath was huge in his chest. Blind panic thrummed through him and he had no idea, none whatsoever, of the direction he was heading in.

Something shot through the air from his left, and then to his right an arrow appeared in the trunk of a tree, its shaft and feathers vibrating, the *thunk* of its contact seemingly unrelated to its arrival. Then another arrow thrust through the air into another trunk, and then a third arrow hit him in his left-hand side, his chest exposed by his madly reaching arms which were up in front of him to try and claw away the undergrowth.

He felt the arrowhead grind into his chest, between his ribs and then, impossibly and impertinently, it entered his heart. Something else too; a sense of a dark cloud enveloping within him, shooting through his blood and climbing up into his brain, and he thought of the Arawak poison he'd learned about in Santa Fe. And then, as the humming seemed to stop and an Indian's laughter rang out like a parakeet in the trees, Billy died.

*

When I woke up, from a dream of women and riches where the only sound was of a constant humming, the arrow was still in my side. I could still hear things in the trees: voices chattering in unknown languages, a scream, a cackle of laughter, the screech of a bird. But eventually all the noises stopped, and all that was left was the sound of the sea somewhere nearby. Even that awful sound of rushing water had stopped, as if somebody had turned off a mighty tap.

There was pain, enormous pain. My heart felt like it had been torn into pieces, and the Indian poison had done something to my sinews and muscles such that they all felt as if they'd been stretched to a breaking point. I reached down and pulled the arrow out of my side, and after an explosion of an even greater pain I felt relief. It was passing extraordinary, to feel my heart restart itself as the arrow came out.

I did not question what had happened. I was alive, it seemed, despite everything. I thought briefly of the fountain of youth, and that sound of water. I got myself to my feet, and started walking towards the sound of the sea. Before very much longer I got to the beach.

I waited an hour or two, sitting in the sand and considering my fate, and then I went back into the trees, and found the clearing again. I did not feel brave or afraid going back in there; merely a flat sense of obligation. I dragged Reynolds back to the beach, which was surprisingly close to the clearing – we must have wandered in an almost complete circle. The feet of my dead shipmate re-established the marks which had been left by the dead Spaniard and whoever had dragged him here, however long ago. There wasn't a mark on him.

I didn't eat or drink that day, and I didn't sleep that night either. I just sat, my hands moving in and out, in and out of the sand, my thoughts on Kate and England and not, definitively not, on the words of the old Indian woman and what they might or might not mean, nor on the obvious fact of my survival. There was no moon, only starlight, and at some point in the night there were more noises from the trees, and what sounded like a scream.

On the second day, in the middle of the morning, I began to notice that I did not feel thirsty or hungry any more, though the pain in my side was as great as ever. My heart felt like there had been a hole punched into it. I fixed my eyes on the horizon and thought of Kate, but somehow her face had faded and that strong pull, which had felt like a rope around the world dragging me back to Stanton St John and her, weakened (but still there nonetheless, an intense little tug on my sore, poisoned heart). And then it seemed to me that the dead Spaniard started speaking to me.

So here we are.

The voice was loud and clear and entirely in my head. It had a thick Spanish accent. I considered the possibility that it must be coming either from the dead Spaniard or from inside my own head. I had heard tell of this, of men at sea imagining voices were speaking to them, particularly men at the extremity of thirst and hunger, who had seen things they did not think to ever see. But was I at such an extremity, given I felt no thirst nor hunger? I decided to speak to the dead Spaniard.

'What has happened to me?'

Do not fear, your boat will return. Your destiny is not on this island.

'What has happened to me?'

You met the old woman? She seems to have presented you with a gift which was not offered to me.

'A gift? What is the gift?'

The gift of fulfilling your destiny.

'What is my destiny?'

Ah, who can answer this question? All I mean to say is that you must have confidence in your immediate future. You appear to be blessed, Billy. You have travelled far and many men have died around you, and yet here you are, a pearl in your pocket, a slaving share waiting for you and a woman at home who cannot sleep with worry for you. Reynolds is dead, you are alive and perhaps that humming in the forest was hungry Indians or perhaps it was the fountain of youth. It is enchanting, is it not, to think on destiny?

'Are you real? Or are you in my head?'

What is the difference?

I grew tired of listening to the Spaniard speak. I moved down the beach and put my feet into the cold water. Were mine the first English feet to be washed by these particular waves? Was my emaciated kidnapper's arse the first to feel this wet sand? My buccaneering boots were lying on the sand behind me. I was tired and hot and afraid. I was an abandoned sailor, a marooned adventurer suspended on the edge of a peninsula which these past fifty years had been called Florida.

And yet, I was alive.

Something was happening to my vision. The edge of the horizon, which had been straight when we first arrived, was now distinctly wavy. The colours around me were beginning to wash out. My eyes were aching and sun-dotted and dried-out and locked on the liquid horizon. Out there were Hawkyns and Drake, or at the very least the pinnace which had dropped me here in the first place. They should have been here yesterday, which wouldn't have saved me or poor Reynolds from the Indians. But I wouldn't have had to sit here with a dried body and a fresh one for company.

My fingers pushed wet sand around in between my legs, probing and releasing, probing and releasing. My eyes kept watch on the horizon while my brain churned through all that had happened to me in the eight months since I had arrived in Plymouth. Gulls were screeching, reminding me of the first time I heard that noise. And then the voice spoke to me again.

Billeeee.

I looked around at that, my tired dried-out neck snapping slightly as my head whipped left and right and my streamed-out vision came momentarily back into focus, the greens and the yellows of the island pouring back in.

Billeeee.

'I do not understand how you can be talking to me.'

Of course not. This does not happen.

'You mean hearing the voices of dead men in my head?'

I have things I need to tell you.

'How is Kate?'

Your wife? You still have concern for her, then?

'We only married the week before I left for this trip. Of course I have concern for her. I need to return with money. She is the reason I sailed with Hawkyns.'

She being Kate? Or she being money?

'Kate, of course. But I am stranded on the other side of the world. I didn't bring back the money I said I would and she will die alone and destitute. Because of me.'

And what of the terrible things you have done? Will you tell Kate of these?

'Terrible things? What terrible things have I done? Is it not a husband's duty to provide for his wife, to secure her future?'

In Our Lady's name, you are a naive fool. You will get off this island.

'Really?'

Really. I have told you already. Your destiny is not to die on this island. That has all changed now.

'Changed?'

Yes, changed. Did you not listen to what the Indian woman said?

BOOK 2

Morgan

Thus they order for the loss of a right arm six hundred pieces of eight, or six slaves; for the loss of a left arm five hundred pieces of eight, or five slaves; for a right leg five hundred pieces of eight, or five slaves; for the left leg four hundred pieces of eight, or four slaves; for an eye one hundred pieces of eight, or one slave; for a finger of the hand the same reward as for the eye.

John Esquemeling, *The Bucaniers of America*, 1678

19 DECEMBER 1811

Thomas Anderson, a constable of the parish of St Paul's, Shadwell, pulls on his cherished old pea coat and opens the door of his little house near the top end of New Gravel Lane, just south of its junction with the Ratcliffe Highway. The house is dirty but cosy in the way that only a house occupied by a single man can be. He steps out into the street. *His* street.

The evening is warmer than it has been for weeks, and the lane is relatively quiet after a long period of busy, clattering days when it seemed that every Londoner, rich or poor, had decided to pay this part of Shadwell a visit. There have been similar outbreaks of public interest in the bloody tragedies of the poorer districts of the metropolis, but never one like this. The funeral of the Marrs was the high tide of this clamouring attention, but it is now fading off. The newspapers remain watchful, the story now shifting in nature to a more political subject – the complete failure of the local magistrates to find the killers. The wealthy have returned to their apartments in the West End and the city. The poorer people left behind in Wapping and Shadwell have seemingly decided that, for the time being, they are safer in their beds than in the local alehouses. Which is odd, thinks Anderson in his slow solid way, when you think that the Marrs were massacred in their home, not in any tavern.

New Gravel Lane runs north to south, from the Ratcliffe Highway down to the wharves that line the river, parallel to and east of its sister thoroughfare, Old Gravel Lane. Both get their name from the gravel which for centuries has been taken down these streets to the river to be used as ballast for the empty colliers returning to the north-east, the same gravel which makes up the raised terrace on which the Highway sits, an ancient feature left behind by the Thames as it meandered north to south and cut down into the earth over the millennia. The land is higher and drier here than it is down by the river, and in some cases the ground-floor windows of the houses are at the same level as the top of the dock wall to the west.

Before Wapping proper was reclaimed, this is where the original community congregated. The higher ground could be more easily built upon and required no Dutch experts to facilitate its draining. The southern ends of the Gravel Lanes continue to form the beating heart of Wapping; despite the development of the dock they have kept their ramshackle, squeezed-in nature, and now have the character of a cut-off island. Houses, inns and shops line both sides of New Gravel Lane; at the southern end, these buildings sit in front of warrens of lodging houses and other dwellings of evil reputation. This is the place where grim-faced sailors in meagre shared dwellings nurse terrible hangovers and frightful dreams while their heads knock against their sea chests.

But here at the northern end the dock has changed things. For one thing, there is nothing behind the houses which line the street, only flat wasteland now owned by the London Dock Company. Within living memory, this open land had been meadow. The company has no doubt reserved this land for some great commercial undertaking of the future, perhaps an extension to the dock (a project already being discussed in the London Tavern, where the re-imagining of the lower Thames as an international entrepôt is a vivid dream of rich and ambitious men). At a time of intense and growing over-crowding, when the available living space has already been brutally squeezed by the grand new dock, this huge plot of empty land feels like a criminal self-indulgence on the part of the mercantile rich. A few of the most militant local souls have tried to extend their properties into this wasteland, normally at night, and within days they have found their untidy little lean-tos and huts smashed to pieces by person or persons unknown.

Anderson's own little house backs onto this wasteland, but for some days he has been carefully not looking out across that empty space. It used to be a source of endless interest, that view westwards towards the dock and the city, but in that direction also lies the Marr house, way over there behind the hulking darkness of the dock warehouses. The wasteland is now a dark vacancy between here and there, and at night Anderson's overactive imagination (often spiked with a good quantity of cheap ale from the King's Arms, just a few doors down the road) is prone to imagining the comings and the goings of all sorts of creatures with malign purpose out there on the deserted mud. A thick curtain, the only one in the house, has gone up on the upstairs rear window just in the last week.

A man living on his own does not freely admit to night terrors, least of all to himself, but the truth is that, like many of the constables of St Paul's and St George in the East, Anderson now lives his days and nights in a grim state of shallow panic. At times this suffocating anxiety could even be characterised as terror. It is perfectly clear to him that the magistrates of the Shadwell office, despite their grandiloquent airs and ostentatious public hearings, are stumbling about in a procedural gloom. Constables like Anderson have little if any understanding of 'procedure', if such a thing can be said to exist within London's fumbling attempts at institutional law and order. But they can smell incompetence and prevarication as keenly as the salt on the riverside wind.

Everyone in Shadwell and Wapping knows this one thing: that somewhere out there, in the wasteland or in the street or nestled in the enclosing warrens of the lodging houses, there dwells a monster (or even monsters) with sufficiently depraved appetites to eviscerate an entire family, including a baby. The central fact of the baby's death has taken on a flavour of doctrinal law in the past week. The saloon bar magistrates and justices are convinced that none of the drunks and fools and thieves who have been arrested since the murders (most of them, it is often noted, Irish) bear the supernatural countenance of a baby-killer, so *ipso facto* the monster is still at large, just waiting for more chances to carry away the souls of more sleeping infants.

Several constables attended the coroner's inquest, and brought back lurid tales of exposed bones and lumpy brain matter clinging to freshly plastered walls. The coroner's dispassionate anatomical descriptions have been embellished by the street's own demotic imagination, and these macabre pictures have soaked their way into the minds of many of the residents, including Anderson. This is a community which has already grown spiritually fat on strange stories from faraway lands. For Anderson, as for the other constables, the murders of the Marrs have become a new local mythology, all the more powerful for being vividly real.

Many of the constables, already well soaked in gin and beer, have been drinking more and more in the face of this spreading malaise. The watchmen, one step down on the official ladder from the constables, have their own stocks of cheap liquor in their little roadside sheds, from which they creep every half-hour during the night to yell the all's-well. Anderson is by no means the worst drinker among the constables and watchmen, because he is by no means the least educated, and he at least has his own house, the result of a fortunate marriage which is now a dim distant memory. But even for Anderson there is an edge which needs wearing down, and liquor provides the best sandpaper of all.

So, it is time for a drink, and there is nothing in the house which will serve. Anderson steps out into the street and walks the two doors down to the King's Arms, nodding at John Lee, the landlord of the tavern opposite, the Black Horse. Lee nods back and then resumes his anxious pacing, his eyes constantly returning to the north end of the street, waiting for someone to appear. Anderson pauses to consider asking him what the matter is, but the call of ale is too strong. He carries on down the street and turns to go through the door of the King's Arms.

It's eleven o'clock at night. The Arms is one of the area's most popular taverns, and normally at this time the place would be almost full, but it is empty, the quiet atmosphere in keeping with the watchful peace of the street outside. Mrs Williamson, the publican's wife, is standing behind the tavern's recently installed wooden bar, on which gleams a single new pump, evidence of the investment the Williamsons have made in the place. Beneath the bar, Anderson knows (because Williamson has talked of little else for months now), lie the workings of a new beer engine, allowing the pumping of ale up from barrels in the cellar direct to the taproom. No other tavern or alehouse in Shadwell or Wapping can boast this new technology, although many are stretching what resources they have to follow the King's Arms' lead.

Mrs Williamson greets Anderson with an open smile, unaffected by the sombre air outside.

'Evenin' to yer, Tom Anderson. I'm takin' it it's still pretty quiet out there?'

'It is, Liz, it is. Your trade will 'ave been slow today, I'd be thinkin'.'

'Slower than the Regent gettin' into last year's breeches, Tom.' She laughs at her little joke, and Tom chuckles willingly. Always willing to smile at a *bon mot* from the attractive landlord's wife, is Tom Anderson. 'John's in the kitchen, if ye'd like to go through.'

'Much obliged if you'd pour me a pint, Liz. I'm blessed parched.'

'Think you mean *pull* a pint, Tom. Don't forget John's new toy.'

They laugh, and she pulls out a rough glass tankard from beneath the bar.

'Go on through, Tom. He's been wantin' to talk to you. I'll give a shout when your beer's ready.'

She starts pulling the pump handle towards her and after three or four pulls beer starts sloshing into the glass. Her arms are bare beneath the simple cotton dress she is wearing, and the broad muscles tense as she pulls on the handle. Fine-looking woman, is Liz Williamson. And a good wife. It's been a dozen years since Anderson touched a woman, and for a wistful moment he ponders on what it would be like to lean towards her, stroke that magnificent upper arm, feel it solid yet soft beneath his lonely, peeling fingertips.

He steps into the kitchen, which doubles as the tavern's parlour, and here's John Williamson, rising from his old brown armchair to grab Anderson's arm and hand and speak at him in the confident, bruising way of a London publican. He's a bear of a man, all bristles and bluster, twice the size of Tom Anderson.

'Tom! Just the man!'

'Liz said yer wanted to speak to me.'

'She pullin' you a pint?'

'She's at it right now.'

'Well, listen. You're an officer, and there's something I think you should know. There's been a bloke 'angin' round, big tall fella, wearin' a brown coat.'

Anderson doesn't react to this. For the last week he's had a dozen of these conversations each and every day. People are watchful, but more than that people want to be part of the drama that has unfolded since the killings of the Marrs. If he'd followed up even a tenth of the things people had told him about, he'd never have slept or eaten. Or had a drink, come to that.

'Brown coat, you say?'

'Yes, like a sailor's jacket. You know, pea coat, bit like yours. He was listenin' at our door.'

Williamson speaks with some urgency, watching Anderson closely as he does so.

'Listenin' at your door? When was this?'

'This mornin'. About nine.' Williamson pauses, still looking intently at his friend. 'Yes, about nine, I'd say. We weren't open yet. I came out the side door and found him 'angin' about, as if he'd just 'ad 'is ear up against the door. Loiterin', if you take my meanin'. I said somethin' or other, and he just stood and glared at me. Then 'e walked off.'

'He didn't speak to you?'

Williamson looks down at this, breaking his gaze. He shuffles back around his chair, keeping his eyes away from Anderson. His manner strikes the constable as suddenly, unfathomably, odd. There is something creeping and guilty about it. This big bristling man is taciturn most of the time, but is gregarious when his position demands. Tonight, he seems edgy and nervous.

'P'raps it was one of Bridget's friends?' Anderson asks. Bridget is the servant in the tavern, a fearsome battleaxe from the West Country who has been known to flatten drunken miscreants on a Saturday night with a swipe of a swinging pewter jug. Even as he says it, Anderson thinks the idea preposterous. Could old Bridget even have any friends?

Williamson looks up from his musing, as if the idea strikes him in the same way. He still seems distracted.

'No, no, Tom. I know all Bridget's friends. This was a stranger, no question about it.' The emphasis is very marked, and Williamson slashes the air with his hands to underline the single word: stranger. 'Tall fella, young man, bad limp. Almost lame, I reckon. Black hair. Didn't say anything, just made off down towards Wapping. I'd have made after him, but Bridget called me back to the kitchen about something or other. When I came out again he'd gone.'

The words tumble out onto one another, deliberately yet messily, as if they've been half-rehearsed. *Tall fella, young man, bad limp, almost lame, black hair.*

Liz shouts from the bar that Anderson's pint is ready.

'Right, that's me. Now don't fret, John, I'll 'ave a look into your lame pea-coat bloke.'

'Right you are, Tom. 'Ave a quiet night.' Williamson shakes his hand, still looking tense.

'You too, John.'

Williamson sits back down in his old leather armchair, picking up a pipe and staring at the rear door to the house, as if on watch. Tom watches him for a moment, wondering why this big, gruff man is apparently so nervous, but the call of the ale (and the woman who has been pouring it for him) is too strong, and he leaves the kitchen.

He goes back to the bar to pick up his beer, and is disappointed to find that Liz isn't there any more. He shouts his thanks, and hears her cheery reply from somewhere inside the building. He sips the beer to make it easier to carry and leaves with his tankard, thinking about her strong attractive arms and the way her simple dress exposed the tops of her breasts.

Outside in the street John Lee is greeting his wife and daughter. Anderson nods again at him, and notes the man's relief. The two women are dressed for a night out. Lee's earlier nervousness is explained: they'd been perhaps a few minutes late, and he'd scurried into the street to watch for them, imagining any number of horrors that might have happened to them on their way home.

The girl, Alice, waves excitedly at Anderson and starts singing a song, which he vaguely recognises as being from the new show at the Royalty Theatre on Wellclose Square. The mother joins in, and Anderson smiles with honest pleasure as he carefully carries his pint jug into his house. The voices of the two women have added a lightness to the street which has been missing for a long time.

He has a small fire going in the front room of his house, and he sits in the only chair in the room to enjoy his drink. He sips at the ale, which is as cold as the night air, or rather as cold as John Williamson's unheated cellar, which is almost the same thing. He lights a taper in the fire, and uses it to light the pipe which he'd made ready before walking to the King's Arms, and puffs away contentedly.

He's been working all day, and will be back working as a shipwright in one of the yards on the south bank of the river tomorrow. His unpaid post of constable is something he is proud of, unlike most of those men who are offered it (many of them willingly pay the customary ten pounds to get themselves out of the obligation). He takes his duties seriously, from setting the nightly watch (which means handing pocket money to old men like Olney up on the Highway, who simply drink the pocket change away, even while on duty) to arresting prisoners and presenting them before magistrates. Anderson is unusual, though: a property-owner with no wife and a steady, skilled job. He can afford some time to be a diligent constable.

On his floor lie several handbills, the detritus of a headless investigation: the initial handbill produced by the parishioners of St George in the East (*Fifty Pounds Reward. Horrid Murder!!*); the handbill published by John Harriott, the great river magistrate himself, offering twenty pounds for information about men seen outside Marr's shop (for a moment, something resonates inside Anderson's mind, something about men loitering outside); and finally the Home Secretary's own, unprecedented, handbill, which took almost a week to appear and offers the unbelievable sum of £100 for information leading to an arrest. One hundred and seventy pounds' worth of reward in total. Someone is going to get rich on this sickening business, that is clear. He has heard tell that the Home Secretary's reward has been raised even further.

He considers the handbills as he puffs his pipe. For him, only Harriott's is worth the candle, entirely because of the man who offers it. All the constables and watchmen of Wapping, St George's and St Paul's know of Harriott: the one-man whirlwind behind the River Police, the man who had stood down the lightermen rioters in 1798, the man who had reclaimed an island from an Essex river only to see it overcome years later by the rising waters. There were rumours of shamen in North America, of concubines in the Indies, even of buried treasure and an abandoned woman in Canada. But these picaresque tales hide a deeper truth: the magistrates of Shadwell,

Anderson's official district, are pale shadows of the imperial Harriott, the quintessence of English drive and energy. If anyone will solve this case, it will be Harriott. Anderson has no truck with those who talk of jurisdiction, who point out that Harriott's remit does not extend inland to events on the Highway. Such matters are for bureaucrats and pettifoggers.

He finishes his ale, and then his pipe. The fire is still burning strongly. He looks at the clock, and decides there is probably still time for another beer. He is wide awake, and will not sleep for some time. And perhaps another glimpse of Liz Williamson and her magnificent décolletage will put pictures in his head to take into his dreams. He puts down his pipe, stands and heads for the door.

As he opens the door, the pint pot is knocked from his hand by someone rushing past. A sudden crowd of people is streaming past, collectively screeching and squawking as it approaches the sound of a man shouting, down the street to Anderson's left. Anderson catches a glimpse of one of his watchmen, Shadrick Newhall, who has been pushed by the surging crowd down towards the King's Arms. Newhall is gaping at something high up, on the building, and Anderson looks in the same direction.

A near-naked man is swinging there, right next to the sign for the King's Arms, frantically scrabbling down a rope made of knotted sheets, his bare feet seeking purchase on the walls, his arse hanging out of the back of his tattered nightshirt. He is shouting as he spins in the air:

'Help! Help! Help! Murder! Help! Fucking hell, murder! Fucking help me!'

He is beginning to lose his grip on the sheets, and his voice is hoarse but clear over the shrieks of the crowd.

'Catch me! Fucking catch me! Fucking catch me!'

His hands lose their grip, and he falls, landing on top of

Shadrick Newhall, his arse almost in the watchman's face. The two tumble to the ground, the knotted sheet landing on top of their heads. Newhall groans slightly as Anderson shoves his way through the crowd towards him, and the man in the night-shirt gets up. It is John Turner, lodger at the King's Arms, a man Anderson has supped with half-a-dozen times. Turner grabs Anderson's arm, recognising him as what passes for authority in this shouting mob. He is breathless, his eyes wide, his skin white in the winter night.

'They're killing them . . . inside. They're killing them all!'

Some people are already beginning to batter on the street door of Williamson's inn, which looks ominously dark and locked. Anderson, clear-headed, gestures to three men to help him force open the cellar hatch in the pavement in front of the tavern. John Lee, the landlord from the Black Horse, is one of them. Another is a local butcher, Edward Crestle. The third man Anderson doesn't recognise, but he notices the man has a poker, as if he's rushed out into the street with the first weapon he could lay his hands on at the sound of Turner's screams.

They heave at the cellar door, and with a cracking sound it opens up. Anderson steps down into the gloom, but by the light from the street he can already make out the shape of a body lying on the floor of the cellar. It is Williamson. Anderson hurries to his side and kneels down to his friend, bending in closely to try to see him in the gloom, and then someone at the top of the cellar ladder lights a gaslight and he sees that the man's throat has been severed through to the bone, that his head has been smashed in, that one thumb is hanging off a hand by a piece of skin. An iron bar, coated in hair and matter, lies next to the body. Twenty minutes ago, he was talking to this inanimate bundle of dead flesh. Twenty minutes.

After some moments of contemplation, Anderson stands, his chest heaving, his stomach determined to vest itself of the ale he so recently took from this tavern. The butcher, Crestle, has followed him down into the cellar but now stands stock still, whimpering. The man with the poker is frozen on his way down the ladder, looking down onto Williamson's body as it lies illuminated by the glow from the street. John Lee, also already in the cellar, has been sick against one of the empty barrels Williamson keeps – kept – down here. Anderson steps over the publican's dead body, taking care not to slide in the pooling blood, and climbs the stairs up to the kitchen. He sees the shape of Williamson's old brown leather armchair heaving into view as his ascends.

There are still lights burning in the kitchen and he finds Liz straight away. Another crushed skull. Another throat sliced down to the gleaming bone. She lies against the stove, half-sitting, and he clearly sees a series of perfect parallel lacerations in her perfect upper arms, deliberate and artisan in their application. Her dress has fallen away from one breast, and swearing and half-whimpering under his breath, he pulls the dress back over her shoulder to cover her up, feeling Williamson's ale rising up his throat once again. He steps backwards into the bar and sees old Bridget on the floor in there, her skull smashed again and her throat, again, torn apart by a blade.

Anderson hears a sound at the door at the back of the saloon, which leads to a staircase up to the first-floor apartments. He glares at the door fiercely and starts towards it. The door begins to open, and as he is preparing to launch himself at it a girl of about twelve peeps sleepily into the saloon. Kitty Stillwell, Williamson's granddaughter. Anderson doesn't stop moving, but instead of raising his fists he opens his arms to embrace the girl, whose eyes widen and shimmer as she sees the body of Bridget.

'Bridget? Bridget! Where's my gran'pa! Nan? Nan!'

MARCH 1603

The shadows were falling. They fell both on the little house in Stanton St John and on the great palace of Richmond, 40 miles downstream. As Archbishop Whitgift and the great counsellor Robert Cecil fussed around the bed of the ancient Queen, swapping interpretations of signs and sending letters north to Scotland, upstream in the quiet village a slow parade of men and women went in and out of the silent house. The women were weeping, the men grim-faced. Some children came as well, and halted their chatter and games at the threshold of the house, quietened by its calm dignity and the mourning of the adults.

All these people stepped directly into the front room of the house, and there on an oak table was a coffin containing the body of a woman. Her eyes were closed, her long grey hair fell onto the silk cushion at her head, her long and slender fingers (still so young!) were crossed on her chest. Even as plans were being made to sail the dead Queen's body down from Richmond to Whitehall, Oxfordshire women touched their fingers to their lips and then to the forehead of the dead woman in Stanton St John. These women still held memories of the time spent by the young Queen in their own village decades before, when this dead woman was in the flush of youth, newly married and with her own hopes for the future.

Some of the women whispered of that marriage, even now, years and years after Kate Ablass was abandoned by that strange, beautiful giant who had adventured on the high seas all those decades before. He had come back rich, had young Billy. He had built this house, bought pigs, and had made something of himself. For some years, the village's respect for the hardworking son of the Polish sailor had waxed along with his fortune. He kept his looks, said the women. He remained the beautiful young adventurer even as the other villagers aged, their bodies and their faces racing towards the inescapable decrepitude that was forged by their hard lives.

No one could tell when and how the happy domestic picture of the Ablasses had changed. But there came a time when the handsome young pig-farmer was no longer the pride of the village. Maybe this decline was triggered by the legendary fight outside the village's alehouse, when Billy had nearly killed his fellow pig-farmer and friend Nathan Whitwell in an argument over land access. Those who were there (and a great many claimed to have been there) said Billy had pulled a knife on Nathan, and had to be restrained by a dozen men from slicing the other man's head from his shoulders. 'He was strong as a bull,' said old George White, cousin of the tenant-farmer John White of Manor Farm and thus a relative of the beautiful woman in the little house, sitting by the fire some ten years later, recounting the story as he had dozens of times before, the vowels stretching in his mouth. 'We could barely 'old him. And he 'issed at old Nathan, he did, like an angry snake. And there was a terrible sound in the air, like bees humming, it was. I'll never forget it. Nathan made himself scarce after that, sold up and headed over to Forest Hill, and I reckon that wasn't far enough for him, neither.'

Or perhaps the villagers remembered the time that Kate, now almost forty and childless, had emerged from the little house one morning with a vivid, creeping bruise across her eye, the colour of a crow. She didn't hide it, but nor would she talk about it. The women looked, the women talked, and the women drew their own conclusions. A black eye on a woman was by no means an uncommon sight in the village. The men barely noticed it, and those that did probably approved. But Kate's face had always been as unblemished as her character, and whatever people had started to whisper about Billy Ablass (and the whispers had become dark things themselves by then, full of witchcraft and magic), the one thing they acknowledged was his devotion to his wife. And now, that wife had a black eye.

Then, suddenly, Billy Ablass was gone. Kate acknowledged his departure but discussed it with no one, not even her close friends Mildred Weathers and Jane Robinson. But if the villagers believed Billy's departure would be a relief to Kate after the changes in him in the preceding months, they were quite wrong. She entered a period of mourning just as she would have done if he'd died. She adopted black clothes and walked through the village with her head down out of respect for the departed. She talked about him in the past tense, and embellished his now-complicated legend with tales of the past as if enjoying the memory of a cherished but deceased relative. No one questioned her behaviour, though privately, inside their own houses, the villagers wondered why there had been no funeral for Billy Ablass. Those whisperings continued.

They were comfortable years for Kate Ablass, after Billy left. She became a cherished matriarch to the village, advising young women approaching marriage, teaching them how to run a household for a working husband, looking after children whenever she was asked, attending church devotedly even as the new traditions of the Church of England pushed their roots down into the people's souls. She had money and she still had pigs, and she paid for one of the local men to husband her livestock, and lived comfortably enough on the proceeds. She was not free with her money (her husband had taught her that) but she was not miserly either. When the illness came and took her, it did so mercifully quickly, and she died at peace and alone in her sleep. She took God into her heart, said the villagers, and he had taken her to his.

So they came and paid their final respects to this beautiful grey old lady, every single family for two miles around making their way to the little house. They kissed her brow with their fingers, looked a final time around the inside of the house, so well known to most of them, and walked out into the dark with that steady sense of good-fellowship which comes from the acknowledgement of a life well lived.

Eventually, the last of them left – the family of Nathan Whitwell himself, who had travelled the four miles from Forest Hill. There were tears in Nathan's eyes when he came out of the house, though for what he did not or could not say.

Silence descended on the little house, and Stanton St John slept. In the churchyard near the house, the two dozen or so headstones stood guard on the now proudly Anglican building. The moon had come out, its light the only thing keeping out the complete blackness up here in the hills outside Oxford. Two white owls circled the ground of the meadow up the lane from the church, and paid no heed to the tall, black figure who emerged down the lane. It paused outside the church and looked up at its squat little tower, a silhouette in the moonlight. Then it tramped on. It stopped outside the house of Kate Ablass.

It stood for a while, its head moving up and down, left and right as it took in the front of the little house. After several minutes, the figure stepped through the unlocked door and went inside.

A mouse scurried away into a corner as it heard the presence come in, and hid in a hole in the still-fresh brickwork. The figure ran one hand along the wall of the front room as it walked. Although the house was dark, it navigated its way to the coffin without difficulty, seemingly aware of where the furniture was without any light to guide it. It approached the coffin.

From within its long coat, it took a tiny sphere and held it up to the moonlight, which shimmered across the object's milky surface and, for one magical moment, seemed to light up the room. A pearl. With infinite care, the figure put one hand beneath Kate's head, lifted it up, and placed the pearl beneath the coffin's pillow. It placed her head back down on the pillow, and then it placed its hands on the coffin's lip and leaned against it, its head down and gazing. The shoulders began to gently spasm and then the tall legs seemed to give way, the figure now kneeling on the floor with its hands still grasping the edge of the coffin, its forehead pressed down on the wooden rim. It was sobbing in great oceanic heaves, and for some time it hung there, as if it were gripping on to a great chunk of driftwood on a dark, cold, lonely sea.

20 DECEMBER 1811

The Chief Magistrate of the Thames River Police Office presents his compliments to the Magistrates of Shadwell and requests their Attendance at a Meeting to be held at the River Police Office this day at 2 o'clock – to consult together on the most effectual Measures for discovering the atrocious Murderers that infest the Neighbourhoods of their respective Offices, which from the murder of three people in a house in New Gravel Lane last night, gives an appearance of a Gang acting upon a System.

The Thames River Police Office rises almost primly between the warehouses which line the Wapping riverfront. It has the appearance of a well-established gentleman standing self-consciously amongst traders and rogues, having found itself in the wrong part of town after a night at its club. The office is built in the same style as the new villa of a city banker. It does not look like a fortress of law and order for the maintenance of trade and commerce on the river.

A decade before, soon after its opening, this office had been the scene of a terrible riot. Its founder and magistrate John Harriott had already been working for three years to bring some order to business matters on the river, and this had gradually throttled the life out of a centuries-old riverside culture of lawlessness which had involved hundreds of petty thieves and rascals. The riot was the last desperate attempt by these men who'd inherited this way of life to regain their blessed pre-office freedoms. A tattered flurry of Irishmen, Portuguese and Englishmen had flowed down Wapping Street, determined to preserve their God-given rights to extort money from the river's trade.

John Harriott had faced them down, his Essex whiskers quivering with outrage. These were men who under other circumstances he might have been proud to command, but they were now committing the cardinal rule (in Harriott's eyes) of misrepresenting their class. He believed that working men should know their place; if they worked hard and remained loyal and steadfast, they would receive their reward, both here and in Heaven.

As a proud Englishman he saw only Irish coal heavers and Portuguese seamen within the mob (the truth being, of course, that the bulk of them were Englishmen and, what was more, Londoners). In the drama of Harriott's long and extraordinary life this was simply another occasion when, as an unshaken officer of the nation of Great Britain, he'd had to stare down uncivilised savages as they sought to assert their privileges over those of the established order. Be they Sepoys, Indians or even the damned French, he'd always stood his ground and this time he did so again, losing one of his watermen-constables in the process and gaining something which was worth rather more: the steady preservation of the arteries of trade which pumped the world's commodities into London's heart, day after day after day.

Today there is a smaller mob gathering outside the windows of the Police Office. Magistrate Harriott's eyes are directed elsewhere, so it is left to Waterman-Constable Charles Horton to keep a close watch on the growing crowd outside.

Somehow the word has got out that there is a meeting taking place at the office on the subject of the recent murders. As is the way of these things, a few have decided that their presence at the office is required by the emerging situation. These few have been followed by dozens more, and now a single body of angry and frightened men and women (and not a few children, Horton notes) has formed itself in Wapping Street, unanimously demanding that *something be done*.

The fresh murders at the King's Arms – their violence, and their echo of the terrible events at 29 Ratcliffe Highway – have reignited and multiplied the panic. Wapping's residents had become used to the idea of the Ratcliffe Highway killings. The murders had begun to acquire the flavour of local myth, as common in the telling as the great fire of 1794 or the riot of 1798. But the new murders at the King's Arms, as fresh in the imagination as a vivid fireside tale, have brought those first killings back into sharp relief, and the slaughter is no longer a unique moment of horror, depraved but singular. Now people do believe that something evil is stalking the nether regions of the dock, and that they might be the next to feel the cold swipe of steel through their neck.

The cocktail of dread and anger has been fed by the gentlemen of the press, and now the stomachs of the people are chock-full of rumour as well as fear. In one thing, though, the mob is at least coherent. It has chosen to gather outside the office of John Harriott, and not at the Shadwell Police Office. Those people outside have seen the progress of Shadwell's investigation, and have voted with their feet. It is Harriott to whom they are protesting, for they believe it is Harriott who will resolve these awful events.

Watching the crowd from the upper-floor window, Constable Horton finds himself remembering other events in other places. He recalls the crowd on the shore at Sheerness, desperate for a view of the destruction of the mutineers on the Nore. He sees Richard Parker leaping into the air, the rope around his neck, the gasps of the people watching seeming to lift him for a moment before the rope stiffens and that awful snap echoes over the still waters. He feels, once again, the terrible weight of his own guilt, the memory of how he purchased his freedom and a second chance. Are any of his fellow mutineers out there right now in the crowd? Would any of them recognise their old shipmate? Would they know of the names he'd given to the investigating authorities?

For a moment, Horton's reflection in the window is a mask of despair. Deliberately recomposing his expression into a more customary one of watchfulness, he turns away from the window.

If the rage of the people is growing in the street, inside the room anger of a more specifically restless kind is building up pressure. John Harriott's temper has been steadily simmering as, one by one, his colleagues from the Shadwell office have justified their actions: Mr Capper has asserted the unblemished reputation of the Shadwell office; Mr Markland has bemoaned the lack of support and resources from other offices and from the Home Office; and Mr Story has once again invoked the Bible and the End of Days as the explanation for the recent slaughters.

Harriott had summoned the Shadwell office magistrates that morning, after Constable Horton had taken the news of the Williamson murders to Harriott's home at Pier Head; Horton himself had been woken in Lower Gun Alley by another of his dirty-faced little boys, who'd rattled on his door using a pre-arranged signal.

John Harriott had at first seemed emptied by the news, like one of the hot-air balloons which had been all the rage two decades before, but soon his natural energy and impatience reasserted themselves and he set about organising this conference. It seemed to him that the second killings changed everything.

Despite themselves, the Shadwell magistrates have appeared as requested, perhaps in an attempt to extend the circle of their non-achievement, to shift the pointing finger of Whitehall blame from them to another office. How else to explain the way they are behaving? Two of the magistrates are busy covering their backs. Story is sliding into a state of personal transcendence.

'We have been diligent in our undertakings, sir, diligent I say,' asserts the spiky, terrified-looking Robert Capper. 'We have interrogated countless ne'er-do-wells and vagrants, pursued untold lines of inquiry, I have barely seen my poor wife and children this past week. Your assumption that we have been found wanting in application is most disconcerting and ill-conceived.' The little Hertfordshire man twitters in a high-pitched voice, his hands in his lap and his pinched, pale white face spotted by two dots of red in his cheeks.

'Sir, no one is asserting an absence of application,' says Harriott, his rage under control but, to Horton at least, as apparent as the presence of a cold wind before a storm. 'There has been a great amount of application. But thus far there has been an unaccountable lack of any progress. Those who have been interviewed can, in my view, almost certainly now be discounted, for what kind of impudent devil would be questioned and then go on to commit more murders? And as for motive . . .'

'Motive?' exclaims Story, his ancient jowls quivering. 'The Devil needs no motive, Harriott. These are the works of the Devil, I say, the undertakings of fierce demons with only one thought – our extermination and our eternal damnation.'

'That is two thoughts, sir,' says Harriott, and Constable Horton, despite himself, smiles. Story looks confused for a moment, as if his demons were dancing in the air behind Harriott's head.

'My dear Harriott, your own efforts in this case are to be applauded,' says the third Shadwell magistrate, Markland, the dandified Yorkshireman whose deep mellifluous tones are suggestive of the vaguely dissolute landowner he once was. 'Yet you cannot deny the simple fact that we are fighting this outbreak of violence like a man whose limbs are unaware of each other. We are all over the place, a whirlwind of frantic action. But we do not have the requisite tools for the job. We cannot watch every lodging house, every tavern, every . . .' He looks at Story somewhat squeamishly. '. . . every house of ill-repute.'

John Harriott does now begin to lose his temper.

'There are, no doubt, any number of excuses as to why our progress has been so poor,' he says. 'You lay these reasons out articulately, and they have been well rehearsed. Too well rehearsed for my liking, sir. Too well rehearsed indeed. We have clues. We have a direction. Why have we not followed it?'

'Which direction are you referring to?' asks Markland, in a tone of voice that suggests Harriott has just cast some dark aspersion on his wife.

'The maul, dammit, man, the maul! The demonstrated instrument of at least two of the Marr murders, and we have had the initials of its owner, JP, since the very start of this case. The very start! I have had my man Horton here seeking out this JP in Wapping, but he has had no assistance from your office!'

'Well, sir,' says Markland, smiling now. 'Well, sir, your office does have the distinct advantage of being operated by those with particular interests in the operations of other districts.'

'Meaning what, exactly, Markland?'

'Meaning just that, Harriott. You have taken it upon yourself to pursue this case with zeal, energy and passion. Your willingness to involve yourself in the affairs of other offices, while your own is neglected, is to be applauded for its public-spiritedness.'

'Neglected? How neglected, sir?'

'The windows of this office face out to the river, Harriott. They do not face inwards. Your realm is the water and the shipping upon it. While you busy yourself with events which have taken place outside your realm, I hear tell that the number of larcenous events out on the water have begun to rise.'

'A fact no doubt unrelated to the general air of anarchy which has been building in this area while you gentlemen sit upon your hands and wait for a solution to present itself.'

'An elegant suggestion, Harriott, but also a self-serving one. Why on earth are you so fearsomely exercised by the lack of progress in an investigation in which you have no official standing?'

'Because, Markland, any right-thinking gentleman should be exercised by it. Not once before have we seen murders like these. Not once, I say! They are unique in their barbarity, their random nature and the sudden way they have fallen upon us. They will be written about and pored over by future generations, and our actions here, today, will be subject to the verdict of history.'

At this, Markland smiles to himself.

'Well, sir, we have read your memoirs and are aware of your position in history. It is a fine thing to wish to preserve.'

Constable Horton wants to step in at this point, because

John Harriott's face has gone a dangerous shade of purple. Horton is becoming concerned that the old magistrate will do himself mental and physical harm. The old man's face expresses frustration as well as anger, and he is reaching for something to grasp on to; Markland's throat would serve pretty well. He catches Horton's watchful eye, and seems to deflate, as if in the face of an unanswerable assertion. Still looking at his constable, he begins to speak again. He seems smaller, suddenly.

'Mr Markland. Mr Capper. Mr Story. My apologies. I have grown hot with you here, and that does nothing to help this case. I admit to a sense of personal frustration and weakness. You mention my memoirs, Markland, somewhat cruelly. I would say this, simply. My memoirs speak of a man who has been accustomed to solving problems through the undertaking of something, through some action. And yet every action we take in this case seems to drag us further into a fog of misunderstanding. We have arrested a great many people, gentlemen, both here and throughout London. We have suspected Portuguese sailors, Irish soldiers and Scottish shopkeepers. We have detected spies, smelled out murderers and seen monsters out of the corners of our eyes. We have, in short, been flailing, gentlemen. Myself as much as any of us. And I begin to perceive that a different kind of activity is required by this. An activity more careful and considered than we have perhaps been used to. We are not in the business of simply knocking together the heads of Irish coal heavers here, gentlemen. I believe we are in the business of something else, something we might call detection. It is a species of police work to which my constable Horton here has given much thought.'

For the first time, the eyes of the Shadwell magistrates look at Horton. He looks back, calmly, despite his customary discomfort with any form of attention.

'Horton?' says Harriott, cooler but still diminished, as if he were handing on a mace to a successor. 'Perhaps you would share your thoughts on the matter with the gentlemen here?'

'Sir.' Horton steps towards the desk behind which the old magistrate has now sat down, and looks at the three magistrates seated before him. 'Gentlemen, our resources are limited to a half-dozen police officers and perhaps two dozen constables. At present, these resources are undertaking to speak to local people, and to act on what they find. This has led us into confusion, gentlemen.'

'Confusion?' says Markland, the only one of the three who seems to be listening carefully. Capper continues to look terrified, Story somehow bored, as if waiting for the conversation to take on a more divine quality.

'Confusion, sir. By relying on the testimony of individuals, we have exposed ourselves to the prejudices of those individuals, and we have thus been chasing our tails. It is an easy thing, gentlemen, for a man to inform on another, with no evidence and no motive other than envy or irritation. Across London, I estimate close to a hundred people have been arrested and brought in for questioning in relation to these incidents. Three men are currently being held at Coldbath Fields. One, Sylvester Driscoll, was arrested the day after the previous murders for being in possession of brandy and bloodstained trousers, and has been in custody ever since. I need hardly point out that makes him innocent of these more recent murders.

'The other two are Portuguese sailors against whom I can discover no evidence of any kind other than that they were in the area of Ratcliffe Highway on the night of the Marr murders and there is some uncertainty over their legal status. Gentlemen, I will say that if these are our standards of proof we will need to arrest hundreds if not thousands of men in these districts before we even come close to arresting the right men, and even if we do arrest the real culprits it will be as much down to luck as planning. This is not a part of town where men can always account for their movements or provide papers. The population is transitory and often below and outside the law. If we continue in this vein, the streets of Wapping and Shadwell will have to be cleared and the jails of our offices extended outwards and upwards to accommodate the intake.'

Horton speaks quietly but forcefully. Markland looks furious and turns towards Harriott.

'Harriott, I may take a certain level of . . . criticism from you. Your experience, your years and your standing require me to do so. But to accept such words from a man like this, a man for whom the accepted propriety of superior and subaltern have been proven to be unfamiliar and who has long been tainted with mutiny, is really quite beyond the pale.'

John Harriott glances at his constable at that. Horton hears the word *mutiny* thundering in his mind and looks at Markland with acute attentiveness, like a gazelle near a lion that may or may not be waking up.

'Markland, hear him,' says Harriott. 'Hear him for a while longer.'

'I can see no . . .'

'Markland!' In the voice is the bark and rasp of the navy and the army, and Markland stops his tongue. 'A minute or two longer.' He nods to Horton to continue.

'Gentlemen, I propose to you that we should follow evidence, not hearsay. The evidence is clear. We have the maul, and its initials. We have the ripping chisel, left on the counter at the Marr murders. We have certain eyewitness accounts, which place two men at the scene of both murders, one tall and one short. The taller of these men is said to be lame, with a distinct limp. We have the reports of men heard running through a house out onto Pennington Street, and the reports of voices at the scenes of both crimes. We have clear footprints across the London Dock Company's land behind the King's Arms. We have the facts of the murders themselves: their brutality, their suddenness, and the apparent lack of connection between them. As Mr Harriott says, we have the fact that a second set of murders occurred despite the arrests from the first murders, and so why are we holding Portuguese sailors when they were under lock and key during the fearful events at the King's Arms?'

By this stage, even Capper is on his feet and Markland is beyond rage. Capper exclaims in a stretched, high-pitched voice that Horton's knowledge of the facts suggests an outrageous breach of trust, and the constable must have bribed officers of Shadwell to gain all these pertinent facts, else how could they be known? John Harriott points out, heatedly, that all the facts have been in the newspapers over the previous days, and did they not read these papers? When it becomes clear that the Shadwell magistrates in fact do *not* read the newspapers, there is a brief, uncomfortable moment of calm into which Constable Horton jumps, feet first.

'Gentlemen, I urge you to consider a reallocation of resources. I urge you to rely less on hearsay and more on witnessed evidence: on what people have seen and what they have heard, rather than on who they know and what they infer. I urge you to follow the logic of the case: that these people were murdered with instruments that can be traced, that there seems to have been at least two men involved, that one is tall and one is short, that . . .'

It is Story, emerging from his meditation on demons and their evils, who cuts him short.

'Enough! Harriott, enough! Call off your dog! We have heard a very great deal about how best to conduct an investigation.

But these crimes are beyond investigation, Harriott. They are evil and bestial and foul things, and the best we can hope for is to maintain our dignity in the face of them. The perpetrators will come to us, either through the grace of God or through his actions within the local community. We do not propose to *investigate* these atrocities in the way your man here describes. We must pray and we must have faith in the humanity of the populace. And with that we end this meeting.'

The three Shadwell magistrates rise, Capper and Markland looking at once embarrassed at the outburst of their superior and aghast at what Constable Horton has laid before them. Harriott says nothing as the magistrates march out. He looks tired and done with. As the door closes behind the Shadwell magistrates, he gets up and looks out of the window.

'*The humanity of the populace*,' he says, more to himself than to his constable. 'God help us.'

Constable Horton nods, again more to himself than to Harriott. He feels in his pocket for the rough edge of the Potosí piece of eight he found at the empty house, and gives a small silent prayer of thanks for dishonesty by omission.

SPRING 1664

At the top of the wooded hill above the island's settlement – the French fort, the small cluster of houses and the little harbour – there was a clearing, and within this clearing two men lay in each other's arms, sheltered by the shadow of the trees which seemed to grow out of the rock and straight into the sky. A light breeze brushed their skin and stirred their long hair. A large brown dog slept nearby, its head twitching as it dreamily chased wild boar through the mist of its memories.

It was a clear blue Caribbean day. The air was warm, not quite hot, but held within it the promise of broiling hurricanes and burning afternoons in the weeks to come.

From down by the sea came the distant crack of a shot, followed by an echo as the noise bounced off the rocky edges of the island. The taller of the two men snapped awake and reached for a gun by his side. He was dark-haired and bearded, his skin browned by the sun, and as he stood and raised the musket towards the source of the gun-crack his true height became apparent. He held the weapon to his shoulder and scanned the trees, alert and tense and naked.

For a moment, the stillness and silence returned. Some of the island's gigantic population of pigeons started to coo again. Then, gently, the other man raised his hand to stroke the standing man's ankle, his eyes still closed.

'*Apaise-toi, Guillaume.* There are *always* guns on Tortuga. And you always spring to your feet like a scared whippet.'

The tall man ignored him, still sweeping his gun across the trees. The dog had also woken up, and gazed at the standing man, his eyes dull.

There was no other sound for a good while, but then a crackling of gunfire erupted somewhere down the hill beyond the fort, or perhaps at the fort itself. The Frenchman now sat up and looked towards the sound of the shots, his blue eyes flat and uninterested. He stretched his legs out in front of him on the ground, and his arms out behind him, leaning back on his hands to look into the sky, even as the gunfire boomed below. It appeared to be coming closer. The Frenchman looked to be the same age as his companion, but where that man was tall and dark-haired, this man was blond and small and intricate. He sat up straight again, wrapping his legs to one side like a woman and hooking one arm around the standing leg of his companion, hugging himself into the other's thigh. He started to stroke his hand up and down the other's leg, a smile on his face, his eyes distant.

'Now, Guillaume, you must learn to . . .'

Men appeared through the trees, a small group of four, dressed in rough leather breeches, thick cotton shirts and a variety of coloured hats and neckerchiefs, all of which had seen better days. They came to a halt within the ring of trees and, to a man, began to laugh.

'Wot a *sight*, fellas,' said one of them, resplendent in a red hat that had kept its dye but lost its shape. 'Wot larks for a forest by the sea.' His accent was London, his sword looked

Spanish, his musket was undoubtedly French. He smirked as he stepped into the clearing, full of the cockiness of a male in a group despite the dark-haired man's gun, which now rested steadily on the newcomer's face. 'So it's true, fellas. The so-called Tortuga Brethren are too busy fucking each other's arses to be of any use in our escapades. Let's leave these two to their cuddles.'

He winked at the tall man.

'You want to get to Port Royal, mate. They've got plenty of cunt there. No making do with your little friend here.'

He made to leave, but the seated Frenchman spoke to him and caused him to turn back.

'You are *English*, I think?'

The red-hatted Londoner looked at him, still with his splendid grin. His teeth were whiter than the teeth of a rogue sailor had any business being. His skin was red and burned.

'So, here's a French poof with a tongue in his head,' he said. 'The very worst kind. We always thought you bastards were a bunch of queers. Perhaps he fancies a taste of some Wapping cock?' This to his friends at the edge of the clearing, who laughed heartily.

The Frenchman looked equable, despite the supine nature of his pose, squeezed against the long flank of his companion.

'You are English, yes?'

'And you are French. What of it, you bugger?'

'I know a man who knows a man who has enjoyed the physical delights of your new king. I believe Charles *le deux, non*? He told me your new king likes to call the men he fucks Oliver. Personally, I do not understand the reference.'

The Londoner's smile vanished and his musket began to rise as he started to say something, but he failed to find the *mot juste* because at that moment the front of his face fell in on itself as the sound of shot ripped through the clearing. The

Londoner collapsed, and the standing naked man put his musket back down to reload it, careful not to knock the butt into the head of his reclining French companion.

The dead Londoner's comrades stared down at the fallen shape of their shipmate, and then started to raise their own weapons, only to hear a click as the reclining Frenchman raised his own gun, as if from nowhere, an elegant bejewelled thing which twinkled like his eyes as it caught the beams from the sun. He was now on his knees, his cock swinging audaciously.

'*Alors, messieurs*,' he said, one eye closed and one eye staring down the barrel of his rifle, which was aimed directly between the eyes of one of the men, before moving on to the next, and then the third, and then back again. '*Mon cher* Guillaume has dealt with your English friend, using his French musket. I too have a French weapon, and while *mon cher* Guillaume reloads his own gun I am pointing mine at the three of you. It is already loaded. You may shoot, but one of you will die, perhaps not even the one who fired the shot. Your odds are three to one. Do you feel lucky today, *gaffeurs*?'

As he talked, his tall friend continued reloading his gun, under the watchful eyes of the three remaining intruders.

'And now,' said the Frenchman. 'Some introductions. This attractive fellow here is Guillaume, an English friend of mine. And my name is L'Ollonais. I understand this is not an easy name for you English to say, but you have perhaps heard it before today?'

All three of the men shivered. After perhaps ten seconds, one of them moved his foot back slowly, as if walking away from a snarling lioness. He started to inch back towards the perimeter of the clearing. Eventually, his two companions began to do the same. By this time, the tall man had reloaded his musket and had raised it to his shoulder, wincing slightly as an old vivid wound in his left side was stretched by the movement, something only his French companion noticed.

'*Formidable*,' says the Frenchman. 'I see perhaps that you have heard my name. Now, *messieurs*, your odds have worsened to two in three. But your retreat is sign enough that you understand your situation.'

The first of the three men reached the perimeter, then the second, then the Frenchman fired and the last of them was flung back into the other two, his chest open and red. One of the men yelled something obscene in what Guillaume registered as a Midlands accent before the two remaining invaders disappeared back into the forest at a gallop, leaving their two fallen comrades to the pigeons and the mad French bastard.

The tall man looked down at his companion.

'They were leaving. You crazy little turd,' he said, a long-forgotten Oxfordshire accent lending a little humanity to his flat, dispassionate voice. The Frenchman smiled sweetly before laying down his gun on the ground and standing. He was shorter and more muscular than his English companion, his back scarred and pockmarked. He walked over to the two dead men, and picked up the Londoner's red hat from the ground. He put it on, grinning to himself and whistling a French air. The Englishman watched him as he sauntered over to the second dead man, picking up the man's rifle and his leather purse, which was almost empty. The Frenchman pretended to pout at this.

'I wonder where they came from?' he said, chucking the purse back on the ground.

'You mean after England?' asked the tall man.

'*Bien sûr*, I mean after England. They did not sail over the Atlantic just to visit us.'

'They mentioned Port Royal.'

'*Oui, bien sûr*. Your little English *boudoir*, surrounded by the Spanish scum you stole it from.'

'Wherever they came from, they'll be back here soon enough, with more men and more guns.'

'You mean, *mon cher* Guillaume, that we do not have time to fuck again before fleeing into the hills.' Again, the pretend pout. 'This is a shame. I am quite aroused.'

The Englishman looked at the Frenchman, and there was nothing in his expression. Despite the Frenchman's psychopathic sangfroid, L'Ollonais did consider for a shivering moment the distinct possibility that his lover might just kill him, here and now. Out of boredom, perhaps. Out of *l'amour*, even. L'Ollonais even readied himself for the moment of death, as he had countless times before. The Englishman was capable of it. His still grey eyes were always startlingly cold, and the Frenchman had awoken several times to see those eyes gazing at him, as if calculating the colour of the blood in his neck, while Guillaume hummed to himself absently.

Guillaume started putting on his clothes. The Frenchman was grinning still, though there was no joy behind the grin now. The shots from below had ceased. L'Ollonais started dressing as well. The dog watched them both.

They made to leave the clearing. The Frenchman headed north, towards the hill and the abandoned plantations above. The Englishman turned south, towards where the surviving interlopers had headed. They stopped and looked at each other.

'You are going to them, *mon cher*?' asks the Frenchman.

'Perhaps. I know I'm not going with you.'

'So this is *adieu*.'

'If you say so.'

'I do not say so. I say *au revoir*, Billy.'

'Say what you like.'

'Then *au revoir*.'

They went their separate ways.

*

I walked out from the wooded uplands of the small island of Tortuga, dressed in my simple Tortugan Brethren's outfit of dark cowhide stiffened with thick dried blood. I felt nothing about leaving Francis. He'd introduced me to the *boucaniers*, the self-governing community of Godless scum who split their time between lazing in the hills of Tortuga and raiding Spanish towns and forts across the Caribbean. He'd introduced me to other things, besides, things which I participated in simply because they offered the possibility of some kind of sensation. Any kind of sensation at all. I had been with no woman since Kate. Decades before this celibacy had seemed a noble proposition; it now seemed pathetic and pointless. Nevertheless, it was the echo of a commitment I'd made. I still would not enjoy a woman, and the pleasures L'Ollonais had offered seemed to have lost their flavour of obscenity (at least to me) as the years rolled by. But the man was an empty lunatic, as dangerous as a cornered dog but with infinitely more intelligence. It was time to go.

I had spent some two years with the *boucaniers* since meeting L'Ollonais. I had crewed on dozens of raids, and had grown somewhat rich on the proceeds. While my shipmates squandered their takings in the fleshpots of Port Royal, I carefully husbanded my growing resources. I sometimes disappeared for weeks to horde away my treasury in among the trees of a hidden cove on the north coast of Jamaica, near a place the English already called Cockpit County. My treasure was watched over by a small group of Maroons whose reliability had been bought by the murder of a Spanish plantation owner a decade before, just before Penn and Venables arrived to begin the process of co-opting Jamaica into the empire about which England, even then, was dreaming.

So despite my appearance, I was now a moderately wealthy

man. I had near a century's experience of rapine, from barges on the Thames to the treasure ships of Venezuela. I had no ship. I was no captain. But I did have a reputation for fearlessness which went some way before me. Long Billy some of them called me, unaware of the irony of such a name to one whose life had been long indeed.

For now, Tortuga was my home. It was here the *boucaniers* had established themselves, as a loosely held confederacy under the inconsequential governorship of France. When L'Ollonais had first come here, the core of the *boucaniers* had been French and Spanish, but that had been changing since I arrived. More and more Anglo-Saxon flotsam and jetsam had washed ashore, many of them refugees from a Restoration England, men who'd fought under the old Protector and had seen early visions of a Commonwealth of men under God. Poor fools. There was no God, and now there was no Protector. I fought under him, too, for a while. But revolution, like sodomy, was just another form of desire.

So these old Roundheads and Ironsides had ditched their God in favour of money, but their silly dreams of Commonwealth remained. So the *boucaniers* were reconstituted as the Brethren, a free society of delinquents living in the sun thousands of miles away from the new Stuart monarch and his bastard Papist brother. Their language, not mine. They imagined themselves a set of sun-kissed dissidents under a Caribbean sun, freedom in their hearts and gold in their pockets. It was an attractive dream, I supposed. But it was just a dream.

There was no leader – no emperor of the Brethren (although the man I would shortly be meeting would come closest to holding that title). But there was ample opportunity for a bunch of well-organised men and there were very few disincentives to piracy. For myself, I took pleasure where I could find it, and I husbanded my stock of gold and (mainly) silver. For now, piracy was suiting me extremely well.

Any captain with ambition could find willing accomplices among the Brethren, as long as he timed things properly. He needed to be offering adventure and rapine just as the takings from the previous raid had begun to dry up, when lazing in the sun and drinking and fucking had begun to lose their allure, when the bloodlust began to whirl and men started to remember the feeling of a sheet in one hand and a sword in the other. Throughout Tortuga, pockets of Brethren had been considering for days the options for a new raid, and today as if by magic a small fleet had appeared down in the harbour below.

I could see the fleet in the harbour now, dominated by a fair-sized vessel, one of the biggest ones of recent times, forty guns at least. There was something compelling about her. She was perky and somehow magnificent. I sniffed the candlewood trees for the last time, as I always did before the start of a new journey, and headed down.

Almost a hundred Brethren had already gathered at the harbour, mingling with the island's small community of traders and prostitutes, the ageing remnants of an army of whores a former French governor had imported to try to break Tortuga's reputation as an island of sodomy. A few of the Brethren noted my arrival and, as usual, cleared an area to avoid physical contact with me. They appeared to be looking for L'Ollonais as well; several of them visibly relaxed when they'd established that I was alone.

A large tender was tied up to the harbour wall, and a group of men from the ship had gathered themselves at the quayside. They were not in any kind of uniform; but they were upright, clean-shaven and their clothing was neat. They seemed organised. They looked like the men who'd disturbed us in the woods. The two who'd run away from us were nowhere to be seen.

One stood in front of the others. He was short, broad-shouldered and barrel-chested, a scarlet kerchief was tied around his forehead, and his red-brown beard was carefully tended. He affected the appearance of none other than Francis Drake, and I smiled at that. His natural authority made it clear he was the captain. His leer, the rings on his fingers, and that blatant red kerchief, all made it clear that he was also a buccaneer.

'So, this is Tortuga.'

His accent was rich and musical. Welsh, like that of old Tillert a century ago, only this man's voice was more cultured and more capable of fine words and manipulation than even that old rogue's. He had a charisma and a power that was so apparent I knew instantly where the perky attraction of the ship at anchor stemmed from. The same thing shone out of this man like a beacon above a Cornish crag. I knew then that I'd be joining his crew, and that I'd benefit enormously from doing so.

'Tortuga. Island of the Brethren. And here you all are, in your shitty cowhides stinking of wild boar and buggery. Greetings from Port Royal, you godforsaken bastards.'

There were mutterings in the crowd, but only dim ones. They wanted to hear what the man had come to say. And they knew how recruiting started. This was a dance with which they were all familiar.

'The ship out there shall remain nameless, as shall I, for the time being. No one knows I'm here, least of all the people who are paying for the little trip I'm embarked on. There's three other captains along with me, and they're all waiting off some little islet between here and the Main. They want what I want. They want bounty.'

At the magic word, the mutterings ceased, and attention was rigid once more.

'I can bring you to bounty, my sodomising friends.'

He was now standing with his legs apart and his hands on his hips in a posture which, for most men in most places at most times of the world, would have been ridiculous, but for this extraordinary bundle of energy rooted to the spot on a buccaneer island with a pirate ship behind him was somehow just right. His chin was up in the air, the beard quivering.

'There's bounty, lads, bounty enough to keep the syphilitic inbred Spanish in pearls and women's underthings until the Sun King decides to head south. There's gold, lads, more gold than the entire English stinking Parliament has ever seen, and it's waiting to be taken, lads, waiting to be taken from under the noses of carpeting bureaucrats and councillors who only want to save their own skin and take whatever cut we care to give them. It's all there, just over there' – he pointed vaguely westwards – 'glistening under the jungle trees. And all you need to do is step down into this little boat' – now he pointed down to the water – 'step down, and sign up for the usual terms, and we'll be singeing the fucking King of Spain's fucking beard before the year is out.'

For a moment the mention of beards and singeing caused my breath to seize, and the world seemed to shimmer, as if curtains between decades were shifting in the breeze from the open sea. I half-expected to turn and find Drake standing there beside me, smirking in that belittling way of his at this little Welsh popinjay with his ridiculous copycat beard, yet mesmerised by what he was saying.

For now, the popinjay had stopped, and waited. There was silence. No cheers, no rowdy hail-fellow-well-met huzzahs. He had their attention, that was all. He had still not told them why they, the Brethren, the *boucaniers* of old, should trust this Celtic firebrand, trust him with their lives and their hard-earned reputation. For myself, I'd already signed up and was ready to go. The rest of them still needed to be convinced.

'You know *Mings*, I suppose?'

Quite a few of them stirred at that name. Christopher Mings, son of a shoemaker, cabin boy-to-captain, the man who had raided Campeche harbour in broad bloody daylight, who'd seized over a million pieces of eight, who'd been taken back to London for refusing to give a single shred of it to the whoresons in the Admiralty, who'd come straight back out here and had then taken Santiago, the second largest city on Cuba. Mings was a legend amongst the Brethren, the first English captain and privateer with the balls and the backing to seize entire towns and not just ships. Christ, Mings was more a king out here than Charles would ever be.

'Ah, Mings I see you've heard of. Good. Well, Mings was my admiral, fellows. I was captain of one of his ships. I've got several thousand pieces waiting to be spent back in Port Royal, where the whores know me by the size of my purse and the length of my cock. I can drink any of you catamites into an early fucking grave, but I need you, or rather I need your sordid, vicious greed. Henry Morgan's the name, fellows. And tearing great big fucking holes in the Spanish Empire is all the bounty I need.'

21 DECEMBER 1811

Abigail Horton ties up the buttons on the front of her husband's coat, humming softly to herself as she does so. Constable Charles Horton gazes at the top of her head, and smells the fine strawberry-and-straw odour of her blonde hair. He leans forward, and kisses her gently.

She stops humming and steps back, looking into his eyes. It is one of her measuring looks.

'Are you happy, faithful husband?' she asks at last. Her mouth is shaped in a familiar half-smile, half-pout. The question is lightly asked (that *faithful* an old joke between them) but seriously meant. Horton knows she is referring to his distracted air of recent days. He has rarely been able to stop his mind calculating and reasoning upon the current case, and several times has looked up to see her looking at him with one of those measuring looks, not untouched by sorrow.

'As happy as I have ever been, faithful wife,' he replies, instinctively.

'Ah, but you have indeed never been a happy person, Charles Horton,' she says. 'So that is saying very little indeed.'

'Well, then. As happy as I have been at my least unhappy moments. Such as our wedding day.'

'Ah, our wedding day.' She brushes invisible bits of something off the front of his coat. 'Yes, you were happy then, I think. For the first time in a long time.'

'Indeed I was.'

'You are worried about what the magistrate said to you. Markland.'

A man who is suspected of mutiny . . .

'I am not worried about what he said.'

'But you are worried about what he knows.'

'To be accurate, I am worried about what he might do with what he knows.'

She smiles again, and now he smiles as well. It amuses her when he is so deliberately precise.

'You are worried he will inform on you.'

'Like I did on my shipmates, you mean.'

His voice is harsh, and she catches her breath at that for a moment, and looks away. Then she looks back at him.

'We have not spoken of this for some time,' she says, and her voice is soft, though her eyes are hard and determined.

'And I would not have spoken of it now, Abigail. Had you not mentioned it.'

She does not speak for a second or two, and continues busying herself with imaginary dirt on his coat.

'Listen, Charles,' she says at last. 'Listen to me. You had no choice other than to act . . .'

'Please, Abigail.' He is pleading, now. 'Please, not again. I cannot bear it.'

'But you cannot allow this *poison* to remain in your heart!' She is gripping the tops of his arms now, and once again he smells her hair. It is impossibly evocative.

'Abigail, enough.' He does not shout, but the words are spat out with such force that her eyes widen and her hands drop from his shoulders. 'You cannot simply demand that this leaves me. It is with me. It is part of me. My actions stay within my heart. There is no feat of memory by which I can erase them. I must carry them with me. It is part of what makes me Charles Horton.'

'I understand . . .'

'No, Abigail. You do not. You sympathise. There is a difference.'

And with that he claps a thick woollen hat on his head and walks out into the winter air, leaving his wife to look after him for a moment, her eyes softening and her brow furrowed. After a moment she turns to sit down before the fire. She picks up the book she has been reading these past few days, a new edition of Bonnycastle's *Introduction to Astronomy in Letters to his Pupil.* Abigail Horton buries her concern for her husband beneath dreams of the stars.

The first of his visits that day takes Horton in a coach towards the east, out along the Ratcliffe Highway, past Shadwell, Limehouse, Ratcliffe and across the top of the Isle of Dogs. The crowded edges of London begin to give way to countryside around Ratcliffe, before commerce and development return with the new docks at the top of the Isle of Dogs and then disappear for good out to the east. The coach is driven by the brother of a fellow River Thames waterman-constable, his time paid for out of River Office funds, despite the jurisdictional niceties.

As the houses give way to green and brown (mainly brown, out here on the flat, open river borders) the air opens out and the crowded nooks and crannies of Wapping are shown to be what they truly are: an astonishing aberration in a still overwhelmingly rural England. Out here, it is almost impossible to imagine a place like Wapping existing on this rolling foggy earth.

Horton is taking his own advice; he is following the evidence. Today that means talking to the two living people who were physically closest to the Ratcliffe Highway and Gravel Lane murders. His first stop is a house on the edge of the village of Tilbury, right on the banks of the Thames, out near the sea where the river is three times wider than it is at Wapping, at the edge of the estuary itself.

It takes more than an hour to reach the neat, austere little house, as neat and austere as the woman who opens the door to Horton's knock. He introduces himself, and explains his business. She looks sceptical, but she is not the type to resist official authority in any form and lets him in.

The front door gives straight onto a single room, with a well-tended hearth. There is a door to a small kitchen, from where there is a delicious smell of poultry being readied in preparation for the upcoming feast day. Unusually for a house this small there is also a staircase, and Margaret Jewell's mother calls up it, tenderly but anxiously. Within half a minute her daughter appears.

The girl is wearing a simple white cotton dress, and her hair is pinned up roughly, as if she has tidied it just to come downstairs. She is pale but composed, Horton is relieved to see. He has a vivid flash of recollection: a young girl, sitting on a pavement, weeping uncontrollably, her hair red and dishevelled. The girl who comes down the stairs looks very different now, as if she's aged ten years in a few weeks. She no longer seems the hysterical type.

He introduces himself. She sits down in one of the two ancient chairs in the little room. He takes the other. The old mother retires to the kitchen, but hovers near the opening between the two rooms, listening and watching.

The girl speaks with a fierce nervousness. She is barely more than a child, after all.

'You were there. That night. You were there at the house.'

'Yes, I was,' he says. 'Miss Jewell, I am here as part of our investigation into the murder of your employer Timothy Marr, and his family.' The words sound strange and officious on his tongue. He rehearsed them several times in the coach. He does not quite know why.

'And Jim.' She looks into the fire, as if to say she has finished with looking at him for the time being. She holds a small brooch in her fingers, which she turns slowly.

'Jim? Oh, yes. James Gowen. The shop boy.'

'No one asked me any questions about him.'

'Should they have done?'

'I don't know whether they should have done or not. But people forget, don't they? They forget the servants. Like they're not important.'

'So you're not implying that James could have been ...'

'No, sir. No I am not.' She seems irritated by him now, and he is conscious of not acknowledging the point she is trying to make. It is true. He has not previously found himself asking anyone questions about Gowen's murder. Thinking about it now, it seems like a potentially enormous oversight.

He waits for a moment, watching her. He has begun to lean forward, and Margaret Jewell's mother, watching from the kitchen, is disturbed to see something almost predatory in his pose, and is on the point of interrupting them when Horton begins to speak again.

'Well, I am investigating the murders, and ...'

'What does that mean?'

'What does what mean?'

'Investigating? You are investigating. I don't understand the words you are using.'

He hesitates. Her manner is quiet, but there's a wilful, young intelligence about her as well. He recognises it as something which could be useful to him, if he can find a way of exploiting it.

'All I mean is that I am trying to uncover facts about the crime which may have been missed by others.'

Margaret looks at him now, and she almost smiles. The expression is startlingly adult.

'But I thought the Shadwell magistrates were *investigating*, as you say. They have certainly talked to a great many people. Locked quite a few of them up, I hear, as well.'

'Indeed they have, miss. But, so far, they have not established a reason for the killings.'

'A reason?'

'A . . . motive. A circumstance which would lead to somebody wanting to kill Timothy Marr.'

'Or his wife. Or his baby. Or James.'

He is startled. Once again, this insight has not occurred to him.

'Or those, yes.'

'I answered all the questions the magistrates asked me.'

'You did, miss, you did. I would like to speak to you about matters which may not seem directly connected to the events themselves.'

'How so?'

'Well, were there perhaps people . . . in recent times . . . who were particularly memorable.'

'Memorable?'

'Yes. People who came to the shop.'

'A great many people came to the shop, Mr . . . Do I call you "mister"? Or something else? Are you like a soldier?'

'Nothing like. I was a sailor once. Constable Horton is correct, I suppose.'

'Well, Constable Horton, a great many people came to Mr Marr's shop. Why should I remember any particular one of them?'

'I cannot say, miss. Perhaps this means something to you.'

He pulls something out of his pocket: the Potosí piece of eight. He hands it to her. He is not quite sure why.

'What is it?' she asks.

'It is a piece of eight.'

'Ah, yes. Spanish money.'

'Normally, yes. But I understand it is still used in some far-flung parts of the world.'

'Still used in London, too, Mr Horton. Mr Marr took payment for quite a few orders with Spanish money.'

'So I understand. Were there any orders paid for with Spanish money recently?'

'Well, there was one that was going to be. I heard Mr Marr complaining about it.'

'What do you mean, going to be?'

The mother is making no pretence of working in the kitchen now. She stands in the opening watching the two of them talk.

'Order came in two weeks ago. Funny little fellow came into the shop with it, Jewish I think he was. Said he'd be paying in Spanish money. Mr Marr was grumbling about it.'

'He didn't want to be paid in Spanish money?'

'No, he said not. I heard him talking to Mrs Marr about it. Said it was a flipping liberty, but it being such a big order he'd put up with it.'

'What was the order for?'

'Plain cotton clothes, mainly. Osnabrück cotton. Various sizes. Some cloth shoes, too.'

'And what happened to this order?'

'What do you mean, what happened?'

'Did Marr complete the order?'

'Oh. Well, no. I never heard about it again to be truthful with you.'

'It was never mentioned again?'

'No.'

They talk for a while longer, but not a long while. Margaret relaxes and talks freely, but nothing much of what she says seems pertinent to Horton. A great deal of it is complaining about her treatment: by the magistrates, by the villagers of Tilbury, by her mother, who is still listening at the kitchen door and sniffs with affronted sadness to hear her daughter's grumbles. As he leaves, the girl touches his sleeve and whispers to him:

'Will you find me a position? Or help me? I cannot stay here a great while longer. It is stiflin' here.'

And her eyes glitter with the memory of being a London girl, surrounded by the clamour of maritime possibilities.

Horton says he will see what he can do, and heads out to the waiting coach. They head back westwards. The old coin is hard against his thigh, its edges impertinently sharp. He thinks about what he has heard, and the order book he had taken from 29 Ratcliffe Highway.

Returning into Wapping, the coach edges down the Highway through the early evening crowd, then left onto New Gravel Lane and thence into the warren of boarding houses, inns and shops crammed between the lane and the dock. He tells the driver to slow down quickly, looking up at the names of the houses, before finding the one he is looking for. He gets out and sends the driver home. He knocks at the door and is let inside, where he is shown up to a door on the second floor. He knocks, and for a good while there is no response. Eventually a quiet, shaky voice asks: 'Who's knocking?' Its accent is local but also educated, the rough corners rubbed off by books.

'Constable Horton. River Police Office.'

'River police? What do you want?' The voice still sounds tremulous, but is a little more sure of itself.

'Let me in, Mr Turner. It should be obvious to you why I am here.'

Another long pause, and then the door slowly opens. The pale face of John Turner looks out and peers into Horton's face, exploring it for confirmation of his official status. Turner seems satisfied with what he sees, and lets Horton into the room beyond.

An open wooden chest containing Turner's belongings is in the middle of the room. A bed, part-covered by some nondescript material, is along one wall. An old piece of sailcloth serves for a curtain. Turner is a man who has not yet made a firm commitment to his new lodgings. There is not even a chair to sit on, so Turner indicates the bed. Horton seats himself, and Turner closes the lid of the chest and sits on that. The position is awkward, especially for a man wearing only a nightshirt, as Turner is.

He seems not to have left this dusty little room for some time, if at all. He is unshaven, dishevelled and smells of dust and sweat and hunger. It occurs to Horton how odd it is, showing up at a stranger's door and asking to be let in to ask questions. And then it occurs to him how odd it is that this has only just occurred to him. Somehow, it seems that some simple small talk is required. They are both adult men. He is not talking to a child. And yet it occurs to him that he has no idea what to say. Small talk is not something Charles Horton is comfortable with. Perhaps he should have brought Abigail.

'You seem to have found somewhere adequate to live,' he says. This sounds clumsy and witless, and Turner looks quizzical. His expression makes his confusion clear. *Why is this man making conversation with me? Why doesn't he get to his point?*

So, enough small talk, then.

'Mr Turner, I want to ask you some questions about the events you witnessed at the King's Head.'

'Witnessed? What do you mean by that?'

'Saw. Heard.'

'I saw a man busy cutting Mrs Williamson's throat.'

Turner is belligerent if still somewhat afraid. Horton takes a breath, and tries again. Steering the conversation towards ... what, exactly?

'I would like to find out more about the details of that night, Mr Turner.'

'Details? What details?'

'Well, for instance, did you hear anyone talking?'

'When?'

'Immediately before you came down the stairs. Or immediately after.'

'Well, immediately after I was busy legging it up to the bedroom and out of the window.'

'Of course. Of course. So before then?'

'I don't understand the question.'

'Well, let me try and explain. Imagine you're back at the inn.'

'You police fellows have some strange ideas.'

'Possibly.'

'Well, as I hear it, you've arrested half of London. Arrest the other half and you'll have the bastard. Makes sense, don't it?'

'There have been a great many arrests, it is true.'

'Too bloody many, by all accounts, but you still haven't caught them, have you? Too bloody busy arresting people to look at what's in front of your bloody noses.'

'And what is it that's in front of our noses?'

'I don't know, do I? Not my job to know, is it?'

The man's voice is now insolent as well as belligerent. The change is startling. A sudden insight occurs to Horton: Turner feels this room, this whole situation, is somehow beneath him. He feels his presence at the murders of the Williamsons gives him something like celebrity, or what passes for it in the poorer parts of London. It's like a kind of power, and this makes him feel essentially superior to Horton, and indeed the magistrates. *I was there*, his sneer seems to say. *You can't possibly understand.* The man won't be charmed. A different approach is required.

Horton stands and suddenly Turner looks afraid again, leaning back away from him. Horton feels something powerful and exhilarating, seeing Turner cringe like that. He is conscious that this power flows from his position as a *policeman*. It feels oddly and dangerously wonderful. He folds his arms, his earlier tiredness washed away, and glowers down at the other man.

'Listen to me, now,' he says, in a low, cold voice which he barely recognises. 'I know how bloody clever you think you are. I've heard it all before. But I know that six nights ago you were swinging over New Gravel Lane with your yellow arse hanging in the wind, whimpering like an old lady. I know you did nothing – *nothing* – to save those poor people. I know you saved your own skin while Williamson and his wife were cut to pieces. I know you locked yourself in your tiny little bedroom while they had their throats slashed and God knows what else done to their dying bodies. While you whined away like a little helpless puppy. So don't pretend you're anything special. Don't. I'm here to do my job, and my job is to find out what happened to these people, not to sit here while you show me how very clever you are, Mr Turner. It's a simple question. Did you hear anything? Did anybody speak?'

Turner's face is somehow both pale and flushed red at the same time. He looks sick, close to fainting, dizzy from this unexpected presence in his room. For a single moment, Horton seems to be channelling the entire authority of the British Empire, and Turner can smell that power, can feel the heat of it coming off the man standing over him. Nothing like this has ever happened before. No soldier or police officer or guard has ever bullied him before. He simply collapses under the weight of it.

'Sorry,' he mutters. Horton says nothing, still enjoying the magic but also feeling an itch of something. Guilt, perhaps? Surely not guilt again?

'No apologies, Mr Turner. Just the facts.'

Horton steps back and sits down on the bed again. He unfolds his arms and puts his hands back in his lap.

'What do you want to know?' Turner asks, looking at the floor, miserable but amenable.

'Did you hear or see anything unusual on the night of the murders?'

'Only what I already told you. The noises in the inn, which I went down to investigate. I saw what was happening, and that's when I escaped out of the window.'

'Well, then, I need you to think about anything else you might have seen or heard, either on the day of the murders or in the days and weeks running up to it.'

Turner looks at him in some despair.

'Mr Horton, it's an alehouse. There's people coming and going all the time. There's arguments and fights and strange undertakings going on from dawn till dusk.'

Strangely poetic, Horton thinks.

'I understand that, Mr Turner. What I want you to do is think of anything that stands out. Did you ever hear Williamson arguing with anyone?'

'All the time. He wasn't scared of a shout, was old Williamson.'

Horton pauses. Perhaps this is a fool's errand, after all. He searches his own memory for something which might make a connection.

'Did you ever hear Williamson arguing about business?'

'You mean the business of the inn?'

'Perhaps. Or something about business outside.'

'No, I never heard him arguing with anyone about that.'

Horton scratches around in his head once more.

'There was something going on between Williamson and his wife, though, come to think of it. Something to do with some bit of business Williamson had going on outside.' Turner speaks with a crisp formality now, the insurance clerk in him coming out.

'Tell me about that, then.'

'I heard them arguing about it a few nights before ... the recent events. Mrs Williamson was crying when I came in from work that night. I only remember because that was exceeding unusual, that was. She never cried, that woman. She was kind to me, but she was formidable.

'But this night, she was terrible upset. She tried to hide it from me when I came in, but I could see she'd been crying and probably still was. I asked after her health and she said she was fine, but she wasn't. I went upstairs. Bit later, I went out to the privy outside the kitchen at the back of the place.'

'No chamber pot in your room, Mr Turner?'

'Yes, there's a chamber pot. But I needed ... well, I needed the privy. I haven't been well. But that's probably not relevant, is it, Mr Horton?'

'No. Carry on.'

'Well, from the privy you can hear people talking in the kitchen, especially if they're talking loudly.' Which probably better explains why you were in there, thinks Horton, who is realising how much he dislikes this man. 'Mrs Williamson was shouting at her husband, and she was still crying too. Her voice sounded all broken up, know how I mean?'

'Yes, I know.'

'I couldn't hear everything that was being said, but they were talking about some kind of a deal that old Williamson had done. She wasn't at all happy about it, and she was letting him know it. He seemed to have done a deal to supply a big old load of food: beans, peas, rice, stuff like that. He knew how to get things, did Williamson, and he was always getting hold of stuff for people, usually in the victualling line. Made as much money from that as he did from the inn, he told me once.

'But for some reason she didn't like this deal. Maybe the size of it scared her, I don't know. But I do remember her screaming at him at one point. *Sin sin sin*, she was saying, over and over, and she was really crying now. And then she said something about Sheerness.'

'Sheerness?'

'Yes. She said if she had her way she'd take those peas and beans and throw them in the sea at Sheerness, and then he could see his precious victuals float down to the bottom of the ocean, like those poor blessed niggers had done.'

Horton blinks at that.

'She talked about "niggers"?'

'Well, she might have said Negroes or blacks or some such, but you get my meaning.'

'She talked about Negroes drowning?'

'That's it. That was p'raps what was upsetting her. But she finished with that, with a big shout, and then it was all over. I finished my business, and went to bed. Never heard it mentioned again.'

As the story ends, Horton sits for a good while, ignoring Turner while he thinks about this. Eventually, he stands up and makes his way to the door, not intending to say goodbye, still somehow angry at the man before him, who seems weak and deceitful. But he looks back at Turner, whose head is drooping over his feet and whose shoulders slump in something like dejected surrender.

'Did you tell anyone else this?' Horton asks.

Turner looks up at him, and almost smiles.

'No, mate. No one ever asked,' he says.

JUNE 1668

The two of us stood on the poop watching the sun go down on the South Cays: the little Welsh admiral, and his quartermaster. A small ship was inching its way into the island's natural harbour. Outside the harbour vicious ocean waves swirled around, strong enough to break a ship's anchor chain. Inside, the water was calm. This was the ninth vessel to creep into the harbour, and it was the last one we expected.

Admiral Morgan, as he liked to call himself, sighed. By now he was almost formally the Admiral of Jamaica, though such a title was new and not widely recognised. But he was also very much (and very unofficially) Admiral of the Brethren. Morgan always insisted he was no pirate, preferring the word buccaneer. He saw himself as fighting for England and its king, and demanded that ranks on his ships mirrored those of the Royal Navy. He was not, and never would be, a whoreson pirate. By now, after four years of plundering and adventuring, I was very much his lieutenant. Billy Ablass, commonly known amongst the Brethren as Long Billy, quartermaster.

The Brethren, now. They didn't care at all whether anyone called them pirates. But they did care about authority, and who held it. They'd evolved a dainty little system of checks and balances, under which the quartermaster held almost the same authority as the captain while the fleet was harboured. During a raid – when the guns were firing and steel was flashing – the men would follow every command of the captain, as obedient as any drilled foot soldier. But once the smoke dispersed and the take was being distributed, the men didn't want a dictator. They chose a quartermaster to represent them, a piratical tribune to look after the interests of the crew in the face of a cocksure captain who probably thought he was master of the world.

And on this fleet, they'd chosen me. There'd been no election and no hustings, just a fearful midnight visit from a few of them and a hurried plea and a gracious acceptance. The men were as scared of me – more scared, probably – as they were of Morgan, so perhaps I was the obvious choice. Appoint a bastard to watch a bastard, as it were. Morgan, needless to say, had hated the idea.

So tonight, the captain and the quartermaster, the emperor and the tribune, were viewing their fleet. And the captain was worried.

'Only nine,' he muttered. 'Why only nine?'

The largest of the ships in the harbour, the *Dolphin*, only had eight cannon and carried barely sixty men. The majority of the boats were simple single-masted things, barely more than pinnaces. The second-largest ship, the one we were now standing on, had been stolen from the Spanish, and I'd picked a new Anglo-Saxon name for her. She became the *Drake*. She only had six guns, but she was fast. I loved that ship, and it was upsetting me that just now Morgan was carving something absent-mindedly into the sturdy rail with a small, ancient knife which he carried with him everywhere and which fitted in his hand like a sixth finger.

Only English captains remained in the fleet, which was why our strength was so pitiful. There had been a good number of French vessels but they'd quit us two days before following a disappointing raid on Puerto del Príncipe. Morgan had barely held the fleet together after that; the remaining English and Irish Brethren had muttered their displeasure and watched with some envy as their French comrades headed for a rendezvous with the fearsome L'Ollonais.

L'Ollonais was now the most feared pirate in the Caribbean, a man whose reputation for extreme and calculating violence had, it was said, reached as far as Madrid. The Spaniards had started calling Morgan *El Draque*, which pleased him immensely, but right now his fame was being eclipsed by L'Ollonais. The Brethren were full of tales about the Frenchman's spectacular raid on Maracaibo, and his seizure of mythical sums.

Morgan knew (as did I) how close the English Brethren had come to joining the French as they left the fleet. The admiral-captain had turned on the bountiful Welsh charm to bring them around, promising them their own glorious trip to the Spanish Main, painting pictures of riches aplenty, juicy golden fruits waiting to be plucked from ill-defended, opulent branches. It was for this glittering adventure that he was now mustering a fleet here, in the South Cays. But even now crucial elements of the plan – including the planned targets – remained only inside Morgan's head, if in fact they existed at all.

'You haven't let on where we're going,' I said as we watched the final ship join the fleet.

'No, I have not. You miss nothing, quartermaster.'

Morgan spat out the words. Ever since the French had left, citing L'Ollonais, he'd acted like a sulky woman with me.

'Violation of the pirate code, that is.'

'Tell me something I do not know, young William. And need I remind you that we are not pirates?'

'Nor did you tell them about the Spanish fleet.'

A new armada had been despatched from Spain to stem the tide of English but mainly French piracy, triggered by the rampages of L'Ollonais. It was now patrolling the Caribbean under the notoriously formidable Admiral Alonzo de Campos y Espinosa.

'If we run into Espinosa, he'll blow this little lot straight to hell.'

'It's a big sea, young William. That's rather the point. If your little French friend hadn't been such a greedy bastard in Maracaibo, perhaps we wouldn't be forced to play hide and seek with the Spanish.'

'Why are you keeping these things from them?'

'You think they don't know about the armada?'

'I think it's possible they don't.'

The *scritch* of Morgan's knife became a little more considered as he finished off his vandalistic carving in the rail of my beautiful ship. His Welsh accent had begun to crack in the Caribbean sun; it was slowly being replaced by something equally mellifluous but also rather odd, a nasal amalgam of London, West Country, African and something else, something new.

'How much money do you have, William?'

'More than I've ever had.'

'But not as much as you need.'

'Need?'

'Your eyes give nothing away.'

'I see no "need", Cap'n.'

'No indeed. No need at all. You just continue on, William Ablass. Like some ship that never loses the wind. Nothing stops you, does it?'

'I . . . endure.'

'But endurance needs money, Billy. That's why you're with me. I've seen you fight. The violence doesn't move you in the way it transports the other men. There's no lust in it. You fight the way an old furniture maker applies varnish: methodically, like you're not thinking. You look like someone who's been fighting for a hundred years.'

'I fight because I have to fight. It's where I find myself.'

'You often say remarkably odd things.'

'I beg your pardon.'

'No pardon needed.'

'You haven't answered my question.'

'Indeed not. Information is power, William. A captain understands that. These idiots were on the point of scampering off with your sodomising French friend. The only thing keeping them away from him is me. If I told them everything I know they'd also know what a big chance I'm taking. And if they knew that this whole enterprise would unravel faster than the underthings of our King's latest mistress.'

Morgan turned towards his cabin, but then turned back, almost as an afterthought.

'He's dead, you know.'

'L'Ollonais?'

'The very one.'

'How do you know this?'

'If not now, then very soon. He's an animal, William, an animal driven by its desires. And animals always get shot in the end. They'll tear him to pieces. Me, I'll die fat and gout-ridden on the veranda of a Jamaica plantation. Just watch me. You need to decide what you are.'

And he strutted off to bed, still fuming in that odd little way of his. I glanced down at the rail. It took a moment to decipher Morgan's carving, but it appeared to be four letters carved over and across each other. *P-T-S-I.*

That explained things, then.

Potosí. That's what Morgan's letters represented. A city, a mountain, but most importantly, a silver mine. A huge upturned rock full of treasure in high Peru, which the Spanish had been hollowing out for more than a hundred years. Madrid was Greater Spain's brain, but Potosí was its shiny metal heart, pumping silver pieces of eight all the way around the empire.

A direct attack on Potosí was forbiddingly unlikely, although Morgan had attacked cities hundreds of miles inland before. But there was a far easier option. Potosí's silver flood needed an outlet on the coast, where it could pour onto fleets of ships which would carry it back to Madrid. For several weeks of the year, one particular orifice opened up to the Spanish treasure fleet and acted as a tap for this silver stream: Portobelo. In those weeks, it was said, the silver was piled up in the streets and the town's mint churned out pieces of eight by the thousand. During the visit of the treasure fleet, the amount of silver waiting in Portobelo was said to be worth more than twice the annual income of England's king and government.

Morgan was surely not considering raiding Portobelo during the treasure fleet's visit. That would have been suicidal. But I wagered he was betting that enough of that fabulous wealth stayed, silted up, in Portobelo for the rest of the year to make an approach worthwhile. The stories of the permanent forts surrounding the town suggested there was something there to protect.

Every Brethren officer knew about the defences of Portobelo: two enormous forts at the estuary, designed to stop ships entering the mouth of the river on which Portobelo stood; numerous sentry houses and lookouts dotted around the shore; and another new fort which was even now being constructed right on top of the harbour itself. Even the coral around the harbour, it was said, was impervious to cannon fire. In the New World, only Cartagena and Havana had stronger defences than Portobelo.

The risks were enormous, the potential rewards gigantic. For an admiral-captain up against it, Portobelo was a target of great distinction. A successful raid would lead to riches, reputation, respect. All equally important, of course, to a short Welsh captain with his eye on posterity and even the governorship of his beloved Jamaica.

And there was something else, a rich, potent fact which had occurred to me straightaway and which, without doubt, was in the mind of my splendidly insecure admiral-captain. The unspeakable wealth and the chance to singe more Spanish beards were reasons enough to attack Portobelo. But on top of that, down there in the waters off Portobelo, his body despatched in full armour into the blue waters, dead of dysentery after weeks of hunting down a small fleet of Spanish treasure ships, lay the rotting bones of Morgan's great precursor, Francis Drake himself.

El Draque, sailing on the *Drake*, to meet Francis. With Long Billy, who had not seen his old friend for a hundred years. Destiny was twitching her skirts in our direction.

The next day, we left the little South Cays harbour and sailed south to Costa Rica. Still Morgan kept his own counsel, refusing to name the target. It would take all the powers of his Welsh persuasion to bring this crew along with him. But I had known, right away, that I would follow the admiral into the mouth of New Spain.

Soon after reaching Costa Rica Morgan did reveal the target

to his officers, to general dismay and outrage. Below decks was a frenzy of near-mutiny. A delegation of four New Model Army veterans came to see me immediately, in my official position. As quartermaster, I was entitled to question strategy, and even to refuse the mission, should I have wished to do so, which I most emphatically did not. They were allowed to ask me this. But they overplayed their hand.

There were a number of Cromwell's old foot soldiers among the Brethren. They still wore their New Model Army red coats with pride. They saw the Brethren fleet as a new model, too; a model for a New Republic. They dreamed of a time when captains would be elected and sovereignty would be vested in the crew. I had heard tell of pirate ships which were already run along these lines, of pirate captains being subject to votes and then being removed when they failed to measure up. I had even heard of constitutions and bills of rights.

These veterans met with me in my cabin, next to Morgan's, right beneath the aft deck. The five of us barely had room to move. I sat on my bunk. My height made standing impossible, and besides hunching up and squeezing caused the old Florida wound in my side to give me pain. The four old Roundheads were crushed together between my sea chest and the door, which they had closed carefully. This was the nearest approximation to a private conversation that was possible on board ship.

The oldest of the Roundheads, a man called Peter Sharp, spoke first. He was an East Anglian, from the Fens, just outside Cromwell's old parliamentary constituency at Cambridge. He had the same stolid immovability of the man he'd served, and whom I remembered.

'Quartermaster. We are here as representatives of the crew.'

I smiled at him.

'Indeed? Would you be *elected* representatives, Sharp? I didn't hear tell of a ballot.'

Sharp did not respond to this. He waited a second, as if to say no, we won't be debating like that, before continuing.

'There is great concern among the crew over the captain's plans for Portobelo.'

He waited again. I did the same. Eventually, Sharp went on.

'The crew is insisting that the captain reconsider. We believe that Portobelo is a dangerous fool's errand.'

I said nothing again, but relied on something else – a slight widening of the eyes, a near-smile, the beginnings of a furrow in the brow at that use of the word fool. I felt a great calmness and a sense that I could make these men do what I wanted, that their fear of me was irresistible. Sharp's face began to redden, even underneath the Caribbean sunburn. He swallowed before continuing. Before, he had been the very image of Old Ironside, remorseless and implacable. Now, he was suddenly uncertain. I was amazed at the speed of the change.

'We ask that you, quartermaster, intercede on our behalf with the captain.'

'Or?'

I said the little word quietly and then I said nothing else. Sharp considered.

'Or the crew may take destiny in its own hands.'

'Meaning mutiny.'

'Yes, quartermaster. If you choose to use the word, meaning mutiny.'

'Are you sure of yourself, Sharp?'

'Sure of myself, quartermaster?'

'There are four of you in this room with me, Sharp. Four old fools from the war. Not enough to take over a ship.'

'We have general support among the crew.'

'Ah, indeed? "General support." You are not used to life at

sea, I think, Sharp. It's not like life on the land, even in that great army in which you served. On land men will think of their futures and their families and their rights and will make judgements accordingly. They are operated on by an invisible hand, as it were. They respond to incentives of a particular kind. A rational kind.

'But this is a ship, Sharp. On a ship men seek something else. They seek security. They seek adventure. They seek something which is halfway between family and wealth. Fellowship, perhaps we should call it. A captain who can offer these things is more than your General and Protector ever was. This captain is their father and their mother and their brother and their general. They might grumble about him, they might shiver like scared women at the audacity of his plans, but get them in front of him, get them to look into his eyes and listen to his words, and all their grumbling and complaining will fall away. They'll sail over the edge of the world for him. And you'll be left on your own, the four of you, with nothing between you and the dark licking flames of Satan but me and the captain you betrayed.'

My voice remained quiet throughout this pretty little speech, but I felt a power surging within me, and a sense of right and entitlement. This must be how a king feels, I remember thinking to myself. And after a few seconds, Sharp's head dropped and he turned to make his way out of the cabin, followed by the three other veterans. They did not look at me, but I spoke to them, looking at the scuffed, dirty ends of my fingers all the while.

'One other thing. It's rumoured that Prince Maurice himself is held captive in Portobelo. Morgan wants to find him and take him back to London and the King. You may have other considerations. Incentives, you see, fellows. The invisible hand.'

I continued to admire my fingers. There was no sound for a moment, not even a whisper, as the Roundhead veterans took in what I had told them. The nephew of a king, within reach of their unforgiving republican hands. Then, the pounding of feet as they trooped out.

21 DECEMBER 1811: EVENING

The King's Head is in darkness, as one would expect. By this time of the evening, New Gravel Lane is a Bedlam of inebriation, but here, ironically right outside the Williamsons' alehouse, there is a little oasis of calm. Or perhaps *absence*.

Charles Horton is pretty drunk, and has not gone home to Abigail. She prefers not to see him than to see him drunk, and she is entirely inured to his night-time wanderings. Between here and Turner's room Horton had stopped at the Prospect of Whitby, drawn there both by its reputation and by the opportunities for information it represents. He has traded the little currency he has – stories of dried peas and beans, cotton shirts, Sheerness and pieces of eight – and in return he has learned some things, been disabused of some other things, and been roundly insulted for his pains by many of those he has approached. He asked questions of most of the people in the tavern, and was met either with puzzlement, laughter or rage (and near-violence, on occasion). He poked himself into a patchwork of other people's business, and he grew increasingly drunk as he bought gin and ale for shady men sitting in shady corners.

And so he has come to the King's Head, swaying silently in the dark, his mind beer-barrel hazy. The door to the deserted inn is a heavy one, but it has glass panels, and these glass windows are not shuttered. However, even in his current state he does not necessarily wish to be spotted smashing his way into premises which are still private and which are heavy with the aura of slaughter.

He heads uncertainly around the side of the building, down a dark and stinking side alley. The source of the stench, the privy described by Turner, is at the end of the alley, facing out onto the ridge of ground and wasteland behind. There is another door into the tavern here, and through it Horton can see a kitchen. So here, out of the view of the common throng, he smashes his way inside.

The kitchen is dank and cold. He tries to remember the layout of the place from his visit immediately after the murders. The sturdy brown leather armchair still sits in the middle of the room. As he walks in he feels something sticky underfoot, and a wave of boozy bile hits his throat with the thought of what it might be.

He needs some light. There is little prospect of finding any in here, so he goes out into the alley again and walks back into New Gravel Lane and down the street to a small shop, one of the general stores which scrape a living from the local boarding-house women. He buys four small candles and a taper, which the old shopkeeper lights from his own fire and which Horton carries back to the side alley and into the kitchen.

His head is beginning to pound. He still feels vaguely like vomiting.

He lights one of the candles, and its flame flickers across the kitchen, picking out strange angles and unexpected vectors.

His horror at what might have been on the floor is unconfirmed by the jittery gleam. There is only a suggestion of a darker area down there, and he cannot remember having seen anything when he visited in daylight. He steps over it anyway, towards the door that leads into the public bar. He knocks his thigh on Williamson's old chair, and pushes the door into the bar open with his free hand.

A sensation of a larger, more open space greets him. The candle flickers up into a higher ceiling and more distant walls, where shadows dance as the candle flame is buffeted by the draughts. He feels for the edge of the bar, and then along it. Jugs and bowls and tankards sit on shelves beneath the bar, and his hand feels around behind them, seeking, seeking.

There's nothing of interest there. He puts the candle down on the bar and walks around the other side, his head beginning to clear as he starts to consider the task at hand. He turns around and around within the place, mentally checking off things until a thought occurs to him.

Of course. The cellar.

He picks up the candle again, then thinks better of it, placing it back down and lighting one of the other three from its flame. Best keep this room as light as possible. He goes back behind the bar and into the kitchen and finds the door at the top of the steps down to the inn's cellar. The door is partly open, and he pushes at it with his toe.

A square of black opens in the wall, and he shines his candle down there. He remembers Thomas Anderson's story of the body down there, clenches his jaw, and steps down.

The ceiling is lower, of course. The barrels of beer sit along one wall, raised off the floor on wooden frames. From one of them runs a pipe, via some odd-looking contraption and then up through the ceiling to the bar above. One of those new beer engines, thinks Horton, filing away a thought that Williamson was a man of some means if he'd been able to afford such an innovation. The ladder up to the street is broken in two places, presumably from when the men clambered down here on the night of the murders.

He thinks. And thinks. And looks. And thinks.

A box, there in the corner. He goes towards it, and notices that the box is a metal sea chest, the kind every merchant sailor in Wapping would recognise. For them, it contains their life: clothes, tools, weapons. What did it contain for Williamson?

It's secure, of course. Otherwise someone, perhaps even a police officer or constable, would have nicked it by now. So how to get into it? Except of course he doesn't have to get into it. He just has to get it back to the Police Office.

The box is attached to the wall by a chain and Horton, a little drunker than he thinks he is, makes a decision. He places the candle on the floor and pulls the box out to make the chain taut. He stands on the box, and stamps down on the chain with all his weight. On the third stamp the chain suddenly wrenches out from the wall, and he stumbles forward with the momentum, hitting the side of his face against the brick. His feet scrabble on the stone cellar floor for a moment, and he nearly slides backwards, which would drag his face down the wall's masonry, but then his boots grip and he is still.

His face is pressed up against the wall, and he can see behind the beer barrels, where the flickering candlelight picks out something silver on the ground beneath the barrel nearest to him. He peels his face carefully from the wall, and then goes down on all fours, kicking the freed steel box behind him, taking care not to knock the candle over. He reaches beneath the barrel, his fingers moving in and out of the dirt and dust beneath it, and he tries not to think about the material his hand is picking up. He is just about to give up when he feels the hard edge of something metallic, and pulls it into his palm and then removes his hand and stands.

It is a coin, a heavy silver coin, and even before he has picked the candle up from the floor and shone it over his palm, he knows what kind of coin it will be. A piece of eight, here in the cellar of the King's Arms.

JULY 1668

Peter Sharp had seen a great many things in his pursuit of the good old cause. None of them were a bit like what he saw up against the walls of the Santiago Fort in Portobelo.

His middle-aged bones had been bent and broken in the service of God and Man (he drew no distinction). His scarred face was a map of English struggles. He'd served under Cromwell in the Eastern Association, and then under Montagu in the New Model Army, but Sharp was one of the thousands of soldiers left behind – morally, emotionally, theologically – by the amoral complexities of the Restoration. How was one such as he to understand one such as Edward Montagu, who had destroyed a king but had then commanded a fleet to retrieve the son of that very king to sit on the throne?

Montagu's betrayal was a sign. England must itself be damned if such a return to the old ways could be permitted by God. So Sharp had fled the slippery moral landscape of Europe and re-established himself among the Brethren of the Caribbean, where a man might make his ethical peace with the whoring and drinking and thieving in return for a spiritual freedom unavailable in Europe. Sharp prayed with passion, took no whores, drank no liquor, and when he followed Henry Morgan into battle the old bloodlust was on him and his sword parted flesh and bone in a way that felt once again sanctified.

Sharp was astute when it came to leaders. He knew what the plan to seize Portobelo was about: L'Ollonais, and Morgan's reputation. The scheme was preposterous, as if the Welshman was beginning to believe in his own myth, and Sharp had seen the danger of that before. He had seen it on Cromwell when they'd stood beneath the walls of Drogheda and Wexford – the sense that the cause had its own life and its own needs, the belief of a leader that he was chosen by God.

So Sharp had allowed himself to talk of mutiny, and had led the delegation to the strange quartermaster, as Brethren tradition dictated. Sharp felt the same awed fear of Long Billy Ablass as the rest of the crew. It was that fear which had caused so many to elect Billy their representative, for even Morgan must surely smell the danger which hung around Long Billy like the electrical crackle after a thunderstorm. Dark tales girdled the tall young man: how he'd tortured women in the service of the dread L'Ollonais; how he'd thrown babies from ramparts; how he and L'Ollonais had lived together in the woods above Tortuga, joined in some Satanic blasphemy of marriage, sacrificing children and sheep and smearing themselves in blood beneath a red Caribbean moon.

Sharp didn't believe half these things. The Brethren were notorious storytellers. He saw, though, the essential truth: Ablass was a crazy cold bastard who nonetheless had Morgan's ear and Morgan's trust and perhaps even Morgan's fear.

But watching the quartermaster's face during their disastrous conference, Sharp had believed every single word of those tales about him. The man's eyes had been as empty as shells. Looking into them Sharp had become a child again, wide awake in a Fenland night, the wind howling off the North Sea outside and demons and spectres wriggling in the shadows of the room in which he and his brothers slept.

He'd backed down, and because of that he was now standing on the deck of the *Drake*, only days away from Portobelo. Sharp told himself he was here because of Prince Maurice – if the old dead king's nephew really was in Portobelo, Sharp and the other old Ironsides in the fleet needed no further excuse to justify their sudden disinterest in mutiny. But Sharp knew why he was really here: he was afraid of what Billy Ablass would do to him if he wasn't.

An ancient rowing boat was inching its way around the coast, away from Portobelo and towards the ship. Two or three of the men on the boat were signalling wildly. Morgan and his quartermaster appeared at the rail, and the captain ordered that the boat be allowed to come alongside.

Six men were inside, so weak and frail they needed to be carried up to the ship. Sharp lifted one of them himself; as he pulled him over the rail the man's head rolled back and a pair of half-mad eyes stared up at him, as if they were looking at Satan himself.

Another one of the six began talking, quietly and with urgency despite his condition, kneeling on the deck. Morgan made his way down to the waist of the ship, his silent quartermaster beside him, to listen to what the man had to say.

He was English, he said, as were all six men. They were the remnants of an earlier Brethren fleet, under Edward Mansfield, which had taken the island of Providence two years earlier. Mansfield had left it under the guard of fifty English Brethren but the Spanish had retaken the island, locking up the surviving Englishmen. These six men were some of the survivors; there were still more in Portobelo.

As the man spoke, Henry Morgan became visibly excited, and as the story of the Providence Brethren came to an end, the captain placed one hand on the head of the kneeling man and turned his face to his crew, for all the world like a priest offering benediction. He carefully looked into the eyes of each and every pirate, weighing them up and nodding occasionally. Then he breathed deeply, drawing in the energy of the moment.

'You heard the man, lads. There's English Brethren locked up in Portobelo, dying by the day, their loyal bones broken and shattered by Papists and inquisitors. They need rescuing, and who's going to wait for the King's navy to do the job? How many of them will still be alive by the time the Admiralty bureaucrats fill in all their bits of paper? None of them, I'll wager. Not one. So are you with me? There's treasure in Portobelo. All the treasure of Potosí, silver lying in the street. But that's all a secondary consideration. There's good hearty Brethren need us to rescue them, shipmates. There's us and freedom on one side, and idolatrous bastard gaolers on the other. And there's treasure scattered *all around*. So do we go in, fellows? I say again: who's with me?'

An enormous *huzzah!* rose from the crew, answering Morgan's question with no further doubt. Some of the old Ironsides may have muttered their concern, but Morgan had the rest of the crew once again. The Welshman's luck had turned. He grinned at his quartermaster, took his hand off the head of the rescued man as if he was now forgotten, and walked back to his cabin.

As the crew dispersed, each man moving to his usual position with adventure sizzling in his head, Sharp squatted down alongside the rescued man, who remained, head down, kneeling on the deck.

'What of the prince? What of Maurice?' Sharp asked. The

man looked at him, but appeared confused, as if he didn't recognise the name. The excitement he saw in Sharp's face caused his expression to change; something cunning came into his eyes, and he forced a smile.

'Yes! Yes! He was with us! He is there still!'

Sharp felt his heart surge, despite that change in the man's expression. He would choose to believe this desperate man and his tales of prisoners and princes. He would follow Morgan and the quartermaster into Portobelo.

Morgan ordered the fleet to be anchored some miles to the south-east of Portobelo, wary of the two imposing forts which protected the harbour mouth. Twenty-three small boats had been towed from the South Cays, and most of the men climbed into them, leaving only skeleton crews on the larger ships. The boats started to make their way up the coast.

For four days they travelled, only at night, cutting through the dark blue water; during the day, they pulled the boats up on shore and slept under the trees, terrified of snakes and burning in the heat.

On the fourth night, the little flotilla of boats came across a fishing boat. In it were three men. Morgan stood up in his boat and yelled something at the men, but they replied in a hail of Spanish and some other language no one recognised. Morgan sat down again, and after a few moments Long Billy spoke to the men in Sharp's boat (the quartermaster had spent most of the previous four days in Sharp's boat, watching the old soldier with calm eyes and causing the other men in the boat to whisper and pull away from Sharp, as if he was diseased in some way).

'Take me alongside the admiral, lads,' said Billy. They began to row over to Morgan's boat. As they came alongside, the quartermaster stood and called across to Morgan's boat.

'They may know a way into the town,' he said, his voice

clear on the still water. Morgan did not answer. 'It would be wise to question them, at least.'

Sharp saw the admiral look up at that, and hold Billy's gaze for a few seconds. Then he nodded sharply and looked away as he spoke.

'Then question them.'

The quartermaster grinned. 'Let's go and get them, fellows,' he said as he sat down, his flat Oxfordshire accent uninflected. They began to row again, the man at the tiller steering towards the little fishing boat. The quartermaster kept his eyes on Sharp, a smile painted on his face.

They seized the fishing boat without resistance, and the quartermaster beckoned half-a-dozen men into it, starting with Sharp, and sailed it into the shore. In the boat were two Negroes, and a *zambo*, half-African and half-Indian. The Brethren took these men up the beach, where they were held down, a pair of sailors to each captive. Sharp held down the arms of the *zambo*. Torches were lit and pushed into the sand, as if for a ritual. At the back of the beach, the trees moved their leaves in the sickly night breeze.

The Negroes squirmed and shrieked, but the *zambo* was silent, staring up at Billy, who was standing at the feet of the three captives. He was not looking at the Brethren or at the captives. He was gazing towards the back of the beach. Sharp felt the wind pick up, and then heard something from behind him, from within the trees. It sounded like people humming.

The quartermaster looked away after a moment, knelt down at the side of the first Negro, and pulled out his knife. He muttered something in Spanish. The man's response was a splatter of yelled words in his native tongue, unintelligible to any of the Brethren. The *zambo* was silent. Billy tried English.

'We need a guide to take us into Portobelo. Will you help us?'

There was no change in the Negro's chattering, not even a

shift in register. He had no idea what Billy was saying. But it occurred to Sharp that Billy was not speaking to the African; he was speaking to the *zambo*. Through a break in the African's shrieks, Sharp could hear the humming noise from behind them growing in intensity. Were there people in the trees, watching them?

With deliberate care, the quartermaster leaned across and cut the Negro's throat down to the bone, from ear to ear. The blood squirted up his arm and into his face, as well as across the body of the second Negro and over the hands and arms of the Brethren holding both the blacks down. Two of them shouted and started to lift their hands.

'Hold them!' yelled the quartermaster, his voice booming across the beach, and the Brethren grabbed the arms and legs of the prisoners again, even the now-dead one. Sharp looked at the man opposite him holding the legs of the *zambo* and saw that he was staring into the trees behind them, not even glancing at the chaos of blood and bone where the first Negro's neck used to be.

He hears it too!

For a moment, the screams of the surviving Negro were echoed in the woods behind by the shriek of some hunted creature, which roared in fear and hunger. The creature's shrieks were cut off with a high-pitched yelp, as if something else there in the jungle had picked it up and ripped its throat. The hum continued, growing louder and broader and deeper.

The quartermaster rolled the dead Negro over and along the beach. Sand stuck to the sticky blood on his front, arms and neck, creating huge orange swirls on the black skin which flickered in the light from the Brethren's torches.

Still the *zambo* said nothing. Looking down at his upside-down face, Sharp saw the man's eyes were closed and he was frantically whispering some kind of catechism.

'Open his eyes,' said the quartermaster. Sharp looked at Billy. 'Do it.'

Sharp knelt on the *zambo*'s arms to keep them in place, and placed the thumb and forefinger of both hands over his eyes, forcing him to look out. His eyes rolled up and around, a frenzy of colour and white. Sharp turned his head to look at the sticky black-and-orange skin of the dead Negro.

Billy leaned over the second Negro, and showed him the bloody knife. Blood from the blade dripped down into the black man's face.

The *zambo* was starting to moan, a moan which turned into a shriek as Billy gently pushed the end of his blade into the second Negro's eye. The humming from the woods now had loud human shrieks within it, as of women dying in the trees. One of the Brethren leaned away and was sick, and then, like all his fellows, he looked back into the trees in terror, as if something with claws and teeth was about to burst out onto the beach. The Negro screamed and screamed, the *zambo* screaming with him, and the quartermaster smiled, as if just noticing the *zambo* again. He flashed his knife across the Negro's neck, and once again cut it down to the bone. More blood spurted into his face. He leaned into the *zambo,* dark drops falling from his chin into the sand.

'Now,' he said. 'Now, you. Are you going to help me get what I want, or am I going to cut your skin from your bones?'

The *zambo* was gibbering, but one word could be made out. 'Sí . . . sí . . . sí . . .'

The quartermaster stood and wiped the blade of his knife on his rough cotton trousers. He looked back into the woods, which were now suddenly almost silent, only speaking in whispers as the breeze moved through the leaves. Billy looked at Sharp again, and smiled that empty smile. He pulled out a purse, and from his purse he pulled out a coin, a piece of eight.

He flicked it into the air and it landed on the body of the first Negro he'd killed. No one moved to pick it up.

They took the *zambo* back to the flotilla.

The following night, under the *zambo*'s direction, they beached their boats three miles outside Portobelo, and the final march by land began.

Caridad was woken up from a dream of jaguars in the woods by her father shouting and stamping around outside her bedroom door. She was wide awake in an instant. Her father's noise was unusual enough, but even more arresting were the sounds from outside the little house which she had heard immediately upon waking. She clambered over her bed to the window to look down into the street, ignoring the protests as she trampled over her two sisters who were still dozing beneath the covers.

Outside in the street people were rushing out of their homes and shouting, but in a funny way, like they were still half asleep. She laughed to herself as the old man who ran the tavern across the street lurched out of his front door still in a nightshirt. How extraordinary, to see an old man outside in his night clothes! What on earth could be happening?

Her two sisters joined her at the window, chattering with excitement. Their father was still shouting as he clattered down the stairs and their mother burst through the bedroom door, her hair in disarray. She dissolved into sudden tears when she saw the three girls clustered at the window and swooped down upon them, her arms stretched wide to gather them up.

'Quick, we must hide, we must hide.'

She squeezed them tight, weeping and speaking of strange men and imminent danger, and Caridad wondered how this was supposed to help, if indeed there was somebody coming to seize them. She wriggled out from under her mother's arm

(Josefina and Perlita remained where they were, crying in sympathy with their mother now, no longer excited by the commotion in the street), and went back to the window.

She got there in time to see her father burst out of their front door, his musket in his hands. He rushed down the street, glancing back once at his family, seeing Caridad looking back at him. He raised his gun above his head, waved at her with his other hand and shouted – 'Caridad! Be my brave one!' – before disappearing into the stream of men which was making its way down to the fort at the edge of the river. She felt her heart surge with pride and excitement, and filed the image of her heroic father disappearing into the crowd for a later painting.

Caridad saw what was happening. The forts of Portobelo – the new one, still being built and unnamed, and Santiago Castle, the big fearsome place out towards the mouth of the river – were manned by only a few full-time soldiers. Most men in the town bore some responsibility for assisting those soldiers in times of crisis, and her father the grocer was one of the part-time guards. Someone had raised an alarm, and now the men were running towards the forts to fight off whoever or whatever was out there.

Her mother and sisters were still sobbing behind her. Caridad thought about going out into the street to find out what was happening. This kind of alarm wasn't at all unusual – whenever a strange ship was seen off the estuary, the people of the town would prepare themselves, and her mother would sob and worry herself about 'strange men'. Portobelo was a rich place, Caridad understood, one of the richest places in Greater Spain, and while she was too young to understand what this meant, she saw its results all around her: the tension during the weeks of the treasure ships; the carts piled high with silver and cob coins coming down from the fabled Potosí. And these moments of running and tension, when the town seemed to fear for itself without truly believing it was in any real danger. It was like the games the boys played after school, all this running around and shouting and shoving. Games she always tried to join, and which were always forbidden to her.

'Can I go out, mama?' she asked, not turning away from the window. There was a break in her mother's sobbing, and she did look round then, and saw that old sign of disbelief in her mother's eyes, like she was a stranger's child that had been accidentally left in the house. Her mother shook her head, open-mouthed, before resuming her position, head bowed, sobbing along with her two other daughters. Caridad sighed, and looked back out of the window.

Up and down the dusty street, women, children and old men – those left behind by the exodus to the forts – were throwing their shutters closed and barricading their doors. There were slamming sounds from all around, and shouts from mothers to children. She saw one boy – she thought it was Hilario, the naughtiest boy in their school – running down the street towards the fort, and she thought she could hear the echo of Hilario's mother shouting after him, begging him to come home.

A few minutes of silence. Caridad began to wonder if this was really some kind of pretend game, perhaps a way of practising for a real invasion, when suddenly there was an enormous BOOM from down by the river, followed by an echoing splash of water. It made her jump, that gigantic sound, and her mother and sisters sobbed even louder. Similar cries of fear could be heard from behind the closed shutters of the other houses. Only a few windows were open now, and most of them had a child of about Caridad's age in them, looking out excitedly into the street.

Another moment of silence followed, but then came an even

more fearful noise, as a great company of men began shouting and, Caridad thought, *laughing*. It was a devilish sound, as if a company of demons had disgorged itself onto the shoreline and was even now firing up cauldrons and sharpening tridents, preparing to throw the locals into the inferno. For the first time, she felt afraid. Even her sisters and mother became silent as they listened to that terrible din.

She heard musket fire behind the shouting and laughing, and saw torches dancing their way up from the river and into the town itself, followed by more of that alien shouting and laughter. There were screams from behind the shutters now, and the angry shouts of old men who sounded desperate to be out there, in the fight, face to face with the invading demons. Caridad thought of her father, and silently prayed that he was safe within one of the forts, firing his musket down into the demons below, perhaps sending them into the next world with a bullet of lead between their horns.

The first demons appeared in the street beneath the dancing torches, scruffy demons who looked like they hadn't eaten properly or washed in weeks. A few dozen of them ran from house to house, apparently randomly, shouting and laughing and smashing in the occasional door. They would rush into these unlucky houses and Caridad could hear screams and shouts from within, and then the men would emerge with various bits of treasure – jewellery, plate, clothes – in their arms, dragging behind them the occupants and proceeding, cackling, back down the street to stash their gains and their prisoners. Or perhaps they meant to kill them? Caridad frowned at this puzzle. Why not kill them then and there? Where were they taking them?

Somehow, they missed Caridad's house in this first frenzy, and she was careful to hide herself every time one of the demons looked up at the window, unwilling to draw attention to herself. Her mother, hearing the noises outside, whispered fiercely at her to step away from the open window, but Caridad ignored her, as was her wont. For perhaps fifteen minutes the invading demons busied themselves with most of the other houses on the street, but then it came – a knock at their window, a shout, and she could look down on three or four of them as they tried to get in through the heavy front door. She thought about dropping something on their heads, but then with a rip their door gave way, and the demons were inside.

Portobelo was taken almost without a fight. Most of the townspeople, including its mayor and other dignitaries, were dragged from their homes, spluttering with dismay and astonished by the sudden appearance of Anglo-Saxons. The invaders simply ignored the massive Santiago fort just outside the town, and the defenders inside the fort fired only a single cannonball into the sea which did nothing but make Morgan's buccaneers laugh delightedly at their ineptitude.

As well as seizing the place's riches, Morgan planned to ransom the townspeople, so there were strict orders to leave the people unharmed. The locals were taken from their homes and poured into the town's new gaol, where they were forced to listen to the sound of New Spain's silvery entrepôt being emptied of its abundance.

Sharp and the other Ironsides went in search of Prince Maurice. It took less than an hour to find the Brethren prisoners from Providence, still in chains in a decrepit old dungeon beneath an empty armoury. It was immediately clear that the prince wasn't there; some of the prisoners claimed that a 'great man' who had been taken in Puerto Rico had been removed from their prison months before and taken to Peru. There was to be no Roundhead revenge in Portobelo.

The Ironsides freed the English prisoners and rejoined the main body of the Brethren, which had by now gathered near the still-dangerous Santiago fort. The town was in their hands, but the fort remained. To get the full fleet into the harbour to remove Portobelo's riches Morgan needed to secure the place, but the walls were impenetrable, and a determined force of local men remained within.

The Brethren were hunkered down on the beach near the fort, behind a motley collection of fishing boats, rocks and sheds. Most were looking expectantly at their admiral, who stood with the quartermaster just a little up the beach, sheltered from the guns of the fort by the hull of an old pinnace which had been dragged onto the shore. The quartermaster was talking urgently into Morgan's ear, gesticulating towards the fort. Morgan was saying nothing, and for a while the Brethren's excitement and good cheer was tempered by the sight of their admiral's indecision. The quartermaster grew more and more animated. Eventually, Morgan snapped something at the quartermaster and then turned his back on him and stomped towards the Brethren. He approached Sharp and the old Ironsides.

'He wants you,' said the admiral. 'Do whatever he says.'

And then Morgan walked away.

Caridad burned with frustration. They were crowded into a windowless room inside Portobelo's gaol. She could see nothing, couldn't even hear that much – the walls were thick, and all that came through them was the occasional crack of a musket shot, presumably from somewhere close to the gaol. There were no shouts, no demonic laughter. In fact, everything was drowned out by the endless sobbing of the women and children in the gaol. Where did they find the tears, to cry so much?

She wondered where her father was. She hoped he had killed some of the demons. She was sure he had – he was without doubt the best shot with a musket in the town, a fact she had asserted with some physical force during a smart fight with Hilario only two weeks before.

With that thought, Hilario himself appeared at the bars of the cell, and seeing her he shouted excitedly.

'Caridad! They're taking us out!'

Hilario was standing with a half-dozen other children, all of whom she knew from school. Behind them stood a man she recognised even though she could not see his face: the schoolteacher, Gonzalez, with whom she'd struggled incessantly for two years now. He was a young man, who'd come fresh from Madrid with high ideals, but whose stuck-up ways and obvious dislike for the hard colonial life made him a figure of fun and contempt among the schoolchildren. Caridad hated him, but for now she could only feel something like sympathy.

Gonzalez looked terrible. He was held up by two fierce-looking demons, who wore odd-looking round helmets and fearsome chest plates. The teacher's face was sunk down upon his chest. Another demon wearing the same armour as the first two, with a terribly scarred face, stood next to them, and behind this little group stood a fourth, young and tall with dark black hair, who stared into the cell with hooded eyes which made Caridad shiver and think of the dream of night-time jaguars which had been interrupted by the arrival of the demons.

This tall figure muttered something at the schoolteacher, in the strange language of the demons. His voice was quiet but everyone fell silent when they heard it. It had an unsettling quality.

The schoolteacher raised his head, and several of the

women gasped as his eyes met theirs. His face was empty, as if all the energy within him had been drained away. The eyes gazed into the cell, but they were flat, unseeing. Only when they fell on Caridad did they show a flicker of humanity.

'Her,' said Gonzalez. 'Her, and her sisters. God forgive me.'

The scarred demon took some keys, opened the cell door, and grabbed for Caridad and her sisters. Their mother screamed and jumped up to scratch at his face, but he shoved her back into the throng of sobbing bodies and pulled the three girls out. The other two armoured demons shoved the schoolteacher into the cell, where some of the women moved towards his prone body, as if determined to hurt him. The demons, now with nine children, marched out of the gaol.

In procession they made their way to the fort. Caridad's sisters were crying, but quietly, as if they were terrified they would be punished for making a noise. Hilario burbled away in Caridad's ear.

'I reckon they're taking us back to our fathers,' he said.

Caridad frowned at him.

'What do you mean?'

'Well, look who's here. Me, you, your sisters, Christóbal and Diego there, their old man's a guard at the fort . . .'

'You mean, all nine of us have got fathers who work at the Santiago?'

'Looks like it to me.'

'Oh.'

Caridad looked at her sisters, and for the first time in her young life she understood the fear they always seemed to feel.

They approached the beach, and there Caridad saw dozens of the demons, most of them hunkered down behind boats and other obstacles, watching the group approach and then stop. It was quiet on the beach, deathly quiet. No guns were firing, and up ahead, rising up at the water's edge, was the stone face of the Santiago. Caridad could see the heads of men moving up there, and wondered if one of them was her father.

There was a shout from the fort, but no response from the Brethren on the beach. Caridad felt strong arms grab her beneath the armpits, and she was lifted up by someone impossibly strong and held in the air before him as he started to walk down the beach. He spoke to her then, in her own language, and she heard a humming sound in the air, and the words he spoke were the worst things she had ever heard:

'Be still, little one. You are beyond rescue.'

From behind her, she heard Hilario shout something, and her sisters scream. She expected they were being lifted and carried, just like her.

Without warning, a volley of shots was fired down from the Santiago, crashing into the water which lapped the shore. Caridad felt something hot and agonising flower in her chest, barely ten years old, and just before she died she heard a familiar sound from the ramparts above them: the sound of her father shouting again, shrieking really, his distraught words the loudest sound in the world.

'No! My brave one! Oh, in God's name, stop firing!'

That night the Brethren celebrated. They would bleed Portobelo and its hinterlands dry over the coming days, and Morgan would negotiate a ransom with the governor of Panama which would see Spain pay handsomely for the return of her stronghold and her people. It would be a triumph, Morgan's greatest triumph, but for now the Brethren contented themselves with drinking Portobelo's fine brandy and eating its fine food. The women were largely left alone, as was their custom.

Sin stalked Portobelo that night, and Sharp shrank from it. He watched his fellow Ironsides fall, one by one, into their cups. He took his prayer book into a small deserted house, climbed up to the first floor and knelt down beneath a window which looked up at a starry, clear South American sky. The householder would have been a Catholic, but Sharp prepared his own simple Protestant ceremony in this undecorated room. He prayed for his immortal soul, the memory of the dying children who'd shielded them hot in his head, the terror of that humming in the trees thrumming in his memory. There had been evil on that beach and evil in the town that night, and Peter Sharp could smell it on him. He washed himself in prayer.

Wrapped up in contemplation, he did not hear the steady feet on the stair, nor did he see the moonlight shadow of the shape appear on the wall beside him. He was allowed to finish his prayer. Only when he had done so did the quartermaster speak.

'Did he answer?'

Sharp stood up quickly, turning towards the voice, his hand on his bloody sword. The quartermaster stood at the door of the room, his pale face floating in moonlit gloom. He was smiling.

The question was asked again.

'Did he answer?'

'He answers every day,' said Sharp, in a whisper.

'He does, does he? You hear his voice?'

The voice was ghostly and dry, like the dusty remnants of a dead, desiccated bird. Sharp said nothing, waiting. His legs and arms shook, quivering with anticipation.

'You hear him, like you hear me now?'

Still nothing.

'Why do you not answer?'

'Because I do not understand, nor recognise, the question.'

'Ah.'

The quartermaster stepped into the room, his long coat brushing the door frame as he entered.

'You did well today, Sharp. You followed your orders to the letter. And you heard it, didn't you? Tonight, and the other night, on the beach?'

'Heard what?'

'Well, you know what I'm talking about. You heard what I heard. You all heard it.'

'I saw . . . I *saw* evil on that beach. An evil perpetrated by you.'

'Ah, indeed? I got you into this town. I made you rich. And, still, you heard something.'

'And what if I did?'

'Well, it is of some importance to me. That others can hear it. It means they are perhaps damned as well. I have heard that infernal humming before, you see. When I was damned.'

Sharp's eyes widened at that, and his hands tightened on the sword.

'Damnation is important to you people, as I understand it. Your religion has always been something of a closed book to me. Of late, I admit to being sorely offended by it.'

'You are stating that I . . . am damned?'

'Sharp, would you really expect a benevolent creator to allow you into heaven after today?'

Sharp's scarred, leathery cheeks grew wet. His eyes swam with a bitter knowledge.

'But who can tell, after all?' said the quartermaster. 'Who knows what comes after this? If anything at all? I have to say, it seems unlikely to me that there is any hereafter, sweet or otherwise. But if there is, my dear old soldier, I fear it is not welcoming of vicious old murderers like ourselves, who crouch behind children to avoid being shot.'

The old Ironside pulled out his sword, and pointed it at the quartermaster.

'I am not damned, curse you.'

'Possibly none of us is, Sharp. But if any of us is, after today you most assuredly are.'

The Ironside ran at the quartermaster, and his sword cut through Billy's stomach and rammed itself into the wall behind. Sharp heard an *ahhhh* whispered in his ear, and then felt something cold and hard against his throat, and there was a deep, familiar hum.

'Consider this a gift,' said the quartermaster as he cut the old soldier's throat. 'I'll take your life for you. Your senseless book of rules permits no suicide. No reason to take chances with eternity. Is this not kinder than the consolations of preachers?'

The Ironside fell to the floor. After a moment, his sword clattered down beside him. A piece of eight was dropped on the floor and the quartermaster went back down the stairs, his gait no longer quite so certain.

BOOK 3

Sloane

In the sugar-islands Negroes are a very important object of attention. The following observations, therefore, are worthy to be remembered:

The Congo Negroes are comely and docile, but not hardy enough for the labour of the field, they should therefore be kept for household business, or taught the mechanic arts, and they will then turn to very good account.

The Pawpaws from the Gold Coast are the best for field labour, but no Negroe should be bought old; such are always sullen and unteachable, and frequently put an end to their own lives.

A Cormantee will never brook servitude, though young, but will either destroy himself, or murder his master.

All Negroes are subject to worms, and other disorders, arising from change of climate and food; they should, therefore, when first purchased, be blooded, and purged with vervain and sempre-vive; they should be allowed plenty of food easily digested, and treated with kindness, they will then take to labour by degrees, and perform their task with chearfulness.

'How to Maintain "Negroes" on Plantations', *The Gentleman's Magazine*, October 1764

23 DECEMBER 1811

The funeral of the Williamsons is held at St Paul's Church, Shadwell. The venue is not auspicious. The old place is forgotten and increasingly ignored, and is no longer accustomed to any kind of public attention. The church authorities are already considering tearing it down, and it is almost dead even now. For years, bits of ceiling have been known to fall in on the congregation. The outside is blotchy and unkempt. Squat, plain and unregarded, it is the short ugly idiot cousin of the awesome St George in the East, a few hundred yards down the Ratcliffe Highway. St George's is all Power and Glory. St Paul's is more Decay and Sheepishness.

These days, the church is only opened for baptisms and for burials, though why anyone should want their new child welcomed into God's family inside the ratty confines of St Paul's is beyond the understanding of most of the local people.

Burials are a different matter, as this is a seagoing church, and seagoing folk like a good send-off. Dozens of captains and quartermasters and bo'suns and midshipmen lie under the ground around the sad old place, their rotting bones the dry echoes of lost limbs, ripped-out eyes, crushed lungs and broken, blighted dreams. The little crooked churchyard is a history book of the maritime dead, an index of Britain's global sprawl.

No one decided the Williamsons should be buried here, except perhaps old Williamson himself, pondering intimations of his own coming destruction. There seem to be no next of kin to take responsibility. With no one around to decide for them (only Kitty Stillwell, their distraught granddaughter, and she is not old enough nor, just now, sane enough to take on the responsibility), St Paul's it is.

The send-off is conducted under the haunted eyes of the Reverend Mr Denis, the father of a hollowed-out congregation. His impassioned eulogy to the fine couple has been rather too overwhelming for his own weak spirits, and he has had to stop the service on a number of occasions to allow himself to recover. The people in the church are rather steadier in their emotions. A good number of the women are weeping, but quietly and with little public display, shoulders sobbing and faces held in handkerchiefs.

The reverend aside, calm mourning is the prescribed order of the day. This has been the stated wish of the magistrates of Shadwell (still burning with indignation over the meddling of John Harriott in their affairs), who have been uncharacteristically decisive and deliberate in ensuring that the Williamson funeral is carried off with the formality and consideration they feel it is due. They have arranged for their constables and officers to watch the service and, more to the point, to guard it. They have decided they want no repeat of the wailing scenes of dismay that accompanied the burial of the Marrs. Shadwell must be seen as an altogether more mannered place. A place of discretion, balance and piety. Magistrate Story has led the planning of the operation and has made it clear in no uncertain terms to Reverend Mr Denis and his skeleton church staff that no public displays of hysteria will be countenanced; that such displays are simply impious. The reverend's own grievous outpourings are in this context frankly undesirable. Capper and Markland, while ignoring Story's more transcendent obsessions, are in full agreement that emotions must be held in check. Panic is raging around the streets of Shadwell, and a funeral such as this can conduct panic as effectively as any electrical experiment at the Royal Institution.

The Reverend Mr Denis is now reaching the end of his heartfelt sermon, and there are audible tears in the congregation. The constables and watchmen remain stony-faced (some of the watchmen are in fact swaying slightly under the influence of alcohol, but even these are sufficiently well drilled to keep their mouths turned down and their brows furrowed). Denis leads the congregation in one more prayer, and then the pallbearers pick up the coffins of John and Elizabeth Williamson (Bridget Harrington has already been buried, at a small family occasion on the south coast). The congregation follows Denis out of the church into the damp air outside. Shadwell itself seems to have caught the subdued mood; all the shops and inns have closed out of respect, and quiet crowds hang around the gates to the churchyard, their combined breath rising into the air and becoming one with the deep London fog, just as it had done when they'd watched the Marrs being taken away to rest. It is as if London itself is breathing. The funeral entourage tramps over the damp earth to the two open graves, which are squeezed in between dead sea captains and expired shopkeepers. The coffins are lowered, while Denis reads his prayers and women weep more deeply, their sobs dampened by the wet fog, as if they are coming from the far Surrey shore of the crowded, busy river, where the forests of masts make their own congregation even in the face of Shadwell's mourning.

Among the local constables dotted throughout the crowd are Hewitt and Hope, a double-act of righteous heavy-handedness well known to the local people, several of whom have felt the fists of Hewitt upon their face while Hope pinned their arms behind them. Backhanded payments and violently extracted confessions are very much their stock-in-trade. As the ceremony begins to reach its conclusion a young man in a greatcoat, who stands at least a head taller than those around him, approaches Hewitt and Hope and starts talking to them quietly, towards the back of the large crowd around the open graves. A few people turn to look, scandalised by the lack of respect, but most of them turn hurriedly away when they see the two officers who are doing the talking. The tall young man is pointing to someone in the crowd around the graves and Hewitt-or-Hope is nodding vigorously while Hope-or-Hewitt follows his pointing finger to look at the subject of their conversation. After several minutes of muttered talk the tall young man limps away, leaving Hewitt and Hope to glare into the crowd as the ceremony comes to a close.

The mourners within the churchyard and around its perimeter begin to disperse, and Hewitt-and-Hope follow one particular man – a rather attractive, if somewhat dissolute-looking, young man with long hair and an easy manner – back along the Highway, down New Gravel Lane, through some winding streets and to the door of a boarding house called the Pear Tree. Here, the young man stops, turns and speaks to them, and looks startled as Hewitt-and-Hope, moving as one deadly organism, arrest him.

Thus John Williams is taken, and to his great surprise becomes the principal object of Shadwell's spatchcock investigation.

Hewitt and Hope take Williams back to the Shadwell Police Office, barely a quarter-mile away from the boarding house. There he is interviewed immediately by the quiet, terrified but periodically effective Capper. Having placed Williams in a room with Capper, Hewitt and Hope seek out a rat-faced man in decrepit breeches and coat who has been hanging around the offices. This is Your Correspondent from *The Times*, and he has been reporting on the case under a special arrangement with the Shadwell magistrates (it had been Markland who had considered, in his canny self-serving way, that a tame reporter willing to print what he is told might be just what he and his colleagues needed, given the absence of any real progress). The officers lead Your Correspondent to the small room where Capper and Williams are, and Hewitt-and-Hope whisper something into his ear as they lead him inside. Your Correspondent nods his understanding as the door closes.

The interview with Williams lasts two hours – at least four times as long as previous interviews in the case. At the end of it, Capper scurries away to discuss matters with Story and Markland. He finds them celebrating the success of their efforts to keep the Williamson funeral quiet (Markland is enjoying a sherry, Story does not drink but in any case is comfortably high on his own righteousness). Capper reports the particulars of his interview with John Williams. Markland pours himself another sherry to celebrate, and hands one to Capper as well. Story kneels and prays, something to which his fellow-magistrates have become well used.

Your Correspondent, having observed the interview with Williams and having been given additional 'background material' by Hewitt-and-Hope, disappears into the late-afternoon twilight to put a story together. After some back-slapping and another sherry (and another prayer) the three Shadwell magistrates call in Hewitt-and-Hope, who then hoist up their trousers and paint on their official faces before retrieving

Williams from the interview room and telling him he is to be remanded in Coldbath Fields Prison. He protests, violently, asking on what evidence this is being done. Hewitt-and-Hope look at each other, and shut the door to the room. A few minutes and a handful of dull thuds later the door reopens and Williams, his head bowed and his arms held, one each, by the two officers, is escorted out of the office.

The next day is Christmas Eve. *The Times* breaks its story with little fanfare, on page three.

MURDERS IN NEW GRAVEL LANE etc. SHADWELL POLICE OFFICE

Several persons were examined yesterday at Shadwell Police-office, charged on suspicion, but no positive proof could be brought home to any of them.

A seafaring man, named John Williams, underwent a very long and rigid interrogation. The circumstances of suspicion alleged against him were, that he had been frequently seen at the house of Williamson the publican, and that he had been more particularly seen there about seven o'clock on Thursday evening last; that on the same evening he did not go home to his lodgings until about twelve, when he desired a fellow-lodger, a foreign sailor, to put out his candle; that he was a short man, and had a lame leg; that he was an Irishman; and that previous to this melancholy transaction, he had little or no money; and that when he was taken into custody, he had a good deal of silver.

These suspicious circumstances having been proved against him, the Magistrates desired him to give an account of himself. He avowed that he had been at Mr Williamson's on Thursday evening, and at various other times. He had known Mr. and Mrs. W. a considerable time, and was very intimate there. On Thursday evening, when he was talking to Mrs Williamson, she was very cheerful, and patted him on the cheek when she brought him some liquor. He was considered rather in the light of a friend than a mere customer of the house.

When he left their house he went to a surgeon's, in Shadwell, for the purpose of getting advice for the cure of his leg, which had been a considerable number of years disabled in consequence of an old wound. From thence he went to a female chirurgeon in the same neighbourhood, in hopes of getting his cure completed at a less expense than a surgeon's charge. He then went farther west, and met some female acquaintance, and, after visiting several public-houses, he returned to his lodgings and went to bed.

The circumstance of his desiring his fellow-lodger to put out his candle, arose in consequence of his finding the man, who was a German, lying in bed with a candle in one hand, with a pipe in his mouth, and a book in the other. Seeing him in that situation, and apprehending that the house might be set on fire by his carelessness, he told him to put out his lights, and not expose the house to the danger of being burnt to the ground. He accounted for the possession of the money found upon him, as the produce of some wearing-apparel he left as pledges at a pawnbroker's. He never made any mystery of his having been at Mr. Williamson's on Thursday evening; and on the contrary, he told his landlady, and several other people, that he had been with poor Mrs. Williamson and her husband a very short time before they were murdered, and remarked how cheerful Mrs. Williamson was.

Under all the circumstances of the case, the prisoner was, however, remanded for further examination.

By Boxing Day, Williams will be the most famous man in London. By the day after that, he will be dead.

CHRISTMAS EVE 1687

I celebrated the eve of the birth of Our Lord at the table of the former Deputy Governor, the former Admiral of the Brethren, the former Lord High Almighty of Jamaica, Henry Morgan himself. I thought it extremely odd to be invited, but Morgan was not seeking to renew the acquaintance of his old quarter-master. He just wanted a final view of me before his end, and as it turned out there was another who wanted to look upon me.

Morgan had practically disappeared from public life in Jamaica by this time. Within recent memory he had been a fixture of the Port Royal taverns, ensconced with his few remaining friends in some private room or unlit corner, muttering bitterly about the new governor and his own betrayal by the King, or celebrating his achievements, both as buccaneer and latterly as a fearsome scourge of the pirates. As Deputy Governor of Jamaica, he had become a vicious pursuer of his former Brethren, taking a positive delight in victimising his former crews from his new position of official power.

But trips down to Port Royal were beyond him now. A new

doctor, called Sloane, had appeared from London with the new governor, reportedly to attend to the governor's wife, Lady Cavendish, who was said to be weak in the head. This Sloane was supposed to be one of the foremost medical minds in England, but he'd drawn a blank with Morgan. I'd heard stories of the admiral spending his days in a hammock like some resting whale, his stomach hanging over the side, empty bottles of sack and wine rolling on the floor.

Meanwhile, his plantation had fallen on hard times under its owner's neglect. When I rode over there for the Christmas Eve dinner (and what a pretty ride it was – Jamaica is so like Oxfordshire at times one can forget it is on the other side of the world) a few blacks were trimming the trees and bushes on the drive up to the house, but I saw little sign of any economically productive activity. The mill was still, there were no field gangs out, and the cane had bent over on itself, unharvested and unloved.

It was a stark contrast to my own dear Woodperry, which continued to thrive under the careful stewardship of my attorney Isak Naar. Isak was my right hand, my eyes and my ears. Our relationship was unusual for Jamaica. Plenty of Jews worked for Englishmen on the island, and many of them effectively ran plantations on behalf of their absentee owners, who grew fat and rich in the fleshpots of London, Bristol and Liverpool. Isak did much the same for me, but I was not quite such an absentee. I was present, but largely invisible. My reputation preceded me, particularly among the blacks, and to keep the plantation doing what it needed to do – generate wealth – I had decided the best place for me was deep in the shadows. Potosí silver may have been the seed for everything that grew on Woodperry, but it was Isak who did the tending.

And he did make the place sing with profit. He took no

nonsense from the blacks and their overseers, and I was told the sugar which was produced from our cane was as fine and as pure as any in the Caribbean, even that of the most famed plantations of Barbados. Isak had proven his worth time and time again. His knowledge of the techniques used in plantations in Brazil meant we were more productive, with cane of a higher quality, than any other plantation on the island.

Jamaica itself was a wonder of energy and invention. Barbados remained the richest of England's Caribbean islands, but all of the planters on Jamaica were seeing their income grow relentlessly. It seemed that every week a new sugar plantation opened somewhere on the island. Good-quality slaves poured into Port Royal, most of them from the dead King's Company of Adventurers, but a good few of them from independent traders as well. If old Hawkyns could see how well-oiled the transactions between ship captain and plantation owner now were, with the slaves washed and greased and gleaming on the quayside, his old Plymouth heart would have swelled beyond the confines of its chest.

The blacks in Woodperry knew their place and mostly behaved. In recent months there had been many escapes from other plantations. Most of the escaping slaves, it seemed, were joining with the Maroons up in the hills and in Cockpit County, and there were constant rumours that they may have been planning to take some kind of stand. Isak told me that this was much in the minds of the local Jews, and the limited contact I had with other plantation owners showed me that they, too, were worried lest the Maroons grew in sufficient numbers to threaten the emerging sugar economy.

No one, including Isak, knew of my own dealings with the Maroons, who for years watched over my own particular treasure trove in Cockpit County, the trove which had allowed me to build Woodperry and buy so many of the highest-quality slaves in the first place. Potosí silver had been transmuted, first into black labour, then into sugar, which attracted ever-growing prices back in England, where chins were multiplying beneath aristocratic faces as the rich and powerful shoved the sweet stuff down their pampered throats. While England grew fat, Jamaica grew rich. Sometimes I even thought there might come a time when England's government was moved to Jamaica, where the landscape was pleasant, the sea was blue and the air smelled of an exotic Sussex.

Morgan's manservant answered the door when I arrived at the house. I recognised him immediately from the Portobelo campaign, an ugly serpent of a man, as ruthless and cunning as any among the Brethren. The man's customary scowl fell away when he saw who was at the door, and he bent his head to the floor, muttering that Sir Henry could be found in the garden room. I followed the man through the house. Everywhere I looked there was careless and neglected opulence: elegant paintings sitting on the floor, leaning against the wall; vases still in wooden crates; expensive furniture left in strange alcoves and nooks. The house felt like something half-occupied and half-neglected. There were house niggers everywhere, dressed in rough Osnaburg cotton and bumping into each other as they moved things from room to room, under the influence of some unseen motion which I could not fathom. The house niggers in Woodperry were never this chaotic.

I went into the garden room, and saw Morgan. The rumours had led me to expect to find him in a hammock, surrounded by food and drink, but today the old admiral was in a massive throne-like chair, apparently plated in gold and upholstered in purple silk and cotton. His bottom half was covered by a blanket. His stomach was enormous, as big as a folded-up sail, and his old red beard was still finely groomed in the best Francis Drake fashion, but was now pushed out by his inflated chins and cheeks. His eyes seemed to have climbed back into his swollen face, like little crabs disappearing beneath a rock.

He did not stand to greet me. Two other diners were already there. One was a fellow captain of Morgan's, who had also been involved in the Portobelo campaign but who made no move to greet me, and seemed to have become suddenly intensely interested in the grain of the floor. The other I did not recognise, but this second guest did stand up and take my hand, looking at me closely as he did so.

'Sloane,' said the other guest. 'Hans Sloane.'

'Of course,' said I. 'The doctor from London.'

The man made a slight bow of the head in acknowledgement before returning his gaze to mine. His eyes held no welcome in them, but were fiercely penetrative. They seemed to be absorbing information from my face. He did not look straight into my own eyes but rather roamed all about my head, face and shoulders, as if looking for a particular sign or badge. I broke the chain after a few seconds by walking over to Morgan, my hand outstretched. I found this young London doctor disconcerting. I felt as if he had been waiting for my arrival – as if I was a specimen and he'd requested a special viewing.

Sir Henry refused to take my outstretched hand, and seemed to shrink back into his seat, if such a massive creature could ever have been said to shrink into anything.

'God's teeth,' he said, and his voice was a cracked vessel, his Welsh accent barely discernible, his breath odious. 'God's fucking teeth. William Ablass. Your mother must be fucking proud she spawned an evil fucking monster like you.'

I smiled at him, my professional smile. My profitable smile. It was a mechanical thing, like an anchor dropped into the water or a pulley guiding a sheet. The smile appeared from nowhere, and went back the same way.

'We are both monstrous, admiral and deputy governor,' I

said. 'Indeed, your monstrosity is somewhat more immediately apparent than my own.'

Morgan did not return my smile. His eyes were fixed and had something in them I had never seen before, even when the French had deserted him in Tortuga, even years later when the news had come from England that he was to be arrested and shipped home for trial. It looked very like fear. Morgan's breath came in short, ragged bursts, and with each of them his belly quivered.

'I had to see it,' said Morgan. 'Had to see it. I suspected it. But now I have seen it.'

'Yes, admiral,' said I. 'You have. You have seen me. The weapon you used so effectively for so long. And the weapon has kept its shine and its edge. But now it is used for other purposes.'

'No. The same purpose.'

'The same?'

'The getting of money. It's the only purpose there is, William. The getting of money is what keeps us human. The spending of it is what makes us monsters.'

'Ah, but then there's the question of how we spend it, admiral. You once described an associate of mine as an animal driven by its desires. And you also told me you'd die fat on the veranda of a Jamaica plantation. I heeded your advice. So, it would seem, did you.'

We ate, not at table, but on small wooden planks which we perched on our laps, so that Morgan did not have to rise from his chair. I had known for years that I did not need to eat or drink, even though I could and did feel hunger and thirst, so Morgan's food was as welcome to me as to his other guests. At one point, the old manservant crept in and went behind Morgan's chair, and knelt down behind him, manipulating something mechanical. Morgan's face reddened slightly and there was a soft, moist sound, as of wet mud hitting rock.

Morgan's face resumed its normal state, and the manservant pulled a chamber pot out from beneath the chair and removed it from the room.

Nothing was said of it, and Morgan barely interrupted his reminiscences. He was speaking of his interview with King Charles years before, at which Morgan had laid out a new Western Design for the Stuart King, grander and richer than old Cromwell's original. Charles had been delighted and had forgiven him all his transgressions and knighted him and made him Deputy Governor of the island of Jamaica.

Morgan always had been a ridiculously loyal old royalist. It had been his good fortune not to have been born a decade or two earlier, as he would have been a dangerous anachronism to Cromwell. The author of Cromwell's original Design, Thomas Gage, had emphasised money and slaves and God's work when laying out his plan for England's western expansion, and Cromwell had lapped it up. But for Morgan, the New World was about the clothes, the adventure, and the drink, much more in keeping with the sensibilities of the Stuart who was now two years in his grave. No mention was made of the idiot brother who now sat on the throne in his place, who had fought on the same side as the Spanish and who was thus an unmentionable on Jamaica.

The guests ate four or five courses, and Morgan drank three or four bottles of wine and became disgustingly drunk. His fellow captain left in a huff after Morgan made a revolting allusion to his wife's activities down in Port Royal a couple of decades before, and the doctor fell asleep in his chair soon after. Morgan and I were to all intents and purposes left alone, though the manservant could be heard banging around in the kitchen and in the hallway, and blacks continued to stream in and out of the room, unnoticed and unheeded.

Sloane was snoring softly. It occurred to me that the snores were a little theatrical, as if this strangely observant young doctor was pretending to sleep while the old admiral and his quartermaster reflected on their past. Morgan was gazing at a bottle of wine with the maudlin aspect of a drunk who has reached the limits of his capacity and is mournful of it. I stood at a bookshelf, marvelling at how a man who had never read a book in his life (as Morgan had repeatedly asserted with a defiant pride) still seemed determined to surround himself with dusty volumes.

'What is it like?' asked Morgan suddenly, his bleary eyes now resting on the ceiling, gravy and cream and wine drifting down the steep sides of his belly.

'What is what like?' I asked, already knowing what he meant.

'What is it like to never grow old?'

'I have grown old.'

'Don't be ridiculous, man. You know what I mean. You still look like a man of barely twenty years.'

'But I grow old, Morgan.'

'Old how, Billy? Old how?'

I tapped the side of my head. Morgan didn't look at me, but seemed to understand the movement nevertheless. He nodded into his chins and spoke with some sorrow.

''Tis true. Our innocence is a fragile and short-lived thing.'

Now he did look out at me.

'Know when I lost my innocence, Billy Ablass? Know when my mind decided it was no longer young and sprightly? Do you know when I puked up onto the ground and out came all my joy?'

I knew what he was going to say even then, in the silence that hung in the air after his question. I grew angry as the doctor snored.

'Portobelo. That child awaits us both at the gates of Hell, quartermaster.'

CHRISTMAS EVE 1811

For the second time this grim and gruesome December, John Harriott is dining with his friend Aaron Graham. This evening Graham is the visitor, travelling east to Wapping to attend his old friend in the fresh-faced apartments at Pier Head. Harriott's wife, Elizabeth, prepares the evening, planning it carefully with the servants and ordering them about mercilessly, but then retires to her own rooms for the duration, leaving the two magistrates to enjoy their meal and drink their port in glorious masculine isolation.

Harriott's dining room looks out onto the river from the second floor of the new building, and their meal is accompanied by the distant shouts of men, the rumble of barrels, the splashing of water and the vertical splendour of masts moving in and out of the dock, plainly visible through the window.

Graham sees immediately upon arriving that all is not well with his old friend. Harriott is as smartly dressed as ever, his belly carefully sequestered inside white breeches, white waistcoat and a dark coat. His clothes are about a decade out of fashion, but such is always the way with Harriott. Graham (whose clothes are hours, not even days, old, and whose tailor is one of the busiest tradesmen in Jermyn Street) normally finds this consistently smart but out-of-date sartorial approach charming, but he barely notices it this evening. He is more preoccupied with how very, very old his friend suddenly appears.

Such has been the change in him, in fact, that Graham audibly gasps when he is shown into Harriott's drawing room to see the old man sat by the fire with a glass of malt whisky. Harriott gets up slowly to greet his guest, and for the first time in his life Graham finds himself urging the older man not to stand, to take things slowly. As the words leave his lips he regrets them. Harriott continues to rise, now with a look of dismay on his face, combined with a flush of embarrassment and, possibly, anger at his friend's well-meant impertinence. John Harriott, the Engine of Empire, too tired to stand up? No, sir, no!

But there is no disguising the man's exhaustion. As they move to the dining room and start to work their way through the evening's seven courses, Graham finds himself having to work hard to maintain any kind of intelligent conversation. Fortunately he is used to this, and can pepper any company with a variety of suitable anecdotes and observations that would keep a party of the dead amused. But even in the face of Graham's charm Harriott's answers are this evening monosyllabic, and occasionally he appears not to have even heard what Graham has said. During one lengthy between-course anecdote relating to the daughter of a senior official at the Admiralty, Harriott's eyes are so absent, his face so nonregarding, that Graham finds himself wondering if the man has not perhaps had some kind of a disturbance of the brain.

Only when the talk turns to the Shadwell investigations does Harriott gain any kind of enthusiasm, but even then he seems more to mourn the details than discuss them.

'So, my dear Harriott, your investigations. How do they develop?'

'*My* investigations, Graham? Would that they were!'

'Ah, of course. Shadwell continues to take the lead, I take it?'

'They do.'

'So. How go *their* investigations?'

Harriott lets out one enormous sigh, sips his port, and answers.

'As of this evening, I believe my colleagues in Shadwell would answer that their investigations go exceedingly well. They have a new suspect.'

'Indeed? There have been so many! Does this one possess any unique qualities to make him stand out from the army of those arrested?'

'It would appear so. To Shadwell's eyes at least. The man is called John Williams.'

'Ah, yes, Williams. I read about him in *The Times*. Arrested only yesterday.'

'Indeed. Arrested for the astonishing crime of being an Irish seaman with an eye for the ladies and a fondness for a drink.'

'A not entirely *singular* individual.'

'Indeed not, Graham. When I heard of his arrest, I confess that I rolled my eyes. In recent weeks we have arrested enough Irishmen to form a new regiment. And enough Portuguese to crew an East Indiaman. I had little confidence that this new suspect would amount to anything. And yet, today, events have moved rather quickly.'

'So this Williams is more promising as a suspect than you imagined him to be?'

'Certain discoveries have implicated him more than I would have forecast.'

'Discoveries?'

'Yes. You remember the maul?'

'Of course. That awful instrument has stayed in my brain like an echo of hell, my dear Harriott.'

'Did you see it?'

'Not at all. Merely your description. It was enough.'

'My words cannot have done the vicious thing justice, Graham. My God, it was an instrument of pure evil. I have seen similar tools in the succeeding days, and all of them have made me shudder.'

'It had letters imprinted on the face, did it not?'

'Yes. "JP" were the letters. Much time has been spent searching for the owner of those initials, and thus the owner of the maul. Our searches, both here and in Shadwell, had proven fruitless until recently.'

'You have found this "JP"?'

'Capper from Shadwell believes he has, yes. A John Petersen. German sailor.'

'Capper identified the man?'

'He claims so. He took the maul to a prisoner in Newgate, who claimed to know it. A Mr Vermilloe, landlord of the Pear Tree boarding house in Wapping. Vermilloe identified it as belonging to one of his lodgers, this Petersen.'

Graham sips his own port, and ponders before speaking again.

'Why on earth did Capper take the maul to Newgate?'

'To show it to Vermilloe.'

'But why the connection, Harriott? Why the connection with the Pear Tree?'

'The connection is Williams himself. The Pear Tree is where he lodges.'

The fire spits suddenly, causing Graham to jump slightly before recovering himself. Harriott is facing the fire, but he is not looking at it.

'Does this Petersen know Williams?' asks Graham.

'Petersen is currently at sea. He left his tools with Vermilloe and his wife for safe keeping.'

'And Vermilloe was in prison when both sets of murders were committed?'

'Meaning is he a suspect? Yes, he was in Newgate.'

'And yet his is the evidence on which the case against Williams turns.'

'There is one other thing. Williams was a shipmate of Timothy Marr.'

'A shipmate? On what ship?'

'An East Indiaman, called the *Dover Castle*.'

'And does anything link him to Williamson?'

'He was drinking in the King's Arms on the night of the murders. And he is somewhat lame. Some people reported seeing a lame man escaping from the crime, although most seem to think it was a tall lame man. Williams is, by all accounts, rather short.'

'You have not seen this Williams?'

'No indeed. I left the investigating of all this to my constable, Horton. It is his information I am relaying to you.'

'And Williams has been remanded?'

'Yes. To Coldbath Fields. But tonight he is at Shadwell, being interrogated again. They have been busy rounding up people who know him, according to Horton.'

'You did not wish to go?'

'Horton is there.'

'Is he now?'

'I'm not at all sure I like your tone, Graham.'

'My tone is as it ever is. I am perhaps surprised at your lack of interest in the proceedings against this man Williams, given how very involved you have been in the investigation to date, old friend.'

Graham is aware of the sharpness in his voice, and thinks with wonder: *My Lord, am I chastising this man for a lack of application? How the world has turned these past weeks!*

Harriott's face has flushed red at his friend's aspersion, but the flush is fleeting. He breathes out suddenly and his head drops, so Graham can no longer see his eyes.

'Do not let me detain you,' says Harriott, softly. 'If you wish to witness the humiliation of this accused man, it is barely a half-mile from here.'

Graham does not rise. He does lean across the table and put his hand on the older man's arm.

'My dear Harriott. You are spent. Your years have caught up with you. One day they will do so with me too. You are an old man, Harriott, and your internal fires have burned hard and strong. But they are spent.'

Harriott looks up, and Graham's world spins again at the sight of tears in the old man's eyes.

'Graham, I should strike you down for saying such a thing.'

He leans back into his chair, as if surrendering to something.

'But you are right, by God. It is Christmas tomorrow. In January, I believe I shall retire. My work is finished.'

A gull squawks outside the window, as if in agreement.

AUGUST 1688

The old buccaneer Morgan was dead. Preparations were being made in Port Royal for his funeral. The doctor from London, Sloane, had not succeeded in curing him. He didn't even succeed in stopping the stubborn old fool from resorting to local remedies and to black magic. Nothing worked. I thought at the end he must have died of boredom and disappointment. The lack of adventure and the lack of advancement swelled up in his Welsh belly until it exceeded his corporeal bounds. He had to die.

His death affected me, I confess. I had known Morgan for as long as I had known anyone apart from Kate. Since I had made my final visit to Stanton St John, so many people around me had died; shipmates and slaves alike. But Morgan had seemed to endure even while he raged at my inability to age. He had seemed to be made of different stuff. And his presence had made me feel really alive. Not this grey shadowy presence which I seemed to occupy most of the days. Truly warm and truly alive.

He had angered me on that Christmas visit, with his talk of

atrocities in Portobelo, as if I had been the only perpetrator and he (like all his crew) had not benefited from the transactions there undertaken. I am at peace with myself. If I find it within myself to commit those melancholy extremities which Morgan claimed had affected him so, why it is just a result of my lingering time on this earth. I see the truth of things. I see how the world is. I know that there is evil all around, because I see it, taste it and, most of all, I hear it. And I know that others hear it too. The old Roundhead did. I saw it in the naive fool's eyes.

Morgan's death had left the island effectively headless. The doctor Sloane had turned all his medical attention to that mad fool the Duke of Albemarle, who was supposedly running Jamaica as its governor. Look to the doctor on these occasions. Sloane spent more time with Albemarle than anyone did, and was also closest to Morgan in the weeks before he died. I would not have been surprised to see him take over the post of governor, if it came to that. And he was a very, very young man.

Woodperry, meanwhile, was going through one of those intermittent phases when the introduction of new blacks disturbed the natural order of the place. Productivity had declined; the field gangs in particular had become uncooperative and even on occasion downright disobedient. I'd branded the new batch of blacks myself on the quayside in Port Royal, marking them with the same *PTSI* which Henry Morgan had once carved into the wood of the *Drake*. My own private joke. These new blacks had proven harder to tame than their predecessors, and their behaviour had infected all but the oldest slaves on the plantation. In recent days we had even lost some of the slaves, following others from other plantations into the hills of Cockpit County to join the Maroons. Some – the ones with children – had even returned to Woodperry by night to steal their offspring.

Today, I was to travel to Port Royal, a journey of twenty miles or so, to attend Morgan's funeral, which would take place any day now. I was waiting on the veranda of Woodperry. The great house was on the highest point of the plantation, so I could see the hundreds of acres of waving green cane and could also, if needed, defend the house from any attack by the field slaves. A dirt track led out from the house to the edge of the plantation, but in front of the house it was bordered by white stones and, behind them, patches of green lawn which were watered regularly by the household slaves. Beyond the garden the sugar cane began, and I spent some time watching the backs of a field gang cutting away at it, dressed in various shades of cotton, their hats drooping in the sun, the cane towering above them like a wall. Some of them were even singing.

I had long ago left the house's garden to one of the slaves, a giant of a man called only Newton after the great scientist (it amused me more than I can say to name the slaves after the Fellows of the Royal Society, for whom my presence on earth would have been as unwelcome as the discovery that apples fell upwards and not down). Newton spoke no English. He had been brought from Guinea five years before, and I had bought him two years ago from a neighbouring plantation that was going bankrupt.

I watched Newton now as the shining black giant gently planted something green and sharp-looking into a patch of earth behind the lawn. The slave stood back from it, and for a moment stood still before dropping his head and wiping something – perhaps tears – out of his eyes. I had seen this kind of thing often. A slave would see something everyday and ordinary and would suddenly, unaccountably, become upset by the memory of whatever. I found it both charming and amusing.

Isak Naar stepped out onto the veranda and watched Newton for a moment alongside me. The slave had not noticed us.

'He is a fool, this one,' said Isak. His voice had kept much of its Portuguese harshness, despite his years in Brazil and then Jamaica. To my ears it sounded almost Russian. 'He stands and he weeps like some old woman, all the time.'

'They have some sensibility,' said I. 'Sometimes they remind me of intelligent dogs with their sad eyes and hung heads. Now, Isak. I will be gone several days for this funeral.'

'Yes, Mr William.'

'You have taken the measures I suggested against the interlopers onto the plantation?'

'I have, Mr William. There is a new fence on the north-west side. And I have undertaken a careful audit of the slaves. All names have been verified. We shall not be surprised by anything.'

'Surprised?'

'I have attempted to calculate the probability of the remaining slaves escaping, Mr William.'

Isak always spoke with this slow, elaborate formality. To start with it had irritated me, and there had been occasions when I'd snapped at the man and told him to speak more directly. But now I found it comforting. History seemed to inform the way Isak spoke, and history was a quality of which I was minutely aware.

'So who is likely to try to escape first?'

'By my calculation, Robert Boyle is the most likely.'

I racked my brain, trying to picture the slave mentioned. I was unsuccessful.

'I have taken the precaution of having Boyle locked up as a warning. We have interrogated him forcefully.'

Isak's face was blank as he said this. But I knew what

spectrum could be covered by the word 'forcefully'. I also knew about the little solitary gaol Isak had had constructed down at the southern end of the plantation, for the imprisonment of Negroes who might be causing a disturbance. Some nights I wandered down there myself and looked in at the porthole in the door, and wide white eyes would stare back at me, sometimes shouting in terror (I was always recognised), sometimes weeping, sometimes defiant.

'Well, you have things under control as always, Isak. I can leave Woodperry with no anxiety.'

'There is one other thing I would discuss, Mr William.'

'Hurry, Isak. I can hear the carriage approaching.'

'It is a matter I have been meaning to raise with you for some time. But,' and with this Isak's face stiffened, and his eyes filled with tears, and his hands started to shake, 'but I fear I must leave you.'

'Leave me?'

'Yes, sir.'

'For how long?'

'For ever, Mr William.'

'Why on earth would you do that?'

'My wife, Mr William. She is . . . with child.' His hands were still shaking, and now there were real tears rolling down his cheek.

'And what of it?'

'She does not wish . . . sir, she does not wish her child to be born in Jamaica. She believes it to be a place of evil, Mr William. She wants to go to London.' The words tumbled out as if vomited. Isak raised one shaking hand to his face.

He is afraid, I thought, with some wonder. *He is so afraid of me that he shakes and he cries. I believe he thinks I will reach out and snap his neck. I believe I might.*

A carriage appeared in front of the house, with two men up

front, obviously assuming a long bumpy ride that would require a change of driver. Old Newton was looking up at the sky, his massive hands pressed to a pain in the small of his back. From beside me, Isak snorted a string of snot back into his nose. Really, the man was in suppressed hysterics. For a moment, I imagined myself suspended in the air above Woodperry, looking out on the fields of cane and the Negroes bent over before them in supplication, men and women both, small children running around their feet, and I believed that I would be looking at paradise. The only paradise available to me. Why would anyone want to leave paradise?

I turned to Isak, and placed a hand on his shoulder. The man's shoulder was a mess of tense knots and shaking muscle. He felt like a slave did when I put my hand on them: terrified yet frozen in place.

'Isak, you have been a loyal friend and fellow traveller these last few years. Woodperry would be no place at all without you. Go to London, my friend, and raise your family. And who knows? Perhaps we will meet again.'

And with that, I walked down the steps of the plantation house and climbed into the carriage. It was an open-top affair, as were most of the carriages in Jamaica, and the engineering was not of the highest quality. The two men in the carriage said nothing as we set off down the driveway of the plantation house and out onto the road, if a road it could truthfully be called. The carriage groaned on the ruts and rocks beneath and I found myself being shaken violently from side to side as I pondered Isak's news and began planning a future without him. We continued in this way for an hour, and Woodperry vanished over a hillside. Soon after, the man holding the reins swore and pulled the carriage to a halt.

'Bloody wheel,' he muttered, and they both climbed out to look at whatever had caused the delay. I gazed over the land beside the road, struck (as I often was) by the immensity of the fact that this entire vista belonged to me, Billy Ablass, son of a Polish sailor, Oxfordshire pig-farmer, river pirate and buccaneer. What a very strange world it was in which to endure. Then there was a noise from behind the carriage, and a man shouted, and perhaps a half-dozen pairs of hands grabbed my shoulders and arms and pinned me from behind to the back of the carriage. I heard someone speak.

'Compliments of the doctor.'

I could not move, there were too many of them, and as I saw them for the first time – three white men in addition to the two who'd met me, and perhaps a dozen slaves, a real gang of lionhearts – one of them placed a sack over my head, and the world disappeared behind a cotton screen. Seconds later, I felt a cosh thumping into the side of my head, over and over again, as they tried to knock the senses from me. Thick rope was tied around my hands and feet, to the fierce rhythm of the cosh and the frightened shouts of my captors. I never saw my Woodperry again.

CHRISTMAS DAY 1811

The small dinghy drifts away from the jetty in front of the River Police Office. The early morning water is grey-black and near-freezing. Further up the river, past the old bridge where the big ships cannot go, the water is already beginning to settle and freeze. People are starting to talk about another Ice Fair on the river in the New Year.

Here, downstream and in front of the Wapping wharves, there is no ice, but the water is still a thick, blood-like liquid, like cold Russian vodka. The chill air and ever-present fog dampen the working noise of the river – the men's voices, the wooden-and-metal clanking of board on stone and chain, the occasional splash as something heavy falls into the water, and the ever-present creaking scream of rope pulling away on timber and iron. Warm breath rises in clouds from the ships anchored, side to side, across the river. On some days, it is said, a man can walk back and forth across the river stepping on the anchored ships. Not so this morning. There is still trade on the river, but it is cold and resentful, as befits a freezing Nativity.

Charles Horton rows the little single-masted Police Office boat into the middle of the river, picking his way between the ships and the lighters, and then over towards the opposite Surrey shore. When there is some room (not much, barely enough to turn the dinghy in and out of the wind, but for a skilled sailor like Horton it's sufficient) he raises the dinghy's sail, which catches the sharp wind immediately. The wind is blowing downstream, and the little boat picks up some speed ahead of the breeze. He stows the oars down the sides of the vessel, and sits back with his hand on the tiller.

The dinghy moves more confidently downstream, away from the clamour of vessels along the Pool and in front of Wapping. Ships are moving steadily in and out of the dock, and the Wapping wharves bending away around the curve of the river are a hive of activity. Watermen ferry goods from the ships which have been anchored on chains in the middle of the stream, transporting barrels and crates and sacks to the riverside wharves.

The wharves present a uniform front on the north side of the river, broken occasionally by steps. In contrast, the Surrey side is more open; many of the old wharves have been pulled down to allow ingress to the emerging Rotherhithe dock complex, built around the Greenland Dock, where for decades enormous whales were cut to pieces and rendered down into their constituent parts. Houses and warehouses have begun to spring up around the new docks, like flies on a gigantic piece of whale meat.

The river curves to the north, and the wharves of Wapping give way to the ramshackle houses and factories of Limehouse and then, as the river bends south again, Horton sees the western edge of the Isle of Dogs, the peninsula which has been hollowed out to create the East and West India Docks, behind the old windmills which give the Millwall its name.

Wapping, Rotherhithe, the Isle of Dogs – the scale of the dock-building in the last decade has been breathtaking, and all while the country has been at war with Bonaparte. Goods are pouring in from the markets of the empire and are being magically transmogrified, by the alchemy of trade, first into gold, then into currency, and then into the mercenary armies who are even now crossing swords with wild-eyed French revolutionaries in distant central European fields. English money flows through the veins of Austrian and Russian armies, and is spilled into fields at Ulm and Austerlitz, but no matter – new money is being created, at an ever-increasing rate, out here on the river.

Around the river there is little time for culture or religion or politics: there is only trade. Every man, be they the richest financier or the meanest dock worker, is seeking to turn something – be it the labour of their hands or the finest Indian textiles – into cash. The recent cessation of the slave trade, which together with the massive sugar industry had been the prime mover in generating this great economic machine, seems to have done little to dent the headlong rush to the banks. This two-mile stretch of river is an engine of wealth – the wealth of the rich men, but also the thinner, less nourishing wealth of the scurrying humanity which swarms around it: the sailors; the dock workers; the shipbuilders; and their attendant armies of wives, children, whores, publicans, pawnbrokers, spies, funeral merchants and shopkeepers. Even on this dark, dank Christmas morning, the noises of this place are evidence of the buzzing energy behind the wharf walls. This is the economic point on which the wide world turns.

Horton sails on for another half-hour before crossing the physical turning point of the globe, the boundary of zero longitude at Greenwich, where he passes dozens more ships, each making their way upstream to the docks. He is in definitively military waters now. Wren's hospital glides into view, as if floating on the river itself, and Horton feels a twinge of nostalgia and anxiety. He has seen this building so very many times before, but now it seems almost unbearable to find himself approaching it, exiled and outcast as he is both from the navy he mutinied against at the Nore and the mutineers he betrayed. He has not been this far downstream in years, and the emotions are as sudden as if he had run into a reef under the river's surface. The hospital (the fingerprints of its co-designer Hawksmoor all over it, echoes of his pale creation St George in the East, whose heart beats along the bloodied Ratcliffe Highway) glowers at him elegantly, as if hidden old admirals were scurrying to its windows to watch the traitor float past, muttering dark naval curses under their breaths.

He passes the hospital and approaches the great shipyard at Woolwich, where gigantic engines of war are being constructed. An enormous man-o'-war is rising from the dry dock, only its masts left to be attached. Outside the docks sit two more enormous ships, and Horton realises he recognises one of them: the *Inflexible*, one of the mutinous vessels from the Nore, although it appears its name has been changed to *Obedience*, one of many little jokes the authorities have had at the mutineers' expense in the last fourteen years. Horton cringes back into his boat at he passes between the two ships, his head kept down. It is not impossible that a face might lean over and recognise him.

After Greenwich and Woolwich, the river begins to move back to its natural state as it shakes off the invasions of commerce and war. The landscape is indistinct and brown-green, with muddy banks, islets and the occasional small hill rising back and up, either into Kent in the south or Essex in the north. The horizon is like the smudge of a child's pencil on the damp air, painted in with occasional masts. Horton keeps close to the south bank, remembering the channels here but not looking forward to what is coming: the estuary, with its treacherous sandbanks and muddy non-edges, where even the newest charts can be out of date within a year or two.

It is approaching lunchtime, so he pulls his little boat in at Greenhithe, where a small cluster of well-to-do houses are squeezed between a hill and the river. He buys some ale and bread at the inn, watching small boats load up with chalk and lime from the pits inland.

After a half-hour of sitting, eating, watching and thinking, he climbs back into his dinghy, and sets off again. Gravesend passes by, and a small child out for a Christmas walk waves at him from the steps leading down to the river. Horton waves back, the small pinch of sadness at the sight of a child like a draught on his neck. He thinks of Abigail, back in their sitting room, probably reading one of her endless books on science or history while the fire crackles and families all around toast the Saviour's birth again, and again, and again.

And now, finally, he is out in the estuary, and his innate sailing skills begin to fail him. His instinct for the water is as strong as any man's, but the currents are wild here, their shapes new and unrecognised. He is torn between the safety of the land, with its treacherous mudbanks, and the safety of the deep river stream, with its equally lethal currents and enquiring eyes.

He puts down a line to keep an eye on the depth, but the wind has picked up and he is doing more than eight knots now, a crazy speed for this little craft, and he has little capacity for doing anything other than keeping the boat upright and himself out of the water. The far Essex shore has dropped away as the estuary opens, and he clings as close as he dares to the Kent shore, aware that he is being pushed from the edge of the deep water of the central estuary onto the sandbanks which reach out from the blurred landscape to his right.

He sails in a state of panic for the best part of two hours, creeping eastwards along the shore. The land is almost empty, farmland and marshes mostly, with the occasional squat Norman church, encased in an ancient graveyard, to tend to the souls of the local farmers. On the little beaches he sees a few grounded boats, usually heavy gnarled things dragged up from the sea by experienced hands. Smuggler territory, no doubt. The writ of the River Police ended miles before upriver, and since the advent of policing on the river these wild, desolate lands on the edges of London have seen a surge in illicit activity. In some of the houses up there Horton knows that ex-shipmates are involved in this grey trade, sheltering inside little houses and looking up at night from the raised land to see lights signalling from ships out in the estuary, meeting rowing boats from those ships down on the beaches and taking up the smuggled goods, shaking hands and exchanging coins in the night-time sea wind.

Up ahead is the Nore, the ancient sandbank which stretches out from Sheerness and the second estuary, that of the Medway. The Nore where navy ships would group together like a gang of well-dressed dandies out for a night on the town, gold-glittered and boastful with their bright new sails. If the sun was shining, they were a marvellous sight, a panoply of marine construction, power and wealth, prepared to set out for battles off Spain, off Egypt, in the Indies East or West, or to push home advantages in Gibraltar or Malta or Newfoundland. This would be their final sight of England, a view back up the Medway into the guts of Kent or over the flat, sightless fields of the Isles of Grain and Sheppey.

His thoughts have become distracted by his return to the scene of the mutiny, and he misses the odd mess of ancient groynes and ship-wood lodged into a sandbank off Hoo All Hallows. The rope he's been using to check for depth suddenly snags, impossibly, and then the wind catches the sails and veers the boat suddenly starboard and southwards. With a shearing wrench, an old piece of the ship-beam which formed the groyne tears into the side of his dinghy and immediately, to Horton's horror, the seawater starts pouring in.

The boat is doomed, it is clear, and barely two miles from his destination at that. He is only twenty yards from the sloping shore, an unpromising combination of mud and sand, but the old sailor's panic of swimming has surged through him. He's been in the water only twice before, once off Portsmouth and once on the Nore. But now the dinghy is already half into the water. He keeps enough wits about him to pull down the sail, which is now as one with the wind and is churning the boat round wildly. He grasps his old leather bag, and holding it above his head he commends his traitor's soul to God and jumps into the water.

Cold rushes into his skin and bones like remorseless fire and for a quarter of a second, as his feet descend through seawater, he imagines a bottomless depth below him, an impossible tunnel of dark water rushing straight down into Hell, but then his feet touch bottom, or at least a kind of loose, ill-defined boundary which will serve as a bottom, and he comes to rest with the water up to his chest. Then, another panic as he tries to lift his feet and finds them sucked down into the mud. He sets his eyes on the church of All Hallows, up there on the hill above the shoreline. Once again he mentally begs a favour of his creator and then yanks both feet out of the mud and starts an uncomfortable, freezing walk to shore.

He reaches it in minutes, but it feels like hours. Hours of a crushing cold which deadens his muscles and causes his brain to slip and slide in between memory and present. He even considers surrendering to these waters, within sight of the mutinous transactions of 1797, the events which have defined him. But then he sees the church again, and the edge of something massive around the promontory, towards the point where the clear waters of the Medway empty into the grey-brown muck of the estuary, and he pulls himself ashore. The images of Abigail reading a book and the child on the riverside are the memories which finally get him out of the water.

'Ashore' is only a comparative term here, of course. The edges of the land and sea are overlapping things, a sequence of gradations between liquid and solid. His feet continue to be sucked down into the mud, but the water is now below his knees and the panic is subsiding. The lizard self is pushed back down; the public Horton, calm and secret, starts to re-emerge. After a few minutes of yomping across damp ground he finally reaches dry land, properly dry even though still surrounded by swampy marsh, and only then does he remember to bring his arms down. The leather bag is dry. He feels inside gingerly, and the rough metal edges of the coins meet his grasping fingers inside one of the many customised compartments.

It is perhaps half a mile to All Hallows Church, up the hill, and from there he can get his bearings, as the land is higher. The church is squat, flat, around five hundred years old, surrounded by a bleak little churchyard containing a few new graves in amongst the old. There seems to be no one around, but he can hear the turning of wheels from somewhere, and a distant sound of metal on stone.

As he passes the church, the rudimentary track he is on forks, running westwards one way down a fairly substantial track, while the track he is on bends away towards the south. Where the track splits, there is a tiny wooden sign with lettering burned into it, naming the westward route which has presumably taken people back towards London, 25 miles away.

The sign says Ratcliffe Highway.

The cold that has been sitting in his bones since the boat sank deepens a notch. He looks back up this other Ratcliffe Highway, which skims the high ground on top of the Hoo peninsula, across to the grey infinity behind which is the Thames and London. For a moment, this ancient church seems to stand at one end of a primitive line of power which connects this grim shore with the smart little house at 29 Ratcliffe Highway, that other Highway where the impoverished hordes gather for work on the docks and spend their wages in a desperate dance with death and deprivation. For a moment, the bodies of Timothy Marr and his family could be lying here, in this cold churchyard, whispering their secrets to him.

He turns his back on this new discovery, and sets off down the other track, south and eastwards towards the Grain Marshes.

It is a walk of perhaps three or four miles, less direct than the sea route, the road taking him around Yantlet Creek and across the Grain Marshes, towards a small hamlet around the Church of St James. There he hopes to find someone who can take him across to Sheerness.

Beyond this second church is the point at which the Medway pours into the Thames estuary, its clear blue waters giving their name to Sheerness, the harbour, fort and town on the far, eastern side of the Medway from where he is now walking. The huge southern bend in the Medway hides the great towns of Chatham and Rochester, back upstream, where another great naval dockyard churns away in the face of an opposing world. Sheerness was intended to be the staunch guardian of the Medway's mouth, its Garrison Point Fort fortified in a panic under Charles II soon after a Dutch fleet sailed, without obstruction, down the Medway and deep into Kent, to the despair of a cavalier court.

For a century and a half since then Sheerness has been a bastard port, a hacking-together of wood and mud and old men-o'-war deliberately beached to form a breakwater. A town of sorts has formed onshore, but many families still live in old hulks out on the water, their masts hewn away like the blasted limbs of sailors, their decks roofed over with cheap timber. Half a dozen of these massive floating workhouses line the edge of Sheerness, which like the Hoo peninsula is on the boundary between sea and land, its mudbanks extending out a hundred yards into the estuary before suddenly they drop away into deep water, the deep water which allows enormous men-o'-war to sail out of Chatham and muster out on the Nore, just offshore.

The sound of metal on stone is louder up here, and Horton knows where it is coming from. Back behind the fort the great dock builder himself, John Rennie, is once again working his bricked-in alchemy, carving out a massive stone dock within Sheerness, just as he gouged out the guts of Wapping to create the London Dock. Sheerness is being turned from a bastard hybrid, a make-do naval base, into something more in keeping with Britain's ambition. Work on the new base had started less than ten years after the Nore mutiny.

He walks down into the little hamlet. The walk has warmed him a bit, even in this cold Christmas air, but he is still freezing, possibly dangerously, and the memory of that other Ratcliffe Highway has supplied its own kind of chill. There is an alehouse here, and inside he finds an old waterman who is prepared to take him across to the other side, and a fire he can warm himself by while the old man prepares his boat. The flames breathe life back into Horton's bones. He recalls tracking a whale off Newfoundland, seeing it rise and sink into the freezing waves and marvelling at the heat in its blood. He needs that heat now.

Eventually, the old man's boat is ready. It's a sad thing, its sail full of holes and its hull covered over in repairs both professional and amateur. It creaks out into the deep water of the estuary, and in a matter of only minutes it ties up to the side of one of the great hulks, which Horton has pointed out to the old waterman. It is the *Sandwich*. One of the Nore mutineers, now emasculated and home to a few dozen families down within its depths.

It is Horton's old ship. It is like rediscovering a beautiful young girl, now in her dotage, her hair gone and her eyes dull and her hands rough as they churn through another woman's washing.

A ladder is let down for him. Someone has been charged with watching out for the visitor from London. The old waterman from the alehouse heads back across the estuary to his beer and the fire. Once up on the now-covered deck Horton looks around him with a nostalgia so intense that it actually feels like a presence in his stomach, but it is only for a moment. The roof that has been built over the deck is low and it no longer feels much like a ship. More like something from which the life has departed.

He is taken below decks. The man he wants is living, with his family, on the spar deck.

This man, probably the same age as Horton but looking much older, greets him warmly, and his wife reaches up to kiss Horton on the cheek before showing off her children. Horton musses the hair on their heads and feels a familiar pang in their presence. He is generous with his time for them, kneeling down to be at their height and talking and laughing with them. After a while their father shoos them away, and the two men turn brusque and businesslike. Horton shows the other man the coins in his bag, and then the man opens a purse and shows him another, identical, coin.

They talk for a while, the man's wife and children looking on. They are hunched over the coins, comparing them minutely, and they talk of boats and sails and preparations for voyages. Eventually, the two men leave the woman and children, and climb down into another little boat which takes them into Sheerness proper, to the old harbour, little of which is left as Rennie's new masonry encroaches.

Several ships are moored up in the old harbour. Some are unloading, but most are being subjected to some kind of activity: repairs, cleaning, even (for one of them) apparent demolition and decommissioning. The man leads Horton to one of these ships, a vessel which begs not to be looked at, which seems to hide behind its own lack of distinctiveness. They call up to the ship from the quayside and, when no answer comes, they cross a gangway onto the deck, and disappear down below.

JUNE 1741

Old Dr Sloane woke to the familiar panicky symptoms dancing in his chest: shortness of breath; a heart galloping away like a terrified three-legged horse; a catastrophic tiredness which served to convince him, once again, that he would never again rise from his bed, that this morning had indeed brought The End.

The doctor has long been a student, a correspondent and, he trusted, a friend of the great Italian anatomist Morgagni. Now, as his dry and anxious mind considered the parts of his old body which seemed to be turning themselves off, one by one, he calmed himself by recalling those inner realms which were already coming to be known by the name of his friend: the *sinus Morgagni* in his heart; the *columns of Morgagni* in his anal canal; the *foramina of Morgagni* in his throat; the *hydatid of Morgagni* in his testes.

Hmm, thought the doctor. *A theme I need to weave into my talk. Morgagni has to a great extent annexed my body by naming it!*

These considerations gradually eased his breathing. His

heart settled down into something resembling the steady but perceptibly weaker rhythm which would be the norm for the rest of his day. After perhaps ten minutes he was able to sit up. After twenty minutes he could call for his manservant and get ready to face the extraordinary day ahead of him, combining as it did an intensely pleasurable task with a painful, even terrifying chore.

A breakfast first, laid out for a hearty sailor but in fact barely picked at. Each day his servants repeated this performance, setting the table for a man in his forties rather than his seventies, for a robust man with robust appetites, not this wizened echo of the man who once shouted down a Jamaican pirate captain and called him an overindulgent idiot. Jamaica had been much on his mind these past few weeks, and today more so than ever. He had brought a lot more than memories back from that beautiful island, and now he faced having to deal with the most terrible of its exports.

After breakfast, he went back up to his chamber with his quiet manservant. The Negro's father, Sloane's original manservant, had caused outrage in polite London society when the doctor had brought him back from Jamaica. His use of a Negro manservant had not been unprecedented, but it was certainly rare and had thus been moderately scandalous. Nevertheless it had been very much the *right kind* of scandal, a *coup de théâtre* which had done the doctor a great deal of good in the long run. 'Get the doctor with the nigger,' went the polite society refrain. 'He's good, and he tells the most wonderful stories while he's draining your blood.'

The original servant had died a decade before, and the man's son had taken over in the same role. The mother had been left in Jamaica. Neither of the Negroes ever mentioned her to the doctor, although both wept separately and secretly at their particular memories of her. The son was almost silent, dutiful, hardworking and beautiful. He and Sloane had never exchanged more than half-a-dozen sentences at a time with each other. The Negro knew what the old man wanted, when he wanted it, and was always there to supply it. No one, least of all Sloane, had ever asked why it seemed so important to him that the job be done so well.

The manservant laid out the doctor's clothes while the old man made his toilet, then helped the doctor into those clothes, a particularly fine set for this particularly important day.

After another hour the doctor was ready. The manservant followed him slowly down to the front door of the smart mansion, carrying the thick leather bag which contained the doctor's self-prescribed battery of curatives and palliatives. Outside in the driveway stood an elegant coach-and-four. The small but immaculate mansion house was surrounded by fields and orchards, its proximity to the new developments of the West End making it convenient for visits to expensive clients while meeting the doctor's desire for more bucolic surroundings. Indeed, on this warm spring day, the landscape reminded him more than a little of Jamaica, that luscious place where he'd first made his name and which still, every day, was in his thoughts.

The air was sweetly scented and clear, the sky was sharply crystal-blue and the sun had that newly minted quality of an English spring. The manservant quietly raised his face up to the limpid light, while the doctor fussed around getting into the carriage, assisted by the driver.

With the doctor and the manservant safely embarked the driver climbed up to his seat and guided the coach out into the lane that ran towards town. There was little other traffic to consider. At the edge of the estate, the great city started to encroach. They passed several new and opulent houses, and some plots where new buildings were being constructed along the same lines as those already there: stucco double-fronted villas with solid wooden front doors and four or five floors. Birds chirped in the plane trees, and the horses pulling the carriage grumbled at each other politely and swished their perfectly dressed tails.

The coach trundled through the developments of Chelsea and Belgravia, before turning down into Whitehall to start its journey along the great east-to-west riverside processional route of state: past the remnants of the great palace which had burned down half a century before and the government buildings which had sprung up around it; then up and around to the Strand, where the palaces of the great and good had congregated along the river for three hundred years. The road was wide and straight but as it approached the Temple Bar it became narrower and more uncertain of its direction, as if in anticipation of the more ancient city and its older intricate ways, up ahead on the other side of the Fleet.

The coach turned into Crane Court on the left-hand side of the road and came to a halt in front of a small crowd of well-dressed men. Some of them noticed the coach arriving, and there was a little ripple of applause in recognition of the doctor's approach. The manservant got out first. The crowd stopped chattering and watched the black figure, dressed discreetly yet expensively, as he pulled out the steps from within the coach and, with one arm held out, supported his old master as he climbed down.

The doctor felt his knees almost buckle as he stepped down onto the ground, and for a moment the manservant took almost all his weight and prevented him tumbling to the ground. The old man leaned into the manservant for several seconds, the Negro's arm strong and secure and unyielding beneath the doctor's frail, almost absent grasp. *Resolution, resolution!* the doctor told himself. He closed his eyes for a moment and took several deep breaths, bringing his body back under his control, locking out his knees and leaning back towards his own centre of gravity. After another handful of moments, they were on terra firma, and the old doctor, leaning on the young manservant's arm, stood for a moment, and turned his eyes to the top of the building before him, wondering if the awful thing that was up there, the Monster in this place's attic, was even now looking down on them. With that thought, the old doctor made his way for the last time into the residence of the Royal Society.

The Society was based in two houses acquired under the presidency of Isaac Newton thirty years before. The buildings were four storeys tall and looked like older, more worldly wise versions of the houses now going up on the edges of the doctor's estate. They had been adapted by Wren and now accommodated a library and a discussion chamber. A red light outside the building showed when the members of the Society were meeting to discuss the systems of the world, and it was shining this afternoon, even in the bright daylight. The windows of the buildings reflected back the gentle sun, welcoming in the famous doctor, Sir Hans Sloane, President of the Royal Society, for his final lecture to the Fellows.

The doctor made his way into the Society's cramped discussion chamber, followed by the men who'd been smoking in the street. A great many more darkly dressed men were already inside, and as one they stood and applauded the doctor as he made his way towards the tiny stage to take his place behind the lectern. Some even whistled. *Not very distinguished*, the doctor thought to himself, secretly pleased with the reception. *One needs to keep a sense of proportion.* His breath was steady, but he had a headache and felt clammy and cold. But then, he always felt clammy and cold.

The steps up to the stage seemed to be miles away, and

didn't seem to be getting any closer, but with another mutter of *resolution, resolution* he reached the bottom of them, and with one final effort (and a gentle, discreet shove from his manservant), the doctor dragged himself onto the stage and reached the sanctuary of the lectern. He gripped the wooden edge as hard as he could, and turned to face his audience.

The men in the room were noisily taking their seats, removing their hats and arranging their wigs. The doctor held on hard to the lectern. He looked down before the stage and saw his Negro manservant gazing up at him, apparently unconcerned, his dark skin like an exclamation mark amid the grandeur of the Fellows. The Negro's calm stare seemed to calm the doctor, as if it was providing encouragement.

So the Fellows of the Royal Society waited for the final lecture (or, perhaps it would be better to say, the final *sermon*) from their old president, and for a moment (for several moments, actually) he forgot that his body was eating itself, he forgot the incessant pain and the daily humiliations, he even forgot the monstrous thing that waited in the attic, and he remembered that for centuries to come this building and this Society would acknowledge that the president who followed the great Newton had gloried in the name Sloane.

He smiled at the crowd. He had a few things to say.

'My friends,' he said, his voice quieter than he would have wanted but unwavering and clear, for which he was grateful. 'It is almost beyond my capacity for speech to tell you how much pleasure it gives me to stand here – within this blessed building, the cherished carapace for this noble Society – and to see the familiar faces of England's finest creatures arrayed before me. In none of the salons of the King can such a collection of beautiful minds and fair understanding be encountered. Not since the days of glory in Athens has so much knowledge and understanding been collected in a single place. If this building were to crumble into the earth, and all of this genius were to disappear with it, what a fall that would be. It is an awesome thought.'

Some frowns at this. Perhaps the image was blasphemous; the Society's philosophers falling like angels into Lucifer's domain. Milton would certainly not have approved.

'This grandeur and this awesome possibility serve to remind me of how far we have come. When I first visited this Society I was recently returned from adventures in the Americas and the Caribbean. I was a young man with the most vivid memories of amazing sights and picaresque peoples. I believed that I had seen the very edge of the world on my travels. I had certainly seen things which no educated man had seen before.

'When I saw those things, they were all of the nature of mysteries to me. The flora and fauna of that great island of Jamaica, for instance, presented themselves as an exotic combination of the oddly familiar and the profoundly strange.'

The old doctor paused. Some of his delight had left him. His reference to Jamaica had done nothing but remind him of the terrible cargo he'd brought from that place, and as he had done every day for the last fifty years he faced a familiar despair: that everything he had worked for, everything this building represented, was made ridiculous by the thing he had hidden upstairs. This despair had flooded his mind so often that he had become practised in first facing it, and then deliberately ignoring it. He had even learned a little mantra to help him through these moments: *there is an exception needed to prove every rule.* He turned back to his speech, determined to talk that despair back into its cave.

'During my travels, I wrote down what I saw, and I drew it, and where possible I brought back jottings and specimens. These I took to my esteemed fellow-members of the Royal

Society – to you! You, who have been busy cataloguing this world of wonders ever since our crown was restored. Between us, we have documented and detailed and delineated a world of precise geometric solidity, a world in which arcana and superstition have been buried beneath an architecture of knowledge which celebrates reason over mystery and experiment over unquestioning faith.

'When I look at this great room, and these great and beautiful men within it, I can perceive the same process: one by which mankind grapples with and makes sense of the world, shaping it into forms which he can understand and control. We have done this, my friends. We have shaped a world in our own image. Everything we see is explicable, every reality has a provable cause. Celebrate our wisdom, friends, and enjoy its rewards!'

A significant outbreak of applause at this.

'I am an old man, my fellow Fellows, and an old man becomes acutely aware of the operations of his own body. We old men are pursued by a dozen little daily humiliations. But this morning I awoke, and I started thinking of the operations of my own body, and I found a language for these considerations. The language of anatomy, the language of the great Morgagni himself.'

A cheer from one section of the crowd at this, and a middle-aged, dark-haired man is shoved to his feet by those around him, and for a moment Sloane feels tears even in his own dried-out eyes, because here is Morgagni himself, the great anatomist, who must have travelled all the way from Italy just to bid the old doctor farewell. The Italian bows to the stage, and Sloane, a huge lump in his throat (did Morgagni have a name for that?) bows back.

'My gratitude for the great Morgagni's presence is boundless. You are welcome, sir, and may I take this opportunity to thank you for your efforts in the service of knowledge and of health.

'But to continue with my theme. This very morning, when I awoke, I felt I had no control over my own bodily processes. Age had taken the helm, and I was helpless in the face of mortality. My body was in the process of declining into decrepitude. But then I started a naming. I ran through a concordance of anatomy, picturing the words and their matching properties. I pictured a map of the body in which the anatomists have named the countries and cities. And, sure enough, as I did this, I regained control and I took back ownership of myself.

'This is my point, gentlemen. For in naming is power. By discovering, cataloguing and naming a plant, a creature, a river or a tree, we do more than grow our knowledge. We extend our dominion. As the Lord told Adam, mankind is in power over the beasts of the earth, and in naming those beasts we both reflect our power and we deepen it.

'I said earlier that I believed that in Jamaica I was at the edge of the world. But we know, of course, that this world has no edge. We also know that our maps have great areas of uncertainty. Indeed, some of them have more white in them than blue, green or brown. There are worlds waiting to be discovered. And in naming those worlds, we will take ownership of them. Ownership in the name of this great new Britannia, of course, but also ownership in the name of mankind itself, whose dominions have been extended by the thrusting explorations of Britons, with so much yet to be discovered. I shall not be there to see these discoveries, but I know that they are there, shimmering over the edge of the world.

'And with that redemptive thought I leave you, my fellow wanderers.'

It was a long speech, and by the end of it his voice was hoarse, his heart was racing and his headache had turned from a thud into a glass-like stabbing. And he was of course conscious of the great irony running through the speech like a watermark only he could see, the irony of the unnameable thing in the attic. Nonetheless he felt exhilarated as the crowd raised a cheer, and he managed to step back down to the ground almost without aid, apart from a final little lurch which the manservant anticipated and caught. *That was Fear and not exhaustion*, he thought. *The Fear of what is to come*.

He walked through the crowd, the one great task left to complete. Various Fellows slapped his back (he rather wished they wouldn't, such were the vibrations these slaps set off throughout his ancient bones), and Morgagni was shoved at him to kiss him on both cheeks in the alarming Italian manner. And then he was out, and as quickly as it had arisen his exhilaration faded, leaving only the now-familiar sense of dried-up exhaustion.

Immediately, a problem presented itself. Sloane needed to get to the top floor of the building, but his exertions had ended his capacity for climbing for the day, and possibly for all time. He looked up at the staircase and suddenly his little scheme seemed stupid and half-baked. How had he ever imagined he would get up to the top floor?

'Sir,' said the manservant, his hand respectfully on his master's forearm. 'If I may suggest.' He leaned forward, and indicated his shoulders.

Sloane paused at the prospect of this. On the one hand, the prospect of being dragged physically up the stairs by a Negro was not appealing, however well mannered and genteel the Negro. On the other hand, there was no other way of reaching the summit of the Society's headquarters, and the alternative was a loose end which could not be countenanced. He really did need to speak to the thing that dwelt on the fourth floor.

When it came to it, there was little need for squeamish consideration. With a glance around to check that no one was watching, Sloane reluctantly acquiesced to being carried, and the impeccable little black manservant gently leaned the old man over his shoulder, his feet in front of him and his head behind, and began to climb the stairs. Sloane allowed himself to go as limp as possible, and barely glanced behind him as they climbed, pondering what he would say as the trunk of his manservant swayed from side to side. For himself, the manservant hardly noticed the weight of the old man; it was like carrying a great plucked battered old bird with hollow bones and smoke for lungs.

Eventually, they reached the top floor, via a narrowing series of little staircases which curled in and around each other as if architected by some imaginative child alone in a dusty nursery. At the top the manservant carefully placed Sloane back onto his feet. The doctor nodded his thanks, with a frown to suggest they would never speak of it again (and little thought for how he was going to get downstairs again). Reaching into his frock-coat's pocket, the doctor pulled out an old key, placed it into the lock of the only door of the landing on which they stood, and went into the room beyond. He gestured to the manservant to remain outside.

The room was only dimly lit by a single window, despite the spring daylight outside. It contained a bed, a chair, a small table, a small set of shelves filled with books, and a tall young man with dark hair, who was reading and not, as Sloane had earlier imagined, gazing out into Crane Court. The man was chained at the ankle, and the chain was itself connected to another chain which ran through iron eyelets around the room. This other chain was thick, and the eyelets through which it ran were welded into thick metal squares which were bolted into the wall at intervals of eighteen inches. However, the chain which held the man's ankle to the chain on the wall was finer, and the anklet from which it hung also had a refined elegance about it, as if it could be worn with comfort, unlike the clunking metalwork which currently held malefactors to the walls of Newgate. Both chains would have evoked different images in the head of the black manservant who waited patiently outside.

At the sight of Sloane, the young man stood up from his chair to allow the older man to sit down, and walked to the window. He was tall, and walked with a limp, which Sloane has diagnosed as a side-effect of the weight of the chain on one leg at all times, or perhaps of the blocking of healthy blood flow through the ankle to the foot on that side. With a sigh, Sloane sat down. Neither spoke for a moment; the tall young man crossed his arms and watched the doctor, while the doctor leant back in his chair and closed his eyes. For a moment, he looked like he was sleeping. Then his eyes opened, and he began to speak.

'First of all, my apologies,' he said, not looking at the young man but instead examining the fineness of the ironwork which bound the chain. *Who worked on that? I cannot remember. My God, the work is exquisite.*

The young man had still not spoken.

'I have not been able to visit for some time,' said Sloane. 'My time as President is coming to its natural end, as indeed is my life. My days have been spent more on my properties to the west of the city. I have missed our conversations.'

Still nothing from the young man.

'This degradation of responsibility is of course made worse by the fact that there is news for you. And I must admit that the nature of the news has added to my reluctance to come here. The Fellows who know of your existence have reached a conclusion. Indeed, we did so at our last session, and the Fellows have agreed to accept my proposal.'

Now, Sloane did look at the young man. The man's eyes were set steadily on him. As ever, Sloane found himself terrorised by the dead stillness he saw in them.

'The Fellows have spent many hours and days examining your case, William. The finest philosophical minds of modern times have disputed your existence and have carefully monitored you over the past decades. We have maintained copious records and drawings, and we have, where possible, sought to discover the knowledge of other cultures on the matter of your continued existence and the unassailable fact that you do not appear to age.'

The young man unfolded his arms and shifted his weight, and the chain screeched gently, like a dying crow.

'Fifty years,' continued Sloane. 'Half a century of investigation and disputation, and we have reached no conclusion. And soon, I will die. The man who brought you from Jamaica. The man who exercised the full intellectual armoury of the Royal Society to understand you. I will die any day now, William. And you will live.'

He sighed, as if with longing.

'I cannot deny,' he said, 'that this voyage of discovery began with a hope that uncovering your secrets would uncover knowledge and arcana which might have proved useful to me, as I approach death's horizon. I cannot deny that I envy you, now. This very evening my Negro manservant has had to carry me up the stairs to your room. Age and decrepitude have reduced me to this, William. To riding on a Negro's back. And still, you remain young.'

'If the curse were transferable, Sloane, I would transfer it willingly.' Lord, that voice, that awful, cold, deep, well-spoken, dispassionate voice. The voice of a renegade God walking through an apocalypse.

'So you have said, repeatedly, and I have no cause to doubt

it. But know this, William. Not ever having to feel age creep into your bones. Not having to feel the rocks on your chest when you wake in the morning, or the creaking of your joints as they painfully fold and unfold, or the dull, dry headache that is one's companion for every waking moment; not having to feel these things would seem, if you were in my position, a prize worth any price.'

'These things you have told me. And still I say: the curse is yours if you can take it.'

'And alas, I cannot. And soon, I will die.'

Something compelled him to stand, and walk to the door. The young man's dead eyes followed him across the room, and for a moment old Dr Hans Sloane was terrified, because the eyes were those of a simple predator, gazing at its prey pitilessly as it gauges the distance needed for the spring and imagines the taste of flesh and sinew beneath its teeth. In that moment, Sloane realised he wanted to squeeze every drop of life out of the allocation that remained to him, and he also realised that the young man in the room with him would pour that allocation out with no remorse whatsoever. His old ears began to pick up that annoying hum which always accompanied these interviews. Even his hearing was dying.

And then Sloane reached the door, and turned, ready to run.

'Our decision is that you cannot be, William,' he said. 'You are an aberration, even an abomination. There is nothing rational or demonstrable about your existence and your state. Should people learn of your existence, they would question everything – *everything* – this Society has fought to cherish and maintain for nigh on a century. We will not let that happen. You are to remain here, a secret known only to the Fellows of the Society. And we shall see what we shall see. You and I, however, will not meet again.'

And with that, the doctor let the young man be.

27 DECEMBER 1811

John Harriott had known that his Waterman-Constable Charles Horton had been planning a Christmas Day trip to Sheerness, but had not been expecting to hear from the man so quickly. When Horton's note arrived post-haste the previous evening it took the magistrate by surprise. Its contents surprised him even more:

> INFORMATION UNCOVERED IN SHEERNESS RELATING TO MURDERS. DO NOT WISH TO LEAVE, NOR TO PASS INFORMATION VIA THIRD PARTY. SUGGEST YOU ATTEND WITH ALL SPEED. HORTON.

The words were crisply written, the handwriting precise, the tone perhaps just the wrong side of respectful. It occurred to Harriott how much he now relied on the fellow, how his odd dark intensity had become something in which the old magistrate placed enormous faith and trust. There was never any question of not going to Sheerness.

Aaron Graham was of similar mind. Harriott had gone to his residence immediately on receiving Horton's note, planning to ask his fellow magistrate to attend at Shadwell today in his place, while he sailed to Sheerness. Events were moving quickly in Shadwell and he felt the need for a reliable witness to them. John Williams, still locked away in Coldbath Fields following his arrest on Christmas Eve, was now the single focus of attention of both the Shadwell investigation and of London's press. All three Shadwell magistrates were adamant that Williams was the killer, an Irish monster, despite the gaps and contradictions in his testimony, and despite the apparent lack of any accomplices, which contradicted much of the eyewitness evidence at hand. Harriott, whose doubts about Williams's guilt were already widely known and who was, in any case, *persona non grata* in Shadwell, was worried about not being in London for a day or two while things developed. He would have liked to have asked Graham to keep an eye on things.

Graham was having none of this. When he had read Horton's note, he shouted for his manservant and immediately began plotting the trip. He'd ordered a servant out to assemble a hamper of provisions for the journey, and sent Harriott away, promising to meet him at the River Police Office at eight o'clock sharp. He had an urgent appointment that evening for dinner and drinks, but this would not delay him in the morning.

Which is how two of London's magistrates come to be standing on a cutter sailing downstream towards the estuary. The *Antelope* is the River Police Office's only vessel of significant size. Harriott purchased her from a merchant specialising in trade with Holland only months before. He has sailed no further than Millwall on her, and is relishing a longer trip. Aaron Graham is less certain. Graham is a city man these days, his naval career a long way in the past, and he has little interest any longer in the salty arcana of the sea, unless it be on a pleasure yacht above Richmond with a hamper full of fine food and wine and, if possible, some music.

The decision to travel by water was Harriott's, and Graham, despite himself, was forced to agree. The road journey to Sheerness is a complicated one, requiring a great loop of travel to cross the Medway and reach the Swale Ferry just to get onto the Isle of Sheppey. It would have taken perhaps two days by coach, though the horse which Horton had sent to London, carrying his urgent message, had travelled it in a single day. A post-chaise might have been quicker, but would still have been uncomfortable, cold and uncertain.

And, as Harriott pointed out in the urgent discussions they'd had following receipt of Horton's message, he did own a boat (or rather the River Police Office owned a boat, but as his enemies have previously pointed out this is not a distinction that Harriott dwells upon). His eyes had sparkled when he'd knocked on Graham's door early yesterday evening, Horton's note in his hand and finally, at last, some concrete action to take.

The smart little cutter glides downstream, elegantly and effortlessly avoiding the clusters of ships around the docks and wharves on both sides of the river. Its tidy trim and blood-red sails stand out in the crowded river mist, and some of the watermen looking at the vessel from the boats and wharves appear to actually doff their caps towards it, so regal does it appear, before remembering who now owns the ship and scowling at it.

Harriott and Graham stand in the stern of the ship. The crew consists of half-a-dozen men and a master. They are busying themselves with the sails and the helm, leaving the magistrates to consider the day's undertakings. Harriott is obviously enjoying himself. Opportunities to get onto open water are few enough these days, and he still relishes the feel of salt water on his face. Graham is uncomplaining, but his green face and desperate grip on the ship's rail tell of his acute discomfort. Last night's dinner and drinks weigh heavy upon him.

They pass smoothly downriver on a falling tide, past Limehouse, Deptford, Greenwich, Woolwich, Gravesend and out into the estuary. Even here, where the water is choppier and the wind sharper, their progress remains unhindered. The Dutch-designed boat is sturdy as well as trim, perfectly at home in the North Sea, and Harriott is delighted with her. Having departed the Police Office steps at eight o'clock that morning, they are approaching Sheerness by early afternoon.

The two magistrates now watch as the half-built port of Sheerness comes into view around the corner of the Isle of Grain (the sunken remains of Horton's little dinghy pass by on their starboard side, unreported and unnoticed). Graham expresses surprise and some delight at the way the clear water of the Medway creates a deep blue contrast with the muddy brown of the estuary. He has begun to recover his typical bonhomie and claps Harriott on the shoulder as the skipper manoeuvres the vessel around the half-dozen hulks which surround the entrance to the new harbour.

'Which one do you think it is, Harriott?' he asks.

Aaron Graham's natural intelligence and curiosity has taken over. Sheerness, the salty sea, the gusty wind, the dark forlorn hulks on the water and the masts dotted in and around the harbour mouth – he takes all this in with the excitement of a very smartly dressed puppy, his queasiness increasingly forgotten.

For his part, Harriott feels a sense of awesome nostalgia. The sea is one thing but here, at Sheerness, he is almost transfixed by naval memories. The hulks, with their missing masts and roofed-over decks, make him feel unaccountably sad, while the new dock rising out from amidst the mess of hulks and houses seems to point to a glorious maritime future in which old sailors and superannuated colonels will play no part. He feels at once redundant and unaccountably excited.

The cutter comes to just outside the entrance to the dock, waiting for a brig to make its way out. The brig picks its way around the hulks gathered around the entrance, and after it has passed the master of the *Antelope* shouts a question at Harriott, who indicates they should continue.

They creep into the half-built dock. There are two or three hulks in there, a pair of matching frigates, a smattering of Thames barges being unloaded onto the dock walls, and a large dark ugly three-masted thing which stands over to one side of the dock, against a quay below a half-built harbour wall surrounded by half-built warehouses. On the aft deck of this final ship, waving across to them calmly and slowly, stands the dark still figure of Constable Horton.

Where the ships outside the dock had sparked nostalgia and some sadness in Harriott, the one on which his constable stands conveys something altogether different. It is devoid of personality, of any poetry at all which might inspire a sensitive response. Its lines are stout and practical and ugly. One of the three masts is missing a top-piece, and what is left of the rigging hangs from the spars and masts in a drab, inconsequential sort of way. There are gaps in the rails around the deck, and patches of unpainted or untreated wood down the sides of the hull. There is no figurehead, and no name that Harriott can see. It flies no flags. It is functionally, as far as the maritime authorities are concerned, invisible. It is a non-ship.

Close to the harbour wall at the stern of the dark ship the cutter comes to, and the crew throw ropes onto the quayside to allow a gangway to be put in place. Harriott and Graham, followed by a waterman-constable from the *Antelope*'s crew, walk across the plank to the dockside. Harriott feels an enormous weight of reluctance weighing him down as he steps onto the quay. The dark ship seems to exert an awful sense of itself.

There is another plank connecting the waist of the dark ship to the quayside, and Harriott crosses it first (his old sea legs returning unnoticed, despite a growing tightness of his chest from the unaccustomed exercise), Graham close behind. The attending constable, at a nod from Harriott, waits on the quay.

Constable Horton offers Harriott his hand for the last few feet but the old man knocks it away peremptorily, noticing that no such help is offered to Graham.

Now they are on the ship Harriott can get a real feel for just how parlous the vessel's condition is. The aft deck is a wobbly, shifty-looking thing, cracked and uncared for. The same effect is apparent across the waist of the ship, and there are fragments of broken wood at the edges of most things. Most of the wood is pale, dry and obviously rotten. There are small piles of freshly packed provisions dotted here and there, apparently awaiting stowage. From below decks comes a regular metallic grating noise, in rhythm with the water in the dock. There is no one else aboard.

Horton formally greets his two superiors, then beckons them down below decks via a wide and still-secure ladder. He lights a candle, and in the flickering light Harriott sees the internal structure of the ship for the first time. He feels a great sense of awe and wonder wash over him.

The innards of the ship are split into three levels: two lower decks, and the hold. Crumbling ladders go up and down between them. Both lower decks are open, with limited space for guns at either end of the ship. This is a cargo ship, not a warship. The deck space is encircled by a deep wooden shelf, some three feet off the floor of the deck and some six feet deep. Something about the layout gives the sense that it has been adapted from a previous purpose. Perhaps it was a prize; it does remind Harriott of the ugly utility of many Dutch vessels.

Ringing the inside of the deck in two rows, one above the deck floor and one above the wooden shelf, are iron loops bolted into the hull. Some are missing, and some are hanging loosely, but the ones that are still intact are as solid and timeless as rocks. From many of these loops hang ancient, dark iron chains which swing in time with the ship's own movement. It is these chains knocking into each other which create the metallic sound Harriott heard outside.

They climb down a ladder to the lower deck, which replicates the layout of the one above but is darker: the open deck, the space for guns, the large wooden shelf, the iron loops, the chains. Another ladder goes down to the dark hold. No one says anything. Horton's candle picks up enormous moving shadows down on this lower deck, as if night-time wraiths were themselves locked into the chains and the loops, wailing their captivity.

They climb outside into the afternoon gloom, onto the waist, and John Harriott walks back towards the stern to investigate the captain's quarters behind the quarterdeck. He walks through another compartment with iron rings in the walls and goes through a small door into the captain's cabin.

There are some signs of life in here. Constable Horton has followed him in, and stands in the door while Harriott sits down on the wooden bench and looks at the scattering of bottles and candles which litter the floor. The constable indicates something carved into the wood alongside the bed. It looks like four letters superimposed upon each other.

'P-T-S-I?' Harriott asks.

'That's my guess, yes, sir,' says Horton.

'This is a slave ship,' says Harriott, to no one in particular, perhaps to himself.

'Yes, sir.'

Graham steps into the cabin, which now seems inordinately crowded with three men in it.

'My God, I thought we'd seen the last of these,' he says. 'Five years since the Act, and I imagined they'd all been scuppered or repurposed by now.'

'Not this one, sir,' says Constable Horton. 'In actual fact, not many of them were scuppered. Most are being used for some kind of trade, though I'm told these ships were never intended to last more than ten years. But so far, this one's been left alone.'

His intonation suggests a question, and Graham asks it.

'Why not this one, Horton?'

'It's the *Zong*, sir.'

John Harriott looks at him, open-mouthed, and then lets out a single, disbelieving *ha!*

'Are you sure, Horton?' Graham asks, his urban poise replaced by an excitement and urgency which Harriott at once recognises and misses from himself. All he feels is the old torpor returning to his bones, part exhaustion, part horror. *Not this, my Lord. Surely not this.*

'Yes, sir, quite sure,' Constable Horton says to Graham. 'I know several of the people here, and they have traced its history. It was to be turned into a hulk; these old slavers make good hulks provided some more room is made for English tastes. They got almost 450 slaves on here on that . . . last voyage, in a space for a dozen English families.'

'So why hasn't it been hulked?' asks Harriott.

'Somebody bought it. Three months ago.'

'Who? Who bought it?'

'I'm still waiting for the papers to appear, but I've got a

physical description of the main buyer. And there's something else. He paid with Potosí pieces of eight.'

'P-T-S-I,' says Harriott, and Constable Horton looks pleased at the speed of his thought.

'Yes, sir. Precisely.'

Harriott leans back against the wooden wall of the benighted vessel. The *Zong*. In the Lord's name, the *Zong*. Here in Sheerness, this close to London, this damned vessel of Liverpool. How the hell had it ended up here? The cursed slave ship, the spur to abolitionist rage, the catalyst for laws that had banned slave trading (though not slave ownership) in the British Empire. They'd slept there, on those awful wooden racks and beneath them, their faces up against the underside of the deck or the shelf above, more slaves lying below them, their women and children amassed on the floor at their heads, chained and dying.

And then one day, on that final voyage, a decision had been made and the ship's crew had grabbed the sickest of them and had thrown them overboard out at sea. Almost two hundred of them. An insurance scam. They were no use to them ill on land, fetching a poor price or even dying before they got a chance to sell them. So they discarded them in order that they could claim full-price against them. And when the *Zong* crept back into Liverpool and reported back to its owners, they disappeared into an office and began filling in the claim forms. Dead human beings, claimed on insurance.

That had been thirty years ago. This empty vessel gave no clue to its history. Nothing breathed in its wood. It had no business at all being here. But yet here it was, as if nothing could kill it off, as if the memories of what it had done were sustaining it into permanent existence. Any emotional resonance that remained was inside the heads of those with the imagination to picture the scenes which played out on this death-ship. Yet the resonance is there.

Harriott is not a sentimental man. He holds no firm views on slavery. Having travelled extensively in America, he has seen how hard it is to find suitable farming labour, and as a good practical Christian sincerely believes that a slave with a humane God-fearing owner is better off than a free man running with the Godless, cannibalising savages on the dark continent. In this he is the same as a great many important men in London, not least the brother of the Prince Regent himself (the Regent's views, if he holds any, are not known).

But Harriott is also a man whose personal history encapsulates entire worlds, who has encountered more races and more cultures than perhaps any man in London. Harriott values life, even the life of a poor, dying Negro out on one leg of the dread Triangular Trade, and for a while the wails of the children, the moaning of the women and the sickening flat rage of the enslaved men fill his head, and he sees their black faces plunging into the waves, their black limbs pointing up towards the sky, and dread, slack-jawed sea creatures ploughing towards them, mouths opening wide. It was as clear and as awful as a gigantic painting.

And here, in this cabin, had sat the captain who had made the decision to throw those dark, damned creatures into the waters.

'Potosí pieces of eight,' says Graham at last, the first to struggle out of the imagined scenes which are playing out in their heads. 'You imply that is significant. I confess I do not see it.'

'Potosí pieces of eight were found at the scenes of both murders in Shadwell, Graham,' says John Harriott, after a significant moment of silence. Until now, Horton has shared this information with Harriott alone. He did not trust Graham sufficiently to divulge it. Harriott has had to step in before the silence becomes too rude and yawning.

'I dare say,' says Graham. 'But pieces of eight are not unusual in London, Harriott. There are more species of coin swilling round the inns of Wapping than there are unmarried young women in Bath.'

'*Potosí* pieces of eight, mind.'

'Well, that narrows it down somewhat. But not enormously.'

Their voices echo slightly out on the cavernous deck beyond the captain's cabin. The ship creaks, but it is a dead sound, as if she were scared to draw attention to herself. And with good reason, thinks Harriott.

'Is there nothing else, Horton?' says Graham. Horton looks at Harriott, and the old man waves his hand resignedly. Let the blighter speak for himself, for a change.

'The ship was sailed into Sheerness by a skeleton crew a few weeks ago,' says Horton. 'The captain is described as a tall man, young, with a limp, by several witnesses and by the harbourmaster. He told the harbourmaster that the ship was going to be refitted somewhere on the south coast, but needed to remain here while he organised for supplies and sundries in London. He said he would return here in the New Year with new sails, rigging and victuals.'

'And no one thought to ask this man his name?'

'They did. He signed the documentation as Henry Morgan.'

'So, presumably we look for this Morgan.'

'Well, sir, I rather suspect that's an invented name.'

'Invented? Why should it be invented?'

'Because I'd think it unlikely that anyone would use their real name in so public a fashion if they were going to do what I think they intended to do.'

'Which is what, man?'

'Trade slaves, sir.'

Graham stops at that and glares at Constable Horton, as if the man was guilty of some terrible social *faux pas*.

'A somewhat inelegant theory, my dear constable,' he says, the words polite, the tone anything but. 'You cannot extrapolate from the *Zong*'s previous history to that theory without some more thought.'

'There's been no work to re-adapt the ship, Mr Graham.' Horton's voice is polite, but a slight change in emphasis bespeaks growing insubordination. 'This boat is useless for the carrying of anything other than slaves.'

'But trading slaves has been outlawed, constable.'

'Indeed so, Mr Graham. But only these past five years. And new laws take time to make their way around the world. There are still plenty of buyers for slaves in Cuba and Brazil. You can find many buyers in America. It will be a lucrative trade for some years to come, perhaps even decades. Made all the more lucrative by the fact that most British traders have abandoned it. It's perhaps a highly auspicious time to launch a slaving enterprise.'

Graham considers this. He looks at Constable Horton in a new way.

'By God, man, you've thought this through,' he says.

'Aye, Mr Graham. That I have. I spent last night on this ship. It has a powerful way of stirring one's considerations.'

Graham pauses, unaccountably annoyed. He glares around the inside of the captain's cabin, defying it to give up some of its secrets.

'I still don't understand why you assume that Morgan is an invented name. It seems perfectly normal to me.'

'I have found evidence of a connection between this tall man and Jamaica, Mr Graham.'

'What evidence?'

'An entry in Mr Williamson's order book. An order had

been placed for victuals sufficient for a journey to Africa and then Jamaica, with sufficient for trading in Africa. The order also included sacks of peas and beans, which I understand was for long years the common sustenance for feeding Africans during the Atlantic crossing.'

'Jamaica was specifically mentioned?'

'It was, sir.'

'And it's Williamson's order book that ties this ship's captain to the murders?'

'Not just Williamson. Marr also. A Henry Morgan appears as a buyer of Osnaburg cotton in pages I removed from Marr's order book. Again, the order includes hundreds of cotton shirts and trousers, which I also understand is common for a slaver; they need the slaves to look the part when they sell them. Again, Jamaica is mentioned. Indeed, it's given as his address.'

'The man is from Jamaica?'

'It would seem so.'

'So how hard can it be to find a Morgan from Jamaica?'

John Harriott speaks up, irritated by Graham's dullness.

'My dear Graham, I think you need to stop and think for a moment. Henry Morgan? Jamaica?'

Graham's bad mood evaporates instantly. He smiles, almost with delight.

'Our man has a sense of humour, it appears.'

Neither Horton nor Harriott respond to this. It is perhaps too genteel a remark for the circumstance, and Graham speaks again quickly to mask any embarrassment.

'So, why didn't this "Morgan" buy his supplies in Sheerness?'

Constable Horton answers again.

'I think that's what he intended, sir. But the chandlers here in Sheerness has been closed for some time. It burned down in a fire.'

'So why not sail the ship into London?'

'The cost. It's far cheaper to have the ship ported here; while the new dock's being built, rates are low and there's plenty of labour on the ships. I spoke to an old shipmate of mine who told me this "Morgan" had been recruiting people to work on the ship, and they have been waiting for supplies and money to get started. Also, he probably did not want to draw attention to himself. Sheerness is ideal for him, in some ways. It's still a bit of a backwater.'

'Linen and victuals,' says Graham. He runs his hands along a small wooden shelf, a kind of decorative counterpoint to the dread compartments and chains in the deck beyond. He scuffs the greying decking gently with one elegant shoe. 'So the question becomes: what went wrong? And why did it end in murder?'

JUNE 1780

I heard them crash into the door three times. The chain was tight around my neck, and no air entered my body, and once again I felt that strange, almost unbearable lightness of being come over me as the old curse took grip and forced encroaching death out. The chain bit into the skin, and there was a great deal of pain, of course. But there would soon be air breathing into me again. I would be able to make my way through the living world.

I had tried this trick a dozen or more times before, but Sloane had been careful in his arrangements, passing down instructions about the Monster in the Crane Court attic only to a trusted circle of young Fellows who had been charged with the responsibility of both observing me and keeping me secret.

This little circle of Fellows had aged as Sloane had done, and as they did so all of them took the opportunity to come up to the little attic room and beg of the Monster the secrets he held, the secret of Eternal Life, and one by one they threatened to eviscerate me to unlock my mysteries before falling into a final despairing acknowledgement of the horrors of Mortality. They never seemed to extend the circle of those who knew about the Monster. The same familiar faces appeared again and again, the skin around their face sagging and their backs thinning out and bending, until finally only one of them remained, an unimpressive gentleman called Lambert who had made an accidental alchemical discovery decades before which had earned him a Fellowship but who had failed to improve on this early success in subsequent years (this was his personal biography, as he related to me on one of the endless evenings when he wept for his own approaching doom). Lambert, of all the Fellows, took Sloane's pronouncements on secrecy the most seriously, and often said that the secret of the Monster should die with him, that he should arrange for the Monster to be taken out of the country and left on some island somewhere to rot in a foreign sun. He said this to me without embarrassment. He made a great show of hiding the papers describing the various investigations into my Existence and Enduring in a cupboard in my room, so they would remain hidden with me. I sometimes took them out, those papers, and cheered myself up with their fruitless attempts to explain, in their new language of Natural Philosophy, a Monster who did not die.

But then Lambert appeared no more. Perhaps he had succumbed to a sudden poisoning, the result of a final experimental effort to unlock an arcane corner of natural philosophy and silence those Society whisperers who said he had singularly failed to achieve any discoveries of note since his first accidental breakthrough. He seemingly left no arrangement for me, and I waited out my chance for seven more months, hunger and thirst raging through me but still, even now, a long way from death. Then the workmen arrived.

I had heard them clambering around Crane Court for

almost two weeks, working their way up the house, chests crashing onto wooden floors and glass chandeliers tinkling into storage. A move was underway, apparently.

Slowly, the workmen made their way towards me, room by room and floor by floor. Last week, they were in the room below my chamber, and were so close that I could even hear them speak, their conversation a rough one of beer and women and poverty and work. Three days ago, I heard footsteps on the stairs outside, and the door into the chamber had moved as someone had tried to force it open. It was then I'd begun to prepare my little tableau, placing the chair in the middle of the floor, looping the chain which was attached to my ankle over a beam above, such that it hung down in a great U, while still remaining attached to the thicker chain which ran around the reinforced walls.

There were no further footsteps on the stairs for some time, and then today I heard them again, three or four men climbing the stairs and talking to themselves, of what I could not hear. So I climbed onto the chair, put a small loop in the great U of the chain, placed my head and neck within it, and kicked the chair away, and allowed myself to hang, the air departing my body (soon to return) and the chain biting into my undying flesh while pulling on my lame ankle.

One, two, three crashes came from outside as the men tried to force their way in, and on the fourth the door flew open and I closed my eyes, listening to the men below me as I hung there (just as I had once listened to a Dutchman on the banks of the river two hundred years before).

'Oh, my Lord Jesus Christ! Fuck!'

The voice was deep and London and heavy, and I could picture the heavy man who spoke it, the one who'd successfully crashed through the door.

'Get the bloody chair! There! Get the bloody chair!'

Scuffling sounds as unseen hands moved the chair back beneath my feet, then the feel of arms on my legs as they lifted me out of the metal noose.

''Anged by a chain!'

'How long 'as 'e been 'ere?'

'Fuck!'

'If you stopped fuckin' cursin' and helped, we'd get this done quicker.'

'Watch your fuckin' mouth, you floggin' cully.'

'Well just get on wiv it!'

The hands brought me down with great care and laid me down on the floor, on my back, and I heard some discussion. My chest did not move. It was simple to feign death.

'Leave 'im 'ere. I'll go and ask what they want doing wiv 'im.'

'I ain't stayin' in 'ere wiv 'im.'

'Well come wiv me then, he ain't goin' anywhere.'

They went out through the door, and clumped down the stairs. I waited, my eyes remaining closed, my lungs not moving. I waited and waited. Finally, more men entered the room. Their voices were refined and educated.

'Must be one of these . . . I wondered what these keys were for . . . Never been up into this attic before, always assumed it was just storage . . . So, try the keys . . . No, not this one . . . Nor this one . . . Nor . . . Ah!'

And the hated lock around my ankle sprang open for the first time in a hundred years.

Later, after much discussion and chatter, these new men left the room, resolving to return to bring the body down. And then I did open my eyes, and sat up, only to find that a young thin dark-haired boy of no more than sixteen had remained in the room and was watching, wide-eyed, as the hanged man came back to life.

I stood up and limped over to where the boy was standing, looking him in the eye all the while. The memory of the iron pain around my neck was already starting to disappear, but the older pains – the wounds in my chest and in my stomach – were as present as ever, hovering like bats, and it appeared the damage done to my ankle by that obscene chain would be permanent also. All I saw was a boy, a witness, and behind him the emergence of a plan for the future.

'Jus' ... jus' ... look, jus' ...' whimpered the boy and I smelled something then, a urine odour, fresh and sharp. I heard something too, that old familiar hum, as once again the curse enfolded me. I did not look away from the boy's eye. The old calmness settled on me as I approached the boy, and my mind was already on the next few minutes – the walk down the stairs, the escape through the courtyard and then, perhaps, a ship, flight to Jamaica, the chance to find my treasure – as I took the boy's head between my hands and with a simple crack! smashed it against the brick wall of the room. The boy sank to the floor, a vertical thick line of blood and brains smeared on the wall behind him, and I turned to leave. I cast one more glance around the room that had contained me for almost a century, and then I went down the stairs and out into London, and beyond.

27 DECEMBER 1811

The three of them stay in Sheerness the night after visiting the ship, planning to sail back on the rising tide the following morning. But the next day dawns to appalling weather, a harsh, cutting wind rushing across from Holland and squalls following one on the other, as if the elements have sensed the obscenity within the harbour and are determined to send the black old thing down to the depths.

In any case Graham now seems determined to speak to every resident of the Sheerness hulks, to 'add some colour to the painting' as he puts it over breakfast with Constable Horton in the snug little inn in which they spent the night. John Harriott has not appeared to eat with the two men. His constable asks after the old man with the inn's staff, and is reassured that his breakfast has been served in his room. Horton goes out into the howling wind to pursue his own unheralded enquiries.

Harriott lies in his bed for some time. The breakfast which is brought into him by a pinch-faced little Kentish lad is allowed to go cold on the side table, as the old man wrestles with a growing sense of despair. The wrench of being aboard the *Zong* has stung him profoundly and he had woken to a black mood. He finally rises from bed two hours after Horton and Graham have departed on their own errands, and wanders aimlessly about his room for quite some time before deciding to take a walk along the straight stretch of flat, dreary beach that drifts eastwards back from the new dock, facing north across the estuary and out to the Nore.

It is not pleasant walking. The wind continues to whip up alarmingly, and squally winds pour themselves back into his face. The conditions bring back memories of that terrible night in Essex when the river had flooded out his little farm, on the island he'd reclaimed by sheer force of will from the waters around it.

He walks for perhaps an hour along the empty shore, until the masts of ships in and around the dock are barely pencil-thin scratches on the grey air. He comes to a stop, and stares out at the flat, grey sea.

He'd stepped out there on that flatness, decades before, as a boy. Thirteen years old, with a head full of Robinson Crusoe, sailing off from Spithead as part of a fleet bound for New York. He'd felt like a king, that first morning, dashing around on the deck and in the rigging. And then the gale had struck, slashing into the side of the ships as the sailors desperately furled the sails and close-reefed the few that were left. The wind had blown for hours, and the horror of that night was still with him: the signal-guns blaring in the dark; the shouts between ships (the terror was not of sinking but of crashing into one of the other vessels, so close were they to each other); the breathless, dashing madness of it all.

And in the morning, the ruination of the fleet. His ship had escaped unscathed. Others were de-masted, or had run afoul of each other and two had sunk beneath the waves. Dozens of lives lost. His first taste of death.

He'd seen other things. So many things. But that blood-rushing mixture of death and crashing violence and crazed activity was what had brought him to the sea, and what kept him there for years. And by God he'd tasted life! Plagues and girls and islands in the Mediterranean, Indians in America, tigers and Gentoos and rajahs in India, sultans in Sumatra and duchesses in England. His crippled leg, destroyed in action in India, followed him around as a keepsake of those dazzling, startling years. Even back in England he'd maintained a flair for the dramatic, his single-handed attempt to roll back the waves, Canute-like, from his little Essex island only the most flamboyant of a procession of adventures within polite middle-class society. But then there were those two other women, dead young wives in the ground, a melancholy rhythm within the bluster of his life.

Four years ago, he'd published his memoirs at the urging of friends, and had found the whole undertaking a desperate, ridiculous process. The publishing, mind, not the writing. The writing of the memoirs had been almost a cleansing thing, a taking account, a starting anew. And when he'd finished, he'd asked himself: *Is my life now over?* And the gruff, energetic old Harriott had told himself not to be ridiculous, to get on with it, to finish *the job*, whatever *the job* might be.

So he'd worked even harder, pushing onwards and forwards with the River Police Office, determined to be a pioneer in the new practice of policing following his early years as a magistrate in Essex. The office had been his idea, developed with his associate Patrick Colquhoun, and the two of them had been its first magistrates, Colquhoun the senior of them thanks to his political connections. Colquhoun had retired as the new century began, leaving Harriott as the senior magistrate.

But his sons had moved away at around this time, and his dear wife had begun to suffer from an occasional absent-mindedness, which had taken root in the past year and which terrified him more than he cared to admit. She remained the serene, kind and patient creature she had always been, but now there was a darkness between them, the presence of something just over the horizon which could sail into dock and destroy them in their sleep. His financial affairs, while steadier after his years in London, remained in some unspoken disarray. Dead wives and an absence of money. His daily realities, as they always had been.

And then, finally, these despicable murders. Harriott was again forced to face his growing irrelevance to the glorious project that was Great Britain, because even in the face of abject incompetence, even when the senior representative of investigative authority on the case was Story, a man who believed that Judgement Day was literally in the coming weeks, even when the response of London's nascent police forces was to arrest anyone who fell into an assumed but never-described set (Irish and/or Portuguese and/or Jewish, poor, drunk, male, sailor, lame, tall, short, ugly, missing, *seen in the area*), even when it was his own people who'd found the best clues and made the best connections, even then it was Harriott who'd earned official displeasure, Harriott who'd been told to back off, Harriott who felt that the powers-that-be had used up their capacity to tolerate him and even now were plotting his removal and expulsion from the only social position in which he any longer felt vested with any relevance at all.

The waves had destroyed his farm. Gentoos had destroyed his leg. Circumstances had destroyed his fortune on more than one occasion. And now They were out to get him. He ponders the flat, brown, freezing waters, the thick air and the dimly perceived shapes of ships out on the waves. He remembers the title of his memoirs: *My Struggles Through Life*. Perhaps the time is coming for those struggles to cease.

'Well now, my friend. You do look preoccupied.'

And there is Graham, wandering towards him with an indifferent but welcoming air, smoking a thin cigar and tapping the ground with his elegantly carved cane.

'Morning, Graham,' says Harriott, studiously adopting his professional face, hiding his embarrassment at the directions in which his thinking had been turning.

'Morning, indeed,' his friend replies. 'And what a quite disgusting sight the morning brings, if I may say so.'

'Indeed. The weather is beastly.'

'I was not speaking in reference to the weather, my dear old friend.'

'Then in reference to what?'

'Oh, in reference to the unpleasing prospect of a fat lame old man gazing into the middle distance over the ugly, flat, lifeless sea, looking for all the world as if he feels more sorry for himself than old Robespierre when they came to fetch him to Madame Guillotine. You have solved the crime, sir! Why the ridiculously long face?'

'Solved, Graham? Solved how?'

'Well, this Morgan fellow, whatever his real name is, has obviously been up to no good. Horton's efforts, his – how shall we say – *investigations*, have unearthed powerful explanations for the deaths of Marr and Williamson.'

'But why kill them?'

'I do not understand why the *why* is so important to you.'

'Because without motive, I cannot understand the sequence of events.'

'Oh, I don't know. They must have upset him somehow.'

'But that won't do, Graham.'

Glimpses of the old Harriott were coming back: perspicacious, intolerant of laziness and shoddy thinking, energetic, determined. The old man did not even notice.

'Motive offers explanation, Graham. Men do not kill each other randomly, other than in war. If we seek out motive, we find explanation.'

'Harriott. My dear friend.'

Graham places a brotherly hand on Harriott's shoulder. For a moment the mask of genteel display drops and beneath one can see a warmer, kinder and cleverer person than the public man suggests. His eyes almost twinkle with fellow-feeling.

'Harriott. John. You are cut from a different cloth to the rest of us. You represent an older, braver, and in its way infinitely kinder way of approaching the world.'

'Graham, I . . .'

'No, John, do let me finish. You see, something is being built here. Something rather new and rather grand. Britain will win this war with the French, believe me, and do you know why? Because we know what we are fighting for. Those idiots over the Channel have had two decades of their mouths being filled with talk of liberty, fraternity, even *equality*, Lord preserve us. They have somehow been led to believe that this world can be made better, can be re-forged into something with nobility and humanity. Or rather, they think they believe that.

'But one day they will look at their ridiculous little emperor and say to themselves, "Now, just wait a while. I'm fighting for him? And what do I get out of the deal?" And when the answer comes "The glory of France!" or "Liberty, equality, fraternity", more and more of them will reply: "Not good enough, chum. Not good enough by half."

'Now take your English soldier. He's not fighting for values or philosophy. He's not even fighting for his King. He's fighting for his God-given right to raise his family, till his plot, fill his belly and his purse. That's the new reality, John. We're a nation of shopkeepers. Hadn't you heard?'

'Shopkeepers.' Harriott says it with deliberate sarcasm, yet

Graham's speech has stirred him. The black dog is creeping away, its tail beneath its legs. 'It somehow does not set the heart racing, Graham.'

'Oh, but it does. It certainly *does*. A nation of profitable souls, each fighting for their patch of land, their slice of cake, their chance at riches? The dreams of wealth, Harriott. These are the dreams which propel this nation forward.'

'It is a picture which is perhaps not as compelling to me as it is to you, Graham.' And yet, of course, it is.

'Indeed not, John. Indeed not. Which is what I intended to say when I said you were cut from a different cloth. The world you fashioned is still with us, John. But a new world is being built upon it.'

'An uncaring world.'

'Perhaps. But John.' And here Graham taps the ground with his cane, almost in exasperation. 'This world will not be built on the backs of slaves kidnapped from one country and transported to another for the profits of Liverpool and London and Bristol. It will be built on industry. People like you built an empire, John. But they also built the *Zong*.'

The three men meet again at the inn for luncheon, and the weather has not improved a jot. The skipper of the *Antelope* has already indicated how reluctant he is to head upriver in the current conditions, and how unpleasant the trip would be for his passengers if they forced him to do so. Harriott is now determined to get them back to London quickly and by any means necessary, and takes it upon himself to investigate the stage as an option for the return trip to London. There is one leaving that afternoon which could have them in London by midnight, subject to successfully crossing the Swale in this fearsome weather.

Graham agrees to the plan. The three men get into an empty

stagecoach and proceed south-east (away from London, much to Harriott's frustration, but the coach driver is adamant that this is the best chance for finding a working ferry, and in any case that is where the best road is).

But when they reach the Swale, their plans are again thwarted. The ferry is suspended due to the bad weather, and no amount of shouting by Harriott can convince the old ferryman that a crossing in this weather is anything other than madness. They are forced to take shelter in a small inn on the banks of the Swale, another night away from London. There follows an uncomfortable evening for Constable Horton, during which Graham affects a studied cheeriness while Harriott glowers, staring into the fire and ignoring all efforts to engage him in something like a conversation about anything other than *motive* and *explanation*.

The following morning is calmer, both meteorologically and, apparently, with regard to John Harriott, who wakes seeming somewhat lighter than the night before (in actual fact, he has slept better than he has for months in the quiet, comfortable little bedroom, sheltered from the winds by the shape of the building and from his own concerns by the future visions conjured by Graham). They cross the Swale successfully, and soon reach the turnpike south of Gillingham and Rochester which takes them up and over the steep North Downs, then down into London via the villages and open fields of Blackheath and Peckham, through New Cross and the Elephant and Castle with its new turnpike gate and then over the bridge at Blackfriars.

Here they leave the coach. Graham makes his way west towards Covent Garden, while Horton and Harriott take a hackney to Wapping. The two of them get out at Harriott's residence, and they take their leave. Horton begins his walk westwards to Lower Gun Alley, where Abigail is waiting for him.

The image of Abigail is welcoming, but nonetheless he stops in at one of the taverns on Wapping Street and with a growing, screaming sense of panic enveloping him he pays for a bottle of rum (*Jamaica* rum) and a glass. Where does this panic come from? He does not know. Something about the enormity of his discoveries of the last few days, and the conclusions he is beginning to draw about them. But more than that the panic stems from the suppression of himself which was forced upon him at Sheerness.

He pours a full glass, fully one-quarter of the bottle, and upends it. The strong Jamaican liquor burns his throat and squeezes his forehead, but at least it suppresses the tidal wave of anxiety that has been threatening ever since he climbed into the hulk on Sheerness. For the best part of a week, he has been a visitor to the scene of his own defining moral crime, standing on the spot where his fellow-mutineers were hanged, constantly petrified that someone, anyone, would recognise him, the Judas of the *Sandwich*, the man who'd bought his freedom with information on the conspiracy which may even have led to the capture of Parker himself. Not even thirty pieces of silver. Just a nod, a wink, a look the other way, and he was gone, to build a new life for himself upstream, buried among the crushed-in houses along the river.

He's back now. Back inside the shelter of London. The first enormous slug of dark rum has pushed the panic back down, but it's still there, swirling away in his stomach like a sea snake. Even while he drinks and frets and remembers, his antennae, finely tuned to the rhythms of the chatter in the bar, have begun to take in what is going on around him. He's sat for many evenings inside saloons like this one, minding the conversations and the emphases, picking up fragments which could be assembled into something later on. And he's noticed something now. An excited chatter. At the table next to him, a drunk woman is regaling her male companion.

'Just fink, luv. Just fink. 'is body's out there right now, innit? Festerin' away. He fawt he woz gon get away wiv it, dinnen he? He rilly fawt that. But he won't. He won't. We'll gets our chance to say goodbye to the unholy bugger. Day after tomorrer. I'll be there, right at the front.'

Horton looks away and towards an old couple hunched over a single tankard directly in front of him. The man is speaking.

'It'll be all right, luv. It'll be all right. They got the bastard. They got 'im. It'll be all right.'

Horton turns towards a young buck with his gang of courtiers, dressed to impress in clothes which cost less than a bottle of gin but over which such care has been taken that they could have come from the finest boutique in Covent Garden.

'Well, lads. Well, now. New Year should be summat special, you 'ear me? Lots of young ladies passin' out in the street. 'Ear me. 'Ear me now. Nuffin' a young woman likes more than swoonin' at the evil of it all. When his body passes, mark my words, they'll be fallin' like pins. And who'll be there to catch 'em if not us? Am I right? Raise your glasses to John Williams, lads. We're goin' to be oiling our cocks on terrified fanny well into 1812. Mark my words, lads. Mark 'em.'

Horton looks out. And there are voices everywhere:

'... his body's out there ...'

'... dead in the prison ...'

'... thought he could top himself and get away with it ...'

'... John Williams ...'

'... we'll get 'im ...'

'... we'll get 'im ...'

'... evil bastard ...'

'... we'll get 'im ...'

27 DECEMBER 1811

While Horton, Harriott and Graham are sleeping in their Sheerness hotel, all of them dreaming of a black ship in stormy waters wreathed in wails and screams, John Williams is sleeping in his cell in Coldbath Fields. He is lying on a small bench with only a thin sheet full of holes to keep him warm. The cell is ten feet to the side, with one barred window looking out onto a mournful little courtyard with a single lamp to illuminate it. The window is permanently open, dropping the temperature in the cell by a dozen degrees and causing the breath from Williams's nose and mouth to cohere into little clouds of fog.

Despite his circumstances, Williams smiles in his sleep. Smiling is his normal state. He is an attractive, popular man in his late twenties, with a good hand and a pleasing face. Women like him and this simple fact is the one that has formed him more than any other. With the right clothes and a bit of work on his manner he could even be taken for an out-of-town gentleman from Ireland. Just now he is dreaming a particularly vivid dream, sun-drenched and pleasant.

He is walking along beside a fast-flowing river, crocodiles

basking on its banks. Insects buzz in the thick humid air. As he walks, he sees something impossible: a serpent in the water which is perhaps twenty feet long and as thick as a man's leg.

Ahead of him, his friend Billy is tramping purposely along; he is not aware that John is following him. Their ship, the *Roxburgh Castle*, lies at anchor underneath the fort at Braam's Point. Billy slipped away during the breakout of a near-mutiny against Captain Hutchinson, which had forced the captain to call for reinforcements from the fort. Billy (who has been distracted these past few days, and has done more than his fair share of encouraging mutinous thoughts below decks) took the opportunity to slip away, climbing down a rope ladder and slipping into the water to swim to the shore. John, who had been watching and recording everything Billy does for some time now, followed him. They were the only two men in the crew who could swim. They may also be the only two who can read and write, a fact which had brought them together early on in the voyage. John and Billy, the below-decks scholars, the young man from Ireland and the strange man from Oxfordshire who looks so young but whose stories tell of experience beyond his years.

Billy looked back to the ship once as he walked up onto the beach from his swim, but John was anticipating that, and ducked his head underwater to avoid being seen. Even in his dream he can remember the cool, salty taste of the water.

Since swimming up to the beach they have been walking for twenty minutes or so, from the point at which the river poured into the sea in the little bay. Now, only minutes after seeing the crocodiles and the gigantic serpent, John begins to hear different kinds of sounds amidst the jungle wildlife. From around a curve in the river come the sounds of shouting and singing and the occasional crack as if from a whip hurtling through the air. Also, a new smell comes to him: a sweet smell which hangs rotten and liquid in the air around him. He is near a sugar plantation.

Billy disappears around the bend in the river ahead, and soon John reaches the same bend, hurrying slightly in case he loses sight of the man he is following. But in fact he is nearly discovered, as just around the bend Billy has stopped dead, staring at a rise in some cleared ground on which stands a white single-storey house above the river, surrounded by a white fence and green lawns. Behind it, undulating in their own cultivated echoes of the wild jungle, swaying thickset crops of sugar cane shimmer in the sunlight. At the ridge of a hill John sees a field-gang of black bodies bent over and scything away at the shining green, as if praying to the crop which towers above them. Two overseers sit on horses observing them. As John watches, one of these men on horseback sends a whip sailing through the air, and it explodes against the back of one of the slaves, the sound of the crack reaching Williams moments after he sees the whip come down on the slave's back. The slave makes no sound that John can hear, not even a shout, but simply bends further and moves a bit faster.

John looks back to Billy, who is surveying the scene in much the same way. After a few more moments, Billy begins to walk towards the main house. John follows him, through the open gate and up the neat little drive that climbs up to the house, lined by trees between which John skips to avoid detection. A black child is playing beneath one of the trees and John nearly steps on her and she shrieks, but John reaches down and puts his hand over her mouth and pulls them both behind the tree and waits, not daring to look. After several moments, he whispers fiercely into the black girl's ear and then drops her, leaving her to run wildly and tearfully towards a low single-storey building down at the side of the plantation estate. His heart pounding, John looks back around the tree, half-expecting his friend's furious face to appear from behind the line of the trunk. And in the strange language of dreams, this does happen – Billy is standing there, his face pale and ancient, his hands strong and secure, grabbing John's throat and digging his thumbs in to choke him off, the life running out of him just as the black girl ran, away and off down the hill . . .

But Billy is not there, and that part of the dream splits into another possible future, and in this dream – the one which is mostly memory – John is still there behind this tree, watching Billy standing in the middle of the driveway, some twenty-five feet from where John is now, unmoving and looking up at the house.

The remarkable thing to John, who has never been on a plantation before, is how many blacks there are, and how little notice they take of the two white men walking through the open front gardens of the plantation. Billy actually physically moves one out of his way when he starts walking again, and the slave (a young male, perhaps thirteen or fourteen) just changes direction and continues, like a stream of water making its way around a rock. It's like Billy and John are invisible but still physical presences to these blacks.

Billy has reached the veranda of the plantation house, and he knocks loudly on the door of the house. A black woman answers, and she certainly sees him because she steps back for a moment as if a wild animal has appeared at her door. Billy speaks to her, but John is too far away from them to hear what is said. The slave woman grows agitated, shaking her head and beginning to raise her voice, and she is almost screaming when a man appears from inside the house and speaks to her: a small, neat, dark-haired man with a small circle of cloth on his head. *A Jew*, thinks Williams. *A Jew out here in the jungle.*

Billy speaks to the Jew, and his voice is raised more than the voices of the others and has some anger in it, and the Jew seems to bow before him and says something in response, and then Billy goes with the Jew into the house.

The slaves continue to flow around the house but continue to ignore him, so John feels emboldened and decides to investigate this strange scene further.

He skips out from behind the tree and into the area directly in front of the house, which is organised like a little front garden, though John is barely aware of the neatly trimmed lawn and precise, almost English flower beds, filled with exotic plants with strange sharpnesses from which the gardens of Sussex and Kent would recoil in horror. The steps up the veranda creak slightly as he climbs them, but only slightly – the wood is new and freshly painted, and up close the house has the same quality of freshness. There is a window on either side of the door, and John crouches to peek through the corner of one of these, but cannot see anything inside: the shutters are open, but thick muslin curtains are hanging in the window to keep out the daytime heat.

John makes his way along the veranda to the edge of the house, passing two more curtained windows as he does so. There is no sound from within the house. As he turns the corner to follow the veranda around the corner, his dream once again separates itself from reality, and in this new fantasy he spies a beautiful dark-haired woman in a long, white, cotton dress sleeping in a hammock, three enchanting puppies curled up beneath her. The dream-Williams catches his breath as soft music began to play, and he walks towards the sleeping girl as if in a trance. The puppies smile at him as they wake up, and he leans over her to see her open her eyes and gently open her mouth, revealing soft white teeth and a red-velvet tongue.

'Kiss me, John,' says the dream girl. 'Kiss me, and then . . .'

John Williams wakes up, and shivers. A noise has disturbed

him: a creak (a key?), the sound of wood (the bottom of a door?) on stone (the floor of his cell?).

He sits up on the wooden bench that has been his bed the past few nights. It is completely dark in the cell. All he can hear now is the sound of his own breathing, and from one of the neighbouring cells the distant, muffled sound of a man moaning.

No. Something else. A low, steady dry-as-bones breath, in and out, in and out. From inside his cell.

'Atkins?' The name of the warder sounds cracked and dry on his lips, barely a word at all. His eyes are adjusting to the darkness, and his ears are beginning to locate the source of the low breath. There, in the corner, to the right of the barred window. A tall, thin shape, two legs popping out from beneath a long, dark coat.

By nature a man of positive dispensation, Williams is not immediately afraid. So much has happened to him of late, so much of it unexpected and unpleasant, that this latest episode does not even seem particularly puzzling. Indeed, his first reaction is one of derision.

'Fuck off, whoever you are,' he says to the shape. 'And tell Atkins not to let any Tom, Dick or Harry into my fucking cell.' His voice has a southern English lilt for he is, indeed, an English fiend, not an Irish one.

'Is that any way to greet a drinking partner?' says the tall shape in a whistling, breathless voice, and suddenly Williams is, actually, very much afraid.

'Billy?'

The tall figure does not move from its position against the wall, but Williams has to suppress the image in his head of it looming over him as the room contracts. The figure says nothing else, so Williams fills the silence before it overwhelms him.

'Billy? How did you . . .?'

'The gaoler,' says the figure, its voice still dry and expressionless. 'He is only thinking of feeding his family.'

'The door is still open?' John asks.

'The door is still open,' answers the figure.

Williams looks at the door, and looks back to the shape in the corner. From outside comes the sound of moaning again.

'Why are you here, Billy?' asks Williams, in barely a whisper. He keeps an eye on the door, already planning a desperate rush to get outside and to freedom, perhaps down to the dock and onto a ship, away from London, away from the magistrates and constables and . . .

The figure peels away from the wall and limps softly towards the bench. It passes through the beam of sickly light which makes its way in from the lamp outside, and for a moment Williams thinks this is an old, old man in the cell with him, worn out and decrepit. But then the tall figure sits down on the bench, and Williams sees that, no, it is his friend, Billy Ablass, come to pay him a visit. Perhaps he is even here to rescue him.

Friend? Is he really a friend, John?

The voice in his head is a warning one, and sounds like his mother. It scares him profoundly and he realises that no, indeed, Billy Ablass has never been a friend. A shipmate, yes. A drinking partner, indeed. But never one to share confidences and intimacies. Since their return to London on the *Roxburgh Castle*, they have seen each other barely a half-dozen times, most of them in the last few weeks. Williams finds himself wondering if Billy Ablass has any friends at all, and cannot recall a single one.

Then why is he here, John Williams? Why does he appear now, out of the blue?

Billy looks at Williams now, turning his face away from the

light outside, and the cheerful hail-fellow-well-met spirit within John Williams runs screaming away from that glance, leaving behind it a dull sense of horror. There is no fellowship in that look, no humanity at all. There is nothing behind the eyes, only an implacable look of determination in the face.

Run, John! Run now!

And he does stand, all thinking spent, his instincts taking over in the face of this vision of death. He stands and takes two or three steps to the door, but he is too slow. Billy sticks out a foot, and Williams tumbles to the floor. Before he can rise, Billy is upon him, grabbing him by the hair and pulling him up onto his knees. Billy's hand grips Williams's hair while he fumbles for something in his coat, and then there is an explosion of pain in the back of his neck, and John Williams feels only one thing more.

That comes some time later, when the world falls back into focus for a moment, the light from the courtyard flickers back on, and then Williams feels all at once, in a rush, the leather around his neck, the stool falling away beneath his feet, and the crack of his neck snapping as his weight pulls down onto the belt which hangs him. The door to the cell opens and closes, and John Williams is left alone, perhaps to dream.

YEAR'S END 1811

The year ends with a procession.

The gentlemen of the press have been diligent. In thundering editorials and deathless prose, they have demanded *justice* and have bemoaned *incompetence*. They have gnashed their teeth and shaken their inky fists, and their clarion call has been read and shared and hugely applauded. People pour out onto the Highway as morning dawns. Even men desperate for bread and money are willing to forgo a day clamouring for work on the dock to get their share of the righteous mob.

John Williams was found dead in his cell in Coldbath Fields three days previously. The verdict is suicide, and at a stroke Williams's guilt is confirmed, even as anger grows that he has escaped London's formal justice (the eternal damnation visited upon his soul by his act of self-immolation is a forgotten detail amid the clamour for reparation).

Williams had exited the stage just as the Shadwell magistrates were hardening in their conviction that he was the murderer – indeed, that he might be the only murderer, despite all evidence to the contrary. They had interviewed him for a second time on Christmas Eve, along with a small host of bystanders, witnesses and victims who could do nothing (even if they had wanted to, and most did not) to halt the runaway assumption that John Williams was the Monster of the Highway. John Turner, who had escaped the King's Arms with his life, said he recognised him as a regular at the inn (but added that he could not place him at the murder scene). A woman who for the previous three years had washed Williams's clothes when he was not at sea testified that she'd washed blood out of two of Williams's shirts in the very recent past (she was not asked how often she'd washed blood out of his shirts before the recent past). Two men who'd lodged with Williams testified that he'd returned home late on the night of the murder of the Williamsons, and had asked them to 'put the light out'.

And then there was the maul, the fearsome ugly instrument of the deaths visited upon the Marrs. It had been traced to the Pear Tree boarding house through the good offices of magistrate Capper and his interview of the Pear Tree's landlord, Mr Vermilloe. And the Pear Tree was where John Williams habitually boarded when he was not at sea.

On the strength of these statements, Williams had been remanded again to Coldbath Fields.

London was learning all about the prisoner, and it liked what it saw: a sailor (an Irish sailor, more's the point – Williams's habit of lying about his Irishness has now caught up with him) with a dubious past and a raffish air; ripped clothes; suspicious behaviour; violence; blood. The genteel readers in the West End and out beyond Southwark and Clerkenwell shivered with delicious delight at the prospect of such a violent, ruthless individual dwelling under the same sky as them, little imagining that dubious pasts, torn clothes and blood were part and parcel of life as it was lived in Wapping.

The Christmas Day edition of *The Times* carried the story, but it was overtaken in enthusiasm by the *London Chronicle*, which held its grubby ears closer to the rhythm of the London streets, and which stole *The Times*'s thunder with a crashing editorial of its own, arguing that London's policing was too important to be left to the dilettantes and bureaucrats who currently held the magistracies, and that police needed to become 'inquisitorial and intermeddling' if crime was to be reduced (Charles Horton, had he been reading the newspaper and not sailing down the Thames towards Sheerness, would have approved).

The ordinary people agreed with the *Chronicle*'s leader writer. In Shadwell itself, on Christmas Day, a private association for the 'mutual protection' of locals was formed, consisting of two companies of eighteen men each, armed with cutlasses and pistols, to patrol the local streets. The magistrates might have their man, went the local thinking, but the magistrates had been found wanting again and again. The locals were past leaving the safety of their families to ineffective dullards elevated beyond their capacity.

Despite this, everyone felt that London's panic and fright had changed register, and had turned into a type of fascination. *Here's the likely culprit*, said the newspapers and magistrates. *We've got him. Sleep easier in your beds. The bogeyman is under lock and key.*

And still the Shadwell magistrates interviewed and cajoled, focusing more and more of their efforts onto Williams. On the 27th of December, they assembled for another inquisitorial round. Messrs Story, Capper and Markland re-assumed their positions behind the bench on the raised dais, and a crowd of gawpers pushed their way inside to sit in the rows before the three magistrates, some back for the third day in a row, others frantic to see the face of the Irish Monster, this Williams who was already creeping into the tales mothers told their children to shut them up. The crowd waited impatiently for the arrival of the prisoner, building itself up in delighted anticipation of imminent outrage and hair-rending.

But the prisoner never arrived. A policeman came instead to hand the magistrates a note, explaining that Williams had been found dead that morning, hanging by his neck from a bar in his cell, quite cold, quite dead. Quite guilty. Of this there was no longer any doubt.

After the initial shock, the magistrates did not let the inconvenience of the accused's absence deflect them from their pursuit of justice. All through the day of the 27th they continued to interview people, adding more and more bricks to the folly of 'evidence' they had constructed around John Williams. His landlady, Mrs Vermilloe, already a star of the story and a regular feature of the newspapers' coverage, returned to the stand for a third time. She appeared shaken and disturbed by the news of his suicide. Her story changed once she heard of his death, becoming more and more elaborate, and not to Williams's advantage. Other witnesses added to the developing picture of a ne'er-do-well, a drunkard, a violent rake and ribald. By the end of the morning, the magistrates and the crowd in their office were convinced beyond any human doubt that Williams had done the deeds, perhaps alone, perhaps in league with others. But probably, or preferably, alone.

At lunchtime a note was sent to the Home Office to this effect.

The investigation began to be wound down. There were still unanswered questions and loose ends: a man from Marlborough who had been arrested, and a local man called Ablass (known by the locals as Long Billy) who had been seen with Williams on the night of the Williamson murders and who was brought in for questioning on December 28th. But alibis were offered by these suspects, and these alibis were accepted with no further investigation by the Shadwell magistrates. They had their man, and he wasn't going anywhere.

Further interviews continued on the 29th. Difficult questions were avoided – constables Hope and Hewitt in particular were fretful over what Ablass might tell the magistrates about the source of their tip-off about Williams, but the magistrates took the man's alibi at face value. While all those involved in the investigation busied themselves with its conclusion, a new idea was growing in the newspapers and on the street: how would Shadwell, Wapping and London itself have its revenge on the monstrous creature who had killed the Marrs and the Williamsons? Had he not cheated death and justice by taking his own life? His soul was already in forfeit; how would the souls of the killed (and the appetites of the vengeful living) be vitiated?

On New Year's Eve, London found out.

John Harriott awakes in his own little bedroom. He is alone. His head aches. It is 31 December. Outside, preparations are being made for a final immolation of the Irish Monster.

His wife Elizabeth has slept these last two nights in a separate room, breaking an unspoken pact between them that they would never be one of those old couples who gravitated to their own rooms once the surviving children were grown. They had shared a comfortable, warm bed for decades.

But she had been cold towards him since his return from his so-called 'investigative expedition', which has made her unspeakably angry (her anger masking her very real concern for the health of his old bones). She has returned majestically to her years-old conviction that the mad old fool should have given up all this nonsense years ago. They had eaten a silent supper on the night of his return, the servants whispering in the hallway outside. She had retired early and pointedly to her own room, leaving him to the fire, his chair and his thoughts. And a bottle of brandy.

Towards midnight, there had been a knocking at the door and his manservant had grumbled downstairs to open it, letting in an inebriated and noisome Horton. Harriott had received the constable and had listened to the tale he had to tell, but as if it were being told in a distant room by people he no longer cared about. The fire was warm, the brandy in his head was soothing, and here was this Horton again, this ludicrously passionate man with his bizarre notions and mysterious undertakings.

Horton raved that Shadwell had got this whole thing the wrong way around. That the evidence of the *Zong* and the discoveries in Sheerness proved there was more to this than was apparent, that this John Williams was at best only a part of the crime, at worst a complete innocent. They must write to the Home Office immediately, now, without delay, with all that they had learned. Harriott thought only of his sleeping wife (probably not sleeping any more thanks to Horton's ravings), his sons, and the thin grey line of ocean that separated England from France. He thought about going to bed.

'Horton,' he said, looking into the fire. 'You have been drinking, have you not?'

'Sir?' said Horton, standing in front of the fire with his hat in his hands, rocking slightly from side to side.

'I said, you have been drinking?'

'Mr Harriott, I . . . I . . .'

'Drinking is a ridiculous vice in a man your age. It occurs to me how little I know of your personal circumstances, Horton. Where you go. Who you see. What you do. You are a man of great mystery, it occurs to me.'

'Mr Harriott, the letter . . .'

'Horton, listen to me. The Home Office is not interested in receiving a letter from me. I have tried, Lord knows, to establish some direction in this ridiculous affair, but at every turn I have been rebuffed. I have been mocked, ignored, chastised and disciplined. I have been spoken to in ways I have not experienced since I was a cabin boy off Newfoundland. I have had enough, Horton. Quite enough.'

'But, sir, your duty . . .'

'Do NOT!' shouted Harriott, and rising from his chair he moved to stand immediately in front of his constable, 'do NOT presume to tell me my duty, Horton. My duty to my King, my country and my fellow men is and always has been as clear to me as the fact that holding my hand in a fire will burn it. That duty has indeed often felt like holding my hand to a fire. I have struggled and fought and been defeated and have been victorious for my duty, sir. But these murders did not happen on the river, sir. They did not even happen in Wapping. They are Shadwell's duty, sir, and always have been. And Shadwell has reached a conclusion. It is to Shadwell we defer at this time, and I shall be writing no letters, intercepting no lines of inquiry, and interfering NO FURTHER.'

Harriott was standing nose to nose with his constable at this moment, and could smell the cheap rum on Horton's breath. Horton, on the other hand, could smell the expensive brandy on the magistrate's, and realised even through the fog of his own head that the old man was himself more than a little drunk. Horton's eyes were wide and Harriott could see that it was only by a rigid effort that his constable was containing himself. It was the self-control Harriott had seen before, and again he is rather awed by it, by its ability to hold the man's emotions down even at the height of passion and with alcohol swilling round his brain.

There was a long, long pause, during which all they could

hear was the crackle from Harriott's fire and, outside, the gentle lament of an ignored cat. Even the ships, the dock, the mighty river were silent. Just two men in a room with a fire, encountering infinities of evils.

Eventually, Constable Horton spoke.

'Am I to understand, sir, that this investigation is over?'

Harriott's passions had, once more, been spent, and the old creeping tiredness came over him again. He could no longer bear to stand. He sank back down into the sanctuary of his old chair. With a great heaving sigh, he prepared himself to face duty once more. The germ of an idea had entered his head.

'No, indeed it is not, Horton. No indeed. Let me catch my thoughts for a moment. And for God's sake, man, sit down and stop swaying so.'

Horton sat down, and the old magistrate gazed into the dying flames of the fire to consider things. He saw immediately that the death of this John Williams would prove to be immensely useful to the Shadwell magistrates. It provided them with a ready suspect who was pleasingly unable to defend himself, and no doubt witnesses were already lining up to provide telling testimony as to the poor dead man's evil soul.

The only thing that would stop this procedural juggernaut in its tracks would be the discovery of the so-called 'Henry Morgan' and the complete unmasking of his plot to fit out the *Zong* and sail off on a slaving trip. Also, this plot would have to be tied in – tightly, evidentially tied in – to the two sets of killings. Could that even be done? And under the noses of the Shadwell magistrates, who believed (or would shortly believe) that the case was closed?

And all this time, another concern, one bedevilled by damned compromise: while all this was going on, the normal business of the River Police was being neglected, both by him and by Horton. On the one side, his duty to truth (and, he thought to himself, perhaps to poor John Williams), on the other, his duty to trade and his paymasters.

He decided.

'This is what we must do,' he says, still looking into the fire. 'You must continue your investigations. You must seek to prove the connection between the so-called "Morgan", the *Zong* and the murders, we must take what we know and then we must show it to Graham, and then leave the thing be. And while you do that, I must formally and publicly renounce an interest in the case and return to River Police business. And you, Constable Horton – you need to quit your post. You will formally cease to be a waterman-constable while carrying on this investigation. Any work you do on the case can thus be taken as your own and nothing to do with the River Police. I must protect the office at all costs. Do we understand each other?'

He looked at Horton. The constable had fallen asleep, his mouth open, breathing silently. John Harriott smiled, wrote a note to Horton which he placed on the constable's chest, and went to bed, with instructions that the man sleeping in the drawing room was to be left undisturbed.

And now it is the morning after, and he faces a thick head and the unpleasant prospect of returning to his normal duties while Horton is out there, speaking to who knows who. But first, he must make his peace with his wife.

So the hungover John Harriott, moving slowly and carefully, begins to prepare for the New Year.

New Year's Eve rises like a cold flannel in a bucket of water, and already at sunrise the crowd is gathering. The body of John Williams has spent the night in the so-called 'black hole' of the Roundabout, the watch house at St George in the East, down at the end of Ship Alley. The open dead eyes of Williams have stared meaninglessly into the darkness of the black hole, into which his body had been dumped. Above them rose Hawksmoor's fearsome architecture, stern and atavistic.

It has been light for perhaps an hour when the high constable arrives with his grubby entourage, bringing with them the vehicle that is to be used to display Williams on his journey through the streets to his final place of unrest. It is a vehicle into which much thought has gone: a cart with a platform which inclines downward from front to rear, to allow whatever is placed upon it to be clearly seen by anyone walking behind. Williams is dragged from the black hole of the watch house and laid on this inclined platform, his head at the higher end. He is wearing blue pantaloons and a white shirt with frills open almost to the belly. His eyes remain open.

The paraphernalia attached to the platform shows a strong narrative as well as visual sense, and no little imagination. The maul, which Horton had recovered from the house on Ratcliffe Highway and which had occupied the centre of the investigation for so long, was attached to the platform on one side of Williams's head. On the other was the ripping chisel found on the counter of the Marrs' shop, its presence in the shop still unexplained. Above the head is fixed a crowbar, found next to Williamson's body in the King's Arms. Next to it, without need of explanation, is a sharpened stake.

The honour guard for this little carriage of horrors consists of the head constable and headboroughs of Shadwell, the Superintendent of the Lascars and an extraordinary number of constables, almost three hundred of them, most of them armed with cutlasses. It is an army which is to accompany John Williams through the streets of Wapping.

The carriage and the procession leaves the grounds of St George's and creeps out onto Ratcliffe Highway, where the crowds are waiting.

Some constables, and the Superintendent of the Lascars, tense themselves as the carriage enters the corridor made by the crowd down both sides of the Highway. Hands move towards cutlasses, and violence is anticipated. But nothing happens. The crowd is, as near as is possible in the metropolis, silent. As the carriage makes its way westwards down the Highway, to stop outside Timothy Marr's shop, the crowd is simply *there*. The display of the Monster, here at last before them, has stilled their chatter. They stand in awe and wonder at the Monster, the man whose knife cut through the throats of babies, girls, women and men. If one of the mighty ships in the dock were to disgorge prancing tentacled creatures over the walls the crowd would barely notice.

As the cart stops outside the Marr residence, the motion of its halting causes Williams's head to loll to one side, as if turning away from the scene of his crime. A constable climbs onto the cart, takes Williams's head in his hands and firmly turns his eyes back towards the shop. *Look at this*, the action says. *Look at what you did.* For ten minutes the cart stays in one place, and the crowd remains silent. No weeping or wailing. No public displays. The display is all there on the cart: the Monster and his instruments.

Eventually, the cart is turned around and is walked back eastwards along Ratcliffe Highway. It turns right and southwards into New Gravel Lane, down to Pear Tree Alley, where Williams had lodged. Then it goes back into New Gravel Lane to stop for another ten minutes, this time in front of the King's Arms. And here some real anger is expressed. A hackney coachman who has stopped nearby unfurls his whip and lashes it, three times, across the upturned face of the Monster, cursing loudly and audibly. The crowd sighs and continues to watch.

The cart goes on, north up New Gravel Lane, then left and

westwards along Ratcliffe Highway again. Then north up Cannon Street to a crossroads, where Back Lane crosses the road north to Whitechapel. A hole has been dug here, but not a grave: it is only three feet wide and two feet long. The cart is stopped alongside, and some of the constables grab the Monster's body and shove it, limbs and head mixed together, into the hole. Another constable grabs the sharpened stake from the platform and with a monstrous cry jumps into the hole with the body and shoves the stake into the chest of the dead man, using the maul itself to drive the stake in.

At this scene of sudden and passionate violence, the crowd erupts at last, screaming and shouting its rage and frustration at Williams's escape from justice. Quicklime and then soil is poured down onto the body of the Monster, and finally paving stones are relaid over the hole. Williams is no more, and will live on only in the memories and fury of the mob. The crowd disperses, the taverns fill up, and the prostitutes prepare themselves for a sharper beating than normal from their inebriated, enraged clientele.

Horton waits for the crowd to disperse. It takes several hours. Before long, only two people are left: Horton and a watchman he recognises vaguely (it is Olney), weeping gently into his flask of gin. A third man, a tall young man in a long coat, watches Horton from the window of a boarding house overlooking the street, but the constable does not see him. Horton steps onto the paving stones above the resting place of the Monster. His head carries the aching memory of last night's ale and rum, and his mouth is dry and dissolute. He is still wearing yesterday's clothes and even now Abigail is once again anxiously awaiting his return.

He stands for a moment, his hands in his pocket, watching his feet on the paving inches above the damned body of the Irish Fiend. He can hear Olney crying just down the street.

Then he turns and leaves, passing Olney as he heads south into the Highway and the future.

Olney follows him. After a few moments, the tall young man appears on the street. He waits while the other two disappear around the corner and onto the Highway, and then he also goes to stand over the resting place of the Irish Monster. Like Horton before him, he looks down to where his feet meet the pavement. He takes something out of his pocket and flicks it into the air such that it lands, with a hefty metallic crack, directly beneath his feet. It is a Potosí piece of eight. He admires his handiwork for a moment, smiling as if in memory of other offerings. Then he too leaves that place.

BOOK 4

Ablass

We in the country here are thinking and talking of nothing but the dreadful murders, which seem to bring a stigma, not merely on the police, but on the land we live in, and even our human nature. No circumstances which did not concern myself ever disturbed me so much. I have been more affected, more agitated, but never had so mingled a feeling of horror, and indignation, and astonishment, with a sense of insecurity too, which no man in this state of society ever felt before, and a feeling that the national character is disgraced.

Robert Southey, letter to Neville White, December 1811

JANUARY 1812

At the urging of a desperate and cornered Home Secretary, in the New Year Aaron Graham takes up the case of the Ratcliffe Highway murders. The vicious slaughter of some frankly ordinary folk in the East End has, to the great surprise of the Right Honourable Members of His Majesty's Government, become a matter for debate within the Mother of Parliaments herself. Political firing squads are beginning to line up. The random perambulations of the Shadwell magistrates are starting to look comical and incompetent and who, after all, is responsible for those magistrates? And what does this show of foolishness say for the safety of all Londoners? If monsters are abroad, does the current Home Secretary have a prescription for dealing with them?

Surely, think all those who are still thinking, surely there was more than one man involved in these murders? What of the sounds of men fleeing the scene of the original murders? What of the witnesses who saw two men fleeing the scene of the King's Arms? What of the double sets of footprints across the wasteland behind that benighted inn?

In the second week of the New Year, the Home Secretary formally orders the Shadwell magistrates to give up their prime piece of evidence – the bloodstained, awful maul – and pass it to Graham, who opens up an investigative office at his own headquarters in Bow Street and begins interviewing witnesses, many of whom had already been interviewed by the Shadwell magistrates, in their own fashion. Shadwell's papers regarding the case are all transferred to Bow Street. And in the Commons itself, the Home Secretary, his back to the legislative wall, introduces a motion to establish a committee to investigate the need for a reform of London's policing. It is, as everyone who is anyone knows, a classic case of buying time.

Graham is assiduous in his fresh investigations and Harriott, at last, is properly involved in the case, advising and cajoling behind the scenes while the Shadwell magistrates return to their offices, fuming. Graham (like Harriott) is convinced that at least one man must have been Williams's accomplice in the murders, perhaps even two. His suspicion (like Harriott's) falls on Cornelius Hart, the carpenter who had been working on the spruce little Marr shop on the day of the murders and whose ripping chisel was discovered on the counter of the shop. On the 13th of January, Hart is arrested by Graham's officers and kept for questioning.

His is not the only arrest. Four days later, the same William Ablass who had been interrogated by Shadwell is arrested by Graham's officers and, like Hart, is kept at Bow Street. He is *officially* suspected (only Harriott and Graham know of the unofficial sniffing around being conducted by Charles Horton) on the basis of fresh testimony from the mercurial Mrs Vermilloe, the landlady of the Pear Tree boarding house whose evidence was primarily responsible for the assumed guilt of John Williams. Her husband, the man who had originally identified the initials on the maul, is still in his cell in Newgate gaol.

Ablass had been released by the Shadwell magistrates when he claimed not to have known Williams and had produced an alibi from a woman he claimed was his wife. Mrs Vermilloe asserts that he did, indeed, know him, and pretty well. They were often seen together. And it is shown that the woman concerned is not his wife at all, and is prepared to say pretty much anything to anyone in return for a jug of gin.

And Ablass has a limp, a very pronounced one. Several witnesses had seen two men, a tall man and a short one, leaving the scene of the Williamson murders, the taller of them with a limp (this evidence had been used to incriminate John Williams himself, who also had a limp but was, in fact, rather short).

Within days Ablass himself becomes a stick with which to beat the weakened government. Long Billy is discussed in Parliament itself.

Hansard record of proceedings in the House of Commons, 31 January 1812 [edited]

MOTION RESPECTING POLICE MAGISTRATES.

Sir F. Burdett expressed his regret, that he had not received the note of the right hon. gentleman opposite (Mr. Ryder) respecting his Order on the subject of Police Magistrates . . . What had they been doing in the late examinations which had taken place of persons who were supposed to have been concerned in the murder of Mr. Marr's family? What had they been doing, but endeavouring to make men, whom they had ever so little reason to suspect, say that which might criminate themselves? This inquisitorial power they had been in the habit of exercising daily, and what right had they to inflict the punishment which they had inflicted on persons brought before them? What was now the situation of that unfortunate person who was in confinement on suspicion of being concerned in the late murders, Ablass? What was he kept for? Why was he put in chains, immured in a dungeon, and called upon every day to criminate himself? It was stated in the daily prints, that the only circumstance against him was, his inability to account for a quarter of an hour of his time the night on which one of the murders was committed.

Mr. Secretary Ryder assured the hon. baronet, that he had not the slightest suspicion of his not being at the House on Tuesday or Wednesday, or he should not have brought forward his motion on either of those days . . . But the hon. baronet had said, there were many improper appointments of police magistrates; he wished the hon. baronet would come boldly and manfully forward with his charges, and not state them in that narrow, pitiful way, without stating the particular charge, or naming the particular individual . . . he must take it for granted, that there were circumstances sufficient in the opinion of the magistrate, Mr. Graham, to justify and call on him to commit the individual. What reason was there then to impute any improper conduct to Mr. Graham? Instead of any imputation, in his opinion, he was deserving of public approbation and thanks.

The Chancellor of the Exchequer observed, that there never was a motion brought forward in that House with less grounds to maintain it . . . As to the severity which was asserted with respect to Ablass, there were circumstances of suspicion which led the magistrates to believe that he was on a given time at a given place; they did not require of him to criminate himself, though if he could have given a satisfactory account of himself during that period, the case would bear a very different complexion, and the magistrates would not have acted properly if they had not given him an opportunity of accounting for that time. The individual who put an end to himself to evade justice was taken up on mere suspicion; would the hon. baronet say he ought not to have been detained?

While Burdett, Home Secretary Richard Ryder and the First Lord and Prime Minister Spencer Perceval plough their parliamentary furrow, Aaron Graham receives John Harriott as a welcome visitor at his house in Great Queen Street. Harriott arrives a little early, and waits for Graham in the drawing room of the finely decorated house. He reads that day's edition of *The Times*, from which any discussion of the recent events in Wapping is absent. There is an odd extract from the recent book by General Sarrazin, reports of a capture of a French frigate in the Adriatic, disagreements over the maintenance of law and order in Nottingham, where there have been recent riots, and a single sentence on the King who 'continues much in the same state'. In the paper's daily Law Report there is one story with which he is familiar, that of George Bicknell and Bob Barney, notorious street robbers and brothel keepers, whom the Shadwell magistrates have just sent down for six months.

'So, the Nincompoops have rediscovered their level of competence,' Harriott mutters to himself.

'Which Nincompoops would those be?' asks Graham as he walks into the room. His voice is cheerful but he looks tired and rather anxious. Even his clothes seem dreary this evening.

'Our colleagues in Shadwell,' replies Harriott. 'I was just reading the Law Report.'

'Ah, indeed. Our colleagues in Shadwell.' There is an edge

to his voice as he shows Harriott into the dining room, but there is also a welcoming hand on the older man's shoulder. 'I am much exercised, these days, by our colleagues in Shadwell.'

The dinner is all set, and the two men make some idle small talk while glasses are filled and dishes served. Then, with servants still hovering around and in between mouthfuls from Graham's excellent kitchen, their conversation returns to the familiar subject around which their lives have revolved for almost two months now.

'You must understand, my dear Harriott,' says Graham, 'that I cannot hold Ablass for much longer. It has been almost a fortnight. I understand the length of his captivity is being raised in the Commons by the formidably irritating Burdett, who still seems rather more exercised by the rights of criminals than by the rights of those they prey upon.' Harriott, like Graham a staunch Tory, growls in agreement. 'Really, Harriott, it has come to the ridiculous point of my being defended by the Prime Minister and the Home Secretary in the Commons chamber. This cannot go on.'

'But Horton is still looking. He believes he is close to confirming how Ablass was involved.'

'He may be close to confirming *something*, Harriott. But if it does not come in the next week, I'm afraid Ablass will be released by default, since it may be decided my head is somewhat more disposable than that of the head of the government.'

'Graham, you have seen the man. We have both seen him, in captivity and in the streets of Wapping. We know him to be quite capable of these acts. Indeed, I have met no creature more fitting the requirements of such deeds.'

'Indeed so, Harriott, indeed so. The man is monstrous. As cold as a sheet of Arctic ice and as calculating as a Whig on his uppers. But all I have so far is Mrs Vermilloe's testimony that

Ablass knew Williams, and his refusal to account for himself for a short period on the night in question. The formidable Mrs Vermilloe is no more reliable a witness than an inebriated fishwife – her stories shift and change more often than the items in my wardrobe. And, as Burdett is no doubt arguing in the House at this precise instant, Ablass is perfectly entitled not to say anything which may incriminate him. I need *evidence*, Harriott.'

'And I believe Horton will provide it.'

'And I believe you are right. But we are now under the fearsome microscope of the legislators. And it is an uncomfortable place to be, Harriott. Terrible uncomfortable.'

Graham falls silent, and Harriott sees again just how worn out his friend is. He remembers how he himself felt standing on the shore at Sheerness – that terrible sense of torpor, overwhelming in its deadening grasp. He remembers what Graham said to drag him out of it, and begins to ferret around in his own thoughts for some similarly inspiring words in return. Graham's manservant appears with a message on a silver platter.

'Ah, what fresh Hell is this!' exclaims Graham, archly. He reads the note, and what colour there had been in his face (somewhat reclaimed by the excellent wine they have been drinking) falls away.

'What is it, Graham? You look like you have seen a ghost.'

'No indeed, Harriott. No indeed. But someone else may have done. This is a note requiring my immediate presence in Soho Square for a meeting with the PRS for an urgent discussion of the circumstances surrounding my arrest of a certain William Ablass.'

'The PRS?'

'The President of the Royal Society.'

*

At about the same time on the same evening, Charles Horton is standing before a neat, dark little house, into which the neat, dark little figure he has been following for the previous couple of hours has disappeared. The house is to the north of Limehouse, near the Cut, and is tucked away on its own in between a small manufactory and a tannery. Horton has never noticed this place before; indeed, this entire street is new to him, as if it had been inserted into the topography while he'd been looking elsewhere.

He has been walking for several hours in the afternoon crowds, monitoring the neat figure as it zigzagged its way through the streets. The figure was holding an ancient-looking leather bag from which emerged a variety of documents and papers, which were delivered to various addresses in Wapping, Shadwell and up towards Whitechapel. All the while the neat figure kept itself to itself, seeming to disappear into the colours of the crowds. Horton had some difficulty keeping his eyes on this person, who was possessed of the most marked ability to lose himself that the officer had ever seen. Horton barely realises that this is a quality he himself shares with the man he is following. The two of them dart in and out of the East End crowds, barely perceived, like ghostly whippets.

As they'd approached this final little dark house, the figure's zigzagging had become less pronounced and its urgent pace slowed. Which suggested that this was the neat figure's ultimate destination; was perhaps its home.

An address, thinks Horton. *Finally, an address.*

He considers going home and coming back tomorrow. Abigail deserves some of his company. He has been rarely enough at home these past weeks, as his unofficial investigations into the Marr and Williamson murders have intensified and dragged him hither and thither across the districts of

Wapping, Shadwell, Limehouse and Ratcliffe. But the man is there; the man he has been seeking since New Year. The opportunity cannot possibly be passed up, can it?

So Horton walks up to the door of the trim house, and bangs firmly on the door with its heavy cast-iron knocker. There is a pause (perhaps a disbelieving pause, as if whoever is inside does not receive many visitors) and then the door is opened to reveal the face of the neat figure whom Horton has been following all afternoon.

'Benjamin Naar?' asks Horton, and reluctantly the man nods his head. 'My name is Horton. I wish to ask you some questions about a ship currently at anchor in the dock at Sheerness. A ship called the *Zong*.'

There is a pause. A shout comes from the shoe manufactory next door, and from somewhere comes the crash of metal against metal, as if something industrial had been dropped from a great height. The man standing at the door is wearing a plain frock coat and trousers, he is sporting a tidy beard and his dark hair is long and thick. His eyes are like coals. There is a deep stillness about him, in stark contrast with his busy zig-zags of the preceding hours. He watches Horton carefully, as if acquiring data towards some critical decision. His appraising look makes Horton feel uncomfortable, making him (for once) an object of investigation. And then the man seems to make a decision.

'No,' he says. 'Not now. Come back tomorrow.'

And he closes the door in Horton's face.

John Harriott, quietly seething, waits in the coach as it stands in Soho Square, covered by a thick blanket brought from Graham's house for the purpose.

He'd insisted on accompanying his friend on the short trip to Soho Square, to the residence of the President of the

Royal Society. Graham was silent during the ten-minute journey, peering gloomily out at the dark streets as the carriage made its way west from Covent Garden. He'd brought his cigar along with him, and its smoke filled the interior of the coach. Harriott found himself picturing that ghastly old vessel at anchor in Sheerness, its dark interior creaking with memories.

The coach came to a halt in front of an extremely well-appointed residence. Lights blazed out from the house, as if a party had recently come to an end. It looked the kind of house where parties were always starting and ending. Graham stepped out and Harriott prepared to follow him, but his friend barred the door and spoke firmly to the old magistrate.

'You will wait here, John,' he said. 'I cannot take you in. He asked to speak to me, and to no one else.'

'But, Graham, I must insist . . .'

'No, John. *I* must insist. This is for my ears and my ears only. I welcome your company. But you can go no further. If I am to be a long time, I will send word and my coach here will take you back to your apartments.'

And with that the door to the coach slammed shut, and Harriott settled down to being angry, cold and old. Really, this was extraordinarily bad form on Graham's part. The two of them had been leading players in the murderous events on the Ratcliffe Highway for months, and now this intervention from an unexpected source, which promised to reveal much of interest, not least the nature of the Royal Society's interest in the itinerant William Ablass. But Graham had shut this off to him. His frustration was immense – first the Shadwell magistrates had stood between him and a resolution, then the Home Secretary, and now even his friend. Self-pity flowed through him: an old man, abandoned and ignored on the edge of events.

There was twenty minutes of this boiling resentment to sit through, and Harriott begins to think that Graham will send word, any moment, that he must go home. But then his friend appears at the door of the glamorous residence, beckoning to the coach driver. The driver climbs down and walks up the steps to the door of Banks's house, and Graham instructs him to pick something up and carry it to the coach: a small barrel, the heaviness of which is apparent as the driver winces to heft it up on the roof of the coach. A coil of something white sits on top of it.

Graham steps into the coach, and with a 'Hai!' the driver gets them moving again. For a while, Graham says nothing at all, and his face is invisible in the shadows. Harriott feels unable to speak.

'Do you like modern poetry, Harriott?' Graham asks, suddenly. His old friend starts.

'Graham, the question is . . .'

'Some of it is rather good,' Graham continues, his voice soft and quiet and steady. 'I am particularly keen on Coleridge, who is a good friend of the PRS, I understand. Indeed, when I think of what I have just been told, I do wonder whether Coleridge knows rather more of the world than I have ever given him credit for.'

Harriott says nothing, feeling at once exasperated and helpless.

Graham speaks again.

'I must ask Horton to do something for us. And I must tell you of what Banks just told me. But not tonight. Not in the dark.'

Silence, then. Nothing apart from the echoing clip of the horses' hooves on the cobblestones below, the occasional slash of the whip and the thousand little shrieks and calls of the vast near-sleeping metropolis. Harriott finds himself looking at the ceiling of the coach's cab and wondering what is in that little barrel. Graham whispers to himself:

'From his brimstone bed at break of day
A walking the Devil is gone
To visit his snug little farm the Earth,
And see how his stock goes on.'

1 FEBRUARY 1812

Horton appears at the door of the same trim little house the next day, at the same time. It had been difficult walking away from this door the previous day, when the Jew had closed it in his face, but there had been something about the man's calm, appraising stare that had suggested a stubborn resolution. Besides, he had no authority to insist on entry. Indeed, he had no jurisdiction at all. This continued to be a secretive investigation. What was he to do, break down the man's door?

In any case, the behaviour of Naar had excited him, because it had indicated that he might have something to tell. The face of the man, the realisation and acceptance behind the eyes – Horton had seen these things before, and they always betokened at best knowledge, at worst guilt. The initials *BN* had featured heavily in the pages Horton had torn from Marr's ledger book, which had meticulously recorded every order Marr had taken since he'd opened his shop. Horton had investigated the majority of the orders in that book, and had spoken to dozens of intermediaries, agents, factors and middlemen throughout Wapping and Shadwell in an attempt to make a connection between the *Zong* and the tradesmen of the docks, but Naar had remained elusive throughout the early days of 1812. For weeks he was only 'BN'. It took the information of a Norwich trader Horton had met in a Shadwell tavern (following up a suggestion from a cooper in Limehouse) to confirm the man's name.

And so now, after weeks of trudging the streets and checking names against lists, he finds himself here at this door. He has been in a state of nervous excitement all day, barely able to contain himself. An answer to the riddle of 'Henry Morgan' might lie just beyond this solid, well-maintained sheet of wood.

But when he knocks at the door there is no answer, and something about the stillness of the house disturbs him. As Margaret Jewell had tried (and failed) to do weeks before, he suppresses a little sliver of panic as he knocks again. Still nothing. Even the tannery and the shoe factory are quiet. It is as if the residents of this district have all crouched down behind something in order to hide from this visitor from Wapping.

He knocks a third time, and when there is again no response he loses patience and tries the handle of the door. Jurisdiction be damned. With a small creak and a squeak, the door opens and he can step inside. The remnants of the late January afternoon light pick out the shape of a staircase, doors leading off to the right and left, and at the end of a short hallway a door through to a kitchen at the back.

At the foot of the stairs is a new candle, and a clean, dry-looking tinderbox with which to light it. It has been placed there very deliberately. Next to it is a note. Horton picks this up. It reads: *You will find me in the study upstairs.*

Horton uses the tinderbox and its new charcloth to light the candle, and climbs the stairs. At the top there are three doors, one of which is half open. He goes in, and to his surprise finds an opulently appointed bedroom, hung with shimmering threads and carpeted with a deep, rich pile. A four-poster bed resembles some Arabian trader's tent pitched in a Maghreb oasis. Horton half-expects to see the beautiful dark faces of Turkish concubines emerging from the purple-and-yellow drapes.

But this is no study, so he steps out of the beautiful bedroom and tries one of the other two doors. Inside the first, he finds Naar.

The Jewish financier is face down on a desk, his hands hanging loosely at his sides, dressed in the same smart frock coat as the previous evening. The desk is bare apart from an envelope displaying Horton's name, and a fine crystal glass. Horton picks up the glass and sniffs at it. There is a strong smell of bitter almonds. He puts his hand on the back of Naar's neck. It is cold.

Finally, Horton picks up the envelope, opens it, and takes out the letter within. He sits down to read it in the room's single leather armchair, in front of its fireplace.

Mr Horton

My Apologies.

If the discovery of my Body comes as a grievous Surprise to you, or as something in another way upsetting, I am sorry.

How you found me I do not know, although I assume you have Papers from either Mr Marr or Mr Williamson which mention my Dealings with them. My dead Body and my ready Willingness to mention those poor men in this Note clearly implicate me in their atrocious Despatches.

Nevertheless, my Faith does not place as much weight on Redemption as does yours. Even if I were forced to make my Case to the Lord, I do believe I would have one to make.

This note is not a confessional Document. Once again I must apologise if that comes as a Disappointment to you. I shall not be naming Names.

I will just say this – I am not the Killer. I did not kill those Unfortunates. I know who did, and I know what was upon him when he took their lives. He is someone I know well, indeed. My Family has talked of him much over the decades.

I shall offer neither Explanation nor Expiation. My relationship with the Killer – or rather, my Family's relationship – is both long and complicated.

My willingness to help the Individual you seek in his Undertakings is explained by my desperation to protect the surviving elements of my extended Family. That Family is distributed across the Globe, as is sadly often the case with my People. The Individual knows where much of that family is situated, and has threatened on multiple occasions to wreak a terrible Revenge upon them if I did not support him in his efforts.

Also, my Family does owe this Individual a debt of Gratitude, which will sound unusual to you but cannot be explained without further information relating to the Individual concerned, information which I am not prepared to divulge to anyone.

Thus, I sent you away yesterday to prepare for today: to prepare my Death, and to remove traces of my dealings. My Money has been moved to somewhere it can be useful. I leave this world confident that I have, at all times, acted with good Intentions and with only the Resources that God has given me. If He has decided that this is how it must be, I can do no more than make the best of it.

Once again, my Apologies. And please, if you know more than I think you do, if you are closer to the Killer than I can imagine you are, do take Care.

Best regards

Benjamin Naar

Horton folds up the note and puts it in a pocket. He stands up and looks into the fireplace. It is full to the brim of fine ash, a few black curls of paper mixed in.

He goes to a bookcase, and pulls down a heavy leather-bound ledger. Opening it, he sees that a good number of pages have been ripped out, and those that remain contain only general information, and no names. He pulls out another ledger. It is the same. The transactions of Benjamin Naar have, to all intents and purposes, been erased.

2 FEBRUARY 1812

Towards evening, a knock comes on the door and Abigail climbs down the three flights of stairs to answer it. Charles is out somewhere *investigating*, as he calls it. She knows he is working on a case with a bitter flavour of secrecy about it, and she knows better than to ask him the details, even on a night like the one just past when he came home pale and anxious, unwilling to talk about the circumstances which had made him so.

A man is standing on the doorstep, his expensive-looking hat held in his gloved hands, dressed in a marvellous green-striped silk coat, embroidered in a most superb manner with gold and silver spangles all over, with a white silk waistcoat and green-striped breeches. The dress is somewhat old-fashioned, but deliberately so (it is modelled on an outfit worn by George III for his birthday twenty years before).

Abigail is dumbfounded by the apparition on the doorstep. Some passers-by stare at the man, and this alone is enough to embarrass her, careful as she is not to draw the attention of strangers.

'Good evening, my dear,' says the man, amicably enough (though Abigail thinks she can detect a certain tense urgency in his manner – she has, without knowing it, taken on many of her husband's habits of noticing). 'I wonder if I might speak with Constable Charles Horton. I believe this is his residence?'

'It is, sir, yes,' answers Abigail. 'Though I am afraid he is not here at present. He is still out working.'

'Ah, yes, of course. I'll wager he keeps odd hours indeed,' says the strange dandy with an attempted smile, and ponders for a moment. He bites his lip gently, a confused movement in stark contrast to the confidence of his bearing. 'I wonder, my dear – and I would not ask this if the matter were not of some urgency – I wonder whether I might attend his return?'

The request is so brazen that Abigail gasps despite herself. She is about to point out the indecency of the suggestion when the stranger holds up a hand.

'Please, my dear. I hazard that you are Officer Horton's wife?' His voice is so charming, and his urgent gaze so needy, that her outrage is snuffed out in her throat. She only manages a nod. 'Then he may have spoken to you about the recent . . . atrocities in Wapping and Shadwell, which saw out the old year in such morbid fashion?'

Again, she nods.

'Well, my dear, I need Officer Horton's help very badly in connection with those murders. Indeed, I believe he may hold the key to their resolution. I need to speak to him as soon as is humanly possible, and can only stress that I am not the kind of gentleman to make any form of inappropriate request lightly. If you knew me, ma'am, you would realise that my presence here is evidence, in and of itself, of the extreme gravity of the situation.'

Abigail considers the request. The rooms upstairs are in good order, as ever, and she would feel no shame in showing even such a man as this the interior. The neighbours will talk, of course; indeed, they are probably talking even now. But this kind of gossip has never impinged on Abigail. She has no interest in it, and it holds no fears for her. She has only her strong internal sense of moral rectitude to guide her, and in this particular instance she senses a stronger compulsion – to help this man and not to turn him away.

She decides.

'Sir, you may await my husband inside,' she says, with the requisite amount of prim decency. 'This is a mean dwelling when compared to the palaces you are no doubt used to, but if you know my husband, as you say you do, you know that what is within was honestly earned and dutifully cared for. I would ask you to remember that the same applies to his other chattels as well. Including she who stands before you.'

The cloud which had been sitting behind the cheerful face of the gentleman lifts at that, and he grins delightedly. He takes her hand and kisses it, much to Abigail's chagrin (and much to the obvious pleasure of two local women who happen to be walking past).

'Constable Horton is an impressive man, and I am delighted to discover his wife is worthy of him, and more. My name is Graham, ma'am. I am indebted to you.'

When Horton returns, perhaps an hour after this episode, Aaron Graham is seated in an old chair near a small, tidy but adequate fire, gazing through the window at the brick wall of the lodging house next door. Even in these surroundings he exudes quiet glamour and poise, but despite the elegantly crossed legs and the half-smile on the face there is still that pressured sense of urgency that Abigail detected. Horton enters the room (having been intercepted by Abigail on the stairs and told the story of the strange man's arrival) and Graham stands immediately to shake Horton's hand with his spare hand, while the other remains firmly in charge of his hat. Horton feels a direct and vicious anger towards Graham, a clear sense of violated boundaries. He takes enormous care to separate Abigail from his work, even to the extent of refusing to discuss this separation. Abigail is his refuge and his conscience. And yet here is this affable magistrate, in his Covent Garden outfit, his arrival trailed by questions.

'My dear constable, please forgive this unspeakable intrusion,' says Graham, still shaking his hand. 'And can I add my admiration for the charms of your excellent wife, who has kept me entertained and amused despite my unseemly irruption into your domestic arrangements.'

'Mr Graham,' says Horton. 'This is quite a surprise for us.'

'Indeed, Horton, indeed. May I?' indicating the empty chair. Horton nods curtly, trying to be polite, and Graham sits. Horton goes to stand by the window. Like all great men, Graham is able to own a room containing only his inferiors without even being aware of it. For now, Horton feels he is a visitor in Graham's apartments, and not the other way around. It does not improve his mood.

'As I explained to Mrs Horton, I am here on a matter of some urgency,' Graham begins.

'So she has told me, sir.'

'Well, here's the substance of it. It's a damned odd tale, Horton, damned odd. Earlier today I released a man we have been holding for two weeks, on suspicion of being an accomplice of John Williams in the late murders. This man's name is Ablass.'

'I know of the man, of course, sir. I have been much interested in discovering his history these past weeks.'

'Ah, yes, no doubt. You may have also heard that I had been acting on the explicit instructions of the Home Secretary in this matter. He believes, as do I, that the Shadwell magistrates did a magnificently poor job in their investigation of these events. He also believes, as do I, that Williams cannot possibly have been acting alone.'

Horton says nothing. His hands are clasped behind his back, and he becomes conscious of standing to attention, as if he were on the deck of a navy ship and an admiral was coming aboard.

Graham continues.

'I arrested two men in the course of my investigation. One was Ablass. The other was the rogue Cornelius Hart, the carpenter who had been working on the Marrs' shop and who apparently left his ripping chisel behind on the counter there. I believe both to be liars, and strongly suspect either or both of them to have been involved.'

'And yet you have released them.'

'Indeed, I have released them.'

'Why?' The question is perhaps impertinent, coming from a mere waterman-constable and addressed to a great magistrate. But Horton, whose anger has only sharpened, is feeling impertinent.

'Why, indeed.'

And here Graham stops and looks, without embarrassment, directly at Horton. He weighs the man up before continuing.

'There is no direct evidence linking these men to the murders, is the first point. If this were to be tried in front of a jury, we may secure a conviction, we may not. I think, given the still-febrile nature of the populace, that a conviction may be likely. And yet, I released them.'

'Yes.'

'What do you know of these men?'

'Hart I know of from the depositions. Ablass was arrested as part of the Williams questioning, but had an alibi supplied by a woman.'

'He did indeed. And interestingly this woman was arrested some days afterwards.'

'On what crime?'

Again, the impertinence. And again, Graham affects not to notice.

'She was drunk and disorderly.'

'Hardly surprising. It is not uncommon.'

'No indeed. Her mode of payment is, however.'

'Mode of payment?'

'The tavern she was frequenting accepted her payment in a Potosí piece of eight.'

Graham pauses, and watches Horton's face. Horton tries to keep his counsel. He knows a good deal about Ablass from his investigations; this, though, is new to him.

'So, I recalled your own particular interest in pieces of eight, and how they seem to be popping up all over this saga. So I began to ponder this situation, while Mr Ablass sat in my cells. He has an unusual history. Did you know, for instance, that he was a shipmate of Williams?'

'I had heard something of this.'

'Yes. Aboard the *Roxburgh Castle*. Which plied its trade along the coasts of what we used to call the Spanish Main. It was a ship badly served by its crew. Mr Williams was one of the miscreants; he was arrested in Rio de Janeiro pretending to be the ship's second mate and attempting to extort money from locals in such a capacity. And later, off the coast of Surinam, Mr Williams and Mr Ablass were involved in an attempted mutiny aboard the ship. The mutiny was only ended by the sharp thinking of the captain, Hutchinson, who brought the ship to under the guns at Braam's Point, and applied for protection from a naval frigate anchored there. It was touch and go, apparently. There was some danger that Ablass and his associates might have seized the ship.'

'Did Ablass lead the mutineers?' Horton has known of the *Roxburgh Castle* mutiny for some days, and has asked himself this question several times. Now, it seems, is the opportunity to ask it of someone else.

Graham looks at him, bemused.

'An interesting question, Horton. A seagoing question, if I may.'

Does he know about me? thinks Horton. He says nothing, and holds Graham's gaze.

'Well, what sparked the mutiny, as you say, is unclear. But by the end of it the bulk of the crew was implicated, and Ablass seems to have been acting as their *de facto* leader, although his behaviour in the midst of the mutiny was odd, to say least.'

'In what way, sir?'

'He and Williams disappeared for an entire day while the mutiny was in full blood, and said nothing of where they had been when they returned. Ah, my dear Mrs Horton.'

Abigail has entered with a tray on which are placed cups and an ancient jug. Horton leaves her to pour out the coffee while he ponders the evening's developments. Graham looks smilingly at his wife, calibrating his eyebrows and mouth into the exactly correct and decent amount of admiration. When she hands a cup to Horton, Abigail brushes his fingers and smiles, suggesting to Horton that his face has the old mask of concern on it. He follows Graham's example, and sets it into something less severe.

'This is interesting, Mr Graham. Fascinating, perhaps. But it only serves to make your decision to release Ablass even more bizarre. And we have not arrived at your reason to be here this evening.'

'Ah, yes, you are demonstrating the already-renowned Horton investigative technique. Harriott told me I should see it in action. I saw him just last night for dinner. He always speaks very warmly of you, you know.'

'I am pleased to hear it.'

'Yes, very warmly. He knows of my visit today, of course. Indeed he wanted to come, but I impressed on him that it is I, and not he, who must make this request of you. When you know the details I am about to impart to you, you will understand why I do not want Harriott to be any part of this. It would taint a great man. So now we come to the nub of it.'

For the first time, Graham's poise is at question. His hands become slightly more exercised. His eyes look down.

'After our trip to Sheerness at the end of December, I made certain enquiries. It seemed extraordinary to me that a single man, this "Morgan", could have acquired a ship and stayed out of the awareness of the crowd of merchants and insurance-men and shipowners who run things along the river. You know of these men. They financed the new dock, the docks along the Isle of Dogs. They are the men who put today's London together.'

Graham looks at Horton at this, but the officer gives nothing back. Graham mulls this, and then continues.

'But I like to think of myself as someone with decent connections. It did not take long to find someone who knew of this old slave ship and the transaction which took place over it. There is a certain cadre of merchants who have found themselves disrupted by recent legislation.'

'Legislation?'

'Legal changes, my dear Horton. We have already discussed – on that doomed ship, no less – the unavoidable fact that certain previously lucrative commercial activities have become constrained by parliamentary actions.'

'You're talking about slaving.'

'Indeed I am. Indeed. The trade has been legally ended, and we can all I am sure feel tremendously pleased with ourselves as a result. But the stark reality is that this has led to some economic changes for some of these old slave merchants. Most of them are in Liverpool and Bristol, but many of them are in

London. And many of them are seeking to release their investments.'

'So slave ships are becoming available for purchase?'

'My point exactly, Horton. These ships could be refitted for other cargo, of course. But these men have little incentive to make such an investment. They would rather realise their assets, quickly and quietly.'

'Quietly?'

'Quietly, Horton. Whatever some of us may think, there has been a stench around the slave trade ever since that blasted ship came back to England with its sordid little history. Slave merchants may have provided the economic grease for our national machine, but they are not being thanked for it.'

'So, this Morgan acquired an old slave ship, and you found the man, or men, who sold it to him.'

'Just so.'

'Which leads us where, Mr Graham?'

'It leads us here, Horton.' And now Graham stands and walks to the window, turning his back on Horton. He cannot look anywhere else.

'Some men sold the vessel. This we now know. But other men funded it.'

'Other men?'

'Yes, other men. Other men invested in the ship's next mission. Considerable amounts, I am told.'

There is no sound from the room next door, and Horton is convinced that Abigail is listening to this conversation. The fire crackles in the hearth, and Horton watches Graham's fingers as they clutch each other behind his back. The grand green-striped jacket is slightly hunched, almost supplicant. The wig is immaculately placed, but a curl of grey hair is peeking out from beneath it, a shocking sartorial error. Graham dressed in a hurry.

'So, this Morgan got investors for his journey, with help from some quarter or another,' says Horton. 'We could have guessed this much.' He says nothing of Naar and his suicide note. Not just yet.

Graham is still looking out of the window.

'It is rather more complicated than that, I'm afraid.'

Horton waits. The elegant man bows his head, and then turns to Horton, as if by some act of will.

'I have been given certain information by a party which must remain anonymous. The information relates to the history of William Ablass and has led me to a certain conclusion. Ablass is Morgan.'

Horton cannot stop himself. He lets out a single, harsh laugh. Graham looks at him, somewhat sadly.

'Ablass is Morgan?' says Horton to him, all thoughts of social deference departed. 'This is your information?'

'It is.'

'You are informed that a mutinous sailor living in poor circumstances in Wapping has been able to secure backing for a slaving trip?'

'That is the sum of it. But Ablass is rather more than a mutinous sailor.'

'So, what else might he be, Mr Graham?'

'This I cannot say.'

Horton considers this. His mind is racing to incorporate this new information, and one question above all presents itself.

'Why are you here, Mr Graham?'

'Ah, Horton. You have a forensic ability to sniff out the hardest question.'

At that Graham stops, sits back and watches Horton, who looks back at him without blinking or moving, as if waiting for the next act in an extraordinary theatrical drama. There is silence from outside the door, but it is a very full, very watchful silence, the silence of a careful woman with her ear to the door. The fire crackles and squeals in the grate. Horton notices that Graham is sweating, and that a nervous tic has commenced above his left eye. The passion has seeped out of Graham's voice, and the old composed visage, the half-smile and the *mots justes*, they are all gone. He is speaking with great care and great precision but his face is damp and his left eyebrow is dancing like a duck skidding on ice. Horton notes this, and notes with care everything he now says.

'My hands are tied, Horton. I can pursue this case no further because certain gentlemen do not wish it to be pursued. They are fearful for what I may uncover. I have released Ablass because I have been instructed to do so.'

'These being gentlemen who have invested in this undertaking, and do not wish this investment to be revealed, since it is both illegal and immoral.'

Graham says nothing to this.

'I believe,' Graham continues, 'the connections between Marr, Williamson, Williams and Ablass are clear and that Ablass was certainly involved in the killings. I also wish to state that I have my suspicions that Williams did not take his own life in that cell. If he did not, the murderer is even now making his way to Sheerness. And I can do nothing to apprehend him.'

And suddenly, the reason for Graham's visit becomes clear to Charles Horton.

'You want me to deal with Ablass.'

There it is. A loose end to be tied fast before it grasps the ankle of a shipmate and throws him overboard.

Graham coughs discreetly.

'The ... gentlemen who I have been speaking to have suggested an unofficial course of action. This much is true.'

'I will not do it.'

Graham looks down at his hat, which is now whirring through his hands like some portable engine. He does not look at Horton again.

'I suspected you would say as much. You are a man of honour and integrity, Charles Horton, and in that you do credit to yourself, to your wife and to your superior. Harriott thinks this of you, and will continue to think this of you, despite what I am about to say about your past.'

Oh my God. Surely not this.

'Harriott agrees that Ablass must be destroyed. He also agrees with me that this will be impossible through the official channels. He is not here because I will not let him be any part of the mechanism by which the destruction will be effected.

'This is too important to let individual punctiliousness drive us. You will do it, Horton, because if you do not I will ensure that your maritime history is revealed to the world. Those former shipmates with whom you still meet – like that neat little family currently residing on one of the Sheerness hulks – will be made aware of your betrayal, you will be forced to leave Harriott's service, and you and your wife will be subject to two disgraces: the disgrace of the mutineer, and the disgrace of the stool pigeon.

'Arrangements have already been made. You will find what you need to complete the undertaking waiting for you in a private coach which will take you directly to Sheerness. You will leave tonight, and we have no time to wait for tides and boats. The means for the destruction of Ablass have been provided and will be waiting for you in the coach. I have an agent in Sheerness who will report on the success or otherwise of your mission. If I do not hear from him within three days, the information I hold about you will become widely known.

'Good night, my dear Horton. And good luck.'

Graham makes his own way out, his eyes still averted. When she hears his feet on the stairs, Abigail rushes into the room and buries her head in her husband's neck, arms tight round his shoulders, and weeps with rage and frustration. Horton says nothing.

5 FEBRUARY 1812

My, the night is quiet. Cold, certainly, and somewhat bleak with those ugly hulks lurking on the water, but the sky is clear for the first time in days and the stars are as bright as they can hope to be at this latitude. Amazing, how the night transforms a scene. What in the day is pockmarked and ugly can in the dark seem wondrous. After the noise and smells of London, after that dirty little cell somewhere beneath Covent Garden, I begin to feel something like peace. Hart and Pugh are leaving. The two of them are very drunk. We have been busy celebrating the recommencement of our project.

Isak Naar and I had stood much like this out on the veranda at Woodperry, the night before I was taken by Sloane's men. We often met together to swap stories and plans for the future. He sometimes called me his *golem*, when the wine flask was nearly empty and the liquor had worked its way into his blood.

But that night had been different. Isak seemed sad and perhaps even scared; even then he was working up the courage to tell me he was leaving. The knowledge of that future conversation, and I assume his real regret at having to leave, meant he was in elegiac mood that evening, with the wind whipping off the Caribbean and the sound of a slave singing from over by the barrack-house. He spoke to me about his own future and past; how his father had sailed out from Portugal with his own dreams of wealth and had established the family on a plantation in Surinam. He spoke of his own dream: the establishment of a successful trading company in London.

'I left home with similar dreams,' I said to him.

'Ah, yes?'

'Wealth and property, Isak. The Jews don't have a monopoly on those dreams.'

He laughed at that, but it wasn't his usual belly laugh, more an Old World chuckle, full of knowledge and more than a little bitter.

Terrible winds and rains came upon us that night. Jamaica could be wicked when she wanted to be. The Negroes ran wild around the house, screaming and wailing that God was angry with them. Isak and I mocked their silliness. Funny little Christians, with their redemption and salvation and superstitious optimism. The two of us knew that all that mattered in the cosmos was comfort and hard work and money. These were what God consisted in.

The next day Isak gave me the news he had been swallowing for days, but then Sloane's men took me and I never saw old Naar again. He did very well out of my disappearance. He must have changed his plans quickly, and with his complete power of attorney over the assets and chattels I held at Woodperry he sold everything and transplanted his family, the business, everything to Surinam, where his father had first made his riches. Isak never did open his London trading company; but one of his great-great-great-grandsons did.

Two years ago I swam ashore in Surinam and encountered a younger Isak, who told me of his cousin Benjamin and the counting house in Limehouse. Benjamin was now the curator of my little store of treasure, the investment against the future that old Isak had put aside, in Potosí silver. The older Isak had known his *golem* would be back to ask hard questions of his descendants; the silver was Isak's insurance policy, transplanted from its hiding place in Cockpit County (Isak knew of my secret treasury, as he knew of everything) to the counting rooms of a lonely Jew in London's East End. Somehow old Isak's message had been passed down the generations: fear the *golem*, but help him, too.

So, you see trust is something which even monsters must have faith in. Without my trust in Isak, everything I owned would have been lost on that road to Port Royal when I was seized by unknown hands. Under Isak's care, my estate survived and even thrived, and my wealth remained available to me, though the years had lessened its worth. I possessed the capital I needed to invest in my own centuries-long undertaking.

Horton approaches Sheerness across the estuary. The lights in the hulks outside the new dock float in the air above the silent water, full of their own melancholy humanity. Inside those dark arks families are settling down for the night, sharing a flavour of domesticity despite their eerie dwellings. He imagines sharing such a watery palace with his own Abigail. She would carve out a comfortable accommodation, comfortably decorated with cheap oddities from who knows where. There would be candles and cushions and rugs. Collected together, it would feel like home.

He sits on the small wooden barrel, smoking a pipe. His heavy old naval coat is wrapped around him; his head is covered by a floppy, wide-brimmed hat in the French Revolutionary style; a leather bag is across his shoulder and chest.

In Europe, Napoleon is marching towards Moscow. In Sheerness, a guilty old mutineer is sailing towards something that feels a bit like destiny and a bit like redemption.

He had told the London coach to head for the small hamlet in the Grain Marshes, confident this was a more direct route than the great loop round to the Swale. He knew he would find the old waterman again, and he knew how to get from that side of the Medway into the Sheerness harbour without being seen by anyone or anything. The London driver had muttered and complained at the unfinished roads that this route took them down, but Horton ignored him, deep in his own contemplation of the task ahead.

The waterman glances occasionally at the barrel Horton is sitting upon. He had tried to help Horton carry it into the boat but had been firmly rebuffed. Consequently he is now working over in his mind what might be there in that barrel. Not anything liquid, like wine or gin. No sounds of sloshing. Something solid and heavy. Not tobacco. Perhaps smuggled spices to be traded. The ferryman looks towards Sheerness, guiding the little boat between the silent hulks.

From aboard one of them comes the sound of singing, male voices joined together in something foreign-sounding. Portuguese or Gaelic, perhaps, though Horton believes that most of the dwellers in the hulks are English, old families pushed out from London like generations before by harder-working, more-desperate incomers, forced to find a new living out here on the margins. Running away from something and towards something else, unable to articulate either.

These people will soon be edged away even from here. Rennie's dock is rapidly taking shape and the labourers dwelling on the hulks are only a short-term necessity. Soon enough the wharves and warehouses will be completed, and men in uniform will patrol the locked gates and shuttered buildings. Within perhaps a year or two it will be like Wapping out here, the dock sitting in the middle of a community, the only engine of moneymaking, essential yet also somehow alien, tolerated, worshipped and resented.

Into the harbour goes the little boat, in among some hulks and other working vessels now at rest. The growing warehouses around the dock stick up against the moonlit sky like geometrical megaliths, monuments to new gods. And there, up against the half-built facade of a mighty new warehouse, is the *Zong*.

In the dark you cannot see her neglect, so you could if you chose marvel at the lines of her hull and the forthright way she sits in the water. In the dark she has the romantic outline of a mighty vessel of commerce, an engine of British influence and power. You cannot see the name torn away from her bows, the figurehead which has been ripped off. In the dark she is all that makes Britain great. You cannot see what makes Britain terrible.

Apart from one thing. There, towards the stern, a light is flickering and a tall, dark shape is moving on the quarterdeck. Here, on the water, it is impossible to hear if it is making a noise. But the shape is moving back and forth, back and forth, pacing out some urgent question. From somewhere behind the ship a man is laughing. Horton pulls the sleeve of the waterman and places a finger on his lips, then indicates that he should head to the bow of the ship, where he remembers steps which reached down to the water from the quay.

*

I find myself considering something Hart said this evening. We were talking of the new plans we must put in place, of the need to find new suppliers, of how Benjamin Naar can help us once again. And Hart had upended a bottle of wine down his throat, wiped his mouth on his sleeve and said: 'Jews and niggers. I can't figure out which of 'em I hate the worst. But they're the only ones what'll do what's needed.'

So English, that mixture of contempt and resourcefulness, that proud and unthinking hypocrisy. Money is what it's about, says Hart, says England itself, and his greed is why I can trust him. Ever since I left Kate behind and travelled to Plymouth to seek out Hawkyns, I have never deviated from my desire to pursue wealth. At first, my goals were not lofty – enough money to buy some pigs and build a farm. A little rural paradise for me and my pretty wife. But then my pretty wife became less pretty and the years opened out into infinity, and how is a man to fill those years? Motion is essential, but motion towards what? In my case, the answer to that question was simple: the getting and the keeping of money.

Still I burn with frustration at what I missed while I sat, for yawning decades, in Sloane's benighted chamber, chained down and with only books to console me, books through which I gathered a picture of the world that had emerged during my captivity.

I read of a globe becoming encircled by English ships (or I should rather say *British* ships, a shining word which was minted and then traded even while I remained in captivity). New manufactories in English and Scottish cities churned out cotton and guns and machines to be carried from British shores to the edges of the world. I read of the birth of a great Triangular Trade: goods carried to Africa, exchanged for slaves, which were in turn exchanged for sugar, which was in turn exchanged for British goods, and on and on went the great machine. And at the heart of the trade those great West Indian plantations, like my own dear Woodperry, engines running on black muscle and spewing out money and sugar and rum.

How right Hawkyns was in his early imaginings. He knew that the fuel for this mighty endeavour would be the blacks. They were the precious commodity on which England would build an empire. The few hundred we took onto the *Jesus* were merely signals of what was to come. Elizabeth had provided that ship – why, she was the most far-sighted of all! A hundred and fifty years after Hawkyns another queen, Anne this time, was setting up her own South Sea Company to trade in slaves, and that company had made Britain rich. Slave-trading primed the pump which even today drives British factories. Thinkers and poets invested in the enterprise: Swift, Pope, Newton, Defoe, Locke. I think of Newton, the great old alchemist, coming to the realisation that there was one base element that could indeed be converted to gold: the Negro. When I think of those great thinkers, I think also of Hart's hypocrisy, for are they not guilty of the same thing?

And, to borrow from Newton, the effect of the Negro was seen at a distance. Those selling slaves in Guinea needed guns and cotton, and British factories were built to supply them. When I think of those black bodies bent down before a wall of cane on Woodperry, I see the labour of their hands working the great machine of Britain itself.

But I missed this magnificent moment. When I finally escaped this great new trade was coming to an end, in Britain at least. The intellectuals and lawyers in Britain had grown fat, literally and figuratively, on the benefits of commerce but had now become squeamish about the activities which primed the great economic pump. They argued for an end of the trade. Other countries were less weak-willed. It took me some years to discover the new Woodperry in Surinam, where I met Isak's descendants and was turned away from my intention of destroying them as thieves by the revelation that my hidden wealth remained intact, in London, and could be transmuted into gold again. That there was a chance for a final trade, even while the slaving acts were being implemented around the great empire which slaving had built.

*

The boat comes to against the newly minted steps. Horton hefts up the solid, heavy little barrel. He indicates that the waterman should move a little way from the *Zong* once he is out of the boat. He cannot see the light in the stern from here, and has no idea if he can be heard or seen by whoever is on the ship. Step by step, as quietly and slowly as he can manage it, he climbs up towards the quay.

Two men appear on the gangplank between the *Zong* and the quayside, perhaps fifty feet away from where Horton stands, frozen, clutching his heavy barrel. He glances fearfully at the waterman but the old man has taken his lead from Horton and is likewise still and silent in his old boat.

The two men are laughing and unsteady on their feet as they walk across the plank. Even while fear of discovery locks him in place, Horton strains to hear what they are saying.

'Steady, you bastard!'

'Don't bastard me!'

'You can't hold your bloody wine, Hart!'

The first man reaches the quayside and turns belligerently towards the one following him. He swings a half-hearted fist but misses and is shoved to the ground for his pains, out of Horton's sight. Both men can be heard struggling, shouting and laughing.

'Long Billy'll get yer, fucking white-livered turd.'

'Shut it, shut it.'

''Ere, that girl you fucked in Spitalfields, I 'eard she was a bloke, big fat weaver with a beard!'

'Go on, 'ave some of this.'

This goes on for some time, and eventually they quieten and stand. Horton sees their heads appearing over the line of the quayside above him. Cornelius Hart and Thomas Pugh, the carpenters who worked on Timothy Marr's shop. The men now have their arms around each other's shoulders and are swaying gently in inebriated comradeship.

'Lovely, ain't she?' says Hart.

'Thing of beauty,' says Pugh.

They are talking of the *Zong*.

'Reckon Billy's right, do yer?' says Hart. 'Reckon we'll be off by spring?'

'P'raps. P'raps.'

'You know what, though?'

'What?'

'I never did get my fucking chisel back.'

At that a great roar of laughter, and the two of them turn away from the ship, singing some old shanty on their way, the words unrecognisable in their drunkenness.

*

I watch my two accomplices fighting on the quayside. These are in some strange way my friends now, I suppose. Like John Williams thought he was. Yet I feel nothing towards them, only that yawning emptiness which has characterised all my transactions with the everyday since – well, since when? Sometime after that encounter in Florida, but not immediately after. I came back in most ways the same man I had been when I left. But one by one the ingredients of a man's inner life – love, ambition, excitement, lust – were emptied from me. Love I left in Stanton St John, with a pearl beneath a pillow. Ambition died with contentment's rise in Jamaica. Excitement, lust – all washed away in the blood and heat of Tortuga and Portobelo. All that remains is a wish for peace, the kind of peace that only money, and a good deal of it, can buy. I wish to sit once again on the veranda at Woodperry, with the blacks singing in the fields and the house slaves preparing dinner. This shoddy dock at the edge of this half-forgotten town is no place to spend eternity.

So for now I must consort with these shallow men, with their limited view of the riches in store for them. They have been useful. It had been Hart's idea to leave his chisel in Marr's shop as an excuse to be let in later. Marr did not then know me. It was Benjamin who'd made arrangements, and Benjamin who'd told me of Marr's decision to end the undertaking, and his threat to reveal what he had discovered of my plans. The old fury had risen within me; I was reminded of the Ironside, Sharp, and his sanctimonious belief in a preposterous Right and Wrong mediated by some supernatural being. Now this new prig, this self-important shopkeeper, threatened all my plans.

When I saw him at the door of his shop, I heard it again: that relentless, insidious hum. It pursued me into the house, maddening and enraging me. Pugh and Hart waited at the back of the house while I pursued my melancholy transactions within. It was the work of a minute, no more. That blissful music thrummed in time with my heart and filled my head with light as I despatched the merchant and his family, my hands a blur of doing and undoing. I took the maul, the instrument of destruction, upstairs and left a candle as the signal of it. The maul would ultimately lead those seeking the killers to John Williams. I felt a glorious kind of peace coming back down those stairs, as if I was in some way sanctified – for did I not carry my own stigmata, in my side, my stomach, my ankle? And was not that hum the sound of angels singing me to my destiny?

Then I heard the baby's cry from the cellar, and was forced to complete my transactions down there. As I entered the baby's pathetic little chamber, I thought of Kate and the life which we could have lived, and – well, then. The memory was cleaned away.

*

Horton waits several minutes until he is sure Pugh and Hart have left the quayside. He looks back down at the old waterman, who has likewise stood stock-still and silent the entire time. He gestures all's-well to the old man, who nods and sits down in his boat to wait.

At the top of the steps, Horton peeps over the lip of the quay. There is no one there. He looks back at the *Zong*. There is a light shining from the aft-cabin, so someone is still on the ship, though whoever it is has gone back inside. Presumably Ablass. *Hopefully* Ablass. With a small sigh, Horton climbs the last few steps up and makes his way to the gangplank.

It creaks when he steps onto it, but he doesn't worry too much about making noise. An old ship like this is a cacophony of creaks and groans as it rolls on the water, even here inside Sheerness harbour. A dropped barrel, on the other hand, would draw the attention of whoever is on board, and while he is on the plank he will be plainly visible to anyone who happens to look. But he still has his sea legs and gets across the plank with little fuss, stepping down on to the deck at the other end.

He tries to remember the layout of the ship. The steps down to the lower decks are midships, towards the stern, and thus towards whoever is already on board. He looks back down along the deck and can see the flickering light at the other end of the ship. The light moves and by instinct he covers up his face with the wide-brimmed hat, his hands gloved in dark material. He sits on the barrel and presses himself back against the shadows below the ship's rail as the ship's captain steps back out onto the deck.

*

Williamson, now. He was a different case. An older man, not as pious and priggish as young Marr, perfectly willing to trade with one such as I. Only money mattered to old Williamson, the invisible hand of profit. I suppose that, in this, he was much like me, though his domestic circumstances were a long way from comfortable. But he reneged on our arrangement too, for reasons I know not. He told Benjamin that he'd promised another not to pursue the undertaking we had discussed, and that mention of another had chilled me. Like Marr, here was another mouth that needed to be stopped-up. Hart accompanied me to Williamson's tavern, and the fool had panicked before our transactions had completed. We'd made our escape through the back of the tavern, leaving some alive inside, but Williamson himself was silenced.

The magistrates of Shadwell and Wapping pursued me over the weeks that followed. I had been careful in my transactions and had sought the opinions of many of those in the area as to the capacities of the magistrates. Those in Shadwell, it was said, were not fit for their purpose. Those on the river, however, were capable, but had no jurisdiction on the land. My former shipmate John Williams was to be the means of my own escape. It was a simple matter to steal the maul from his lodgings, but even then the Shadwell magistrates were unable to follow the trail I had laid out for them. I was forced to point out the way to them directly, and eventually they accepted the gift I gave them readily. And with Williams dead in his cell, the dead end I had pushed them down ended their investigation.

But then others became involved, magistrates with more imagination and application. I was arrested and kept for days, taken time and again before the Covent Garden magistrate, whose questions were as smooth and dangerous as his face. I began to worry then, for this man seemed in possession of knowledge which might serve to trap me, but then as soon as it started my incarceration ended, suddenly, two days ago. I came straightaway to my dead ship, and she was still here, waiting for me to return.

So the project can now start again. We will make the ship beautiful once more. Within three months I should be off the coast of Guinea once again, like I was all those years ago, with Drake and Tillert and grumbling old Cornelius. This time the Africans will know what a gun is and will not wait for us to shoot at them. They will be wiser, and cannier, but one thing is for sure: there will always be someone there willing to trade, and thanks to my investors I will have no shortage of items to offer them.

The time has come again. Everything is now in place. I walk back to the stern of the ship: my ship. There is no foolish Welshman to deface the rail with a knife and ponder his own glory. There is no Drake to smirk and sneer and then disappear when metal starts to cut into flesh. There are no pompous Royal Society Fellows, begging to be told my secret while desperately denying my very existence. There is only me, Billy Ablass, enduring in the face of time.

The trade may be banned. But the business goes on.

*

Peering over the brim of his hat, desperate to avoid showing any pale skin in the moonlight, Horton hides in the dark. During the day, he would be a hundred feet away from the captain, and plainly visible. Now, he is just a dark shape amidst many.

The captain turns and walks up the ladder to the aft deck, above his cabin, and continues on back towards the stern. He is tall and walks with a noticeable limp. His long coat swirls round his feet, and Horton's mind is suddenly awash with conflicting witness statements and depositions and the common themes that ran through them. *A tall man . . . he had a limp . . . there was a tall man outside the shop the day before . . . a long coat . . . a young man, very tall . . .*

The captain comes to a halt at the stern, his back to Horton.

He puts his hands behind his back. Horton can see them, pale against the night.

His chance. He removes his shoes and leaves them on the deck, places his hat on his head, carefully takes up the barrel, and walks towards the stern, every step adding to the creaking shrieks of the ship's wooden planks. He tries to feel the rhythm of the boat, to make each step in keeping with the language of the vessel, and he must succeed, because within seconds that feel like hours he is standing at the top of the ladder that goes down into the dark lower depths.

He steps down, one step, two steps, and as he passes into the lower deck the edge of the barrel catches the edge of the deck above and he ducks down all the way, unable to see if the captain has heard the noise or not. As lightly as he can he skips down the rest of the steps, the weight of the barrel carrying him into the darkness, before turning back behind the steps and gazing up at the square of night sky above him to see if the captain has taken any notice of the strange noise.

As he stops, he listens and listens. And there is something new, a more regular noise within the caterwauling of the ship's structure. A step then a shuffle then a step. A limping gait, coming towards midships. His heart thumping, Horton moves backwards into the darkness of the hold until something presses against the small of his back: the shelf onto which the slaves had been packed in for the Atlantic journey. As carefully as he can manage, Horton slides under the shelf and covers his face with the hat again, as the captain's foot appears on the ladder coming down.

The long body of the captain shows as a silhouette in the moonlight from above the opening in the deck. He seems more sure on his feet on this ladder than he seemed on the deck, practised at clambering up and down. Steadily but also blindingly quickly he steps down onto the lower deck, and then looks around, peering into the dark shadows.

His face is clearly visible to Horton now in the moonlight, and familiar. It is a face he has seen in crowds at funerals and gatherings ever since the death of the Marrs. A young, handsome, appraising kind of face, far younger than seems correct for the crimes Horton believes he has committed. The cheeks seem too soft, the lips too full to be in the face of a man who has slashed the throat of a baby. The brow is heavyset, though, and the eyes are in darkness. The hair is untidy but also looked after, apparently professionally cut. Something about the man's bearing suggests authority and wealth. It is not the bearing of a young man.

And then the captain speaks.

'Anybody there?'

The accent is odd. Part West Country, part establishment, part something foreign which Horton recognises as distinctly West Indian, the cadence of several of his former shipmates who had grown up amid the islands and reefs and hurricanes.

'If there's somebody there, best show yourself now.'

The captain waits. Five seconds. Ten. Half a minute. A minute.

'Careful, now,' he says finally. 'Careful what you do next. If there's someone there, best be careful.'

Then one hand grabs a step on the ladder, and he turns round and climbs back up again, into the starlight.

Horton waits and then waits some more. He hears that strange half-damaged step walking away along the deck, and then nothing but the waves and the creaking of the hull. Slowly, infinitely carefully, he manoeuvres himself out from underneath the shelf. He stands, hoists the barrel back up to his chest, and makes his way back to the ladder.

Immediately below the ladder from the main deck is another, going down into the belly of the ship, where provisions would be stored for the voyage, lying directly against the outer hull. Horton climbs down, working essentially from memory now – memory of the plans of the *Zong* itself, but also a deeper memory of the essentials of an ocean-going vessel, its contours and its vectors. The ladder has a dozen steps, and somehow Horton's old seagoing legs expect this and are not shocked with their contact with the bottom of the ship.

There are only inches between him and the water of the dock. The darkness is absolute now, although Horton does not need light for what he is about to do.

From his bag he takes out a coil of something like a longish length of narrow rope; it is a fuse, but nothing like any fuse he has seen before, seemingly constructed from a combination of rope, paper and powder. He takes out a knife from inside his coat and works away at a stopper in the lid of the barrel. When it comes away, he works the fuse into the powder within the barrel, as Graham had explained earlier, and replaces the stopper, which has a small gap at its edge for the fuse.

He unwinds the coil, then picks the barrel up and slowly walks towards the stern of the ship, allowing its contours to show him the direction in the dark, unwinding the coil as he goes. After perhaps thirty seconds of slow walking, the barrel hits the rising inner surface of the hull, and he stops himself standing as there would be no room. He is now directly underneath the captain's quarters. He places the barrel down on the hull, picks up the unwound coil and uses it to guide himself back to the ladder.

Once there he takes something else from his bag. A tinderbox, dry as a bone, its charcloth carefully maintained. The one from Naar's house, left at the bottom of the stairs. He settles down onto his haunches to set about the careful business of starting a flame. He strikes the flint on the steel abruptly, directly, acutely aware of the sharp noise he is making. It takes nine strikes before the charcloth ignites, and then he misses catching it on a wood splint and is forced to hold the charcloth directly against the fuse he has uncoiled onto the floor.

For a moment, nothing happens, and then the special fuse provided by Graham ignites in a frenzy of colourful sparks the like of which Horton has never seen, which light up the bowels of the ship, sufficient for him to see to the other end of the hold, where the little barrel awaits the arrival of the flame. 'You will have between seventy and ninety seconds once the fuse is lit,' Graham had written.

For a moment, a destiny suggests itself, a deliberate self-immolation in the face of Graham and those faceless men who have dragged him down here to the hold of this hellish ship. Richard Parker throwing himself from the yardarm, all doubt and guilt vanquished in a single gesture of defiance and glory. Then he thinks of Abigail, and with that, he grabs a step on the ladder, and then strong hands have grabbed his hand and are pulling him up onto the deck above.

The captain has him by the arm, then he has him by the hair, and Horton shrieks as he is pulled up towards the captain's face, towards a shining lethal sliver of knife-metal which catches the moonlight as it hovers before his eye, ready to take it out or slash at his throat. Horton smells the captain's breath and feels the hairs coming away from his scalp and then the captain sees the colourful luminescence from the cavity below them and bellows something deep and ancient before hurling Horton onto that dreadful shelf which rings the lower deck.

Horton shrieks, again, as he slides onto the shelf and hits something hard, sharp and metallic which bites into the space between his shoulder blades. He feels skin break and starts to scrabble away but cannot. He is caught by something snagged onto his clothing, and then recalls with sudden clarity the iron chains and manacles which line the interior of the *Zong*. One of them has him held fast.

From below he can hear the captain shouting and stamping, trying and failing to extinguish Aaron Graham's fuse, and the inside of the *Zong* is humming, as if a gigantic swarm of bees had been released below decks. How much time has passed? Half a minute? More? His fingers scrabble down between his shoulder blades but he can feel nothing there, cannot reach around far enough to release himself, and how many more seconds have passed now?

His shoulders feel like they will pop out as he stretches manically, and fingers scatter across something hard and cold, snagged into his coat in that impossible place in the middle back where an itch can last for hours. *Abigail, I am sorry* he says to himself for the ten-thousandth time since his marriage, but almost alongside that thought he makes one final stretch, the sinews in his shoulders straining like the rigging of a doomed ship head-on to a murderous wind, and his fingers grasp the underside of the devilish iron thing at his back and with a desperate pull he is free.

That humming surrounds him and from the hold comes a sound like an enraged Minotaur held by unbreakable threads and Horton is climbing, climbing into the moonlight, blood running down his face and his arms hanging almost useless by his sides, his shoulders livid with pain, his feet now on the deck and pushing him towards the ship's rail as, from below, first a flare of light, then a ripple of wood and then a roaring, crashing percussion which helps to shove him up, out and into the night, falling into the water below as the old slave ship explodes into its essential parts and pours its guts down on the other ships, on Horton and on the old, watching waterman. The final thing Horton hears is a jolly tinkling, as dozens of silver coins rain down against the stones of the dockside before sinking into the black water, like an offering from heaven.

EPILOGUE

John Harriott watches the river, from his customary position at the window of the Police Office. He stands, as he likes to do, with his weight on his good leg, determined not to sit at the window like some old maid spying on her neighbours. Even at this late hour the stream is full of noise and movement. Lights flicker from ships at anchor and from the dozens of lighters and wherries which are still ferrying goods and people from shore to ship to shore. The river is as busy as any London street.

When he had first looked on this stream, decades before, all he'd seen was chaos. Now, he sees an emergent order, as if a new quality is rising up from these scurrying motions, like honey from a beehive. The quality is prosperity, he supposes. His own, but more importantly that of the country. A prosperity which must be protected and nurtured, like the spark of life itself.

Ah, but at what cost?

There is a discreet knock on the door and his big, ancient heart leaps in its chest. He growls: 'Come in.'

One of the office servants opens the door.

'Mr Graham is here, sir.'

It is the visit he has been anticipating, yet it feels as unwelcome as the bite of a mosquito. He does not turn from the window, leaning on his stick, his lame leg throbbing with exhaustion.

'Good. Send him in.'

His voice is its usual gruff self, calm and measured but with the old excitability bubbling beneath. He hears his old friend enter the room, and wonders if indeed they are still friends, or if the ballast of their recent history is too much for comradeship to bear. He finally turns from the window and sees Aaron Graham standing before the fire, head bowed and eyes looking deeply into the flames. The magistrate has none of his Covent Garden poise this evening. He looks both older and more serious. It is, considers Harriott, probably an improvement, yet it feels like a diminution.

'Well?' he asks, and Graham visibly starts at the sound of his voice. He clears his throat, his face still fixed on the fire.

Is he ashamed to look at me?

'The deed is done,' says Graham quietly.

'There can be no doubt? Ablass was on the vessel?'

'My agent saw him go on and did not see him come off before Horton arrived.'

'The ship is destroyed?'

'I'm told it was the biggest explosion Kent has ever seen. They will be talking about it for years.'

'And Horton?'

Harriott's voice catches a little, and Graham looks up at him then. He looks terribly sad.

'Constable Horton survived. He dived from the ship as it exploded.'

Graham looks back to the fire.

'Thank heaven,' says Harriott.

Graham says nothing to that. He does not look much in the mood to thank anyone or anything. Perversely, Harriott feels some sorrow for him. His political friend has been rather boxed in by events, it would seem. He cannot shout or bluster, as Harriott would. He has too much at stake. Graham has bent his personal morality to the snapping point in recent days. It is unlikely to bend back quickly.

There is an uncomfortable silence. Neither of them is armed with a quip to fill it. Eventually, Graham speaks.

'I am to convey the gratitude of the PRS for your cooperation.'

And, for some reason, that finally sets Harriott off.

'Given the seriousness of his imposition on my office, I would have thought a personal conveyance of such gratitude would have been appropriate.'

'Now, Harriott, that was never ...'

'Has the man any conception of what he has asked and what has been done? Or does he prefer to hold court in Soho Square in magnificent scholarly indifference, while we send men to skulk around in strange harbours for murky reason of political expedience? By God, Graham, we have sent a good man to undertake a demonic task.'

'Horton is safe, Harriott.'

'He is *damaged*, Graham. We have damaged him. We have resurrected a past from which he was trying to escape.'

'He would not have undertaken what was needed without incentive.'

'My God, Graham, you speak as if you were in Parliament. We are not in Parliament. We are in the River Police Office, and you are with an old friend. I pray you, do not speak as if I were an elector. You do me a great disservice. Not as great as that done to poor Horton, but nevertheless.'

'Harriott, your constable will recover. I have a proposal for him.'

'A proposal?'

'Yes. He has been working for you in a semi-official capacity.'

'He has. So much I told you when we began the secondary investigation into the Wapping murders. I did not expect then that this would lead to furtive assassinations on the Kent coast.'

'My proposal is that he keeps working in this capacity. With you as his magistrate.'

'*Keeps* working? For what? The case is closed, though in a brazenly clandestine fashion.'

'There will be other cases.'

'No doubt. Cases which Horton can investigate in his official capacity.'

'Not these cases.'

'Graham, what in God's name are you talking about?'

'Old friend, I have not been honest with you.'

Graham has not once looked up from the fire during this little exchange, but he does now, and Harriott can see, really *see*, how terribly careworn this West End dandy now appears.

'It is late, Graham. Perhaps in the morning . . .'

'No, John. Now. Yes, the hour is late, but darkness is appropriate for the tale I must tell. It is true that the President of the Royal Society himself demanded the cessation of the existence of William Ablass, but not for the mercantile reasons I gave to you and to Horton. That was a fabrication, one which weighs heavy on me but one which I will now try to correct. The PRS knows I am here, and knows of my insistence that you, at least, be told the whole truth. He also knows of my proposal for you and for Horton. We will come to that. But for now, John, sit in that old chair and rest your lame leg. My story is long, dark and fantastic. Neither of us will sleep tonight once it is told.'

And with that, Graham begins.

AUTHOR'S NOTE

There are stories, and there are histories. It goes without saying that this is a story, and what's more a story that takes some liberties with reputations, biographies and events.

That said, I did give myself the task of cleaving as close as possible to the true facts when telling the story of the Ratcliffe Highway murders (as they became known). The dates given within are the real dates; the Marr and Williamson families were really exterminated in the manner described; John Williams really did kill himself in Coldbath Fields; and he really was thrown into a non-grave just north of the Highway. His bones were dug up, legend has it, by a gang of workmen laying a water main in the early years of the twentieth century, and for many years afterwards a skull was on display in a local pub which was allegedly that of the so-called Irish Monster.

The story of the terrible murders and the tragically amateurish investigation into them is told in the magisterial *The Maul and the Pear Tree*, by P.D. James and T.A. Critchley (Faber & Faber). Written forty years ago, it describes London's emerging and chaotic police infrastructure in 1811 (Robert

Peel is still some years away), and the attempts by John Harriott, in particular, to give some sort of energy to the investigation. Harriott's impetuous handbill and his clashes with the Shadwell magistrates and the Home Secretary himself are described as they actually happened. There really was a Billy Ablass in and around Wapping at the time of the murders, and he was mentioned in the House of Commons (the extract from Hansard within is real, but edited). Of course, it should go without saying that the history I have given Ablass is entirely my own invention; there is no suggestion in the historical record that he was, well, *enduring*.

Waterman-Constable Charles Horton, like Ablass, was a real man who did work for the River Police Office but whose historical background is unknown (at least to me). All I have is an address and a name – the character of Charles Horton is an invention, and so is his wife Abigail. The character of Aaron Graham is also a biographical liberty on my part, although Graham really was magistrate at the historic office of Bow Street who took a keen interest in the murders and was asked in January 1812 to undertake his own investigations into the murders, as described within.

John Harriott, now. No one would make him up, and his desperate attempts to find the perpetrators of the Ratcliffe Highway murders were heroic. His memoirs were published as *My Struggles Through Life*, three years before the events of *The English Monster*. He leaps out of the pages of those memoirs as a true archetype, British and bulldog-magnificent. His life was a vivid, monumental struggle, marked by relentless energy but punctuated by tragedy and black despair. Someone should write Harriott's biography, and it would be the biography of Britain itself. His endless struggles with money mirror those of his country rather too closely for any modern Briton's comfort.

As for the remaining 'contemporary' matters dealt with in the book, I should say a word about the Royal Society, whose president in 1811 was Sir Joseph Banks. It can't be dodged – I've implicated both Banks and his great Society in a terrible historical cover-up in the pages of this story. Lest the present Fellows of the Society start devising methods of separating me into my component parts in scientifically interesting ways, I should of course emphasise that, to my knowledge, the Society has long been in the habit of investigating those accidents of natural history it comes across, rather than shutting them away.

I will only add that 1811 is a peculiarly *fluid* time in the Society's history, and in natural philosophy itself. A new scientific establishment will soon appear over the historical horizon, and its offspring will include Faraday's dynamo and Darwin's theory, but in 1811 the Society is rather more like an arm of a government at war, and its patriotic president Sir Joseph would have felt no shame in that. Read more about this amazing period in the history of science in Richard Holmes's mesmerising *The Age of Wonder* (HarperPress).

Just as with the events of late 1811 and early 1812, I've tried to make the historical events which created the Monster chronologically accurate while indulging in a good deal of artistic licence. John Hawkyns did lead England's first 'official' slaving trip, an accolade which should (although doesn't, in my opinion) burn with sufficient infamy to our modern eyes to perhaps blot out his achievements in defending England from a Spanish invasion years later. His lead ship, the *Jesus of Lübeck*, did belong to Queen Elizabeth herself, and she knew perfectly well what he planned to fill its hold with. He sailed three times in total to Africa and New Spain, the third of these into disaster; the events portrayed in *The English Monster* are largely drawn from the second voyage.

It is also a matter of historical record that Francis Drake sailed with Hawkyns on the third voyage, as a senior officer and then as a captain, so his presence on the second, though by no means unlikely, is nevertheless (another) liberty taken by me. The events of the Hawkyns voyages are covered in scholarly yet engrossing detail in Nick Hazlewood's *The Queen's Slave Trader* (Harper Perennial), whose title describes exactly what Hawkyns and Drake were up to.

Some will be shocked that Francis Drake, England's great Elizabethan hero, had dabbled in the trading of human souls. Some may even be annoyed by my bringing it up. This is understandable. The horrors, evils, and crushing inhumanity of the slave trade have been well documented but certainly not as well remembered as they should be. Anyone with a determination to face England's guilt in this regard should read Hugh Thomas's *The Slave Trade* (Phoenix), which plumbs with dispassionate clarity the full depth of England's iniquity. To read more about the specific cruelties of slavery in the Caribbean, and how it primed the great engine of English commerce, please read Elizabeth Abbott's *Sugar: A Bittersweet History* (Duckworth Overlook). All I can do here is repeat George Orwell's remarks from 'The Lion and the Unicorn':

> England is not the jewelled isle of Shakespeare's much-quoted message, nor is it the inferno depicted by Dr Goebbels. More than either it resembles a family, a rather stuffy Victorian family, with not many black sheep in it but with all its cupboards bursting with skeletons. It has rich relations who have to be kow-towed to and poor relations who are horribly sat upon, and there is a deep conspiracy of silence about the source of the family income.

And with that, on to pirates. Of all the ground covered in *The English Monster*, that walked upon by Henry Morgan and his fellow Brethren is the most mythical, not least because many of the witnesses were not, shall we say, the most reliable. Morgan himself, though, is implausibly real and red-blooded: he did attack Portobelo (along with many other places, topped off with a ludicrously ambitious march to Panama), and he did fall into decline on Jamaica. Morgan is the flipside to John Harriott – a bulldog of a man with remorseless energy and boundless optimism, but one inflated beyond all reason by his own greed and vanity and capable of great cruelty. There were human shields used in the attack on Portobelo (women and old men, chiefly). But cruelty was the stock-in-trade of pirates, be they called buccaneers or Brethren. The episode between Morgan's French antithesis L'Ollonais and Billy Ablass is of course invented but the viciousness of the Frenchman is not. For a swashbuckling yet unromanticised gallop through Morgan's career, read Stephen Talty's *Empire of Blue Water* (Simon & Schuster).

The final player in the story is London itself. A walk through Wapping today is a walk through a country that rather seems to have forgotten where it came from; where once the mighty London Dock clattered with the goods of a whole world there is now only some rather average-looking housing and the ugly immensity of Rupert Murdoch's newspaper empire. The streets are quiet and ringed with warehouses which used to hold goods but which now house City traders – which isn't a bad image – and many of the stairs down to the river are gated off.

But there are still walls which recall the frenzy of dock-building which came in with the nineteenth century. You can still stand on Pennington Street and put your hand on the same wall that Margaret Jewell listens against. You can't visit

Timothy Marr's house – it's now a car showroom. The Ratcliffe Highway is an anaesthetised through road called The Highway, as if by renaming it the old poison could be drained away, but it is still watched over by St George in the East. My recommendation: get a seat in one of the riverside pubs (the Town of Ramsgate is my favourite), look out towards the river, and try to imagine.

Docklands today is a glass-and-steel monument to high finance and retail, and that's perhaps an appropriate epitaph for the old mercantile machine which once existed here. What's less appropriate is the dearth of good histories of London's docks; too few people have tried to explain why a river which once buzzed with shipping is now virtually empty. Fiona Rule's recent *London Docklands: a History of the Lost Quarter* (Ian Allan Publishing) goes a long way to putting this right (and is correctly named, in my opinion), but the richest source I found was Sir Joseph Broodbank's *History of the Port of London* (Daniel O'Connor), written in 1921, when London's docks were still the beating heart of global trade.

It's quite possible to get lost in the endless succession of maps which England produced from 1750 onwards, as mapmakers attempted to keep up with the remorseless expansion of London and the endless renewal of its streets, particularly in the East and West Ends. My own guide to those fluid times was *The A to Z of Regency London*, which takes William Faden's 1813 edition of Richard Horwood's map of 1799 as its basis. In the fourteen years between those two editions, London's docks appeared as if from nowhere, while England waged war in Europe and invented the modern industrial society.

The quotations in *The English Monster* were found in the following places:

'They have good ships . . .' which opens the book is from a letter from Guzmán de Silva to Philip II, from London on 4 February 1556, from *Calendar of Letters and State Papers Relating to English Affairs Preserved Principally in the Archives of Simancas*, vol. 1, Elizabeth 1558–1603, printed for HM Stationery Office by Eyre and Spottiswoode, 1892. It is quoted in *The Queen's Slave Trader*, by Nick Hazlewood (London, Harper Perennial, 2004).

'As I was a-walking down Ratcliffe Highway . . .' which opens Book 1 is a 19th-century song, which I found at http://mysongbook.de/mtb/r_clarke/songs/ratcliff.htm.

'Thus they order for the loss of a right arm . . .' which opens Book 2 is from John Esquemeling's *The Bucaniers of America*, which was published in the late 17th century and is widely available online.

'In the sugar-islands Negroes . . .' which opens Book 3 is from the National Archives' excellent online exhibition 'Black Presence: Asian and Black History in Britain, 1500–1850' at http://www.nationalarchives.gov.uk/pathways/blackhistory/index.htm.

The letter from Robert Southey which opens Book 4 is from a letter to Neville White from Keswick on 27 December 1811, from page 247 of Volume II of *Selections from the Letters of Robert Southey*, edited by his son-in-law John Wood Warter, B.D., (Longman, Brown, Green, and Longmans, 1856). It is quoted in *The Maul and the Pear Tree*, by P.D. James and T.A. Critchley (London, Faber & Faber, 1986).

The poem at the end of the January 1812 chapter in Book 4 is originally by Coleridge and Robert Southey and was published in 1799. Coleridge slightly adapted the poem in 1835, which is the version I use here (and thus could not, of course, have been quoted by Aaron Graham in January 1812).

ACKNOWLEDGEMENTS

My thanks go to: my agent Jim Gill; to Mike Jones and Jessica Leeke, my editors at Simon & Schuster; to Danny McLaughlin, who first showed me around Wapping and the ghostly edges of the dock; to Rob Jeffries of the Thames Police Museum (still housed in the building which John Harriott built); to Tim Wright and Andrew Grumbridge, who wandered with me down the same coast Charles Horton sailed along on Christmas Day; to the staff of the London Library; and to my own English monsters Jack and Lily. This book is dedicated to my very own Abigail, Louise.

Read on for an exclusive extract from Lloyd Shepherd's forthcoming novel

THE POISONED ISLAND

Out 28.02.13

SIMON &
SCHUSTER

London · New York · Sydney · Toronto · New Delhi

A CBS COMPANY

ONE

She comes!—the GODDESS!—through the whispering
air,
Bright as the morn, descends her blushing car;
Each circling wheel a wreath of flowers entwines,
And gem'd with flowers the silken harness shines;
The golden bits with flowery studs are deck'd,
And knots of flowers the crimson reins connect.—
And now on earth the silver axle rings,
And the shell sinks upon its slender springs;
Light from her airy seat the Goddess bounds,
And steps celestial press the pansied grounds.

(*from* 'The Botanic Garden', Erasmus Darwin)

TAHITI, 1769

Near the foot of great Tahiti Nui, in the shadow of the dead volcano and beneath the hungry eyes of ancient gods, the young Englishman chased his princess through the forest, despite the best efforts of the forest to stop him. The dipping branches of trees slapped his face and arms. Damp leaves, drenched in the mountain's tears, were heavy on his face, like wet green clothes hung out to dry. The sun had come up after the rain storm and joined the gods to watch proceedings. The air was warm and liquid.

The Englishman's breath was loud but steady in his ears, strengthened by countless rope exercises on the deck of his ship, just one of the many ways he'd filled the endless empty days of his voyage. His bare feet, strong and leathery after weeks on the island, felt solid and sure on the slippery earth. He had stopped concerning himself with the crawling and slithering creatures underfoot.

The princess (favoured by the gods) said nothing as she ran, and neither did he. Both of them breathed and breathed and breathed, their lungs in counterpoint, three of her inhalations to two of his, her waltz to his march. On every third breath, she exhaled a little sigh, and the gods sighed with her.

The chase was in its final stages. It hadn't started in this grim silence punctuated by sighs. When she had first leapt up and started to run from him she'd squealed the same delightful girlish squeal he'd heard so many times before. She'd bubbled with laughter and he did, too, as he'd set off after her. The other Englishmen and the island women seated around the tents had laughed along with them, the men cheering heartily as he crashed into the green wall of trees to follow his escaping quarry. Her laughter had seemed to fill the forest, as if the island itself was joining in on this tremendously spirited romp. Above them rose mighty Tahiti Nui, its smoke long extinguished but its memories as enduring as the sea.

She'd shouted at him a few times as the chase began, and he'd recognized several words in the local tongue, with which he'd made pleasing progress. *You cannot*, he thought he'd heard. *I am fast*, he was sure about. And *No no no* was as clear as day, and he'd laughed at that again, laughed at her games and her delightfully arch modesty. He knew it to be a masque. Was it not just what those charming London courtesans had said on that cherished fishing trip with his Lord S—. They too had lifted their skirts and run away, ankles dappled with mud, eyes sparkling and full of hidden knowledge, the game all part of the essential transaction.

In any case, this coquettish flight was very much not in keeping with the island's delicate intimacies. He was *sure* of that.

They ran like that for some time, laughing and shouting at each other, but at some point the nature of the chase had changed. Her laughter had died. His continued for a while, but it became forced and then it too ebbed away, replaced by the grim metronomic breathing, the liquid trees, the slapping, muddy feet, the little royal sighs of the princess. Then they were only running, breathing together, the wet sound of their bodies crashing through the undergrowth silencing the forest creatures around them.

And as the Englishman ran, his certainty grew.

No more. No more of this. No more teasing and cajoling. The other women of this island have given themselves freely and often, both to me and to my men. They have moaned and sighed and stroked and played, while this one has shared only caresses and the occasional chaste kiss. She knows I want her. I believe she wants me. What is this escape, but the need to find seclusion and privacy for our final consummation? She wishes to be hidden from the eyes of her retinue. Well, let her have her ways. And let me have mine.

His self-assurance grew. So did his desire. He felt he could chase her all the way to Venus.

The ground began to climb, and even with his heart pumping in his chest and the sweat bursting through his skin he knew where they were. They were running south, into the heart of the island, where water cascaded down into pools and birds circled. The trees would start growing ever thicker as they climbed away from the human places and into the green heart of the island, the places where only priests and their adherents ever went. The place where, the Englishman had been told, the Arreoy sanctified themselves with the blood of babies.

Her breath, he could hear, was beginning to sound ragged, and almost without thinking he slowed down. His arousal was by now at a delicious plateau. There would be no refusal. But the pursuit was pleasant and he wanted it to last.

A sound of water close by. They were near one of the many falls. Up ahead he heard a shriek and then a splash, and then he was into the water, and he had her.

She wriggled and scratched like a fish with claws, and for a moment his certainty faltered. *Why so steadfast? Does she not indeed want this? Perhaps whatever faith she has precludes it?* He considered this for a moment, even as he held her around her middle and felt the sharp angular rocks at his feet, one of them biting into his ankle and tearing the skin. He felt his blood in the water and the water in his blood, and he laughed and shouted because of the magnificent feeling of being *alive* that now encased him. Like a bear with a salmon he climbed up the other bank and onto the shore line, where she collapsed onto the ground and he began to unbutton his fine Covent Garden breeches, stained green and brown with the time on the island.

She said nothing for a moment, watching him. Her fine colourful robe, the mark of her nobility, was wet against her skin, and her dark shining hair was flat against her head. The flowers with which she'd decorated herself were gone, washed away down the mountainside by the stream. Her skin – *my God, her skin* – glowed like butter before a fire, wet and bright and alive. He congratulated himself on his refusal to accept no as her answer. Every pore of her, every fibre of her hair, every shining droplet of water on her hot, soft skin, spoke of desire. But then, as he stepped out of his breeches and prepared to lie on top of her, she spoke, in his own tongue.

'No, Joseph. No.'

The words were flat and shockingly tuneless, with none of the melody of the local tongue in them. He noticed her breathing, how it was still dancing along in 3/4 time with that persistent little sigh. There was, for that moment, no doubting the woman's meaning. For a second time he hesitated and his rational self seemed to emerge from the wet trees to find him there, his fine breeches round his ankles and his gentleman's cock high in the air. That self shouted at him, pleaded with him, and its voice was the voice of his mother. He could almost smell her old perfume, and hear her high, tissue-thin voice, and it told him to stop, now, stop, before everything changed forever.

But there was never a chance of that. This was a man of action, of determination and most of all of will. This was, above all, a *young* man whose appetite for women was already the subject of scandalized rumour in the drawing rooms of England. He roared like a bear again, laughing delightedly at the princess lying on the ground (who must, after all, desire him for she did not struggle, only breathed that odd little rhythm), and he fell on and into her.

She had made no new sound as he'd taken her, other than that precise little pattern of breathing and sighing. When he rolled away from her she did not move. Her eyes looked to the sky. Her chest rose and fell. He stroked her face, smoothed her hair and kissed her forehead, frowned in irritation and mild concern at her silence, and then he slept and dreamed. In the years that followed and across the thousands of nights in which she haunted him it became impossible for him to unpick the real from the dream.

In his dream she stood and walked away from him, her damp robes falling to the ground, her black hair unrolling down her back as she walked. His dream-self woke up and followed her close behind, respectfully this time, although even here the desire was still present, impossible to ignore. It was as if their previous relationship of visitor and monarch had been restored. She walked along the side of the pool, then she climbed – or rather, in this dream-state, she seemed to *float* – up the rocks which lined the waterfall. He clambered after her, heavy and clumsy and lumpen, heavier and clumsier the older he got, as this dream repeated and new appetites fattened him, his belly growing as enormous as his reputation, but the dream was always there to remind him. By the time he'd reached the top she was already disappearing into the trees. He followed her once more, occasionally glimpsing her as he struggled to keep up.

And then, she began to sing.

He recognized neither the words nor the melody, and he'd made a careful study of the islanders' music. What she sang sounded different from anything he'd heard, a complicated melange of tones and whistles, and after a moment birds began to sing in the trees around them. And here was something to thrill the heart of a voyaging explorer: the birds were singing along with her. They harmonized, they made counterpoint, they embarked on thrilling little rills which ran through and around and into what the princess herself sang, like crystal water flowing into a blue pool.

He came upon the hilltop clearing suddenly, emerging from the green just as she stopped singing and the birds, one by one, ceased their accompaniment. He picked up his pace now, some new urgency coming over him, but she stopped, finally and completely, her glorious back to him.

There was a crackling wooden sound then, and the ground around her came to life. Tendrils of green burst upwards and wrapped themselves around her feet, her calves, her thighs. Her hair burst open with green light and fire, and her back began to elongate and spread itself up towards the fresh sun-light. Her fingers twisted into twigs which curled out from the branches of her arms. Shiny ovate leaves appeared all around these branches and twigs and then, with a final crunch of wood and bark, her shape disappeared within the new-yet-ancient body of a small, elegant tree, perhaps fifteen feet high, its canopy a neat, shining triangle which caught the brilliant sun and reflected it in a symphony of green, her legs fused into a single straight trunk.

He woke up beside that Pacific waterfall. Only Tahita Nui, its gods and the sun remained to watch him as he stood and dressed. The princess was gone.

For a Reading Group Guide to *The English Monster*,
and a Q&A with Lloyd Shepherd, go to:

http://readinggroups.simonandschuster.co.uk/

SIMON &
SCHUSTER

London · New York · Sydney · Toronto · New Delhi

A CBS COMPANY